THE EARL STRONGBOW

Ruadh Butler

Published by Accent Press Ltd 2018

www.accentpress.co.uk

ISBN 9781910939291
eISBN 9781910939307

On the walls of Waterford, a king will be made…

Glossary

WALES

Abergavenny – castle controlled by Braose family
Aberteifi – castle in modern Cardigan
Afon Wysg – River Usk
Deheubarth – Welsh kingdom of South Wales
Haverford – Haverfordwest
Melrfjord – Milford Haven
Netherwent – Lower Gwent, roughly from Monmouth south to the Severn along the River Usk
Striguil – castle in modern Chepstow
Tyndyrn – Tintern Abbey
Usk – castle in modern Monmouthshire

IRELAND

Áth Skipir – Auskurra, near modern Dunmore East
Banabh – Bannow Bay
Baile an Gharráin – Ballygarran, close to Waterford Airport
Bearú – River Barrow
Brénainn's Hill – Brandon Hill in modern County Kilkenny
Uí Ceinnselaig – a tribal kingdom in modern County Wexford ruled by the Meic Murchada family
Cill Odhran – Killotteran in County Waterford
Cluainmín – Clonmines
Dubháth – the 'Black Ford'; Duagh in County Waterford
Dubhlinn – a city in eastern Ireland (modern Dublin)
Dubhán's Headland – Hook Head
Dun Conán – Duncannon
Dun Domhnall – Dun Donnell, modern Baginbun Head in County Wexford
Fearna – the modern town of Ferns
Fiodh-Ard Liag – 'High Wood of the Slate'; Faithlegg in County Waterford

Uí Geintaigh – Ogenty, a barony in eastern County Kilkenny controlled by the Uí Ceallaigh

Laighin – the modern province of Leinster excepting Counties Meath, Westmeath, Longford, and Louth

Meannán – Minaun; a hill at Faithlegg in County Waterford

Mhumhain – Kingdom of Munster

Osraighe – a tribal kingdom ruled by the Meic Giolla Phadraig family in modern Kilkenny and the southern part of Laois

Sláine – River Slaney

Siol Bhroin – Shelburne, an area of land including the Hook Peninsula

Siúire – River Suir

St Abban's Monastery – Celtic monastery at modern New Ross

St Fiachra's Monastery – Ullard Church just north of Graiguenamanagh

Tuadhmumhain – petty-kingdom roughly equating to modern County Clare and North Tipperary, ruled by the Uí Briain family

Veðrarfjord – Waterford; an Ostman city on the River Suir

Waesfjord – Wexford; an Ostman city built on mud flats

PRINCIPAL CHARACTERS

Alice of Abergavenny – illegitimate daughter of the late Lord of Abergavenny

Basilia de Quincy – illegitimate daughter of Richard de Clare

Déisi – a tribe from modern County Waterford

Diarmait Mac Murchada – Dermot MacMurrough, King of Laighin

Diarmait *Ua Ceallaigh* – Dermot O'Kelly, King of the Uí Geintaigh

Donnchadh Ua Riagháin – Donnacha O'Ryan, King of the Uí Drona

Fionntán Ua Donnchaidh – Fintan O'Dunphy, a Gaelic warrior

Henry FitzEmpress – King of England

Henry the Young King – the heir to the throne of England

Sir Hervey de Montmorency – uncle to Richard de Clare

Hubert Walter – a priest and court official

Jean de Clahull – knight from Strongbow's Hertfordshire lands at Weston

Máel Sechlainn Ua Fhaolain – Melaughlin O'Phelan, King of the Déisi

Máelmáedoc Ua Riagain – Malachy O'Regan, the secretary to Diarmait Mac Murchada of Laighin

Ragnall Mac Giolla Mhuire – Reginald MacGillamurray, King of Veðrarfjord

Raymond de Carew – a warrior in the retinue of Striguil

Richard de Clare – Lord of Striguil, formerly Earl of Pembroke

Roger de Quincy – son-in-law to Richard de Clare, married to his illegitimate daughter

Sigtrygg Mac Giolla Mhuire – Sihtric MacGillamurray, usurper King of Veðrarfjord

Uí Drona – a tribe from Idrone in modern County Carlow

RAYMOND'S MILITES

Gilbert Borard, Thurstin Hore, Christian de Moleyns, Asclettin FitzEustace, Denis d'Auton, Walter de Bloet, Dafydd FitzHywell, William de Vale; Griffin de Carew, Gerald 'Bach' FitzMaurice, William FitzMaurice, Hostilo d'Angle, Gervais d'Alton, Robert de Barri.

Notes

The '**Fitz**' prefix is the Norman derivation of the Latin 'Filius' meaning 'son of'.

A **miles** (one of a number of milites) is a Norman horseman armoured similarly to a knight but not considered to be of the same noble rank.

The **Ostmen** (East Men) were made up of *Fionngall* (Fair Foreigners), presumed to be the descendants of the original Norse invaders who populated the cities of Dublin, Waterford, and Wexford (amongst others), and the *Dubhgall* (Dark Foreigners), who were Danes and arrived a century later following their conquests in northern England. The Danish *Uí Ímair* (the descendants of Ivarr) quickly became the ruling class in most of these settlements and founded the cities of Limerick and Cork.

Irish families were divided into clans (**tuath**) and septs (**finte**), thus Diarmait Mac Murchada was the King of the Uí Chennselaig (*tuath – the descendants of Cennsalach*) as well as the Meic Murchada (*finte – the sons of Murchad*)

Prologue

Ger Castle, Normandy
Summer 1170

The king was dying.

All his doctors were in agreement. He would not survive the fever. For two weeks the sickness had raged through his lungs and ravaged his guts. Henry FitzEmpress was fading. The king was dying.

Royal messengers had already been despatched to his son and heir, Prince Harry, crowned king alongside his father two months before. Prepare, they were instructed to tell the fifteen-year old. Prepare to become lord and master of an empire. Prepare to become the greatest king in all Christendom.

Secret letters telling the same tale also found their way south to the king's wife, Eleanor, at Poitiers, and east to Paris where the exiled Archbishop of Canterbury plotted his return to England.

'Where is Master Ralph?' King Henry raved, and slugged from a wine goblet, spilling most down his chest and onto his bed. 'Master Ralph will return me to health.' The king's light ginger hair clung to his damp, yellowed face and he swiped it away with his shivering hand.

'You Grace, your physician was among those poor souls who perished during your crossing to England in the spring. Do you recall?' The Bishop of Lisieux used the same voice that he employed to calm his hunting dogs. 'Be assured, we have engaged new doctors to oversee your recovery.' His eyes flicked up. One of the new physicians, an Italian, visibly wilted and refused to meet his eyes.

Henry suddenly shot forward from his sick bed and grabbed the bishop by his robes, hauling him close enough so that the bishop could smell the puke and wine upon his breath. The king's eyes danced in his pink face.

'Becket has done this to me,' Henry whispered, 'just as he summoned up that storm to try and drown me during my passage across the Channel. You must protect me from his magic.' A moan of sadness hissed from the king's throat and he meekly punched the bishop in the shoulder as he clung to his robes. 'I extended my hand in friendship to him, tried to make peace as you instructed, and he has conspired to murder me.' The king's head slumped onto the bishop's chest, the grip on his chasuble lessening. 'It's too damn hot,' Henry whimpered as his hands fell away and he flopped back onto his back in bed. 'Why is it always so damn hot in Normandy? I cannot believe I am going to die in this shithole.' The king began rolling around the bed, his arms clutching his legs to his chest.

A smear of sweat had been left on the bishop's rich vestments. The bishop raised his hand to wipe Henry's perspiration from his clothes, but stopped himself from doing so in the company of so many great men. As he glanced around the room though he realised that not one person cared how he comported himself. All eyes were on Henry. Each man was considering how the king's impending death would affect his empire and their place in it. The bishop understood their panic. Like them, he wondered if Henry's death would present him with an opportunity to extend his influence, or with the circumstances that would diminish his power. The bishop had no doubt that Henry's passing would bring great peril upon them all. The Count of Eu had already departed Ger with his small retinue. He had told the bishop that Henry's death would precipitate an attack on his territory from Champagne or Flanders and that he had to prepare for that eventuality. The count would pay dearly should the king recover and learn that his liege man had left court without permission. This king did not forget. This king did not forgive.

The rest of the gathered barons, administrators, and clerics lingered, biding their time, safe in the knowledge that their households were ready to start out as soon as the king died. They would seek to be close to power once the king was gone, the bishop knew. But where would they seek it? The heir was a boy and could not be expected to preside over the kingdom for many years. A regency council would be established, but who would head it? Queen Eleanor? Could a woman – even one who had reigned over Aquitaine and Poitou – possess the ability to rule Henry's empire? The bishop doubted it. He considered a dozen candidates for the role of regent, but as quickly as they occurred to him he thought of reasons to discount them. The bishop began to wonder if anyone had the authority and vigour necessary to hold the kingdom together without Henry.

A sudden shiver ran down the bishop's back. There was one man of great ability who had experience of running the kingdom. The bishop crossed his chest and looked heavenward. What if the new king turned to his former mentor in his father's absence? How would the barons react if Thomas Becket, their errant Archbishop of Canterbury, returned from exile as regent for the new king?

'Get word to Thomas, tell him that I truly do forgive him,' Henry whimpered in his direction, giving voice to the bishop's worst fears. 'At Fréteval he told me that he still believes me a liar. Tell him that I wish him to return to Canterbury and be as a father to my son – as he was before our troubles began. The boy will need sound advice after I am gone.' Tears poured down the king's face as he spoke. 'He may even conduct another coronation, if that is what he wants so badly.' Henry blubbed and panted, and forced his body further down into the bedclothes. 'I have enemies everywhere! I need my true friends at my side now. Get Thomas here, Bishop, before it is too late!'

As the king rolled over onto his stomach to weep into his pillow, the Bishop of Lisieux swapped an alarmed look with the Earl Warenne, the king's bastard brother. Warenne slowly shook his head and gestured for the bishop to remain in the room.

'I will see to it, Your Grace,' the earl stated, but made no move to fulfil Henry's wishes.

At the foot of the king's bed the Lord Chancellor and the Dean of Salisbury shared a whispered and hurried conversation. Whether it was caused by the earl's inaction or by King Henry's words the bishop did not know, but he did know that they, above all others, had more to lose should

Becket be permitted to return to England. He crossed the room to stand by the Earl Warenne's right hand.

'Have you ever seen those two weasels look more worried?' the bishop joked.

'I don't think any of us have,' the earl retorted, 'or more tired. Three weeks on the road with Henry is like a lifetime on crusade. A week ago I would have thanked the Holy Trinity for my brother to be bed-bound for I felt that I could not possibly drag my corpse one more mile. But now, with Becket poised to return, I pray only for Henry to recover and for us to be back on the damned road.'

'But His Grace was in good health before Fréteval?'

Warenne nodded. 'In good health, and in a bad mood as usual.' He lifted his chin in Henry's direction. 'This business with King Louis, the Pope, and Becket has thoroughly distressed him. That idiot son of his is no better of course.' The king was shivering in his bed, seemingly asleep. 'It is Henry's own damned fault. I told him that he had been pushing himself too hard since we landed at Barfleur.'

The bishop nodded in agreement. He had only joined the king's court at Bernay, but had found it almost impossible to keep to the punishing pace set by Henry. It had been a whirlwind journey through Normandy on horseback. Every day had seen Henry's vast itinerant court visit a different city – Rouen, Évreux, Caen, Falaise and Alençon – and every evening had presented a new set of problems for the king and his entourage to preside over. But Henry would not delegate. He had to hear every detail of every court case, had to stick his nose into every disagreement. Left behind at La Ferté-Bernard after the king's conference with the Count of Blois, the bishop had been forced to ride through the night in order to be present at the talks with Becket at the field of Fréteval. Thankfully, he was assured that the king had been able to achieve his main goal: the threat of papal interdict over England had passed. All their souls were safe.

'Yet Henry accomplished what he intended.'

'At what cost, I wonder?' Warenne asked and nodded towards the squirming king.

Before the Bishop of Lisieux could answer the Lord

4

Chancellor cleared his throat so that he could address all present.

'If he was still clear of mind and not overborne by this cruel fever, I am sure His Grace would wish to thank you all for your loyal service and to ask that all your prayers should be directed towards the Virgin, asking her to intercede on the his behalf -'

He paused as the dean stooped to whisper in his ear.

'I mean to say that all our prayers should be for the Virgin to find him in heaven, given his sad and hopeless condition. During our last conversation, the king made it clear to me that his choice of resting place would be in Our Lady's loving sight, in the hope that she will conduct him to Heaven and to speak for him when he meets Lord God's judgement. To honour that wish we must now begin arrangements to conduct His Grace's body to the Abbey of Fontevraud.'

While several of the barons nodded in appreciation at his words, the bishop raised his eyebrows in surprise that none, bar he, had yet grasped the significance of that location. The chancellor had concocted an excuse to force them, the great men of the empire, both lay and ecclesiastical, into Poitou. Obviously the chancellor had decided where power would reside after the king's death, and he would shepherd the barons and court administrators towards it. The Lord Chancellor would throw in his lot with Queen Eleanor! This was her grab for the regency. Her husband's mortal remains would be the bait.

Events were threatening to overtake the bishop. Despite his urgent messages to Eleanor's court in Limoges, he did not yet know if he would find favour with the queen, and so he could not yet commit to her cause as had the chancellor. The Pope might yet insist upon his throwing of support behind Becket as regent. But he had yet to hear from his master to that end. His spies needed time to reach him. He needed news. All he could do was to slow down proceedings.

'The king's supplication to Our Lady of Heaven is admirable, but might not His Grace have meant the Abbey of Our Lady of Bec as his final resting place? It is where his beloved mother lies and is, of course, dedicated to the Virgin. It is also closer to Ger Castle and to His Grace's eldest son and heir, now in England. Bec is not far for his wife and younger sons to travel from Aquitaine.'

The bishop could feel the ire bubbling from the chancellor and his confederates as the meaning of those words hit home. He did not give them a chance to recover. 'I am sure that the Lord Chancellor will recall overseeing His Grace's last will and the distribution of his lands amongst his sons. And of course, as His Grace's chief servant, he will need to return to England to be at your new king's side as he oversees the beginning of his reign. I would suggest therefore that upon the King's passing we should despatch riders to fetch the Seneschal of Normandy to Ger and he can arrange His Grace's final journey to the abbey at Bec while the Lord Chancellor journeys back to England to his appropriate and correct station.'

The chancellor's eyes tightened and he looked ready to launch into an impassioned argument, but at that moment two royal guards entered the solar with the fat Constable of Ger Castle.

'Messengers have arrived for the Lord Chancellor, Lord Warenne and the Dean of Salisbury,' the man announced, silencing the room.

'We will continue this conversation later,' the chancellor stated, casting a venomous look in the Bishop of Lisieux's direction. He strode from the room with the dean in his wake. Other chancery clerks filed out behind them, their arms laden with rolls of paper. The Earl Warenne waited for them to pass and then turned towards the bishop.

'Bec?' he asked.

'Be assured, we shall talk later,' the bishop replied as the earl and his retinue followed the chancellor from the solar. It left the bishop and his own staff alone with the King. The bishop stood at the foot of Henry's bed, staring down, his arms folded and one hand rubbing his thin lips. For several seconds no one said a word.

'I thought that they would never leave! Good God, can someone please open a window? It stinks of royal shit in here.' The voice came from a slim priest who emerged from the bevy of servants on the far side of the King's bed. The priest placed

6

a hand on the King's brow before leaning forward to sniff his hair. Grimacing as he withdrew, he patted the King on the shoulder reassuringly.

'Keep him drinking water and try to get him to eat some red meat,' the auburn-haired priest ordered, his finger jabbing the Italian doctor in the chest. He did not wait for a response but instead turned to address the Bishop of Lisieux. 'I believe that the king is over the worst of the sickness now, Lord Bishop. He will shake this fever in no time.'

'I hope you are right, but I don't recall ever hearing that you had studied medicine, Hubert.'

'Perhaps a prayer from Your Grace will help him?'

Despite Hubert Walter's usual sarcasm, the bishop closed his eyes and mumbled some words to St Peter for the saint's intercession. 'Cast your munificent nets around our glorious and earthly master, and raise him up from the darkness that threatens to drown him,' he urged.

As the bishop extolled his heavenly guardian, the King moaned a curse and a fart squeaked from his backside.

'I thought you would be happy if Henry ended his days here in Mortain, Lord Bishop,' Hubert chuckled. 'He loaned you all that capital to build your cathedral, after all. If he dies you won't have to pay it back for many years, I would've thought - if at all.'

'And I thought that you would send word, Hubert, rather than journey here yourself. Was it simply in order to insult me? Did I not pay you to deliver me swift news! The King could still relapse and I must be ready to act. Where have you been?'

Hubert Walter began counting off on his fingers. 'At Rouen having a conversation with a man in Becket's inner circle who was on his way to take seisin of the archbishop's estates in England; speaking with Sir William de Saint-Jean on Chancery business; to a Danish trader for news from Ireland and Wales, to a Fleming who had been in Aquitaine; and to Walter, the Canon of Rouen, on behalf of Richard FitzNeal and the Treasury.'

'Is there anyone against whom you are *not* scheming?'

Hubert bobbed his head from side to side. 'Those with whom I am currently scheming? In any event, my sources tell me that Pope Alexander will be happy with the archbishop's restoration, and should the chance come he would support Becket as Regent of England.'

'Then God help all those who attempted to negotiate with Becket on the King's behalf.'

Hubert laughed. 'I have friends in Ireland, Your Grace. I can make some arrangements for your escape. Becket would not pursue you there. A small fee might be -'

From the bed by Hubert's back, the King's voice hissed. 'Exactly what friends do you have in Ireland, priest?' he asked as he hauled himself up to a sitting position. His bearded face was masked in sweat and his arms quaked slightly under him as he fixed his gaze on Hubert.

'Lord King,' the priest exclaimed and went to his knee. 'I thought you were asleep.'

Henry scowled and demanded wine from a servant. 'The only men I know in Ireland are rebel knights and pauper chieftains,' he stated before drinking deeply. 'I would not like to hear that a member of my court had been conversing with them without my knowledge or express permission. Did I not make it clear that I wished to have nothing to do with them?' He took another draught of wine. 'So who exactly are your friends in Ireland?'

'Perhaps I misspoke, Your Grace. *Associates* might be a better name for them.'

The king's blue eyes bored into Hubert and he did not speak, instead allowing the silence hang between them.

Hubert turned towards the bishop for assistance, but none was forthcoming. 'The news that they send to me is interesting. Perhaps you would like to hear of it, Your Grace? My associates tell me that Sir Richard de Clare has landed an army on the south coast. Sir Richard himself remains in Wales, but his man, Raymond de Carew, has scored a notable victory over the Ostmen, the Danes, near the city of Veðrarfjord.'

'What?' the king roared. 'That damned cur Strongbow has sent that Raymond to Ireland? I remember Raymond's insolence in Westminster all too well! And he makes war without my consent? How dare he? I'll turn his guts into bowstrings, I'll turn his bones into axe handles, his thick, fat skull into … into …' Henry struggled to summon the words to match his fury and instead he cast his wine goblet onto the floor. 'I gave him no permission! You, priest, get a rider to Strongbow's castle at Striguil. I place a ban on him leaving my kingdom. He is expressly forbidden from going to Ireland!'

The King did not wait for Hubert to obey but signalled to the Italian physician to help him to his feet. His naked legs shook as he leaned on the doctor's shoulders. 'That twice-damned rebel can bloody well swing if he thinks I will let him take what is mine.' Steadying himself on a nearby couch, the King began peeling off his sweaty, linen chemise, launching it at one of his attendants. He stood naked in the middle of the room and demanded more wine.

'What of Raymond, Your Grace?'

'He can damn well climb into his ship and sail back to Wales.' The king threw a clean shirt over his shoulders. 'Get these shutters open and let some damned sunshine in. A man needs fresh air to recover and I have enemies to engage.' He turned to the Bishop of Lisieux and pointed a large finger at him. 'Don't just stand there like a page in a whorehouse – get a servant in here with some water for a bath. I smell like a Welsh latrine. There is work to be done. Go, go, go!'

Both Hubert and the bishop stumbled from the solar, stopping at the top of the stair as the door closed behind them. Inside, Henry continued to shout orders at the bishop's followers. Their hurried footsteps echoed on timber floorboards.

'I thought he had me there. Why are you smiling?' Hubert asked of the bishop.

'Because there will be no regency and no break-up of the kingdom. There will be no power-grab or civil war.'

Hubert nodded. 'Henry is back on his feet.'

'And his empire is saved.'

'So all he needed to recover was a bit of anger?' Hubert remarked and nodded his head in appreciation of the king's resilience.

'No,' the bishop retorted as he made for the stairs. 'The king needed an opponent. God help Strongbow if Henry gets his hands on him now.'

9

Chapter One

He had vomited in the darkness and he retched again as the dull morning sun pierced the gaps in the stone walls. His lips were dry and the sharp smell tingled at his nostrils. His brain squealed like it was being stretched inside his skull. Panting helped lessen the pain and dizziness, but hooves still clattered around his head. When he had finally fallen asleep he could not recall. Groaning, he hoisted himself to a sitting position on his makeshift bed, arms quivering with the effort.

His eyes refused to focus. Everything was confused. The surge of panic was sudden and severe. He searched his memory for answers. Was he in the great stone keep of Striguil? Perhaps he was in a cell at Tyndyrn Abbey, or in a farmhouse somewhere in deepest Gwent Uwch Coed? It would not have been the first time he had woken up in such as place, but this sickness did not feel like a hangover. His palms clawed at his hairline as he urged his mind to concentrate. His head continued to ring, but his vision, as well as his memory, slowly settled. Propped against the wall near his bed was his sword.

'Ireland,' he said. 'The earl sent you to Ireland. You are at Dun Domhnall.'

The journey of several weeks before came back to him. Raymond de Carew had always loved sailing and his memory of the crossing from Wales – the sparkling bright waves below the full-bellied sail, the gulp of the sea on her clinkered hull – helped to ease his alarm. His next recollection was of *Waverider*, the Earl Strongbow's ship, aflame upon the beach below Dun Domhnall's high cliffs, of enemy warriors emerging from the sea, their war axes raised above their heads, and of colourful, circular shields and smoke, so much smoke. His pulse pounded in his head as he remembered the battle; flashes of sunlight on wicked steel, the crunch of axe upon palisade wall; grunting effort and fear; of slick dark grass,

10

carcasses, and distant cattle calls. It made his headache all the worse.

Taking several deep breaths, Raymond climbed to his feet. The door was only three paces away, but he didn't make it that far. Instead his body tumbled to the left, scattering the remnants of his last meal onto the dirt floor. The stone wall felt cold under his palms as he fell against it and clawed for purchase, fighting to remain on his feet, but he slid downwards to land on his backside, crushing scattered biscuit and cooked fish beneath him. His right hand massaged his temple, his left his stomach as it churned like an unruly sea. The swelling on his head had greatly subsided, but it remained delicate under his rough fingers.

A bump; that is all I have suffered, when so many have died.

Images of the battle threatened to assault him again, of friends and foes all fallen, and he turned so that he could rest against the cool wall. Instead of stone his cheek met a blanket of intertwined steel links. It was his hauberk, hanging on a peg on the wall, and Raymond's hand caught its swaying mail skirts. Fourteen years of boyhood spent as a page and an esquire had made him expert in armour maintenance and he could immediately tell that the mail had not been properly cleaned. He could smell the oil that had been worked into its links, could feel where it gathered. His esquire's work was not up to his usual high standards. Raymond felt coated shards of sand tumble between his fingers.

'Geoffrey!'

Voices sounded outside the room, commands and faraway laughter, murmured conversations and, somewhere close-by, a woman's weeping. The noise was compounded by honking geese and bleating goats, metal tools cutting wood, weapon play, and horses. Each irked him.

'Shut up, shut up, the lot of you,' Raymond groaned and hugged his arms to the sides of his fair head. His fingers clipped the bruise above his right ear and he winced.

'Geoffrey,' he roared again.

It was only as the sound of his own voice faded that the memory of his esquire's death came back. The boy had thought to save him when Raymond had been outnumbered and alone,

11

his senses in disarray after his head had been dashed against a wooden strut. While Raymond had been hauled to safety, Geoffrey had been made prisoner by his enemy, Jarl Sigtrygg. His brave, rash esquire had been murdered as Raymond had watched on from behind the defences. He remembered the look on Jarl Sigtrygg's face as he had killed the boy. He had smiled. Raymond recalled Alice of Abergavenny's screams as she was escorted from the walls of the fort, driven to despair by the sight of her brother's murder. He would always remember her furious eyes as she was dragged away from the fortifications.

You did nothing, Alice's eyes had accused him. *You broke your promise, Raymond.*

He had led a hundred and ten men to victory over a grand alliance of Ostmen and Gaels, perhaps thirty times their number, yet he still felt as though it was he who had been routed.

Raymond let go of the chainmail and reached for a wooden mug, flinching as water sloshed down his raw and sour throat. It had been Father Nicholas who had denied him wine, but he could not remember the priest's reasons for refusing its comfort. Emptying the mug at the second attempt, he breathed deeply, his eyes closed. When they re-opened Raymond's gaze settled on the door to the squalid little hut.

'Up.'

The door was a strip of burned hull recovered from the wreck of *Waverider*. Ferrand had placed it over the entranceway and it had proved enough to keep out the breeze off the sea. Raymond clutched the panel and hoisted it aside. Pain seared through his head as the silver glare of sun flashed off the waves, straight into his face. Dazzled, he retreated back into the shadow. It took him several seconds blinking to ready his eyes to pass through the door and into the sunshine.

William de Vale sprang to his feet. 'What are you doing out of bed? Father Nicholas said that you were to remain abed for at least another day.'

Raymond had never noticed how irritating he found William's voice. 'I'm fine. Are you responsible for the condition of my armour?'

'No, no – I've asked Fulk to be your esquire,' he said and

12

indicated to the boy at his side. 'I thought you would -'

'You treated my mail?' Raymond demanded of Fulk.

'Yes, master.'

'Get in there and get it polished again. It is in a disgraceful condition,' he ordered, his arm indicating back towards his quarters.

'I'm sorry, master,' the youngster mumbled as he fled into the hut.

Small houses, tents, and improvised shelters peppered the headland that had become his army's camp. Everywhere Raymond could identify the signs of many men living in close quarters: blackened stone hearths where fires had been set, weapon racks, armour, horse tack, and the remnants of food. Most of the tumbledown stone houses had been roofed with turf. Two others were crowned with spare sails which sagged and ballooned in the small wind off the sea.

Those men not on duty on the main wall collected in groups, chatting and doing whatever jobs they could manage. One, a linen band wrapped thickly around his head, was stripping lengths of yew to use as arrow staves while another, his arm bound to his chest, was rationing out wine.

'Where is Borard? Sir Hervey?'

'What's wrong with you? Why are you being so angry?' William muttered.

'Borard?' Raymond demanded again. 'Sir Hervey?'

William's gaze dropped to his feet. 'I was told to keep my mouth shut,' he said. 'They didn't want to worry you, what with you being insensible and all.'

'Insensible?' Raymond took a deep breath through gritted teeth. 'Well, I am *sensible* now, so tell me what has happened.'

'You've been in bed for a week, since the battle was won. After we charged the enemy, you, well, went into a swoon. I was worried that you might not remember promoting me from esquire to miles …'

'I do.'

William smiled proudly. 'Father Nicholas told me that we weren't to worry. He has seen such things before in warriors who took a whack to the head, and Fulk was to make sure you rested and that you were kept cool at all times. By the time I got back down to the outer defences it was already over.'

'What was?'

'The fight at the inlet. I've told you about it already – you really don't remember?'

Raymond felt hot blood flow to his face. 'Remind me as we walk.'

Crashing surf ground against the high cliffs on all sides as Raymond and William made for the inner gates. The grass had been well trampled by the to-ing and fro-ing of his warriors and he followed the path along the base of the ancient Celtic fortifications. The curving wall was so old that most of the once circular defences had fallen into the sea, leaving only a solid stone stretch fifty paces long at the eastern extreme of the arrowhead-shaped headland. Though most of it had disappeared, the folk thereabouts still remembered that a fort had once stood on the spot. They called it Dun Domhnall, though Raymond guessed that no-one had lived behind the tumbledown walls since Domhnall, whoever he had been, had departed the headland hundreds of years before.

A few minutes walking took Raymond and William from the headland fortifications to a second set of defences. Two huge earthworks, crowned with timber palisades, ran parallel between the cliffs and cut the promontory off from the rest of Ireland. The ramparts had taken his men weeks to complete, but they had proven their worth during the battle against the Ostmen and their Gaelic allies. The King of Veðrarfjord had thrown thousands of warriors against those walls, but they had held firm like a cliff face battered by a wild winter storm. Two hundred paces long, it had taken everyone, man and boy, in Raymond's small army to halt the enemy's advance. To emerge from the battle with victory had required a plan so audacious that Raymond's pulse still rose as he remembered it. St Maurice had guided him, of that he was sure, as he recalled the charge of stampeding cattle, the crash of Norman lance upon Ostman shield.

'So after the enemy were dispersed by the cattle charge, you told me to send Caradog and his archers to help break up a big group of Ostmen that had reformed down at the inlet,' William told Raymond, pointing over the bay and northwards.

Raymond was about to ask a question of William when he was interrupted by a high-pitched and demanding voice. 'What are you doing out of bed? One more day! One more day of rest or you'll be right back where you started.'

'Father Nicholas, I'm fine -'

'If my advice to you is to be wasted then you must at least permit me to provide care for your prisoners. You must talk to Sir Hervey, Captain Raymond, and remind him of his Christian duty. I cannot stand idly by as fellow members of Christ Jesus' flock suffer. Yes, I have prayed for the Ostmen, but I am sure that there are more pressing issues which require my more direct attention.'

Raymond's head pounded, his vision sagged. 'Prisoners? Who are you talking about?'

With effort he followed the direction of Father Nicholas' outstretched arm to where the burnt-out remnants of the marshalsea stood. A large number of men lounged in the summer sunshine, imprisoned between the fire-scorched walls.

'As I was trying to say,' William said, 'after you collapsed we took prisoners. A lot of them, actually.'

Raymond stared blankly at the prisoners, about a hundred by his reckoning.

'These men got caught on our side of the inlet a mile to the north,' William recounted. 'They had crossed to this bank at low tide and didn't realise it was flooding when they fled the battlefield. The Gaels, they just swam across, but these rich fellows refused to part with their mail and swords. They are merchants in Veðrarfjord. So they put their backs to the water and formed a shieldwall.'

'And like all good tradesmen, they tried to make a deal,' guessed Raymond.

William nodded. '"Let us live and we will give you silver. Or attack us now and risk death as poor men". As you can imagine, greed won the day and they were made prisoner. Two were sent back to Veðrarfjord to tell their families that they must raise ransoms. They are to meet our representatives to parley for their release.'

Raymond watched as one Ostman hostage, with long, combed hair and a rich embroidered shirt, told a joke and enjoyed a Norman oatcake. The sight of his already meagre food stores being wasted made his anger threaten to rise. Raymond had an obligation to provide for his master's army when it eventually made landfall in Ireland, and he could not do that if the prisoners doubled the number of mouths he had to feed.

'I must make sure that the Ostmen's wounds are being correctly tended, that they are not suffering from hunger or any other neglect,' Father Nicholas stated. 'The Earl Strongbow would wish it.'

'The Earl Strongbow is not here.'

'These are men of standing, Captain Raymond, not mere spearmen.' The priest dropped his voice and leant in close. 'And I for one do not trust these Welshmen to watch over them.' Father Nicholas raised his eyebrows towards five archers who guarded the entrance to the makeshift prison. Squatting behind a small fence twenty paces from the marshalsea, the Welshmen could keep watch over two sides which had been worst affected by the blaze, where the wattle and daub walls had been scorched, blackened or had collapsed.

The archers were from a band of seventy Welshmen who had taken Raymond's coin and the promise of further riches if they accompanied him to Ireland with their deadly bows. Though they had cost him almost everything he had, and many of his Norman friends had counselled him against it, Raymond would have happily impoverished himself a second time in return for the mercenaries' service. If not for their efforts in battle, his small company would've been annihilated by the Ostmen from Veðrarfjord. Some of them spoke French - of a kind, heavily smothered with the bawdy accent of Gwent - but most could not, and those fellows in particular kept themselves apart from the Norman milites, huddling around isolated fires at night and sleeping in their own shelters as if wary that their allies might yet betray and attack them as they slumbered.

Raymond again asserted that he would keep his promise to Caradog's archers; somehow he would find a way to enrich them. They, who had every reason to hate men of Raymond's kin, the Norman invaders of their homeland, had stood alongside him when it seemed like they must be crushed. They had trusted in his captaincy and Raymond vowed to reward that fidelity with lands and great wealth. How or when he would be able to fulfil that oath he could not tell, but one day he swore that it would be within his gift.

'How many men did we lose in the battle?' Raymond asked the priest. 'What of our horses?'

'God rest them, but we only lost poor Bertram d'Alton and three esquires. The worst of the injured are Walter de Bloet with a broken sword-arm and the page, little Robert Barrett, who was badly burned. All three of Sir Hervey's milites escaped unscathed. I don't know about the horses.'

'Caradog's archers?'

'Oh, eleven dead, I believe, and about twice that injured. The Welsh preferred to treat their wounded themselves rather than seek my help.' Father Nicholas sniffed indignantly.

'So we have, what, eighty men left standing. We are surrounded, in enemy territory, with no idea when Strongbow's army will arrive to relieve us, and no way to retreat since our only ship was torched by the Ostmen. I know that our outer wall was ready to fall down and, as far as I can see, not one bit of work has been done to repair it while I was recuperating. And yet, despite all that, you are telling me that someone thought it was sensible to move a hundred Ostman warriors inside the fort?'

'There are only seventy and we disarmed them -' William began, before seeming to realise the feebleness of his argument. 'Everyone went along with the plan, sir.'

'In return for a cut of the ransoms?' Raymond felt his temper flare. 'And they told you to keep this from me, the man to whom you had – just days before – sworn your service? You should have woken me as soon as they were taken.'

'I told him that you were not to be troubled for any reason,' the priest attempted to intercede.

Raymond shot a severe and incredulous look at Father Nicholas. His men must've known that he would never have allowed them to put Dun Domhnall at such risk. Raymond turned on his heel, purposefully casting his gaze into every corner of the headland behind the defences. 'I see that we have not retrieved even a single cow that stampeded during the battle. So what will feed us once our few stores disappear into the prisoners' bellies? What will feed Strongbow's army when our lord eventually joins us from Wales? Are we to eat grass while we besiege Veðrarfjord?'

'Sir Hervey said that we couldn't leave the fort to round up the cattle for fear that the prisoners might stage a revolt,' attempted William.

'A revolt has already taken place,' Raymond countered. 'Only it is my warriors who are in rebellion against their captain.'

He stared at the tumbledown walls and the Ostmen. If he had been in their position he would certainly have been plotting his escape. Why should they impoverish their families if there was a chance of fighting their way to freedom? They could surely see that Raymond's garrison was only a few more than they. The seventy foreigners were well-fed and rested, and, although unarmed, if an uprising was timed correctly their captors would be hard-pressed to get them back under control. Should they attempt an escape in the unfortunate event of another external attack, it could be disastrous for Raymond's bridgehead fort in Ireland.

'You have made us prisoners within our own walls!' he accused, jabbing a finger into William's chest. 'You will go and find Borard, quickly and quietly, and tell him that he is to attend to me.'

'But Raymond, Borard is not here; none of the milites are, save the sick and injured. The whole conrois was taken north this very morning by Sir Hervey. He is to meet Veðrarfjord's representatives at St Abban's monastery to set a price for the Ostmen's release.'

Disbelieving, Raymond dragged a hand down his face. 'So, not content with making us hungry, Sir Hervey would seek to strengthen our enemy by giving back some of their best fighting men?'

'*Selling* back some of their best fighting men. Perhaps he hopes for -'

'He is only interested in silver. Find Caradog and Fionntán, and ask them to join me.'

The young warrior nodded once and jogged away in the

18

direction of the main fortifications.

'In the meantime I will enter the Ostmen's...' Father Nicholas paused and searched for an appropriate word, 'lodgings to see to their wounds.'

A vision of Geoffrey's brutal death at Jarl Sigtrygg's hands surged into Raymond's mind. 'You will not set foot in there! I will not have you taken hostage. Do I make myself clear?' Raymond had not meant to speak so forcefully, but he was finding his temper too hot, hotter than it had ever been. Nicholas was a good man, a friendly and forbearing priest as well as a decent surgeon, and Raymond lifted his head to begin his apology.

However, he found that the priest was no longer looking at him. Instead he was staring over Raymond's shoulder, a quizzical look evident on his face. Raymond had only half-turned in the direction of Nicholas' gaze when he saw the axe fall on the unprotected neck of an Ostman.

Raymond knew then that his head injury was more severe than he had believed. His sanity, he supposed, had been lost when the giant Jarl Sigtrygg had smashed his head against the fortifications during the battle. He had heard of warriors who had ended up in such a state: young men no longer able to tell dreams from reality after receiving a head wound, left reliant on their family for care, and with no hope of recovery. That he could no longer trust what his eyes were showing him was obvious for if that which they had revealed was true then he didn't know if wished to go on at all.

Alice of Abergavenny had murdered a man.

It had happened so quickly that Raymond found himself unable to move. He had merely watched as his former mistress, still wearing the expensive blue dress which he had bought for her in Le Mans, had skirted the wall of the marshalsea to where one young Ostman was resting his head on the fence, enjoying a jest with his fellow prisoners. How she had found the strength to heft the blade, or the arm to deliver such a blow to kill the Ostman, he did not know. Alice had only needed to hack down once. Then there was blood against the blue sky.

The Ostmen were in uproar. Alice was screaming at them

and attempting to swing the axe at a second of the bearded hostages.

'My brother!' Raymond heard her cry. Tears shone on her cheeks as she missed her target and hit the twisted fence, tearing a large rent in the barrier. The nearest Ostman bellowed as he leapt away from the next swipe of the axe while the five Welsh guards scrambled to their feet, shouting commands in their own tongue, their bows drawn, arrows nocked.

'Captain Raymond?' mumbled Father Nicholas at his side.

But Raymond was locked to the spot. He could not yet grasp the violence to which he had been witness. The prisoner was dead, of that there was no question, but the sight of Alice wielding a weapon did not make any sense to him. Raymond gazed at the woman in the blue gown as she frantically swung the axe, her feet kicking up dust as she spun. In her fury, Alice missed again, burying the blade into the fire-blackened doorframe of the burnt out and roofless marshalsea.

'Captain Raymond!' The priest's voice urged action.

Raymond let out the breath he hadn't realised that he had been holding, a breath that held onto the order for his milites to come to his aid. He found that his right hand had crossed his body as if to rest upon the pommel of a sword at his left hip. The reassuring presence was absent. His balance faltered and everything around him became less defined: the fury of the Ostmen and the fear of the Welsh guards, Alice's rage as she sought to revenge herself on her brother's killers. Up on the fortifications other warriors had clambered to their feet, alerted to danger within their walls. Even on the far side of the headland the Norman horses raised their heads from the grass to flick their ears. Raymond's eyelids slowly folded as the throb of pain returned to his temples and sent him deeper into the swoon.

Several seconds passed until the sound of the fence collapsing caused a surge of energy to pass through his body and Raymond's eyes to open. Three young Ostmen, their forefingers outstretched and accusatory, had pushed through the hole in the fence to confront Alice. Father Nicholas had left his side to be at hers and seemed to be bartering with the prisoners, urging calm and trying to put his thin body between the men and Alice. The Ostmen would not be appeased. Neither would Alice. She screamed profanities, her fingers extended as if she wished to claw out the warriors' eyes.

As Raymond started forward to intercede, more Ostmen spilled through the rent and out into the bailey. Ten, fifteen and then thirty were outside the marshalsea in quick order. Some spat curses at Alice, but more threatened the five Welshmen. Raymond could see the archers shifting their weight between their feet as their aim swept from man to man in the angry mob. The Ostmen might not be armed with steel, but they still had their armour and one had torn a solid length of timber from the marshalsea wall which could lay out a man as well as any sword. Shouting crackled from both groups. Foreign curses flashed in either direction. The kindling was in place, the bonfire built. A single snap of bowstring upon yew stave was the spark. As the Ostman flopped to the floor, an arrow buried in his shoulder, the uproar from his kinsmen abated temporarily, but once ignited it had to blaze. Masonry and wood from the walls flew through the air towards the archers. Then, with a roar, the Ostmen of Veðrarfjord charged the Welshmen. Two more arrows hit home while the rest, shot in panic, flew over their heads and into the sea. Caradog's men were already running but, as Raymond watched, one was tackled to the ground. Raymond took two steps in the direction of the stricken Welshman before Father Nicholas' cry of anguish made him turn. The priest had been floored by a punch while, at his side, Alice, kneeling as if in prayer, was being choked.

Raymond charged.

The first Ostman was of a similar age to Raymond, if a good deal taller. Strong and confidant, the bearded man strode forward to meet the unarmed Norman, his hands stretched out as if wishing to embrace Raymond with a bear hug. At the last second, Raymond reared, moving his body upwards as he lifted his elbow towards his assailant's chest. His forearm struck, throwing the man of Veðrarfjord from his feet and onto his back. His head snapped backwards to thump onto the sun-dried earth. He did not stand again and Raymond stumbled onwards.

The man on top of Father Nicholas was knocked insensible

by Raymond's foot full in the face as he steadied his arm to strike down with his fist. The force of the kick caused Raymond to fall, but he rolled onto his shoulder, crawling for a few paces, and then back to his feet. The Ostman choking Alice had hardly time to lift his hands in defence before Raymond's shoulder slammed into him. Both went down hard. The man of Veðrarfjord recovered quickest, landing an elbow which drove the air from Raymond's chest. Another punch caught him on the side of the head before Raymond felt fingers wrap around his throat. Eyes bulging, Raymond grappled against the Ostman's grip. His vision blurred. Shouts faded into the distance. His head pounded in pain.

Then suddenly, his airway opened and his chest hauled in a glorious breath. Father Nicholas appeared against the blue sky with shock apparent upon his face. The Ostman had fallen onto his shoulder, struck by the priest's hand. There was blood on the foreigner's face and anger in his eyes. He said something in his own sloshing language as he climbed back to his feet and stalked towards Nicholas. A second swing of Nicholas' fist missed. He backed away in the direction of the cliff face.

'I am a man of God,' the priest appealed as he eyed the long drop towards the swirling sea. 'I do not wish to fight you.'

Raymond gulped down air and attempted to rise to help Nicholas. His temples tightened and ached. He felt weak, dim-witted. The priest, now only a pace from the cliff face, unfurled his hands in supplication to the young warrior.

Raymond knew he had to act to save Nicholas. His body would not react.

It may have been that the sudden smash of a wave and sparkle of sea spray distracted the Ostman, but Alice's attack seemed to take him completely unawares. She had recovered her axe and whipped it at his knees, causing the warrior to fall, still grasping for a hold of Nicholas and crying out in pain and alarm. The priest stepped out of range of his clutches as the Ostman collided with the ground and then fell over the edge of the cliff, his leg already broken from Alice's strike.

'My brother!' Alice screamed after the Ostman and then spat over the edge of the cliff. She then turned her eyes on Raymond. There was madness there, an intense widening of

22

her left eye, and tightness to her right. For several seconds it seemed like she could not speak and she merely stared at Raymond, her knuckles white as they wrapped around the bloody axe haft.

'Get up,' she finally demanded of him.

'Alice?' Raymond garbled as vomit rose in his throat. His head rang and he cursed and groaned and spat, clinging onto the grass with both hands as if he might tumble off the surface of the earth and float skywards. He felt Father Nicholas' hands slip under his armpits and hoist him upwards to his feet.

'The Ostmen are in revolt,' stated Alice and forced the axe into Raymond's hands. Evidence of her killings still shone red upon the blade. 'So what are you going to do?'

Raymond turned towards the main wall. Ostmen armed with all manner of rudimentary weapons were already swarming in the direction of the inner barbican and the four archers posted there. Other prisoners were throwing debris at those few men stationed further down the battlements.

'You killed that man.'

'It doesn't matter. What are *you* going to do?'

Raymond shook his head. 'I'll force them to stand down. I'll get them back in the marshalsea!'

Alice frowned, turning her attention towards the priest. 'You should get to safety up on the headland.' When Nicholas began to protest, Alice raised her hand. 'Someone needs to alert Caradog to what is happening. The Ostmen are escaping.'

Father Nicholas paused and looked to Raymond.

'Go.'

Alice waited for the priest to get a few paces away. 'You are one of the stupidest men I have ever met, Raymond. But you are all I have left. And I need you.'

'I -'

'You do not realise the opportunity that lies before you. Nor do you grasp the peril. And so I have decided to guide you, to help you keep in the Earl Strongbow's favour. In return you will help me.'

Raymond struggled to make sense of Alice's words. She had barely spoken a word to him since he had rescued her and Geoffrey from their cousin's murderous intents; since he had

23

brought them to Ireland. If their brief reconciliation had been interrupted by the threat of three thousand enemy warriors coming from the north, it had been destroyed by the death of her brother in battle. Or so Raymond had believed.

Alice looked back towards the ancient fort on the headland, to make sure that Father Nicholas was well out of their earshot. 'You know the Ostmen threaten the success of your mission here. What will Strongbow think if he arrives and there is no food left for his army, or if he were to discover that you allowed warriors to walk free and so strengthen his enemies?'

'That was Sir Hervey, not me.'

'It doesn't matter. Strongbow placed you in command. It is your reputation at risk.'

Raymond's temples squealed with pain as he considered her words. He had come to Ireland from Wales with a tiny advance force and a determination to prove himself to his lord. An army three thousand strong had threatened Dun Domhnall and he had led his hundred men to victory. Yet he still faced the ruin of all his ambitions at the hands of these prisoners. Fury gathered in his chest. He pictured Basilia, Strongbow's daughter. The Ostmen put everything in jeopardy and he cursed them for it. He cursed Sir Hervey de Montmorency for his greed, and his own milites' recklessness in following Sir Hervey's orders.

'Damn them all. The Ostmen should never have been admitted to Dun Domhnall.'

'Yes, they are to blame,' encouraged Alice.

'I was abed, unconscious.'

'They drove you to it. No one would blame you.'

Raymond paused, his wrath interrupted. 'No one would blame me for what?'

'For killing the prisoners. Every single one of them.'

Sir Hervey de Montmorency was sweating. He could feel perspiration gathering under his linen shirt and soaking through at his arm-pits where his gambeson was held together by thick cords. The early afternoon sunshine was high in the sky and roasted his face as they climbed the hill.

'We must stop,' he panted.

The armed men walking ahead of him grudgingly echoed

his command to those at the front of their small column. They ambled to a halt.

It was half a mile from the river up to St Abban's Monastery and Sir Hervey was wheezing at the effort of the climb. Sweat was slick upon his balding head. In an effort to hide his exhaustion from Raymond's ten milites, he turned his back to stare towards the sparkling River Bearú. Clawing at the hot mail coif at his neck, Sir Hervey watched the esquires far below as they joked and tended to their coursers at the riverside. It had been a hard day's riding from Dun Domhnall and he was glad to see that the boys were again rubbing down their horses. If his conference with the enemy went awry, the coursers would need to be fresh, watered and ready to be ridden. Sir Hervey was disturbed to find just how far away the abbot's warriors had forced them to leave their small campsite; it had not seemed so distant when he had stood at the riverside looking up at the monastery and its high stone tower.

Looking to the other side of the wide river, over the fishermen's houses of pointed thatch, Sir Hervey spied a longship. There, the Ostmen of Veðrarfjord had landed their vessel amongst the reeds and mud, leaving a large force to guard her while their leaders had walked upstream to where the river was fordable. Sir Hervey could see that the tide was at its lowest and he wondered if those come to parley were already at the monastery or were still marching down from the north. A turn in the river and a rolling hill blocked his view in that direction.

The abbot's captain, who had accompanied the Normans from the riverside, impatiently stomped the end of his spear into the dry turf by Sir Hervey's feet. He barked something in his own tongue, making it clear that he wished to continue. He jerked his head in the direction of the monastery. The six moustachioed men with him did not wait for the Normans to respond, but began walking uphill again.

'Onwards then,' Sir Hervey told his men, dabbing sweat from his receding grey hairline with the hem of his new red, white and green surcoat. On either side of the path were dilapidated huts, each surrounded by tangled fences where cattle roamed freely or slaves toiled with wheelbarrows of dung. The morning sunshine toasted the naked backs of the labourers. In other fields, grass was cut and raked for hay.

As they walked towards the stone tower, a circular bank of earth crowned with timber posts emerged from behind the farming hovels. The abbot's men did not pause but led them through the gates where they were confronted by an intricately carved stone cross. It stood twice as tall as a man in an open expanse surrounded by tightly packed buildings. Most of the houses looked empty to Sir Hervey, some were ramshackle, and those that were not were being used to house animals. Manure was piled everywhere. To his left, a nun and a monk frolicked in an open fronted alehouse. Their laughter echoed from the palisade and the walls of the other houses. Sir Hervey watched as the monk slipped a hand underneath the nun's clothing.

'Now this is my idea of a monastery,' giggled Denis d'Auton.

The Gaelic warriors did not seem to notice the aberrant behaviour and plunged between two houses, still climbing in the direction of the stone tower. They indicated for the Norman band to follow.

Sir Hervey was panting hard by the time they emerged from the darkness between the wattle and daub walls and into another grassy area at the hill's pinnacle. Oak trees guarded the northern edge alongside the stone tower and monastery burial ground. In the centre were two stone buildings, their roofs acute triangles of sandstone and slate. Another soaring stone cross cut with saints' faces, swirling symbols, and indecipherable script stood serenely before the houses.

But Sir Hervey did not have time to look closer. On the stony path below the cross were thirty Ostmen from Veðrarfjord. At their head was the biggest man that Sir Hervey had ever seen and he felt his heart sag into his stomach at the sight of him. The last time he had seen the warrior had been a week before, during the battle for Dun Domhnall, when he had cut a bloody swathe through the archers and stormed the outer wall of the Norman fort. He was a giant of a man with flaming red hair and a braided beard which sat like tusks on either side of his mouth. His bare arms bulged with muscle. Above him, a

26

banner depicting a charging black boar flapped in the small wind.

'It's Jarl Sigtrygg,' whispered Borard as Sir Hervey attempted to find the words to address his enemy. Before he could speak a bearded man dressed in colourful embroidered clothes emerged from one of the stone buildings and fell to his knees in front of the cross. He was flanked on all sides by a procession of monks, nuns, warriors and harpers, each armed with twirling banners, smoking incense burners, fiery brands, or thrumming instruments. From amongst the cacophony came the voice of the bearded man, who Sir Hervey took to be the abbot, as he began to loudly appeal towards the heavens in the Gaelic tongue. One by one the Ostmen copied his lead, some bowing their heads and kneeling on the ground.

Sir Hervey recognised his words to be a prayer and, not knowing what else to do, dropped his eyes to the ground, his gnarled hands curling around each other close to his chest. The prayer went on for many minutes, although what was said, or to which saints, remained unknown to the Norman conrois. Sir Hervey lifted his chin to steal a look at those who he had come to meet. The Ostmen were bearded with long locks tumbling over their shoulders. They were armoured but seemingly unarmed. Otherwise his enemy looked no different to their Gaelic hosts. Sir Hervey's hand drifted towards the dagger secreted under his gambeson sleeve.

'Friends,' announced a younger monk, disturbing Sir Hervey's study of the Ostmen. 'We are here in full view of God and His servant, Holy Abban, and he who breaks the peace promised by our Good Father the Abbot will surely be struck down, his bowels turned to water, his genitals to porridge oats and scabs, his cattle to dried-up husks, his wife to a wizened crone -'

The man continued his list of punishments, but Sir Hervey noted that the Gael had spoken in good Latin. He was shocked at the vying emotions that rose in his chest at hearing the ecclesiastical tongue, a language he had not heard since departing Wales many months before. He was so lost in his thoughts that Sir Hervey did not realise that all eyes had turned towards him.

'I think they want you to approach the abbot,' whispered Borard.

Sir Hervey edged forward. He could see that Jarl Sigtrygg had also detached from his group and was striding towards the young monk. Sir Hervey quickened his pace so that he arrived at the same time as the Ostman.

'You have sworn to uphold the peace at this parley under threat of eternal damnation from Mother Church if you raise arms against each other before sundown,' the translator spoke in Latin before repeating the statement in the Irish tongue. 'Do you agree to take responsibility for your warriors?'

Sir Hervey nodded.

'I thought I would be meeting Raymond the Fat, not his ugly grandfather,' Jarl Sigtrygg snorted, his French passable if heavily accented. 'As Raymond is too scared to face me again, I promise to keep the peace too.' He said the last seven words in Irish so that the translator could understand.

'I thought that I would be meeting King Ragnall for this parley, so we are both to be disappointed from the outset,' Sir Hervey countered. 'Let us hope that it will not be so at the outcome.'

Sigtrygg's small eyes tightened at the corners. He said nothing for several seconds, but merely scanned Sir Hervey's face. 'The men of Veðrarfjord have decided that a new man will lead our city rather than one disgraced by defeat such as Ragnall. I am konungr now. You do not lead the foreigners. Do you speak for Raymond the Fat?'

'I am Sir Hervey de Montmorency, uncle to the Earl Strongbow, and I speak for him, not Raymond. I have command of Dun Domhnall now.'

Sigtrygg turned towards his own followers and shouted something in his coarse tongue. One spat on the ground in disgust. Several laughed out loud. 'I told them that the fat captain of the foreigners is dead. He was our enemy. They would've liked to have seen him die by my hand.' His hand went to his nose which was turned up, giving him the look of the boar that was depicted on his banners.

Sir Hervey did not correct Sigtrygg's mistake. It suited him to have the Ostman believe his was the final word in their negotiations. 'I command now. And I have seventy of your fighting men as prisoners.'

Sigtrygg licked his teeth. 'All Ostmen of Veðrarfjord, not Déisi warriors?'

Sir Hervey could barely identify a distinction between the native Gael and Ostmen of Ireland. He nodded his head anyway. There ensued a few moments of silent expectancy between the two men as both awaited the other to speak.

'I will not submit to you.' Sigtrygg said suddenly. 'No king would do so for the lives of seventy men. I hold Veðrarfjord, I have powerful allies. You can keep the prisoners and do what you will with them. I will not do homage to you.'

'I don't wish for your submission. I want silver.'

'As tuarastal? You want to hire these men as mercenaries?'

'I do not know what that means. I will give you the prisoners when you give me silver as ransom.' Sir Hervey spoke slowly, as if to a child, gesturing towards his mailed chest.

'If you want silver you can sell the prisoners into slavery in Dubhlinn or Waesfjord.'

Sir Hervey was shocked at his opponent's response. 'They are men of standing.'

'Your ways are strange.' Sigtrygg waved for one of his own retinue to come forward.

Sir Hervey shook his head in despair. He knew the natives of Ireland to be savage, but he was truly amazed at their stupidity – apparently Sigtrygg required help to discuss a simple concept such as ransom!

Sigtrygg's conversation went on for many minutes before he sent his warrior back to join the other Ostmen. 'I have been involved before in a scheme like you describe. A double-dealing Norman forced me to do his bidding in return for releasing my people. In the end I lost crewmen and saw only part of the payment I was promised. I made a vow after that to never make a deal with one of your people again.'

Sir Hervey felt his weight switch onto his heels as Sigtrygg stared at him, stroking the two beard braids on either side of his mouth.

'As I see it I have three choices before me,' the Ostman

said. 'I can pay you in silver and return to my city with the prisoners -'

'You would return to a hero's welcome, and be sure of the love of all your people.'

Sigtrygg bobbed his head from side to side as if considering the truth of Sir Hervey's statement.

'Another choice would be for me to tell my people that the hostages were callously murdered by their captors.'

Sir Hervey's eyes narrowed. 'Why would they believe that we would do such a thing?'

'Your folk have a reputation. Traders from the north have told their tales of Jorvik, of the killing of thousands of Danes there by Normans in the days of their conquest. They would easily believe that you would be savage enough to kill these men, perhaps in order to send a message to Veðrarfjord.'

'What message?'

'That we should submit or die.'

Sir Hervey had thought their parley would be short; a conference with only one subject up for discussion: the price for the return of the prisoners. He had believed that that the Ostmen would fall in line and pay up, that he might already be riding back to the safety of Dun Domhnall. He had not expected the parley to take this course.

'What good would that do you?' Sir Hervey enquired.

'It would unite my people behind my kingship and give all the factions in my city a common cause: resistance against a foreign threat, the threat of the Normans.'

Sir Hervey shifted uneasily. 'I thought we were meeting to discuss the price for the release of prisoners. Is all this talk merely obstinacy? Or is it some sort of bargaining tactic?'

Sigtrygg was unmoved. His pig eyes bored into Sir Hervey and took a step towards the Norman knight. 'I did say there was a third option, didn't I? And that is the one that I choose.' His wolf-whistle was startling and loud. Behind the Ostman his crew understood the signal and began producing weapons, long knives and throwing axes. 'I expect that the deaths of your men here will hurt your army more than losing seventy will do mine. Your heads will be all the evidence that I need to ensure my people see me as a leader worth following when war is on the horizon.'

Sir Hervey was aghast and scuttled away with surprising speed for as Sigtrygg made a grab for him.

'Borard!' the old Norman squealed. Raymond's warriors were already at his side, pushing him out of their way as they drew weapons and made ready to face Sigtrygg.

It was ten men against one, but the giant Ostman's demeanour was anything but fearful. Rather, a smile stretched between his braided beard tusks and his misshapen nose flared as he produced a warhammer and a long, slim knife from amongst his clothes.

'Stay back,' Borard warned. 'You swore to keep the peace!'

'Peace? There can be no peace with invaders of our lands,' Sigtrygg spat back and braced himself to attack. However, at that moment a bellow sounded and the old abbot, armed with a sword, launched his counter-offensive, his robes billowing like wings as he ran headlong into the body of Sigtrygg's crewmen. He was followed into the fray by his six spearmen and his entire retinue of monks, nuns and musicians, still playing madly on stringed instruments. One spun an incense burner around his head before casting it into the midst of the Ostmen. Sigtrygg snarled and turned away from the Normans in order to help his men.

'Back!' shouted Borard and the conrois responded by shuffling towards the gates, their attention still locked on the fight between the abbot's men and Sigtrygg.

'Why did the abbot attack?' Asclettin asked as they reversed.

'Protecting God's peace?' Borard suggested. 'Who knows? Perhaps he is simply insane? Let's just make sure that we get out of here.'

Once through the gate the milites turned and ran downhill through the houses, their mail jangling loudly as it bounced on their shoulders. Sir Hervey was panting hard and he left it to Borard to issue orders and encouragement to the conrois. The thought of running the whole way back to the river appalled Sir Hervey, but he knew it was the only by getting to their coursers that they would be able to escape. Ahead he could see the main wall of the settlement and he redoubled his efforts, swiping sweat from his eyes as he ran between the buildings.

Ahead he could hear shouting and yelling, and he pictured more Ostmen lying in wait to murder him. Letting Raymond's conrois get ahead, Sir Hervey dove to his right and cowered behind the timber posts of the wall. He could hear raised voices and the thud of many horses' hooves.

Trinity help me, he thought. *I am surrounded.*

The sound of laughter and good natured chatter confused Sir Hervey as he pressed his frame up against the inside of the fortifications. He edged out through the defences, glancing both ways to make sure that there was no hidden threat, only to find Borard and Asclettin climbing into the saddles of their coursers.

'Get onto your horse, Sir Hervey,' Borard ordered, 'or stay here. We are making a break for it.'

'The Ostmen left on the west bank have crossed the river,' Asclettin added. 'Thankfully, the esquires were smart enough to bring our mounts to us rather than wait for us to run down to them.'

'Sigtrygg never meant to treat with us,' Sir Hervey exclaimed. 'Well, more fool him – we shall sell his folk to the slavers! We shall still be rich.'

'He always meant to break the peace?'

'He was planning to kill us.'

'Not just us,' Borard stated as he glanced meaningfully at the monastery on the hill.

Sir Hervey turned as he hoisted himself onto his horse's back. Over the rooftops he could hear screaming and the crackle of flames. A battle had overtaken St Abban's monastery. Monks were running uphill armed with whatever they could find to use as weapons. They screamed battle cries. Women, children and slaves poured in the other direction towards the Norman conrois.

'Let the savages kill each other,' Sir Hervey shouted. 'I need to get out of here. I'm going south to Dun Domhnall!' he ordered, kicking his heels to his startled gelding's sides.

Raymond felt Alice's eyes bore into him as he struggled to comprehend her words.

'Kill the prisoners?' he repeated. 'You think me capable of such a thing?'

Beyond Raymond, a fight was raging as the Ostmen climbed the wall to combat the arrows being shot by the few Welshmen stationed on the inner barbican. Raymond knew instinctively that in moments the weight of numbers would tell and that the Ostmen would kill the archers. Then the enemy would have weapons. Then they would have mastery of the gates to Dun Domhnall.

'I can't murder seventy prisoners. It'd be against everything that I -'

'Either you kill them or they escape,' Alice stated. 'Either you kill them or they will destroy Earl Strongbow's trust in you.' Her eyes sparkled with anger. 'Is that what you want? Do you think he will reward a man he no longer trusts? It's you or them.'

The taste of bile still clung to his mouth and Raymond felt another swoon coming over him. He tried to consider what to do. Alice did not give him the opportunity:

'I have given you the excuse you need. They are the enemy and they are in revolt -'

'Only because you murdered one of them,' countered Raymond. The pulse of pain at his temple was becoming unbearable.

'You need to realise that the longer you try to put off the inevitable the more likely they are to kill more of your men.' Alice took a step closer to Raymond and placed her hand over his as he held the bloody axe. 'Are you not sworn to the Welshmen as they are to you?'

Raymond considered the truth in her words.

'No one would blame you – did you not just face them in battle? What are seventy to add to the five hundred that you killed a week ago? It really wouldn't make any difference.'

'It makes a difference to me.'

Raymond wished he had a better argument but he could already feel doubt creeping into his mind. He could not afford to lose the patronage of Strongbow. It would mean the end to all his ambitions; his hopes of winning the hand of his lord's beautiful daughter. And from the barbican he could hear Welsh

33

voices shouting for help. He turned in that direction. Many Ostmen were huddling below the fighting platform on the inside of the wall. There, they were safe from any Welsh arrow. Several were attempting to hoist the heavy timber bar that locked the inner gates shut. More had climbed up onto the allure and were trying to force their way onto the barbican to attack the archers.

Perhaps Alice identified something in his bearing, his hesitation. 'Think of the future, Raymond. Save those Welshmen. Save your reputation and kill the Ostmen.'

He was still struggling with the decision as the thump of many feet announced the arrival of more archers under Caradog ap Thomas and the Gaelic warrior, Fionntán Ua Donnchaidh. Caradog did not wait for Raymond's command but ordered his men to line up and make ready their bows.

'Do you want me to try to talk to the prisoners?' Fionntán asked. 'They must know that they cannot win against a full company of archers.'

'Yes, no, we should ...'

'Raymond?' Fionntán swapped a concerned glance with Caradog. 'Are you all right?'

'Of course,' he attempted and turned to Alice. She offered no further advice. 'No, we need to -'

At that moment there was a scream and all eyes turned towards the barbican. The contorted shape of a man tumbled from the barbican to land awkwardly on the summer-hardened ground, twenty feet below. Those Ostmen still huddled around the gate crept out of the shelter to beat the fallen Welshman with their improvised clubs as he lay stricken upon the ground.

'Raymond?' Caradog demanded, his voice beginning to brim with anger. 'They have already killed four of my people – will you let them murder more?'

He looked from Fionntán to Caradog and back to the scene under the barbican. Doubt and pain assailed him. But his shoulders suddenly slumped and he nodded his head. 'Just kill them.'

Caradog didn't require a second command. He turned back towards his archers. 'Draw,' he ordered and the forty men hauled back their bowstrings, raising their yew bows towards the sky. 'Aim for their balls,' he growled. 'Loose!'

Raymond watched the arrows streak across the headland to smash into the Ostmen clustered under the wooden allure a hundred paces away. Screams and the thwack of arrowheads into timber palisade and human torso echoed around the headland. Men fell on their faces, whether dead or seeking cover, Raymond could not tell. Braver men ignored the danger and increased their efforts to open the gates. A second wave of arrows pummelled into the Ostmen, and then a third, and those that were still alive by the gates had their hands in the air, pleading for the arrow storm to end.

'Draw,' Caradog ordered. His hand was in the air, ready to give flight to another forty arrows.

'Caradog, wait!' interrupted Fionntán. 'They've had enough! They are giving up.'

Horror and resentment mingled in Raymond's mind, a mind clouded by injury, a mind at which Alice's barbed comments still clawed: *it is you or them, it is you or them.* He felt sick. He felt absent.

'Hit them again.' Raymond was surprised to hear the order shouted in his own voice.

The creak of drawn yew bows and the intake of each archer's breath was followed by the snap of bowstring upon stave and the hiss of arrows as they flew towards their target. The Welshmen had not even waited for Caradog's command to shoot. The shafts whacked into bodies standing as well as bodies already fallen, into hard ground and the wooden inside of the fortifications. Screams of fear and pain began and were ended as the arrows struck home.

'They've had enough!' appealed Fionntán from Raymond's side.

'Again!' shouted Raymond and the archers responded by sending another flight into the sky. But Raymond was not finished there. 'Draw -'

This time Caradog added his voice to Fionntán's dissent. 'They are finished,' the Welshman snarled. 'We've few enough decent arrows to waste them shooting at dead men. And I need to see if our folk are alive,' he added as he stomped towards the barbican. His men trailed alongside their leader, arrows nocked on undrawn bowstrings, their eyes on the Ostmen, ready to react to any threat. Raymond followed with Fionntán. The Irishman said nothing as they crossed the headland. Raymond could see distaste on his face. It angered him.

Three arrows were buried in the first body that they came across. A young archer stopped and knelt at the man's side. Producing a short knife from his belt, he stabbed the body close to where one arrow had entered his throat. Blood seeped from the wound, but the Welshman was able to prise free the shaft and, after an inspection, wiped it on the grass and returned it to the quiver at his hip. All around the area below the barbican the archers were doing the same surgery on the dead.

Caradog was already at the barbican and shouted up in his native tongue. In response, three bearded faces appeared and shouted down in a language that Raymond could not understand.

'The Ostmen say that they have taken the guards prisoner,' Fionntán translated. 'They wish to strike a deal.'

'They broke the last deal they made with us.'

'Oh, let's just get on with it,' Caradog replied and turned towards Raymond, a large finger pointed at his chest. 'Just get them to free my men.'

Raymond nodded and swapped Alice's axe into one hand so that he could wave at the Ostmen to come down and talk. Fionntán shouted up in their tongue. A few seconds later one man emerged and climbed down the ladder from the barbican. He was middle-aged with a wispy blond beard and a sword at his side. He glanced nervously at the archers cutting arrows from his comrades' bodies.

'He says that he only wants to be allowed to leave the fortress with his two surviving companions,' said Fionntán. 'He'll let the men they have captured go if you promise they will not be harmed as they depart.'

'Tell him that we agree,' Caradog said.

Raymond laid a hand on Fionntán's arm to prevent him translating. 'Wait.'

'Wait?' Caradog asked.

'I said that you will wait.' Raymond did not mean to get so angry, but Caradog's insistence had annoyed him. With effort, he relaxed. 'If it were you in his position, would you rely on a promise to get free?'

Caradog shook his head. 'I don't understand.'

But Fionntán nodded at Raymond's words. 'Of course you wouldn't. You would keep the hostages with you until you were well clear. Only then would you release them.'

'Well yes, I suppose, I would tell my captors to stay well away or I would kill -' Caradog nodded his head as he began to understand. 'Oh, I see.'

'Tell them that we need to see that our men are unharmed,' Raymond told Fionntán who translated it into the Norse tongue of Veðrarfjord.

'He says that you are to let them go free and then you can see them.'

Raymond sighed and looked meaningfully at Caradog.

'You bastard!' the Welshman cried and raised his bow. 'They are already dead.' He loosed his arrow. It was a point blank shot. The arrow went straight through the Ostman's throat and clattered into the gate behind him. The man was dying, but he did not yet know it. He teetered on his feet for several seconds before collapsing to the ground. Caradog spat on the Ostman and took the axe from Raymond's hand, whistling for his men to follow. He climbed the ladder onto the palisade and then the next to the barbican. Raymond could not see the Ostmen, but he did see Caradog chop down five times with the axe. Blood seeped through the timber palisade and onto the grass before the gates.

Raymond looked around. 'Are all seventy dead?'

'Looks like.'

'They should never have been made prisoner. It was always going to end up like this.'

'If you say so.' Fionntán sniffed and spat. 'Sir Hervey may have something to say about all this.'

'How do you mean?'

'He is in the north setting the ransom with the Ostmen. He won't be happy that you have messed up that deal. Think of all that silver he will miss out on.'

'Sir Hervey is a fool.'

Fionntán nodded. 'A greedy fool, like all Normans.'

Raymond caught the warning in his voice. 'My milites will understand.'

The Gael raised an eyebrow but did not contradict Raymond. 'What do we do with the bodies?'

'Bury them with the rest, I suppose.'

'Sir Hervey ordered the bodies from the battle to be thrown into the sea,' a voice said from behind them. Unbeknownst to either, Alice had followed them down to the barbican. She looked fascinated by the bodies of the Ostmen that surrounded her on every side. 'He waited for the tide to go out and had the Welshmen dump them over the cliffs. They were washed out. I watched them go, all five hundred. And I cursed each one.'

'Thrown into the sea?' repeated Raymond. It seemed an undignified and distasteful method of disposing of the bodies. He gripped the crucifix under his shirt. The throbbing discomfort had returned to his head. 'Oh, to hell with them. If it was good enough for those who died in battle, it will be good enough for these untrustworthy curs.'

'Raymond -' Fionntán growled.

'Just get it done,' he ordered before stomping off. A hand caught his cuff and forced him to turn.

'Let's be very clear about this – I am not one of your conrois,' Fionntán said as he released his hold on Raymond's arm. 'You do not give me orders, certainly not ones with which I do not agree. I like you, Raymond de Carew, but I am beholden to no one, be he king, lord or friend. I am not your servant. I go where I please when I please. Understand?'

'If you serve no purpose, why are you still at Dun Domhnall? Were you not here simply to deliver a message from my uncles in Waesfjord?'

'You needed my help -'

'And you've given it. Perhaps it is time for you to go back to Robert and Maurice?'

Fionntán stared at Raymond without speaking, his grey eyes searching his friend's face for hint of a jest. He found none. 'That knock to your head has changed you, Raymond.'

'I am fine.'

'And I tell you again that you are not yourself.'

Raymond could feel his jaw clenched tight, his fists too.

'Being as I *am* beholden to Earl Strongbow, I am not at liberty to journey to Waesfjord myself and tell Robert and Maurice about our victory over Ragnall of Veðrarfjord. But it still needs to be done. Do you think, going where you please as you do, that you might be able to deliver news of our victory to my uncles?'

Fionntán sniffed. 'I could do – on the way to Fearna and King Diarmait's side. I think that I have had enough of the company of foreigners for a while.'

'Then you should go.'

'And you will be well without me?' His eyes flicked to Alice and back to Raymond.

'Lord Strongbow will be here soon enough,' Raymond replied as he turned to walk away. 'All will be well then.'

Fionntán watched his broad-shouldered friend as he began issuing orders to the Welsh archers, pointing at the Ostman bodies and then towards the tumbling sea. He had met few men in his long life that could match the young Norman captain in battle. He had thought Raymond's uncle, Sir Robert FitzStephen, a great warrior, but the younger man had proven himself superior even to the conqueror of Waesfjord. They were very different in character; one was cold, level-headed and shrewd, the other a boisterous, bawdy brawler. Fionntán prayed that Raymond would recover the charm and disposition that had made him such a great leader. He feared what might become of the young captain if his current dark turn continued.

'Don't worry,' Alice of Abergavenny said from Fionntán's side. 'I'll make sure Raymond is cared for when you are gone. He'll be himself again, better than himself, if I can manage it. Don't fret about that.'

Alice was as beautiful a young woman as Fionntán had ever seen, as striking as the wife he had lost decades before, but as Alice smiled the Gael felt a shiver run down his back. What her plans were for his friend, he could not imagine.

Chapter Two

When he was a boy, Sigtrygg had walked the Merchant's Quay at Veðrarfjord by his father's side. He remembered the day intently. Nestled between the high walls and the shining River Siúire, it had been a tented city brimming with commerce and activity, so different to the wide timber streets and residential abodes inside Veðrarfjord's walls. The Merchant's Quay had been all colours and noise and smells, a swelling, busy festival of strange sights and new sounds in tight, cramped confines. Sigtrygg remembered being jostled from every direction as people moved back and forth between a hundred thatched shops, the tented stalls, and the ships on the shoreline. Everywhere, people bartered, haggled and argued. The noise had been incredible. From every side bargains were struck and commodities changed hands. Twenty different languages had assaulted his ears. Bearded Englishmen negotiated prices with sly Bretons while rich Flemings toadied up to tall, long-haired Danes. Silver was cut and coins jangled on wooden tabletops.

Sigtrygg closed his eyes and recalled prudish Frankish wine merchants and the street-rat children who shovelled animal dung into small carts to sell to tanners further upriver. He smiled as he thought of the hustle and bustle, of bartering fishmongers, of hauliers promising the best rates, and of the cloth-makers, down by the waterside, who pounded and cleaned wool bought from savage mountain Gaels. Animals squawked, honked and mewed, men shouted and begged. Timber docks groaned and creaked under the weight of humans and their cargoes. Wet rope strained and twisted aboard the fleet of merchant vessels. Every one of Sigtrygg's senses had seemed under assault on the Merchant's Quay at Veðrarfjord.

'Lower the sail,' his ship-master, Amlaith, shouted from the stern of *River-Wolf*, causing Sigtrygg's happy recollections to fade.

His back was sore and he climbed to his feet to stretch, grabbing hold of the forestay in order to do so. The crew worked the halyards but he made no move to assist them to stow the sail and then hoist the yardarm back to the top of the mast. Instead Sigtrygg relieved himself over the side and stared at the northern shore of the River Siúire. Wooded and mountainous, it was the territory of the Uí Bruadair and the Uí Dheaghaidh. If Sigtrygg had his way every tree would be hewn down and the savage Gaels forced over the mountains so that his people could add the valley to his city's territory. He spat a long globule in the direction of the forest.

'Get the oars out, lads,' Sigtrygg commanded. The longship rolled around on the sparkling Siúire as his men moved to and fro in answer to his instructions, unplugging the locks and sliding the pine oars into the water. He reached up and grabbed hold of the forestay for balance.

'Pull! Come on, you slovenly bastards. Pull!' Amlaith shouted out the pace from the far end of the ship.

Sigtrygg felt *River-Wolf* lurch forward towards the turn in the river. In his hand the forestay strained and his bicep bulged at each tug of the oars on the water. Seconds later Sigtrygg caught sight of the top of the great stone tower that marked the eastern extreme of Veðrarfjord. It appeared over the trees, sprouting from the vast marsh like the bows of a ship. He could feel *River-Wolf* gather speed. His men knew that they were almost home and as they rounded the bend, more of the city came into view. First, it was the jetties of the Merchant's Quay, jutting out into the river like great oars. Then it was the muddy beach and the heavy timber wall crowning the stone glacis which ran along the shore to Thorgest's Tower, half a mile upriver.

Sigtrygg felt his lip curl in anger. The quayside at Veðrarfjord was quiet, too quiet for midday at the height of summer. He could see only a handful of tented shops on the shore, and perhaps ten masts above the moorings. Where were the traders? Where were the Gaels down from the mountains with their precious animal skins? Where were the butter-sellers, or the slavers? Where were the horse-dealers and silversmiths?

He knew the answer, of course. Everyone knew. Ragnall

Mac Giolla Mhuire, Sigtrygg's father, had been defeated in battle and an invader was loose on Irish soil. War would soon find its way to the city's gates and that was a risk too great for most. The merchants had taken their merchandise elsewhere, to Corcach or Dubhlinn, or another rival town. Commerce was Veðrarfjord's lifeblood. If it did not flow, Sigtrygg knew, the city would stagnate and die. He needed a victory, and soon, or his reign would be over. To get that success, he needed support from the townsfolk. Sigtrygg had always known that the parley with the foreigners at St Abban's Monastery was a fool's errand, but he still worried about returning to Veðrarfjord without a promise from the Normans to release their prisoners. There were few families in the city that did not have some familial link to one of the seventy hostages, whether close or distant, and to have ignored their calls to meet with the foreigners was to invite discontent at a time when his rule was too fragile to survive. At the same time, Sigtrygg recognised that most of the prisoners had served the jarl Sigtrygg Fionn, one of his father's henchmen, who he had murdered. Were they to return to the city, the prisoners would certainly oppose his week-old reign.

He again rehearsed the story that he had concocted at the riverside camp the night before: that it had been the Normans who broke the solemn peace pledges to parley, they who had attacked first; that the foreigners had claimed that they would conquer Veðrarfjord; that the enemy had promised to kill the prisoners if Sigtrygg did not open the gates of his city to them. They had no choice, he would tell his people: they had to follow him, and he would bring them victory.

'Make for the wharf closest to the eastern gates,' Sigtrygg shouted at Amlaith, his arm pointing towards Rögnvald's Tower, the great fortification five ship lengths ahead. Sigtrygg felt a minute shift in his knees as Amlaith edged the ship towards the riverbank. There, at the eastern extreme of the city, where a small tributary met the mighty River Siúire, a wide pool had formed in the marshland. It was where Sigtrygg's Scandinavian forefathers had first made a winter anchorage for their longships, and where they had first thrown up a waist-high stockade to defend themselves from the native Gaels. It was where Veðrarfjord had been born.

Several minutes of effort at the oars brought *River-Wolf* to her berth. Sigtrygg's feet slapped on the timber jetty as he jumped up from the ship. As he made for the muddy beach, ten of his crew immediately tracked his movements, their shields and weaponry bumping against their spines and hips as they formed a bodyguard around him. It was a precaution that Sigtrygg could no longer afford to be without. Four days before, a stranger had attempted to knife him in the kidney as he had walked towards St Olav's Church. His cloak and hauberk had taken most of the damage from the thrust. Unfortunately, the would-be assassin had been killed by his men before he could give up the name of his employer. Sigtrygg could guess who had sent him, however. Gufraid was his father's cousin and a powerful jarl in his own right. He had been amongst Ragnall's inner circle before the defeat at Dun Domhnall and had declared his enmity to Sigtrygg by refusing to make a formal submission to him like the heads of every other family. Whether Gufraid had been making a play for the kingship of Veðrarfjord by sending the assassin, or merely wished to free Ragnall from his imprisonment, Sigtrygg did not yet know. Sigtrygg promised that he would take Gufraid's three sons out of their incarceration and parade them before Gufraid's hall. There, he would slaughter them, one by one, until Gufraid yielded to his kingship. And then, when his authority over Gufraid had been established, he would kill his rival too. That, Sigtrygg considered, would send an appropriate signal to any future opponent.

They still had a quarter-mile walk from the jetty to the gates and the midday sun was blinding as Sigtrygg led the way. Ragnall's warehouse, the sole building on the wharf, protruded from the wall. Only two people could walk abreast under the eaves of the warehouse, unless they preferred to get their feet wet, and in normal times it meant a bottle-neck would form at either end. Sigtrygg's party passed through without breaking stride. These were not normal times in Veðrarfjord.

Mud and marsh began to disappear into tough grass and firm soil as the land rose slightly the closer they got to the gates. Sigtrygg glanced upward at the top of the stockade where a defensive brattice jutted out from the wall. Rather than Ostmen, Déisi warriors patrolled the fortifications of Veðrarfjord. He sucked in a long, slow lungful of air and grimaced at the sight of the Gaels. His people had spent three centuries battling to keep their kind out of the city and to retain their independence. Now the Déisi stood ready to defend her sovereign walls against foreign invaders; to defend his kingship against threats from within. Still, he felt concern at having them inside Veðrarfjord.

The city gates were open. Sigtrygg had made sure that they were guarded by chainmail-clad Ostmen rather than any of Máel Sechlainn Ua Fhaolain's Déisi, but those to whom he had given the responsibility were nowhere to be seen. Sigtrygg fumed and stomped into the shadow cast by the stone glacis, already imagining the punishments that he would impose upon the family that he had entrusted with the gate's defence. Momentarily blinded as his eyes adjusted to the darkness inside the walls, Sigtrygg almost collided with a man as he walked into the small square. The man stood at the back of a large crowd of townsfolk and wilted when he saw the vast figure of Sigtrygg approach.

'What's this?' Sigtrygg shouted and pushed the man aside. There was a general murmur of disaffection and this gathered pace as Sigtrygg barged his way towards the middle of the crowd. Behind him, his bodyguard were even more forceful, sending a boy backwards over the wattle fence of one property as they forced their way through. Most of the crowd moved aside to allow them to pass. As they divided a strange scene emerged: eight bodies lay on the dusty ground. They were Ostmen, of that there was no doubt, bloated and pale, their leather clothes sodden and unkempt.

Sigtrygg's brow furrowed. 'Who are they?' he demanded of those gathered, his finger pointed at the eight bodies. 'Come on, speak up.'

An older man, a mariner by the look of him, stepped out and bowed his head. 'We found them in the sea, Lord, off Dubhán's Headland.'

Sigtrygg knew the area well. It was where the River Siúire spilled out into the ocean, many miles to the south. It was close to where Ragnall had been bested in battle by Raymond de Carew.

'There were more bodies, Lord,' the man continued. 'But we were fully loaded with hops and salt out of Bristol, and could only lift these few.'

'How many did you see?'

'Maybe fifty, Lord. They stretched in a long line on the current.'

'Who are they? How did they die? A shipwreck?'

A cry sounded to Sigtrygg's left and he felt his bodyguard close in around him on all sides. But rather than face an attack, the noise preceded the arrival of a woman to the square. She pushed through and launched herself across one of the bodies. She wailed in pain and dragged his cold hand to her chest.

'Niels, wake up, Niels!' she sobbed. 'Holy Mary, please send him back to me!'

It took Sigtrygg a few moments to realise why the woman had reacted in that manner. But it soon became clear: 'They are the prisoners,' he hissed. 'The Normans killed them.' A smile stretched behind his knotted, ginger beard as he watched the reaction of those in the crowd as they observed the woman's sorrow. Another person, a freeman from a nearby house, ran forward and cried out in anger as he spotted one of his kin. Then a third, and a fourth, pushed through the crowd and identified men who they knew. Sigtrygg could see the shock turn to disbelief turn to sadness. He knew that anger would follow.

'Good people,' he stepped out and addressed the crowd. 'Good people, hear your king now. These men were amongst those brave warriors who were taken prisoner by the foreigners out at Dun Domhnall.'

More people pushed through the crowd to comfort the woman whose husband had died.

'Niels!' she cried again. 'What have they done to you?'

Sigtrygg ignored her howls and pointed to the bodies. 'This will be the fate of all our people should we not unite to oppose the cruel invaders who threaten us.' A murmur of support gathered pace in the crowd.

'Kill them!' the woman screeched. 'Kill them all!'

45

'Will we stand together, my good people? Shall we face this enemy as one crew and send them back into the sea defeated?' He could feel the uproar building. More and more people had joined the crowd in the square. More of his people could see the bodies and shouted their support for action, for a violent response. The noise gathered pace. And Sigtrygg fed their fury.

'This poor woman has lost her husband! How many more must lose their loved ones? We went to parley with the foreigners in good faith, and they told us that unless we threw open the gates of Veðrarfjord, they would kill the prisoners and throw their bodies into the sea. And now we see the truth of their murderous intentions.' He swept a hand over the carcasses.

'Kill them all!' the woman cried again, her head sinking to her dead husband's chest.

'You know me!' Sigtrygg shouted, his voice booming despite the tumult within the city. 'I am the jarl who stormed the beach at Dun Domhnall and burned their ship. I am the warrior who captured the gates of the foreigners' fort. I faced their captain in single combat before Konungr Ragnall and Jarl Gufraid ordered me into a shameful retreat. And we all know how that turned out.' Boos echoed off the timber walls. 'Without me, Ragnall and Gufraid were defeated. But I can beat them, I promise you. If you stand behind me, I will defeat them! I am your captain and Veðrarfjord will weather this storm with me at the tiller.'

They cheered him then, their applause drowning out the miserable moans coming from those who had lost loved ones to Norman treachery. And as Sigtrygg marched away towards his father's hall, they surrounded him, shouting encouragement as they traversed Shieldmaker's Street onto the High Street.

'Sigtrygg, Sigtrygg,' they chanted.

The woman was beautiful. Her black cloak was wrapped around her shoulders like wings, her long dark hair covering most of her face. He could see her red lips as she walked towards him. Behind her the soundless blue ocean chewed at the green, grassy cliffs. Raymond could hear his own breathing and feel his heart in his chest. He was on a mountain top. That

46

he knew, but everything else was indistinct. She stopped a few paces in front of him and opened her mouth to speak.

'Climb.' Her whispered word stretched into a breath and then a rasp and the woman's head fell back onto her shoulders as he watched. Her hair and cloak tumbled from her shoulders, revealing a flock of red-eyed birds of every kind inside. They erupted towards Raymond – ravens, sparrows, herons, swans – and as they did so the sound of her voice transformed into a scream of a thousand birds and the disjointed snap of hurried, flapping wings.

'No, I don't want to,' Raymond cried and threw himself beneath the birds as they tumbled in his direction, covering his head as they squawked their way skyward. He raised his head to see a single magpie left standing where the dark woman had been moments before. The bird had something shiny in its mouth and, as Raymond held out a hand, it hopped forward, dropping a gold coin onto the grass.

'Climb,' the magpie croaked before taking to the air.

He picked up the coin. There were stamped pictures on either side, with writing around the edges. He rolled it around in his fingers as he climbed back to his feet. On one side was a castle and on the other, a face. It was that of Basilia, Strongbow's daughter, and around her it read: *montée*. He turned the coin and the same embossed words were wrapped around the picture of the castle.

A screech sounded from above and Raymond raised his head to see the murmuration of birds return. He watched them wheel and roll in the sky and then turn in his direction. He knew what was about to happen. They swooped low and slammed into him, forcing him to his knees. Raymond closed his eyes and held up his hands to defend his head. He screamed in pain as the flock surged over him. He could feel their beaks impact with his body, a hundred cuts or more. But as soon as it had started it was over. Raymond looked down and began panting. Arrow shafts protruded from his torso and legs at strange angles. His blood was everywhere. He was dying.

'Montée,' a voice called, over and over again. 'Montée, montée, mon -'

'Raymond, Raymond,' his esquire Fulk repeated. His

master mumbled but did not awaken and so Fulk gave his shoulder a shake. 'Master Raymond, they are leaving. You asked me to rouse you when they were getting ready to go.'

Raymond jerked awake. His hand went to his stomach, expecting to find arrows buried in his belly. He blinked as he looked up into Fulk's honest face. 'What?'

'Ferrand and Nicholas, they are leaving with Fionntán. Right now,' he stressed. 'You told me to wake up you when they were leaving.'

'They are leaving?' Raymond was momentarily confused and he sat up, shaking his head and sucking in air through his nostrils. 'Of course. Help me up.'

Fulk had been an apprentice butcher in Westminster before becoming Raymond's servant and then his esquire. It was not the done thing, to promote a boy of such lowly birth to the rank of esquire, but the fourteen-year-old had proven in the heat of battle that he was capable and steady. He would always lack the etiquettes and niceties learned by each esquire, but working with animals and cutting meat had made the red-cheeked boy stronger than most. The other esquires had called him Fulk *le Grand* even before he had been promoted. Now, he hauled Raymond to his feet by his outstretched hand in one swift motion then handed his master a skin of water. Raymond splashed a handful on his face and thanked him.

'Are you feeling any better, Master?'

Raymond could feel his ire rise. 'Some. How long have I been asleep?'

'All night, Master. The sun came up an hour ago.'

'Good lad. Run along and find me some breakfast. I'll also need horses ready for myself and half of Caradog's men within the hour. See to that too, please.' Fulk nodded and walked out of the hut as Raymond dried his face and blinked the sleep from his eyes.

The headland seemed strangely empty without the conrois of horsemen but Raymond could already see a small crowd had gathered within the gates to see off Fionntán and the small group who would accompany him to Waesfjord. The walk took Raymond several minutes but he soon heard the good-natured joshing of Welsh voices as Caradog's men said farewell to the

48

five archers who would guard the Gael and his two companions, Father Nicholas and William Ferrand.

'Nicholas,' Raymond greeted the priest and took hold of his bridle. 'I wish you safe travels back to Wales.'

'You could pray for me?'

'Of course I will – although without your instruction I might do more harm than good.' He leant in close. 'You have the money to barter passage back to Wales?'

'Yes, it is safe.'

'And you remember everything I asked you to tell Lord Strongbow?'

'I remember.'

Raymond shook him by the hand. 'Thank you for doing this, Nicholas. I cannot impress on you how important it is. Convince Strongbow to make the crossing! Remind him that infantry will be next to useless – he must employ archers, a minimum of four hundred, and milites. Urge him to act now. We few left here at Dun Domhnall cannot withstand another attack.'

'I will, Captain Raymond. And I will tell him the tale of the battle as best I can.'

'Not just him, I hope. Tell the story often and tell it loudly, in every church or inn you visit – we could use more ambitious warriors here at our side. Ragnall of Veðrarfjord knows that we are coming and he will be ready.'

'I will do my best.'

'Stop at Melrfjord first. The earl may already be there. If not, make your way to Striguil. Head to Carew, Pembroke, and Manorbier too.'

'I will. And I will tell your brothers and cousins that you need them here. That you need warriors and that they will be rewarded.'

'Odo won't come, but Griffin will, I hope, and perhaps my younger brothers too, though I do not know how capable they are of bearing arms.'

'I will approach your father. He will guide me.'

'Thank you, Nicholas,' Raymond said as he let go of the bridle. He next shook hands with each of the five Welsh archers who would act as the priest's bodyguard as he made his

49

way back to their homeland. Each of the bowmen had sustained a wound in Raymond's service and yet each stated his desire to return to the Norman's side before the storming of Veðrarfjord. Everyone knew that their path led to the Ostman city - the only question remaining was when. Raymond was touched by the archers' admission, more so than he had ever considered he would be. They, above all others, had no reason to trust Normans, the invaders of their country. But even when events had been at their darkest, the Welshmen had stood alongside him.

'Tell your people about the victory at Dun Domhnall,' Raymond told Bryn, the most senior of the bowmen. 'Seek out more archers and to tell them that I will pay well for men of their trade, if they can find passage across the sea.'

'We'll tell them, Raymond. And I'll even teach your priest how to shoot while I'm at it,' Bryn promised. 'Let's go, lads!' he shouted. 'It's a long way to go for a proper mug of ale.' He led the way through the inner gate with Nicholas in their midst.

Raymond found Fionntán lounging beside the inner gate in the sunshine with his eyes closed.

'I'll be out of your hair soon,' he said as Raymond approached. The Gael did not even open his eyes, but kept perfectly still with his head slightly tilted back. At his side was a satchel, a neatly folded long hooded shirt, and an array of weapons some of which, Raymond was sure, had been pilfered from the cache left by the dead Ostmen.

'How did you know it was me?' asked Raymond.

Fionntán smiled. 'You are the only man in Dun Domhnall who doesn't smell of wine or ale.'

'Not because I am the only man in Dun Domhnall who seeks out your company?'

One of Fionntán's eyes popped open. 'I get on well with Caradog too.' A second later, Fionntán started giggling and he started patting the ground beside him. Raymond sat down and for some time neither said anything.

'I stand by what I said yesterday,' Fionntán finally told him.

Raymond nodded. 'I don't. I spoke rashly and -'

'It is already forgotten.'

'So what is next for you?'

'Back to Fearna, I suppose, where I belong. I'll tell Diarmait that you are here and that Strongbow cannot be too far behind. And then? I really don't know.'

'Where is your home?'

'Nowhere anymore. I've lived among my enemies far longer than I ever did my friends.' He sniffed and spat on the grass. 'Be careful of vengeance, Raymond de Carew. It won't bring back that which has been taken from you. It just leads you to lose more.' Fionntán groaned as he hoisted himself to his feet, but turned and offered Raymond his hand, helping him to stand. 'I'll make sure your friend Ferrand gets to Waesfjord safely,' he said as he knelt and picked up his belongings. A sword and an impressive array of daggers and axes went into his belt while a sheaf of darts was secured at his spine in an old Welsh arrow quiver. He placed his pine spear across his shoulders and flexed it. 'I'll also make sure that your uncle Robert treats Ferrand well. They have a history,' he added with a smile, reminding Raymond of the Irishman's first words to him when he arrived at Dun Domhnall two weeks before.

'Thank you,' Raymond said and gripped Fionntán's arm. 'I suspect that we will meet again.'

'Probably,' Fionntán replied and strode away, wolf-whistling in Ferrand's direction and pointing to the gates with his spear. The Gael did not turn as he plunged into the darkness between the double embattlements.

Raymond smiled and shook his head as he crossed to meet William Ferrand on the back of his rugged pony. The leper had deteriorated since his heroics in battle and now permanently wore a scarf around his face and a chape over his head to mask the affliction. Nevertheless, Raymond could hear his breath catching in his chest as he exhaled. His elbows rested on the pommel of his saddle.

'Fionntán is eager to be away,' Ferrand said as Raymond reached him.

'He is. He suggests making camp this side of the Forthairt hills and then crossing to Waesfjord tomorrow.'

Ferrand bowed his head. 'And then what?'

'I don't know. Fionntán says he will keep you right.'

Ferrand turned away and looked out to sea, over the burnt-out marshalsea. 'You'll rebuild it?'

'We will.'

'And you will be safe without me?'

'I will. You've taught Fulk well.'

The warrior fiddled with his pony's reins and looked down at his hands. 'I need to thank you, Raymond.'

'Thank me? Ferrand, you saved *my* life.'

The leper's mottled eyes turned back towards him. 'No, you saved mine. You remember what I said down on the beach when we first made land?'

'You said that you came to Ireland in the hope that you would die in battle.'

Ferrand nodded and turned away again. 'And not one among the horde of Veðrarfjord could accomplish that small feat.' He laughed but Raymond could hear real sadness in his attempted levity.

'That day down on the beach you also said something else. Do you remember?'

'What was that?'

'You asked if this was the edge of the world.'

'I did.'

'And you said that men of God always sought out places like this when they were overcome with the need to consider the condition of their souls.'

Ferrand did not speak for several moments. 'I am not ready to die yet,' he whispered.

Raymond took a step forward and placed a hand on the leper's shoulder. 'I suspect that you are more complete today than you were when you first set foot in this country.'

His friend nodded. 'Yet I must face your uncle Robert and beg his forgiveness for what happened at Aberteifi Castle all those years ago. Then, I will be able to consider my soul.'

'Good, for I have a task for you, Ferrand; one that may take the rest of your life to complete.'

'A task?'

'You will go to Waesfjord and build a church in honour of our victory here at Dun Domhnall. Borrow what capital you need from my uncle Maurice FitzGerald. Tell him that I will pay him back.'

'A church?'

'And beside it you will build a hospital for the care of lepers.'

'For lepers?'

'You will build it as close to the town walls as Maurice will allow.'

'Raymond, I -'

'You will do this for me, Ferrand, for I wish to remember the bravery of the leper that faced down an army of Ostmen when all others had fled before their axes. I want to remember the man who saved my life. And I think it would be good for more people afflicted with the disease to know that their lives are not over.'

Ferrand's expression was unreadable beneath the thick scarf and for many seconds he merely stared out to sea. 'For whom would you have me name this hospital?'

Raymond, having only moments before come up with the idea, shrugged his shoulders. 'I don't know. Lazarus?'

'Perhaps one who thinks that they are damned, but is later forgiven?' Ferrand suggested.

Raymond grunted. Something in Ferrand's answer raised his ire. 'You need to catch up with Fionntán before he leaves you behind.'

'He's a good man. He'll wait for me on the road.' Ferrand insisted. He leant down close to his captain's ear. 'Keep safe, Raymond, and remember that you have friends ready to help you.'

With his advice still ringing in Raymond's ears, Ferrand tapped his heels to his pony's sides and walked her towards the gates. It was only as he was passing through that the leper turned in the saddle and waved to Raymond.

'I'll build your church, Raymond de Carew. And I'll dedicate it to Mary Magdalene. Make sure you live long enough to visit it!'

As the echo of Ferrand's laugh-cough vanished he felt a presence at his shoulder. Alice's arm slipped around his and her head came to rest against his shoulder.

'You are building a church?'

'Ferrand is, on my behalf.'

'Expensive.'

Raymond inhaled through his nose. He could feel Alice's long blonde hair wafting around his chin and mouth. He dared not move to stop it tickling him.

'There are fewer and fewer of us every day,' she said.

He shifted his head to look down at her face. Her hair shrouded it from his scrutiny. 'So it seems.'

'What do we do next?'

'We wait for Strongbow to arrive.' Above him a seagull began to cry and he pictured the woman from his dream. He desperately tried to remember the words and pictures that had been embossed upon the coin. He closed his eyes but the memory would not form. He hugged Alice's arm tighter.

'When will that be?'

'I wish that I knew.'

Sir Hervey de Montmorency was bone tired as he urged his horse down the bank and onto the causeway of slippery black logs which crossed the creek. He was a mile from Dun Domhnall and safety behind the tall double fortifications. The clop of his horses' hooves was dulled by the squelch of mud which squirted up beneath the ancient roadway. He looked to his left, towards the distant river inlet. Each day it flooded at high tide, covering the causeway and scattering the wading birds that hunted in the shallows. Sir Hervey and his men had missed the evening low as they had made their way back from St Abban's and had been forced to camp out in the tumbledown ruins of the homestead overnight. Sir Hervey had barely slept a wink. Every distant scream of a fox, every shuffle of a badger in the undergrowth nearby, had caused him to reach for his weapons, his body alert to any danger that might emerge from the darkness.

At his back were the esquires, chattering as if they were simply out on a hack rather than in fear for their lives. And ahead – a good bowshot away – was Raymond's conrois, the seven heavily armoured milites. They too joked and laughed as if they were at ease instead of on campaign. As far as Sir Hervey was concerned everything outside Dun Domhnall was enemy country. He would not feel safe until his nephew, the

Earl Strongbow, was in Ireland with their army. With Raymond's milites were two of his own warriors, sworn to his service. It infuriated Sir Hervey that they chose the company of low-born men like Asclettin FitzEustace and Thurstin Hore over his own, and he made a mental note to reprimand both when they were safely back inside the fort. His third miles, Rechin, was elsewhere on Sir Hervey's business.

'Come on! Forwards,' he urged his horse and rocked his hips in the saddle. The animal was unsure of its footing on the unstable causeway and edged on one step at a time, ears twitching fearfully. From behind, Sir Hervey could hear the esquires' ponies step down onto the wooden walkway and follow him into the midst of the creek.

'What's the hold-up?' one amongst them asked when their column came to a halt behind Sir Hervey. 'Are you all right, master?'

Sir Hervey could feel hot blood rush into his face and he dug his heels into the horse's flanks. Thankfully, that got the beast moving again. He could feel sweat pouring from his brow and back, and he was not sure if the cause was his fury or the sunshine which already poured down upon his small fighting force from the south-west.

Halfway across, Sir Hervey spied an arrow buried in the rushes. A remnant of Raymond's fight at the causeway just a week before, he supposed. The arrow caused the knight to remember his own experience of the battle for Dun Domhnall: of the savage horde approaching the fort upon the very path that he now ventured, and of the idiocy of the conrois who had allowed their enemy through the outer gates. He dismissed his actions after that, recalling instead how he had been in command when the conrois had taken the seventy Ostmen prisoners. That would be the part which would impress Strongbow, he decided. That would be the evidence he would use to press his claim for high command within his nephew's army. It would be the strategy he would employ to make sure Strongbow lifted him above Raymond. That would put the fat fool in his place.

The sound of sloshing water made Sir Hervey look down. The causeway had disappeared beneath the surface but his horse seemed happier to wade rather than face the slippery timber trunks. The bank was less than twenty paces away in any event. The land rose quickly to form a ridge running parallel to the creek and Sir Hervey did not stop as he left the causeway and began the slow climb to the top. He followed a path that had been greatly expanded since he had first used it and still showed the signs of the passage of many thousands of humans and animals. In parts the path was so muddy and deep that he was forced to move tight to the side, pressing against the thicket of briar and nettle, in order to keep going. Right then Sir Hervey promised that when Strongbow confirmed him to the land of Siol Bhroin, he would replace the barely traversable path with a proper stone road, and the silly causeway with a huge stone bridge. Never again would he be forced to travel in such a backward fashion! Of course a toll would be imposed upon anyone wishing to cross his new bridge, as would a payment from anyone who wished to use the harbourage below Dun Domhnall, or to pass the river leading towards Veðrarfjord. Raymond's silly timber fortifications would have to be replaced too, in order for him to maintain his rule over the entire peninsula.

For a man who had spent most of his life encumbered by debt or destitution, the thought of the riches that were owed to him gave Sir Hervey energy and he even managed to encourage his horse into a short trot which took them to the top of the ridge. There he recovered his breath. He had to shield his eyes from the sun as it climbed in the sky. He stared down across the gently rolling grassland to the walls of Dun Domhnall. Heat radiated above the ground and the air seemed filled with the sound of insects. From a mile away the fortifications looked so flimsy and small, a brown line upon the otherwise green landscape bounded on all sides by the ocean. Out on the arrowhead promontory to the east he could see the small hovels that his companions used for sleeping. He could see people going about their daily tasks. He held his hand out and closed one eye, pretending to crush one small figure between his fingers as he had done with stars when he was a boy.

'I hope you are Raymond,' he whispered as he squeezed shut his thumb and forefinger.

Voices and the sound of horse tack and hooves made him drop his hand. He did not turn his head to greet the milites who joined him on the crest of the hill. He was just about to move on when Borard spoke to him.

'Are you wondering who they are?'

'Who?'

'Them.' Borard's arm was pointing slightly to the west rather than south to the fort and Sir Hervey looked in that direction. He squinted but could make out a small group of people on foot behind two horsemen. They were walking away from Dun Domhnall. They were seemingly in no hurry as they had chosen to go miles out of their way, inland across the peninsula, in order to avoid crossing the causeway.

'One of them is not used to being in the saddle, that's for sure,' Borard added.

'Our men?'

'Difficult to tell at this distance – if we had Fionntán here he could tell us. I've never met anyone with better eyesight than his.'

Sir Hervey grimaced. 'I ordered that no one was to leave the fort until we returned. They were to watch over the prisoners or lose their share of the profits. If that Welshman has disobeyed I will flay him alive.' Sir Hervey did not wait for a response from Borard, but tapped his heels to his horse's sides and started him trotting towards Dun Domhnall.

Borard did not get the message and quickly pulled alongside Sir Hervey. 'Talking of the prisoners, sir, have you come to a decision yet of what we are to do with ours? The boys and I are looking forward to our cut of the profits, you see, and I have this issue where I have to let Raymond have all my-'

'We will take them to Cluainmín and sell them to King Trygve,' Sir Hervey interrupted. Trygve was the leader of a small town a few miles north. Although an Ostman like Sigtrygg, Trygve had declared himself neutral in the fight between Veðrarfjord and the invading Normans. Sir Hervey slowed his horse to a walk as the ground began to slope downwards again. That allowed Raymond's milites to close in around him from all sides.

'Trygve?' Thurstin Hore asked. 'Really?'

'He has silver and a slave market. We will get a good price.'

'Not as good as it would've been to ransom them back to their families,' accused Amaury de Lyvet. The whole conrois had caught up with Borard and Sir Hervey and crowded around them. Another voice – Christian de Moleyns, Sir Hervey guessed – growled his agreement with Amaury.

'What's the rush? We can keep them in the fort and find a ship. Then we could take them to Corach, wherever that is, or Dubhlinn. I hear it is the best place to get a good price for slaves.'

'Raymond wouldn't want us going that far,' Borard warned. 'Earl Strongbow could arrive any day now and he will want us to be ready to move out.'

Asclettin laughed. 'Raymond? Come on, Borard! You know that he'll let us do whatever we want in order to keep us happy.'

'And he knows we have earned a bit of extra pay,' Denis d'Auton insisted. 'Did we not win the battle for him when he was knocked out? Raymond owes us.'

'Hang on!' Borard attempted but was shouted down by raucous appreciation for Denis' words.

'You know as well as we do that Strongbow will reward Raymond and we'll see next to nothing for our efforts. We only want what is owed to us,' Amaury de Lyvet hooted.

'So we are sailing them to Dubhlinn then?' Borard asked and looked over both shoulders at his friends.

In the brief pause, Sir Hervey exploded with anger. 'No,' he cried. 'We are selling them to Trygve and that is all there is to it. You two,' he pointed at Amaury and Dafydd FitzHywell, 'will ride north to Cluainmín today and tell him that we are coming. The rest of you will chain the Ostmen up with fetters on their knees and wrists, and tomorrow morning before dawn we will drive them north over the causeway. We will be in Cluainmín by early afternoon. I will negotiate for a good price with King Trygve.'

'But -'

'No! Do you want to miss out?' Sir Hervey wheezed. 'Because with all your big talk of Dubhlinn and ships that is what will happen.' He turned towards Borard and extended a long, crooked finger in his direction. 'You said it yourself: my nephew, the earl, could arrive any day now. You know him to be a good Christian man – always up at Tyndyrn Abbey praying – and pious folk like Strongbow wouldn't like to know about the selling of men as slaves.' Sir Hervey paused while the weight of his words sank home. 'If you want to get rich off the back of the prisoners we have to sell them now! We can't wait around for a ship to appear in our harbour. Where would you even find a ship big enough for seventy prisoners and the rest of us? Veðrarfjord?' he asked and looked at Christian de Moleyns. 'You'd put us back in danger so soon after that fustilugs Sigtrygg tried to kill us at the monastery? You are a fool for even suggesting it.'

'We could hire a ship out of Waesfjord,' young Dafydd FitzHywell chimed in.

'We'd spend half our profits before we even reached Dubhlinn,' stated Amaury. No one dared argue with him about ships and the sea, but the group nonetheless descended into small conversations about what they were to do.

Sir Hervey sneered and angled his horse further towards the outer gates of Dun Domhnall, now only a hundred paces away. 'We are selling them tomorrow. Is everyone understood?' Silence met his declaration. 'Good. And tonight you can decide what you will do when you have good Cluainmín silver filling your pockets.'

With that Sir Hervey kicked his horse into a canter. There were two figures up on the barbican keeping watch. One was a Welshman and the other was Walter de Bloet, another of Raymond's senior milites. While the archer turned his back on the Norman horsemen, Walter waved and then leant over the spiked timber stockade. He put a hand to the side of his mouth a shouted down towards the conrois as they passed under him and through the gate.

'What?' Sir Hervey shouted up. The thump of hooves and rattle of brass and leather tack, not to mention the chat from the milites concealed whatever it was that Walter had attempted to tell him. As he turned left to make the long trek between the two battlements to the inner gate, Sir Hervey swivelled in the saddle to look back up at the barbican. Walter again attempted to shout down.

'I can't hear you!' Sir Hervey replied. Neither could he stop to enquire, for all the horsemen followed him through into the frigid cold between the walls. He was forced to continue, moving away from Walter. Here and there on the outer battlements were Welsh archers posted as lookouts. Sir Hervey caught a number of them glancing at him as he passed by. Something in their manner made him tense. He had lived long enough to listen to his instincts when they told him that something was amiss and his right hand slipped from the reins across to his left hip so that he could grip the hilt of his sword. Ahead he could see sunlight pouring through the open inner gates. He felt his few remaining teeth grip together and he steeled his body for action. On the inner barbican he could see more Welshmen. Their captain, Caradog, was one. He was statue-still as he watched the conrois walk the last few paces through the gates beneath him. The horsemen emerged into the sunshine within the walls of Dun Domhnall.

'Am I wrong or is something up?' asked Borard as he dismounted.

Thurstin Hore was the nearest man to him. He nodded and looked around him. 'There is definitely something going on.'

Sir Hervey stayed in the saddle waiting for all the milites to gather and climb down from their horses. The esquires took more time to enter through the inner gates but they soon began taking the reins of the horses from the milites and leading them away.

'Master?' one of the youths asked.

Sir Hervey looked down at the boy but did not dismount or answer. Instead he turned the horse to look back up at the barbican. Caradog had crossed from the far side so that he could look down at the returning Normans. Sir Hervey felt his eyes tighten as he returned the Welshman's study.

'Master, may I take your horse so I can give him a rub down?'

He still did not answer the boy. Sir Hervey felt his fingers grip tighter around his sword hilt. His eyes dropped to the wood on the back of the barbican. There was a large dark patch that he was sure had not been there before he had left for the expedition to the monastery in the north. It was dried blood. Sir Hervey's eyes flicked to a point on the ground directly below the barbican where he could see a similar sized patch of discoloured grass and earth.

'Something has happened,' he murmured.

'I'm sorry, master?'

Sir Hervey ignored the esquire and tugged on his reins, turning his horse in a tight circle. He looked into the empty cattle pens and towards the marshalsea. The remains of the building had no roof and from his height on horseback Sir Hervey could see that there were no prisoners inside. He felt his lips curl and his teeth bare in anger. He had been cheated!

'Someone will pay for this,' he hissed and turned his horse towards the ancient Gaelic fort, up on the eastern extreme of the headland. There, dark against the blue sky and burning sun, was a lone figure stood upon the high stone wall. His hands were on his hips and his surcoat and hair whipped around him.

Raymond de Carew had awoken from his slumber.

'You killed them all?' Asclettin accused. 'You knew that we were planning to ransom them back to their families, and you killed them? Are you completely mad?'

Raymond kept his lips clamped closed as more of the milites concentrated their ire in his direction. He had already heard what had happened in the north, but it seemed that none of his men even remembered that their trip to the monastery had been a disaster. Instead they hurled abuse at their captain. Raymond was unmoving. He leaned against a supporting pole at the top of the kitchen tent inside the walls of the old headland fort, his arms crossed on his wide chest. Above him the canvas roof drooped and billowed gently in the wind. He could feel the midday sunshine warming his right shoulder. On the benches below him were his milites, although most of them were on their feet, their arms outstretched to accuse him of wrongdoing.

'What were you thinking?' Denis d'Auton asked. 'Do you know how much money we have lost out on because of you?' He brought his hand down on the table, causing three mugs to spill their contents.

61

Even Borard, his most trusted lieutenant, had refused to speak in his support despite their lengthy conversation before the assembly. At the back of the tent, Raymond spied Sir Hervey de Montmorency and his two savage-looking horsemen. They swapped whispered words, shouting infrequently and only then in support of the milites' accusations.

'We should damn well throw *you* off the cliffs for this,' Christian de Moleyns shouted in Raymond's direction.

'You'll do no such thing,' William de Vale yelled weakly and stepped to Raymond's side. His response earned a number of mocking laughs from the older warriors. Raymond could feel his own indignation bubbling in his stomach and behind his eyes, but he refused to allow another outburst. He clamped down harder on his teeth. That merely made his head hurt more.

'I cannot understand why you would do this.' Thurstin Hore shouted. He did not speak often but when he did he made himself heard. 'Where was the harm in us making a bit of money on the side, eh? Who was it going to hurt?'

When Raymond did not answer it only added to the milites' annoyance and soon their arguments descended into a blur of accusations. Quarrels begun years before began to re-emerge: Walter de Bloet's resentment at Raymond's promotion over him; Raymond's control over Borard's finances; Raymond's absence when Amaury de Lyvet's brother was murdered; and the time, eight years before, that Raymond had broken Asclettin's nose. All the old squabbles were set free and were tossed in Raymond's direction. And still he said nothing to defend his actions.

'Aren't you going to speak?' Borard appealed. 'Do our concerns mean so little to you?'

That finally brought a hush to the tent. Raymond waited for everyone to sit down. 'Your concerns mean a great deal to me, but we are here on behalf of Earl Strongbow and his concerns are paramount -'

He had barely finished his master's name before the incensed shouting began again. Raymond could barely discern a single question or comment amongst the raucous noise.

'Men, men,' he heard Sir Hervey appeal until the kitchen returned to calm. 'Do we actually know that Raymond here killed the Ostmen? Where is the evidence? Perhaps he secreted them out of the fort in our absence and sold them himself. He probably split the money with those foreign Welsh devils with whom he is so friendly.' The French knight raised his thin arm to point at a small group of Welshmen sitting in the sunshine a hundred paces away. Again there was uproar in the tent. Even the esquires – who had to that point remained quiet – were on their feet and adding their anger to that of their elders, shouting that they hadn't been paid in months.

Raymond shook his head and again fought against his rising rage. He looked to his old rival, Walter de Bloet, and, with his eyebrows, directed him to address the conrois. With his injured arm still in a sling, Walter scowled and slowly climbed to his feet.

'Listen! Raymond didn't sell them,' Walter said. 'I saw it with my own eyes as sure as I'm seeing you. He killed them all. I was to benefit from their sale, just like you -'

'Why didn't you stop him?' Asclettin demanded.

'It happened fast.'

'We heard that he murdered them in cold blood.'

Walter rocked his head from side to side. 'I don't know. He definitely ordered the Welsh to throw the bodies into the ocean.'

There was a short pause as the assembled men considered that piece of information.

'Did he do it to hide the deed from us?' asked Dafydd FitzHywell.

Raymond could take it no more. 'I threw the bodies over the cliffs to stop disease from spreading around the camp, you dullard.'

'Sit down, Dafydd, and be quiet!' Borard ordered. He got to his feet and turned towards Raymond. He was angry but reluctant to outright accuse his friend of cheating him. 'Perhaps you could tell us all why you killed them? Was it as the men are saying? That it was jealousy because we captured so many Ostmen and that you were not going to profit from them?'

'Don't be so stupid,' Raymond countered. 'How long have

you known me? When have I ever cared about money?'

'Then tell us why you did it.'

Amongst all the shouts and anger, Sir Hervey's quiet, composed request proved enough to quiet the room: 'Tell us why any of us should trust a word that you say?'

Raymond felt his own eyes narrow as every other face turned to look at him. 'Because I am the captain of this conrois and I adjudged it to be the right thing to do.'

'Ha!' Sir Hervey laughed. 'I have heard that it was your murderous whore who actually did the deed, and that she gives the orders now. Is that how it is, Raymond? Has she unmanned you?'

Despite his attempts to control himself before he knew what was happening Raymond was halfway across the room, his fist raised and a stream of incoherent curses issuing from his mouth towards Sir Hervey. The old man looked shocked and tumbled backwards over a bench. But Raymond did not reach him. Instead his conrois surrounded him and took hold of his arms and hauled him away. He kicked over a table but it was eight against one and they half carried him out of the tent before pinning him to the ground. Raymond jerked his body and kicked his legs, but his warriors restrained him.

'Get off me,' he shouted. 'Get your damned hands off me!'

'Shut up,' Amaury told him, 'and calm down.'

'What do we do with him?' asked another.

'You will not treat me like this. I am your captain!'

'No,' Borard said as he stood up, letting go of Raymond's leg. He indicated that all were to follow his lead. They did it slowly and then backed away. Raymond immediately sprang to his feet. Borard put his hands on Raymond's chest and pushed him backwards. 'You used to be *our* captain. Now you are only the man that delivers Strongbow's orders.' He lifted his chin in the direction of a nearby hut. Raymond followed the direction of his gaze to where Alice of Abergavenny had emerged. 'Or maybe it is her orders? Why don't you go back to your new commander and check?'

Raymond spat on the ground. 'What are you saying?'

Borard shrugged and Asclettin stepped forward. He looked at each of the men who stood opposite Raymond. 'We are saying that we'll have no more orders from you today. You betrayed us and you cannot be trusted any longer.'

Raymond was so shocked that he said nothing as he watched the eight milites – men who he had grown up alongside – backed away from him and vanished back into the shadow of the kitchen tent. Raymond was locked to the spot. He could not believe what Asclettin had said. To make it worse from inside the tent he could hear Sir Hervey de Montmorency addressing his conrois.

'Are you all right?' William de Vale asked.

'No, I don't think I am.'

Sigtrygg did not take his eyes off the gates as he marched forward. At his back were two hundred Déisi warriors and eighty of his own folk. The stomp of their boots on the hard soil was confident as they followed him through the fields. They knew as well as he that there was no chance that the small ditch and earthen bank could resist them. A storm was about to break upon the settlement. To the east, the church at Cill Odhran tolled its bells in warning.

'Too late,' Sigtrygg mocked and banged his axe head twice on the reverse of his circular shield. The Ostmen responded with a battle cry.

The land fell steeply away to a stream in the west but otherwise was open meadow. The inhabitants could not have missed the approach of the force out of Veðrarfjord. Yet Gufraid had done nothing to oppose them. The city was three miles away through the wooded hills and Sigtrygg had expected some sort of resistance along the path. He would've easily swept aside the few warriors that Gufraid could call to his side, but no altercation had occurred. Instead Sigtrygg had led his army unopposed towards the manor on the western extreme of Ostman territory. A mile beyond was a sea of Gaelic princes and chieftains.

Sigtrygg could already see the top of Gufraid's hall above the meagre defences and sitting beside the blue River Siúire. The far bank was forested and hilly. He had his shield on his left arm and an axe gripped in his right. He had an army behind him and he was a hundred paces from his target. He smiled.

'Go,' Sigtrygg shouted to Máel Sechlainn Ua Fhaolain off to his right. The moustachioed King of the Déisi hoisted his spear in reply and wrapped his mustard-yellow robes around his left arm. He screamed for the attack and then took off at a run towards Gufraid's defences. His pack of derb-fine closed in around him. Sigtrygg could see Máel Sechlainn's Tánaiste, Toirdelbach, amongst their number, his long hair flapping behind him like a tail. The Déisi howled like wolves as they ran. They were still thirty yards away when they unleashed their bombardment of darts over the rampart.

Sigtrygg watched their attack, but a sinking feeling had already begun to form in his stomach. The Déisi were almost at the defences yet Gufraid's folk had not responded; no flight of spears had soared over the wall towards the Gaels. There had been no arrows. In fact Sigtrygg could not see one warrior on the walls. He stopped walking and moved his gaze from the manor gates to the field beneath his feet. He grasped a fistful of wheat. Not one stalk bore any grain – Gufraid had already brought in the wheat harvest. He turned to his right and looked at another field, half a mile away. It was ploughed and sown, most likely with a winter crop. Sigtrygg had to shield his eyes from the summer sunshine as he quickly searched the surrounding fields for the signs of animals. He could see none and he cursed out loud. Gufraid had fled. Ahead the Déisi shouted in acclaim as they leapt over the ditch and began to scale the wall. Sigtrygg knew that there would be no defenders to oppose them.

'Follow,' Sigtrygg barked and pushed on through the fields. He could feel his warriors' worry as he made directly for the gates. No one stopped his approach. He stood before the closed gates and then lifted his foot to kick his way through. The gates were not even locked. His warriors crowded around him as Sigtrygg continued into the muddy street inside the manor's walls. There were thatched houses on either side.

'Search them,' he ordered. Sigtrygg did not wait for a response but began walking down the street. To his right he saw a number of the Déisi drop over the wall and into the manor. They still had their weapons raised as if expecting a counter-attack. Sigtrygg ignored them and turned his attention on the biggest building in the settlement, Gufraid's hall, directly ahead. It was only impressive because the houses that surrounded the hall were so small, he decided. Otter skins hung from the eaves of the hall and the door. The pelts shone in the sunshine. Sigtrygg pointed towards them and then to his own wide chest so to lay claim to the skins. He then levered the door open using the handle of his axe. Though he knew the hall to be empty, he kept his shield high as he plunged into the darkness. He sniffed the air. It was stale. His eyes adjusted to the gloom and he could see more otter skins on the beds to his left and right, and more hanging from the rafters.

'They left in a hurry,' he murmured.

'Sigtrygg?' enquired Amlaith, his ship-master, from Sigtrygg's heels.

'Get the pelts. Search the loft and under the beds for Gufraid's hoard.'

He waited for Amlaith to nod and then he strode down the length of the hall and kicked open the door at the far end. Gufraid had built his home on a strip of land near the water's edge and Sigtrygg emerged close to the muddy beach. The distant northern bank of the Siúire shimmered in the heat. The river was at its lowest point and on the far bank he could see many abandoned coracles and faerings, a couple of karvi-sized vessels too. Gufraid's folk had fled into the land of the Osraighe with all the food and possessions they could carry. He wondered where Gufraid could be headed and what he could hope to achieve by crossing into Gaelic territory. Could he be aiming to enlist a mercenary army? Sigtrygg dismissed that thought almost immediately. Gufraid had nothing to offer in payment for such a force. The likely answer was that he would simply remain out of sight until Sigtrygg's army returned to Veðrarfjord. Then they would re-emerge from their hideaway and cross back to the manor. He strained his eyes and searched the far shore for Gufraid's scouts. If they were there, and he was sure that they were, the scouts were well hidden.

Footsteps and chatter from behind Sigtrygg caused him to turn. Jarl Háimar approached with his body of warriors. Háimar had been the chief man from a small steading to the east of the city, out where the three rivers met and divided. He had been amongst the first to throw his support behind Sigtrygg's takeover from Ragnall and his loyalty had been rewarded with a second manor abutting his own at Fiodh-Ard Liag. Háimar had also been afforded the rank of jarl in Sigtrygg's new regime.

'Do you think that they crossed the river?' asked Háimar. He was a short man with earrings, tattooed arms and long brown hair. 'Should we follow? He has women and children with him. They will be slow.'

Sigtrygg's misshapen nose flared. He would've liked nothing more than to hunt Gufraid down and to end his threat once and for all. But he knew that he could not afford to be away from the city for long. Not when so many factions still called him a usurper. 'No,' he told Háimar. 'We will go home. I have a better idea about who can hunt down Gufraid.'

Háimar seemed annoyed at his answer. 'And what about these three?' he asked, jerking a thumb in the direction of three gaunt-looking young men with their hands in fetters. 'What will I do with them?'

Sigtrygg stared at the trio without speaking, his small eyes locked on them. They were Gufraid's three sons, captured as they tried to flee Veðrarfjord in the days after Ragnall's fall from power. None of them could meet his gaze. Instead Gufraid's sons kept their heads down, staring at the muddy beach. Sigtrygg had hoped to use them to force their father to submit. He could feel his anger mounting, his axe seeking vengeance upon the sons because of their father's transgressions. With effort, Sigtrygg relaxed and a smile appeared from behind his braided beard tusks.

'We'll keep my young cousins alive for another few days,' he chuckled and dropped a hand onto the eldest boy's shoulder. The boy's whole body jumped as Sigtrygg touched him. The youngest was weeping and Sigtrygg smiled even wider. 'They may yet come in useful.'

Jarl Háimar cursed. 'They are your hostages, Sigtrygg. Do you want them to go back with you to Veðrarfjord?'

'No. Keep them with you at Fiodh-Ard Liag. There are too many in the city who would use them against me.' Sigtrygg lifted the chin of the eldest of Gufraid's sons - he couldn't remember the boy's name. He looked into his eyes. 'This one is thin. You will feed them more. If they die I will blame you,' he told Háimar and started walking back towards the hall, ignoring the jarl's grumbles about the vast expense of accommodating the three layabout hostages.

'You've been well paid for your trouble,' Sigtrygg snarled. At the far side of the manor he could see Amlaith loading the precious otter skins into a hand-cart and begin making for the gates. 'But as a favour to you I will allow you to have anything you wish from within Gufraid's own hall. Maybe you can feed his sons off the plunder.'

'Thank you, my konungr,' Háimar gushed.

'And when you are done, burn the manor to the ground. Burn the fields and every building. I want Gufraid to have no home left to return to.'

Alice had watched Raymond mope around the headland for two days. She was beginning to lose patience with him. If Strongbow arrived to find his troops in mutiny against him the likelihood was that he would never be trusted with command again. Her attempts to talk to him about the rift that had opened between him and his milites had been met with a sullen silence and as a result he had requested that Fulk, rather than Alice, bring him his meals.

'He won't listen to me either,' William de Vale told her when she had approached him with the problem. William was fishing off the cliffs at Dun Domhnall. 'Raymond just wants to be left alone,' he told her. 'It's not like him. I think it is still his injury,' he added, contorting his face and sticking out the end of his tongue to support his point. 'His mood is up and down. He's happy one minute, then he's sad, and then he is angry.'

But Alice refused to accept that a mere knock to his head could influence him so adversely. 'He needs to do something to keep busy. He needs to take back control.'

'The conrois won't listen to him. They are still furious.'

'We shall see,' she said and hitched her skirts to scale the steep cliff face.

'Why do you care anyway?' William shouted after her.

Alice ignored him. William was little more than a boy and

could never understand the needs or anxieties of a woman alone in a foreign land; a woman whose last family member had been murdered as she watched. He could never understand the choices that were placed before her or comprehend the regrets that stalked her every waking moment.

Alice paused as she climbed upwards and wiped the tears clear of her cheek. 'Keep going,' she whispered.

Soon her hands were tugging for purchase on tough coastal grass rather than rock and she was able to hoist herself clear and onto the headland. She dusted off her palms and looked back towards the sea as it chewed and crashed against the black rocks far below. William de Vale had returned to his sport. She recalled watching him teach Geoffrey to fish just a few weeks before.

'No,' she scolded and sniffed back the tears. 'You will keep going.'

She turned away and walked back to her own hut. She ducked inside and found the large piece of pale folded linen that she had been using as a pillow for the weeks they had been at Dun Domhnall. She had hoped to turn the fabric into a surcoat for Geoffrey, one bearing their father's arms; one that would have declared his right to Abergavenny Castle. That dream had died with her brother. Her usurping cousin had beaten them. She would never go home. Abergavenny would never be hers. Alice held the linen to her chest and closed her eyes.

'I am sorry, Geoffrey,' she whispered to the cold darkness. 'It is time for a new dream.' She breathed in deeply and began nodding. 'Come on now,' she said and set the fabric down on her bed, making sure it was smooth and would not wrinkle. She then hauled on some breeches under her skirts. A cloak was thrown over her shoulders and fastened with a large brooch that Raymond had bought for her from a merchant in Wareham. Her blonde hair was tied back at the nape of her neck. Alice added a knife to her belt and a knapsack to her shoulder.

Raymond, predictably, was seated in the doorway to his own hut, facing the sea, and dozing in the sunshine. Three half-finished wood carvings lay abandoned on the grass nearby. Woodchips were all over his clothes. A knife was thrust into the ground at his side.

'I am going into the countryside,' she told him and walked on past.

It took him a few seconds to respond and sit up. 'What? Why?'

'To find some flowers and bark – I have some fabrics that need to be dyed.'

'Is that really necessary?' he asked.

'Yes, it is. I will take Rufus up to the woods.' Alice flapped a hand northwards.

Raymond climbed to his feet but did not leave his doorway. 'No. It is too dangerous to go that far from our walls by yourself.'

There was an aggression in his manner but Alice ignored it. 'I will be fine.'

'Halt,' Raymond ordered as she passed beyond his view around the side of his hut.

'No.'

She could hear his feet thump on the dry ground as he left his doorway and came after her. He caught her arm and hauled her to a stop.

'It is not safe to go inland. We don't know who may be out there, watching the fort.'

'Oh, for goodness' sake. No one would dare -

'You can't know that.'

Alice shook her head. 'Then send someone with me - one of your milites.'

She watched as Raymond's eyes flicked to the main wall. His warriors had taken to spending most days lounging around on the outer defences just as their captain did out on the promontory out of sight. Raymond didn't say anything in reply but bowed his head. Alice rolled her eyes and walked away from him.

'Wait!' he called.

'No. I am going.'

He spun on his heels and looked around. 'William! Where is that damn fool of a boy? He can go with you. Why is he always missing when I need him?'

Alice did not admit to having seen William down on the

71

cliffs.

'There's no sign of Fulk either. Well, I suppose that I'll have to come with you,' Raymond finally admitted with a slight slump of his wide shoulders.

Alice stopped but did not turn to look at him. 'If you like. I can't stop you.' She marched away again as Raymond ducked into his hut and grabbed a tunic and cloak. Alice could hear the rattle of his weapons as he caught up with her.

'You can't even get a minute's peace to recuperate from a head wound,' he mumbled as he threw his cloak on and slotted his scabbard onto his belt. His complaining continued as they crossed the bailey to where Raymond's esquires watched the horses roam around. Since the marshalsea had burned down the horses had been allowed the run of the entire western half of the headland and they had already eaten almost every blade of grass on the wide acreage. The esquires had been told to watch over the animals in shifts although Alice could see several of the boys asleep in a lean-to against the inner palisade. A 'catch' game involving the rest was in full swing and as a result they did not realise that their captain was nearby until Raymond barked a sudden command for quiet.

'Honestly, you'd think I paid you to sit around all day and do nothing. Find me Rufus and the dun palfrey and get them saddled,' he ordered. 'I need a spear too.' The boys immediately leapt into action with six rushing to the equipment store under the fortifications while the rest went to retrieve the two mounts as instructed. Raymond did not watch their work, but folded his arms and stared out to sea. Several minutes' hustle and bustle saw the two horses caught and saddled.

Raymond offered the boys no thanks as he clambered onto his palfrey's back and began walking her towards the gates. 'Are you sure you would not be more comfortable on this one?' he called back to Alice.

'I'll be fine.'

'Suit yourself.'

Whether it was their voices or the sound of their horses that alerted them, Alice did not know, but as they approached the inner gates faces of Raymond's milites began to appear from buildings and on the wall. They said nothing but glared down at their captain as he left the fortress. Alice felt discomforted enough by their impassive stares that she bowed her head until they were under the barbican. She looked up at the top of the inner wall as they walked the long passageway between the fortifications. The same blank faces appeared above, unmoving.

'Off for some fun, are we?' one voice called out. Another yelped like a rutting dog, earning laughs from more of the warriors. The sound rang in Alice's ears and echoed off the timber walls to either side of her. Ahead, she could see Raymond's shoulders bristle as he urged his palfrey into a fast amble. Alice refused to hurry and allow the milites to see a reaction to their slurs.

'Are you going to give him his orders now, girly?' another shout came, followed by more laughing.

Raymond soon built up a significant gap between them. He did not stop as he exited through the outer gates but maintained a steady pace as they rode. Alice increased her stride to a canter once she was clear of the fortifications and caught him, but as soon as she slowed down again his lead widened thanks to the palfrey's quick gait.

They were travelling parallel to the creek and Alice could feel the bright sunshine on her left cheek. She could also hear the river flowing in the muddy channel and knew that the causeway across would be well underwater. Raymond had also realised that the tide was in and led her on the circuitous western route. With Alice continually falling behind and then cantering to catch up, it took them just over an hour to journey around the stream and then to turn north to where the trees became more plentiful. Soon they were in the midst of the woods and Raymond was forced to slow his palfrey to a walk in order to pick a safe path.

'There's a freshwater stream up ahead,' he told Alice as she drew close. 'We'll stop there to get the horses a drink. We must keep our eyes and ears open. There is a settlement half a mile to the west. They call it Dun Conán and it has a beach which is used by the Ostmen to land their ships.'

Alice nodded her head and followed quietly to a long meander in the stream where a little pebble beach had formed.

73

Raymond dismounted and led his palfrey to the edge of the water. Alice copied him and both horses happily drank down their fill before investigating the bank for grass to eat. Steam rose from both animals' backs.

'What are you looking for in the forest?' he asked.

'Alder bark, oak apples, iris root,' she listed. 'Things that I can use to make dyes.'

'I didn't think you would know how to do that.'

Alice raised an eyebrow. 'It was one of the tasks that I was forced to do when my cousin put me in that nunnery.'

'Oh?'

'I never thought that I would use anything I learned there again, but here we are,' she raised her hands and indicated to the trees around her, 'in Ireland.'

Raymond looked away. 'Sorry. I -'

'No, no – I didn't mean it like that.' Alice paused and began again. 'I am also looking for cow parsley and nettles and foxgloves. That should produce a really radiant yellow. I need a lot of marigold and St John's wort too – if such a thing can be found here.'

Raymond nodded meekly.

'Aren't you going to ask me why I need all this dye?'

He began to slowly shake his head. 'Why do you need the dyes?'

Alice smiled. 'Because I am making a new surcoat for you.'

Raymond screwed up his face. 'I already have two -'

'I'm also designing a new coat of arms; a coat of arms that belongs to you.'

'Why would I need that?'

She ignored his question. 'It will be a golden field with three black lions. Gold because I have faith in you, and lions because it denotes strength and courage.'

'Angevin lions?'

'Welsh lions.'

Raymond looked suspicious. 'And I ask again: why do I need a coat of arms?'

'Because if you pull yourself together and take charge as you did when you disposed of the prisoners, you will be rewarded by Strongbow.'

'Rewarded? What I did ...' Raymond paused and looked distraught. 'The Ostmen are the reason I am in this mess with the conrois.'

'It was the only sensible course of action.'

Raymond shook his head and took hold of his palfrey's bridle, leading the horse off the beach and back into the trees.

Alice fumed. 'The only reason that you don't see it is because I am cleverer than you.'

That caused him to stop in his tracks and turn to look at her. 'You think that you are smarter than me?'

'Yes. By far.' She clicked her tongue three times and Rufus followed her out off the beach and onto the grass. 'And if you listen to what I tell you to do you will be wealthy and powerful and beholden to no one. I am intelligent and I am ruthless and I am -'

'Just a woman.'

Alice turned on Raymond, anger surging through her, but his hands were up in apology.

'I meant no offence. I spoke out of turn.'

Alice blinked many times. 'You are right. I am a woman and that means I need you. And if you listen to me then you will succeed. Strongbow will need a constable once Veðrarfjord is taken. Have you thought about that? I can help you get it. Then you can help me. We can help each other.'

'You mean as man and wife?' His manner held a challenge.

She felt tears form at her eyes and she turned away so that he couldn't see her face. She didn't speak but shook her head.

'You still blame me for Geoffrey's death. I understand.'

Alice breathed in deeply to compose herself. 'I did blame you. For days and days, I blamed you. But then I realised that my anger and sadness will not help me now. Geoffrey's death is not the reason that I will not marry you.'

'Why then?'

She braced herself to tell him the real reason. It seemed the proper time to tell him. But her confidence failed her. 'Because there will come a time when you will have to marry for power and position and I cannot be in the way of that,' she said instead. 'I can provide neither of those things for you now. Any hope I had for recovering Abergavenny died with Geoffrey.'

Raymond looked confused and hurt by her words.

'Of course, it may be that the person who can provide prestige and connections may also be someone that you love.' She had seen Raymond's affection for Basilia, Strongbow's daughter, before their own brief affair. She judged that his mind had drifted to her.

'That's not why I -' He held up his hands. 'Perhaps we should start looking for your plants?'

For some time neither said anything. They found a fallen oak close by and it proved strong enough to secure the two horses.

'I've seen cow parsley, nettles, and foxgloves on the southern bank of the creek near the causeway so we can leave that and concentrate on the other items,' Raymond said. 'We are best looking for alder down by the riverbank.'

They walked in that direction and soon Alice spotted the distinctive catkins and rounded leaves of an alder tree. Bees buzzed around the branches. 'We need the inner bark,' she told Raymond.

Her companion nodded and produced a hand axe from his belt. He put his left palm on the rough bark and paused, looking around the woodland. Content that there was no one around that might hear his work Raymond swung the axe, driving it into the tree. The noise of the impact echoed around the wood. He kept working until he was able to use the blade to lever away a piece of bark as wide as his hand and as long as his forearm from the sapwood underneath. He then repeated the process higher up the tree on the far side, and then lower down on a third side.

'That should be enough,' Alice told him as she returned with her knapsack bulging with marigold and St John's wort. She added the bark to her load. 'Back to Dun Domhnall?' She watched him grimace. 'We still need to find foxgloves and nettles. That will take some time.'

Raymond nodded but did not move. Instead he knelt on the ground and indicated for Alice to do likewise. He then leant close to her ear. 'I see movement in the forest. It looks like cavalry, but I can't be sure.' He lifted his chin in the direction from which they had come.

'They might find the horses,' Alice whispered.

'Come on, stay low,' he replied and darted soundlessly away from the river. Alice followed, her heart beating faster, though whether from nervousness or the effort it took to keep pace she could not tell. She found him crouched behind a bush close to where Rufus and his palfrey were tied. Alice could not see but as she approached she heard a joyful laugh.

'I don't believe it!' he said and turned towards Alice, a smile plastered across his face. 'I really cannot believe it.' Without explaining he stood straight and worked his way around the bush. Alice could hear snorts and whinnies coming from the horses, followed by Raymond's appeal for calm. She pushed through the undergrowth to find Raymond standing by the fallen oak not with two horses but three. He had his arms out from his sides and was speaking in soothing tones to a nervous small, tough-looking courser. Alice recognised him as soon as Raymond laid his hands on the horse's face.

'Look, Alice! It is Dreigiau,' he laughed. Tears were shining at his eyes. 'He's alive.'

Gone were Raymond's worries about the dangers of Ostmen on the beach at Dun Conán. Forgotten were his concerns about the threat of Gaelic warriors in the forest. He whooped and laughed and talked loudly to Alice as they rode southwards again. He even sang a tune, a jaunty part from the *Song of Roland* which he knew so well.

'*The mountain passes in safety tread, while I breathe in life you have nought to dread. Count Roland sprang to a hill top's height, and donned his peerless armour bright.*' Raymond paused suddenly and turned towards Alice. 'I will admit it: I thought that some damned Ostman or Gael had caught Dreigiau and that I would never see him again. I had given up! I fully admit it.' He was beaming. It had been over a week since Dreigiau-Lladdwr had thrown Raymond from his saddle and run away from the battlefield in a panic. 'I cannot believe that we found him. I wonder what strange adventures he had been on since he ran off.'

Alice suspected that the horse had spent the time that he was absent from Dun Domhnall eating grass and wondering why his master had not yet found him and brought him home. 'I am just glad that we discovered him,' she said instead. 'It's nice to hear you singing again.'

'I mean, where has all his tack gone? How did he get his saddle off? Someone must've got hold of him and stolen it. I'm not saying that I am not happy to have him back, but it would be nice not to have to replace all that equipment, or even know what became of it.' He laughed and broke back into song: '*Around his neck he hung the shield, with flowers emblazoned was the field.*' Raymond was still riding the palfrey but had removed that horse's bridle in order to put it on Dreigiau's head. The tough little courser had a number of cuts and bruises and was lame so they did not go above a walk as they made their way towards the causeway and the Norman fort. Raymond led Dreigiau but the absence of reins on the palfrey did not cause him a second thought. He effortlessly used his weight and a light grip on the palfrey's mane to steer. It had taken nearly two hours' riding to gain sight the crossing.

'*No steed but Veillantif will he ride, and he grasped his lance with its pennon's pride.*'

Alice knew that Raymond knew every word of the *Song of Roland* and that he was in the mood for a rendition that would last until they got back to Dun Domhnall.

'How did you come to own Dreigiau?' she asked.

'It was back when I first was given a place in the Striguil conrois by Sir Reginald de Bloet, that's Walter's late father. That was, what, three years ago?' He closed one eye and stuck out his tongue while he thought about it. 'Yes, three years ago. Anyway, one day we all went down to the market in Chepstow to look at the stock that was to be sold out of the Earl of Gloucester's stud. Sir Reginald's elder son, Sir Ralph, bought Dreigiau-Lladdwr as a three-year old. You could see that he was an excellent prospect, but Ralph wouldn't wait to break him in. He was impatient to show off. He even gave him that awful name: *Dragon-Slayer*. It was obvious to everyone except Ralph that the horse was not ready.'

'Poor thing,' said Alice. As they started downhill, she raised her hand to shield her eyes from the sun. Ahead, she could just make out the timbers of the causeway despite the blinding reflections of the lying water. The tide was out and they would be able to cross without delay.

'It made me so angry to see Ralph frighten him and so I used to go down to the training field each morning to try and help him – or at least to stop him from treating Dreigiau too badly. One morning my duties kept me late at the castle and when I came down I found Ralph flat out and unconscious in the field. The gates were open and Dreigiau was nowhere to be seen. I thought Ralph had been robbed! I went and got Sir Reginald.'

'What had happened?' Alice asked, having to strain her voice to be heard over the clip of hooves on the wooden logs and splosh of water as they crossed the causeway.

He clicked his tongue to urge both horses under his control forwards onto the causeway. 'He had scared Dreigiau so badly that the poor horse had head-butted him and then run off.'

'So Dreigiau has precedent for running away?'

Raymond ignored Alice's comment. 'When Sir Ralph came around, he admitted that he had been using the whip on him. I lost my temper and called him an ass for treating a young horse as he had. It got a little heated and Ralph declared that Dreigiau was unteachable and that if I could find him he was mine to keep. At the time I was a bit stuck for money as my father's estate in Emlyn had been overrun by Rhys of Deheubarth.' He coughed and cleared his throat. 'Anyway, I could never have afforded a courser like him. I did know I could teach the horse better than Ralph and I didn't want him getting himself hurt out in the wilds of Netherwent. So I struck out into the countryside to find him. The Benedictines at the priory had seen him headed south and I caught up with him later that morning within sight of Caldicot Castle. Dreigiau tried to bite me at first, and kick me, but he eventually came around when he realised I wasn't going to hurt him.'

'Did you use the trick with the apples? The one you used on Rufus.' Alice leant down and rubbed a hand along her own horse's dark flank.

'I did.'

'What became of Ralph?'

'He's Lord of Raglan, near Abergavenny,' Raymond

realised his mistake a moment too late and tried to re-tread his steps, 'Near Monmouth, I should say.'

Alice smiled and said nothing as Raymond backtracked and began to outline his favoured methods for getting a horse to trust him, methods perfected over months of training Dreigiau, using a line, treats and great patience. Alice was barely listening. The riverbank loomed ahead, the bulging ridge shrouded in shadow by the midday sun which burned high in the southern sky. Minutes more saw them leave the causeway and begin climbing the ridge away from the creek.

Raymond had begun singing again: '*White was the pennon with rim of gold, low to the handle the fringes rolled. Who are his lovers men now may see and the Franks exclaim, "We will follow thee!"*'

'I am with child,' Alice suddenly blurted out as Raymond inhaled to prepare for the next burst of song. Alice felt that she had been holding onto the secret for so long, had missed so many moments to tell him the truth, that it had become quite unbearable. She felt a stinging sensation at her eyes. Embarrassment made her hands shiver and clutch her reins.

Raymond had stopped speaking in mid-sentence and looked shocked at her admission. His eyes drifted to her stomach. 'You are going to have a baby?'

'I think so, yes.'

Alice didn't know what she had been expecting from him when she told him. Hardly joy, she had thought. Anger perhaps? A series of questions over the paternity of the child? Raymond knew that she had been mistress to Prince Harry, the young heir to the throne, during their time in Westminster earlier in the year. But Raymond did nothing. He merely stared at his palfrey's twitching ears.

'Say something,' Alice urged.

'I will in a moment.' He began singing again, but more constrained and slower. '*Roland hath mounted his charger on; Sir Olivier to his side hath gone. Gerein and his fellow in arms, Gerier, Otho the count, and Berengier, Samson and with him Anseis the Old; Gerard of Roussillon, the bold; thither the Gascon, Engelier did speed.*' His singling had dropped to barely a mumble, his lips forming the words more out of

80

frequent practice than consideration. *'"I go," said Turpin, "I pledge my head". "And I with thee," Count Walter said. "I am Roland's man, to his service bound". And so twenty thousand knights were found.'*

Raymond stopped singing at that point and Alice tried to guess what thoughts were running around his head. Their brief affair had been ended by Alice in Westminster when Prince Harry had made known his affections towards her. She had abandoned Raymond in the hope that the prince would help her recover Abergavenny from her cousin, Sir William de Braose – a task at which Raymond had failed. But, in the end, the prince had abandoned her; used her and then let her fall into her cousin's murderous grasp. Only Raymond had cared enough to save her. Alice looked at Raymond's face. His brow was creased in concentration. Or was it resentment? She felt panic rising in her stomach. Had she made a gross misjudgement in telling him?

'In Wales, you promised to protect me,' she began.

'And I will,' he mumbled in reply.

'But -'

Raymond removed his hand from the palfrey's mane and held it up. 'A moment, please.'

Despite the mud on the path they had made it to the top of the ridge and Alice could see the walls of Dun Domhnall in the distance. Raymond eased his palfrey to a halt and pointed at some foxgloves in the hedgerow.

'I'll get the nettles and cow parsley,' he said a slid off his horse's back. Alice nodded and felt tears stream down her face. But she did not make a sound. She scuffed them away with her forearm and alighted on the grass beside the pathway, turning away from him. Raymond had gone to the other side and Alice glanced several times at his back as he worked.

'The child is mine. That is all there is to it,' Raymond said suddenly without turning. He had his small axe in his hand and swung it back and forth to cut down a swathe of nettles. 'If he is a boy we will call him Richard in honour of Lord Strongbow and if she is a girl she will be Isabel for his lady mother, the countess.' He crouched to pick up the cut weeds, his hand wrapped in cloth to protect him from their sting.

Alice did not turn around but kept at her work, pulling the purple foxglove blossoms away from the stalk and placing them gently in her knapsack. She wondered why she felt so disappointed at Raymond's words. Was it not what she had hoped to hear?

'You don't want the child to have your father or mother's name?'

Raymond still did not turn. 'I hardly knew my mother before she died and I grew up at Striguil and Raglan away from my father.' There was another long stretch of silence between the two. 'I will keep you both safe, Alice, and when the time comes the child will have lands or a dowry from me, bastard born or no, I promise to provide that.'

Alice nodded but did not answer. Instead she continued to delicately pluck foxglove flowers.

Raymond hacked harder at a large handful of cow parsley. 'If he is a boy he will bear my new arms and he will be sent to learn to be a warrior with one of my uncles. He will bear the surname of Carew.'

Alice did not turn around. 'What of me?'

He stopped and threw the plants into a pile by his feet. 'You will be mother to my child. And you will help me as you said you would; the higher I climb the better off you and the child will be.' He turned around, staring at her as the three horses milled between them. 'Constable of Veðrarfjord sounds like a good office for us to aim at. Agreed?'

Alice thought him angry as she her eyes met his. She nodded her head. 'I will do everything I must to help you.'

Raymond seemed content by the answer for he dropped to his knees and spread out a large piece of cloth on the ground. He threw the cow parsley down on top and then, more carefully, laid the nettles down as a third layer. Once that was done he began rolling the cloth, encasing the nettles in the middle of the bunch. He secured the plants with a twist of rope and tucked it under his arm.

'Let's get back,' he announced and climbed back into the saddle. 'I have a conrois to bring under control.' He paused and looked across to her as she dropped onto Rufus' back. 'So tell me, how I should go about doing it.'

Chapter Three

William de Vale woke Raymond before the sun had risen, just as he had asked.

'Caradog and the Welsh lads are ready,' his miles told him through a yawn. The torch in his hand trembled as he released the deep lungful of cold night air. 'And I have your horse prepared and saddled down by the inner gates.'

Raymond splashed water in his face and rubbed a finger around his gums. 'Good man. Has there been any sign of life from the milites?'

'None. They were drinking late into the night. They'll be asleep for hours yet.'

He nodded and pulled on his shirt and boots. He had returned to Dun Domhnall with Alice to find that Sir Hervey had dished out a week's worth of wine to the conrois and esquires in honour of the Feast of St Soupierre of Bayeux. The men had been drunk by sundown, singing their thanks towards the heavens for Soupierre's goodwill and that of Sir Hervey. Raymond had wanted to prepare without their knowledge and Sir Hervey's attempt to further ingratiate himself with the milites had made it all the easier.

'You prepared a pack with food to last me a week?'

William yawned widely as he nodded his head. 'I even managed to steal a skin of wine and hid it in your saddlebag. It wouldn't last me more than a day.'

Raymond sniffed a laugh. 'Well done, William.'

'Don't worry! I took one for me too.' The youngster's face stiffened. 'Are you sure I shouldn't go with you? It'll just be you and the Welshmen out there in the wilderness.' The torch flickered and danced as he indicated towards the north.

'It won't be any fun for horsemen, I assure you,' Raymond replied as he lit his candle from the flame in William's hand. 'And I need you and Fulk to keep Alice safe.'

'I'll have nothing else to do?'

'You'll need to look out for the pages, and see if you can talk the esquires around. They might listen to you better than they would me.'

William nodded. 'What will I do if the earl arrives before you return?'

'Tell him the truth,' Raymond suggested.

William looked nonplussed. 'What if Sir Hervey -'

'You will be fine.'

'Do you need Fulk to help you with your armour?' he asked, lifting his chin to the wall where his hauberk, coif and gambeson hung. The firelight reflected dully upon the links of steel.

Raymond shook his head. 'We are travelling light and moving fast – the Welsh way.' He pushed his head through his hooded chape and added his dark cloak around his shoulders.

'You wouldn't catch me out beyond the walls without my armour,' William told him. 'Are you quite certain you need to go?'

'It has to be done.' He blew out the candle and took the torch from William's hand. 'You and Fulk can share my quarters until I come back. You will be far comfier in here.'

'If you say so,' William said as he dropped onto Raymond's bed.

Raymond chuckled and went through the doorway, moving the rudimentary door back into place. He paused to look down towards Alice's hut and could see the glowing embers of a fire and the dark outline of Fulk as he guarded her door. He lifted his hand to bid his farewell, but Fulk did not see him. The wind tugged at his hood and Raymond pulled his cloak closer with his free hand. The last time he had left the headland fort before dawn was on the day of the battle against Ragnall's army. The conrois had been at his side, each one of the ten men willing to follow him north to meet the horde that approached their tiny bridgehead. It seemed like years rather than weeks had passed since that day. But his mission was the same: to hold the ground and to prepare the way; to be ready for his master and his army to join him. He did not know exactly when the Earl Strongbow would cross the sea, but did know that when he arrived his army would need food – and a lot of it. Raymond's meagre stores were already running low and would be exhausted quickly by the thousand men that Strongbow had hoped to bring. Fish from the sea would not be an option. He needed cattle.

A grey smudge on the horizon told him that the sun would soon be up and Raymond knew that it was time to go. He had one last task before he could leave.

It only took him a matter of seconds to reach the huts used by his milites. He drove his heel into the grass outside, knocking away enough earth so that he could prop the torch upright. There was a cloak over the nearest doorway and Raymond ducked beneath it to enter. He didn't know who was using the little turf-roofed house, but he was immediately struck by the stench inside, of wine and bad breath. His hand went to his nose. He could hear at least two men breathing, but in the darkness he could not tell their identity. He lumbered towards the nearest person and prodded him with his foot. The sleeping figure did not wake up. He jabbed him a second time.

'Time to get up,' he said loudly.

'Raymond?' Denis d'Auton's voice asked blearily. 'What do you want?'

'Get everyone awake.'

Denis didn't seem to understand him. He groaned and asked, 'Is it even morning?'

Raymond could hear the other person in the hut shuffling about. 'Leave us alone,' the voice whined. It was Asclettin.

At Raymond's feet, Denis rolled over onto his other shoulder. 'Yes. Piss off and leave us to sleep.'

Denis's insubordination reminded Raymond of his first days as captain of Strongbow's conrois and of his struggles to impose his orders upon the milites. All those frustrations came back to him: every question of his commands, each lonely night listening to distant laughter which he guessed was at his expense; every time one of the older men had called him 'son' or 'boy'. He had been promoted over them, only nine months after joining the conrois, but Raymond proved that he was up to the challenge. He had trained harder than any two other milites combined. He had pulled more picquet duties, mucked out more stables. He had rode harder and further for longer than any other. He had challenged his men to keep up with him, and they had followed or fallen away.

He knew he did not have the time to repeat that process to regain their trust. Instead he had decided upon a different method. He grabbed Denis by the ankles. The warrior was slow to react and was dragged half out the door before he knew what was happening. His first reaction was to reach for the doorframe but that only caused his blanket to go over his head. Raymond laughed at the miles's attempts to extricate himself from under the bundle and to kick out at him. He had a good grip and dumped Denis in the middle of the grass outside.

'What the hell do you think you are doing?' Denis demanded as he finally threw aside the blanket and got to his feet. He was still suffering the effects of wine and wobbled as he stood there. He was taller than Raymond by a head.

Raymond did not speak but stooped to pick up the torch. Denis flinched when he looked directly at the flame. Behind Denis, Raymond saw Asclettin appear, and both shouted at him, demanding to know why he had hauled Denis out of the hut. The commotion drew more of the milites out into the open from the other huts.

'Are we under attack?' Dafydd demanded before vomiting on the grass outside his door. One esquire was sick at the sight of it while another noisily dry-heaved. Thurstin Hore and Christian de Moleyns appeared in various stages of dishevelment. Walter de Bloet looked unsteady but had a sword in his good hand. Borard, a noted drunkard, was nowhere to be seen. Raymond prayed that he had not wandered over a cliff in a wine-fuelled stupor.

Sir Hervey and his two followers were the last to arrive from their quarters further away. 'What is the meaning of this uproar?' the French nobleman demanded as he arrived.

'Good morning, Sir Hervey,' Raymond greeted him. 'It is a fine one, is it not? I must say it is terribly nice of you all to volunteer to help with the work.'

'Work?' Sir Hervey asked. 'What are you talking about, you dullard?'

'We are going to repair the walls of Dun Domhnall,'

Raymond replied, 'since you are all up anyway -'

'We are not taking orders from you any more,' interrupted Asclettin. 'We told you that.'

'Unless you pay us back for our losses,' Denis added.

Raymond shrugged. 'I've given you my orders and I expect them to be carried out. Sir Hervey, you will oversee the work.'

A cackle coughed from Sir Hervey's throat. 'I will do no such thing.'

'That is completely up to you, I suppose,' Raymond responded. He watched Sir Hervey's eyes narrow with suspicion. 'I'll be back in a week,' he said and began walking away, deliberately choosing a path that took him between the milites.

'A week?' asked Amaury. 'Where are you going?'

'I'm going north to recover the cattle we lost during the battle.'

'By yourself?'

'Of course not,' Raymond replied. 'I am taking Caradog and all the Welsh archers with me.'

'They'll never keep up,' Walter de Bloet told him with a laugh.

Raymond had cleared the group and did not turn. 'They will be on horseback, so I think they will.'

Walter had to raise his voice. 'They don't have horses.'

It was Raymond's turn to laugh. 'Of course they do – the ones which you have been using up to now.' He passed through the gates in the headland fortifications. He could see movement at the gate, although it was hard to identify the source with only the light from his torch and the little light the coming dawn provided.

A murmur of discontent told Raymond that the implication of his words had finally hit home with the milites. He could hear feet running towards him from behind. He increased his pace.

'Raymond, wait,' one angry voice ordered.

As he got closer to the main battlements he heard all the familiar noises of a fighting force ready to ride. Nervous horses shook and their cold leather and brass tack chimed against scabbards and steel weaponry. Men spoke in hushed tones as if the dawn might be frightened away by their speaking voices.

'Caradog?' Raymond asked. At his back the milites had closed the gap to twenty yards.

'Over here,' the Welshman replied in his sing-song accent. 'I have Dreigiau for you.'

'Good man. You can get your men moving towards the creek.'

'I already have,' he told him. 'This is only the last ten. We didn't want you getting lost in the dark.'

Raymond hoisted himself upwards into the saddle. Dreigiau skipped a few steps as the weight came onto his back but a rub of his neck calmed the tough little courser down.

Amaury de Lyvet was the first of the milites to reach him. 'You can't take our horses,' he stated.

'Of course I can,' Raymond countered. 'I am captain of Strongbow's conrois and they are Strongbow's horses. The tack and saddles were paid for by Strongbow too. It is only right that the horses are rode by men who are about Strongbow's business.' He could hear Caradog laughing and translating his words for his Welsh companions.

'What about us?'

'What about you?'

'We need our horses!' Amaury told him. 'We are cavalry. What if it comes to a fight?'

'Perhaps you can ask Sir Hervey to help you with that? You seem to be taking his orders now.'

Denis d'Auton still looked hurt from Raymond's treatment up on the headland and held his shoulder with one hand. 'You would leave us defenceless against our enemies,' he accused.

'I've left all your weapons and armour. Consider yourselves lucky that I do – believe me, it is only because the Welsh lads don't want any of it.' Raymond spotted that Sir Hervey had joined the milites gathering before the inner gates. He turned towards Caradog. 'Get the rest of your men moving,' he commanded. 'I'll catch you up.'

Caradog whistled once through his fingers and the remaining Welsh bowmen followed him through the gates. Only Raymond remained, faced by seven of his milites as well as Sir Hervey and his two sworn swords.

'My nephew shall hear of this!' the old knight declared. 'I shall tell him how you abandoned this fort, and rustled all his horses like a damned thief in the night.' He reached for Dreigiau's bridle, but Raymond was too quick for him. He squeezed the courser's flanks with his knees and Dreigiau danced out of arm's length.

Raymond laughed. 'You can tell the earl whatever you like. But before you do you might want to consider this: two-thirds of our fighting force will be gone for the next week, stirring up trouble amongst the Gael and the Ostmen. You'll recall how difficult it was for us to defeat our enemy when you had the Welshmen's bows fighting on your side? Can you imagine how hard it might be without them?' Raymond could see his men considering his words. 'Perhaps you might want to consider your predicament and rather than drink yourselves stupid each day you will do as I ask and repair the walls?' He paused long enough for even the dullest of his warriors to understand. 'It might be all that stands between you and our enemies in our absence. I leave it up to your judgement,' he added and touched his heels to Dreigiau's sides. The little courser broke into a walk which Raymond directed towards the inner gates. Inside was dark but his torch was reflected in Caradog's eyes as he rounded the corner.

'So they'll fix the wall,' the Welshman stated. 'What of us?'

'North for some theft, banditry and cattle-rustling.'

'Brilliant,' Caradog replied. 'It would be a shame to not take a look around the countryside while we are here.'

Raymond crawled forward on his stomach. The undergrowth grasped and tugged at his clothes, still wet from crossing the stream. Above him hung blackberries, ripe and juicy, and he fought the urge to reach up and pick them. His belly groaned in hunger as he moved forward. There was a patch of nettles to his right and he steered away from them. He sniffed the air. *Cow dung.*

'Do you smell that?' whispered Caradog at his heels. 'They are close.'

Raymond responded with a nod. Ahead he could see the tree line and moving shapes. A moan of cow startled him and it was taken up by more. He carefully continued forward on his hands and knees. Sweat poured from his brow and across his back. Even in the shade of the forest it was hot, and the fact that they were coming down out of the mountains did not make their progress any easier. Raymond could feel his fingers and arms shaking as he attempted to control his descent.

A few more minutes of effort brought Raymond and Caradog to the edge of the woods. They stayed as flat as possible as they stared through the thicket into the open pasture. Fat cows roamed around the bight in the trees.

'I count fifty,' Caradog whispered. 'You?'

'Fifty,' Raymond agreed, 'and they are good ones too. I also see cowhands over there.' He nodded to a large beech tree in the centre of the field. In the darkness beneath there were men. 'I think I can see five. One is holding a spear.'

'My boys will have no problem dealing with them. What are those others doing?' Caradog pointed to twenty or so people scattered out in the fields.

Raymond could see that there were men and women amongst their number and they had baskets over their shoulders and wooden shovels in their hands. 'Collecting cow shit for the arable crop.'

'More slaves?'

'I think so.'

Wherever they had ventured over the past days they had come across them. Sad, skinny and dressed in rags, it seemed foreign and obscene to both Raymond and Caradog that humans were kept in such conditions. Even in Wales the church preached against slavery and the practice had all but disappeared under their influence. Three days before, Raymond's raiding party had come across four slaves working a stone-walled field high in the mountains to the east. The field was brimming with oats ready for harvest. Rather than run the men had meekly stopped working and then bowed their heads as the Welsh archers had stripped them of their food and water. There was no master with the four slaves, no reason for them to have remained at their back-breaking labour. But remain they had and as his raiders had rode away, Raymond had turned to see them pick up their spades and begin working again.

'About ten years ago I sold eight men to Irish slavers,' Caradog said quietly. 'They were just boys really, and had stolen some of my sheep. I never thought about them again until I came here.' For many moments the Welshman stared across the meadow at the people in the distance.

'We'll round the slaves up and get them to drive the cattle back to the river,' Raymond told his companion. 'When they have done that we'll send them on their way with one of the smaller heifers.'

Raymond was about to add more when Caradog's hand shot out and grabbed him by the forearm. As he turned to enquire why, he saw a warning in the Welshman's eyes. Raymond went still. And not a second too soon for, less than five steps away, a slave suddenly appeared and set down his basket on the grass. The breath caught in Raymond's lungs. It felt as heavy as mail. He slowly exhaled through his mouth as he watched the man through the scrub. The slave's face was tanned, his beard long, and he was greenish-brown to his elbows. He was close enough that, as he knelt to pick up another cowpat, Raymond could hear his knees creak. Raymond licked his lips nervously. If the slave looked up then he would stare directly into his face – there was simply no way he could not see him. Caradog's archers were still half a mile away, hidden on the eastern facing side of the hill. If the slave saw him and raised the alarm there was no chance that the Welshmen could cross the terrain in time and the opportunity to rustle the cows would be gone. Raymond stayed still and urged the slave to move away.

The man slowly rose to standing, his eyes on the cow muck in his hands. Hardened by the sun, the dung still dripped green onto the grass from its sodden bottom until the slave dropped it into his basket. Raymond could feel relief surge through him as he began shuffling off into the middle of the field with his malodorous load on his back.

Several minutes later, he felt it was safe to speak again. 'Head back across the stream and get the men,' he told Caradog. 'I'll wait here. If they move on I'll track them.'

Caradog did not need a second invitation and soundlessly melted back among the brambles and into the woods beyond. It would take him some time to get back over the hill and back to where their raiders were hiding. The Gael had posted sentinels north and to the south, giving them view over the steep-sided valley for several miles, but none had been set to look east where they thought Brénainn's Hill guarded their backs. Little did they know that a pack of forty Welsh bowmen lurked on the far side awaiting their chance to attack.

When they had first landed in Ireland, it had been the milites who had done the cattle-raiding while Raymond and the Welshmen had constructed the fortifications. His conrois had not travelled far, but had raided the small coastal settlements just inland from Dun Domhnall. No one had known the Normans had landed in Ireland, and they had certainly not reckoned upon the swift attack of the horse-borne warriors. The conrois had quickly built up a herd of fifty cattle which had been driven behind their fortifications. News of their pillaging, and of Raymond's later victory over Ragnall of Veðrarfjord, had obviously spread quickly among the Gaelic lords, for when Raymond and the Welsh had gone north on his raid there was not one cow to be found in the whole of the land of Siol Bhroin. Every settlement was uninhabited, every field empty. The Gael had sought the safety of their upland pastures for the summer. And so Raymond had followed them.

His band had first followed the River Bearú north, past St Abban's monastery, to where the river split in two. He had elected to keep on the northern arm which led them towards the hills which Fionntán had called the 'Black Mountains'. The climb and the terrain were equally hard on the horses and the men, and worse, they had found the mountains devoid of cover. Every day they found signs that humans and many cattle had been there before them – fords cut up by hooves, animal dung, and well-trodden grasslands. But no matter how hard they pushed they could not catch up with the Gaels. They tracked them across ten miles of mountain range for three days until finally Raymond was forced to concede that those they pursued knew the land better than he. Descending down from the highlands, they had entered into a beautiful and bountiful country with forests, streams and fields teeming with life but devoid of people and cattle. There, they again picked up the Bearú and followed it south.

Staying overnight in an abandoned rath, Raymond had decided upon new tactics which he hoped would help them accomplish their task. Rather than move as one body which could be seen from miles away, Raymond decided that he would find a secure site and send out scouts to search for the cattle. To that end he sent a small party across the river during the night to take charge of a monastery on the western bank of the Bearú. The abbot spoke Latin and, following his opening salvo of cursing, had told Raymond that he had entered the lands of the Uí Geintaigh and that their king, Ua Ceallaigh, would soon return with his army to slaughter the raiding party. In his efforts to scare Raymond away, the abbot had disclosed that King Ua Ceallaigh had taken his people and their cattle up to his tribe's summer pastures on Brénainn's Hill. The man had even helpfully pointed out which of the hills around his monastery was that which he had named. Raymond had his target and he had a location. His scouts were sent out within the hour.

That assistance, and the good food and ale that they found in the kitchen, was enough to make St Fiachra's Monastery a fine choice for their base. However, the real prize was the abbot's eighty head of cattle. Raymond could not believe it when he had spotted the long column of beasts, surrounded on all sides by warriors and slaves, being driven into the paddocks just outside the monastery compound the afternoon after they had taken control of the site. As the warriors had approached the monastery living quarters, Raymond's men had surrounded them and forced them to surrender. Suddenly, having spent days without a single success, they had stumbled upon enough cattle to feed Strongbow's army for a several days. And he had a lead on where to find more.

Hands on his chin as he lay in the shady hideaway, Raymond contemplated the herd of King Ua Ceallaigh's cattle. Every cow was white and long-bodied, with black ears constantly flicking away flies. Each had a vast curving set of horns and he had no doubt that each cow would be good for either milk or meat. Raymond could only see a handful of calves and one thick-set bull running with the herd. It looked docile enough, but he decided then to leave it behind rather than run the risk of having the beast run amok as they drove the cattle back to the monastery.

Raymond froze as he heard the rustling of foliage at his rear, but a series of four clicks followed by a run of five told him that it was Caradog. He carefully withdrew from the tree line where he found the Welshman with his archers. One had his knee through the bow and grunted as he hauled the twisted hemp bowstring onto the horn nock. His whole body quivered with effort.

'Ready?' Raymond asked.

Caradog did not even bother responding but merely pointed through the trees and his men followed him at a jog in single file towards the mountainside pasture. Speed was more important than stealth, but the archers didn't say a word as they hopped over bushes and ducked under branches. Raymond followed at the rear of the column, emerging into the sunlight as Caradog led the men a little bit downhill and eastwards to take advantage of the small breeze coming over their shoulders.

They had barely come to a halt when Raymond saw movement from the Gaelic stockmen under the tree. They appeared into the sunlight with spears and darts in hand, two hundred paces away from Caradog's men. There were fifteen in all and they began shouting and waving their hands. Those slaves who were lifting cow dung stopped and instead began yelling, driving the cattle away from the raiders. Some had switches in their hands and they brought them down on the cows' rears to make them move more quickly.

'Caradog, they are getting away,' Raymond snarled, but the Welsh commander did not as much as lift his head to look in the direction of the cattle.

'The air is dry,' Caradog announced in his native tongue.

Raymond watched as each of the archers adjusted their grip on their yew bows following Caradog's advice. Every one of the Welshmen was taller than Raymond by a head, but equally wide in the shoulders and he could see the muscles on their backs ripple as they tested the strength of their bows.

'Nock,' ordered Caradog and each placed an arrow on his bowstring. 'Draw,' he said. The draw of forty bowstrings in unison sounded like the creak of a particularly stiff church door.

'And loose!'

There came a thwack of yew staves and forty arrows flew through the air. Raymond watched them as they sailed towards the men in the distance, but Caradog did not wait for the flight to strike. Instead he ordered the advance.

'Go,' he shouted and his Welshman responded. They did not march but took off at a sprint, some heading south, bounding downhill over the grass in great leaps. Others took off northwards, following the curve of the hillside. Caradog was running too, straight at the cattle with ten men by his side, leaving Raymond standing on his own. Only the Norman saw the arrows thump home. The Gaelic spearmen probably didn't know what had hit them, for they were still shouting orders at the slaves to get the cattle moving when the arrows landed. One second they were standing and the next they were dropping to the ground as if some sudden swoon had come over them. Raymond heard the whack of arrows hitting dry earth and saw little puffs of dust. Only one man was left alive. He stood only long enough for Caradog to pause and shoot him in the belly from a hundred paces away.

Raymond began following the Welshmen, although more slowly. From his vantage on the hillside above them he watched in awe as the archers fanned out, closing in around the cattle like a wolf pack. The slaves were attempting to make their escape, whipping and hauling at the frightened cows. Raymond could already see that they were moving too slowly to get away. Cows mooed and slaves yelled, but it was the whoop of victorious Welshmen that was loudest. He soon realised that he was being left behind and broke into a run to catch his fellow rustlers.

By the time Raymond arrived in the belly of the valley Caradog's men had closed the escape routes to the west and south, forcing the slaves and cattle to run northwards along the edge of a small stream. Each of the Welshman had an arrow ready to shoot and stalked forward at a crouch, ready to draw if any tried to break through. They cajoled and shouted, keeping the cows and slaves moving – not quite a stampede, but on the verge of it.

'Keep them going,' Caradog shouted as Raymond caught up with him. The Welshman ignored his captain and turned to the man on his left. 'Keep the net closed, Ieuan! We don't want to give them any chance of escape.' That archer relayed the message to the next man in the line. While the Welshmen continued to pass orders between them, Raymond found that he could barely speak. He was red-faced and out of breath and struggled to match Caradog's pace. Sweat stung his eyes and his breath burned in his chest. His weapons bounced painfully on his thighs and at his back. He did manage to steal a glance behind him and was amazed to see just how far they had come from the tree line uphill.

'How long can we keep this up?' he gasped in Caradog's direction.

The Welshman laughed. 'All day if you want – but I'm going to guess you'll want some beef left at the end?'

'On me or the cows?' Raymond wheezed.

'We'll tighten the net and get the cattle to bunch up,' Caradog told him, 'then we'll pull back and let the herd slow down naturally. If this valley leads right back to St Fiachra's Monastery as you say, we'll be there in no time.'

'I hope so,' Raymond replied. He knew it was fully five miles back to the monastery and he soon fell back, unable to keep the voracious pace set by the Welshmen. They were well practiced in the art of cattle theft and he trusted Caradog to handle any problem that came about. For his part, Raymond was determined not to allow the archers beat him back to their base by too great a distance. Being left behind had its own dangers. The Gaels would surely come looking for their herd and the cattle tracks would not be difficult to discover. They had stolen a small fortune from the tribesmen. He glanced back towards the hills behind him, to make sure he was not being followed, but the curl of the hilltop hid any enemy from his view. He increased his speed and kept the black water of the stream on his right. After three miles the valley opened up and fell away towards the Bearú in the east. He had entered woodlands dense with oaks, angling downhill to where the small stream met the big river. There was a small, empty fishing homestead at the confluence and, still breathing heavily, that was where Raymond caught up with Caradog. The Welshmen had slowed the herd to a walk, and Caradog kept pace with them at the back of their long column. The coming and going of generations of natives had created a small pathway leading northwards parallel to the river and it was in that direction that Caradog's men forced the herd.

'Welcome back!' the Welshman joked as he fell in at his side.

Raymond noticed that Caradog had felt safe enough to unstring his bow and he took that to be a good sign of their progress. The Norman captain accepted a slog of water from his skin. He could feel the sweat gathering at his armpits and between his shoulder blades. Twenty yards ahead was the rear of the stolen herd. Two slaves were keeping the cattle moving and Raymond could hear the click of their tongues, the infrequent crack of their switches on the cows' flanks. The animals responded with heavy groans.

'How did you get the slaves to help?'

Caradog shrugged. 'They're not stupid. They accept that they have new masters now and they are trying to prove that they are useful to us. What would be the point in making a fight of it?'

Raymond nodded and slugged down more water. 'How far to the monastery, do you think?'

'Two miles, maybe less,' Caradog told him.

He slapped a hand on the Welshman's shoulder. 'A hundred and thirty head of cattle is not bad for a week's work – enough to keep an army fed for a good stretch?'

Caradog sniffed. 'If your man Strongbow ever arrives.'

Raymond didn't reply. His lord's absence was something that had been playing on his mind, even before the battle for Dun Domhnall had been fought. Where was Strongbow? Half the summer fighting season had already passed without his appearance on Irish shores. How much could he hope to accomplish before the winter rains closed in? Raymond tried to dismiss his fears that something had happened to the earl; that Strongbow had lost his nerve, or had not been able to find merchants willing to ship his army across the sea. Might King Henry have changed his mind about granting him licence to leave Striguil? Could he have been attacked by one of his neighbours in Gwent? He pictured Strongbow's beautiful daughter, Basilia, but shook her image from his mind.

'We can only do our best to be ready for him when he eventually crosses the sea,' he told Caradog with as much assurance as he could muster. 'Then the real work will begin.'

That seemed to suffice for Caradog nodded his head and for many minutes they walked on in silence. Where the pathway curled around the base of a small hill it narrowed so that only two cows could pass at a time and that held them up, but they were soon moving again through woods. Pollarded and coppiced trees formed an avenue on both sides as far as he could see. To his right Raymond caught sight the long line of the cloud-wrapped Black Mountains and he tried to make sense of the land into which he had come as an invader. He pictured the River Bearú running north-south all the way from St Fiachra's Monastery to the ocean far to the south. That was where Dun Domhnall stood perched on the clifftop. To the east were the mountains and beyond them were the lands of the Uí Ceinnselaig and Diarmait Mac Murchada, who Strongbow had promised to help win back his kingdom. Somewhere on that east coast, and he only had the vaguest notion of how far that was, were the Ostman towns of Waesfjord and Dubhlinn. Veðrarfjord lay to the south and west, on the River Siúire, which was a branch of the Bearú, in the territory of the Déisi tribe. Everything else on the island was unknown to him, a vast expanse of land full of warriors and strange practices, of forests, bogs, wide rivers and mountain tops.

He was so lost in his thoughts that he hardly noticed a sweaty archer who appeared beside Caradog from the front of the column. He began talking excitedly in the Welsh tongue, too fast and thickly accented for Raymond to translate. He jabbed a hand off towards the west, towards a long sloping shoulder of a hill on the horizon, less than a mile away.

'What is wrong?' asked Raymond.

'Twelve of the cattle broke away from the main herd,' Caradog replied. 'He and ten archers went after them through those hills.'

'Did he get them? We cannot afford to do without that

98

many -'

Caradog raised his hand reassuringly. 'They got them back and killed the four slaves who had made off. But up beyond the ridge is a wide pastureland. They could see for miles from up there.'

Something in the Welshman's bearing made Raymond suddenly nervous. 'What did they see?'

'Ostmen,' Caradog replied.

Raymond stared at the little figure made from twisted and knotted ears of corn. She was one of forty or more that hung on the cave walls that led down to the well. She had eyes made of blueberries and a garland of small meadow flowers around her head. Long hair flowed down her back and she had a dress of gold. Somewhere above him he could hear the squawk of birds and he stifled the urge to reach up and tear the corn doll down from her spot. The stone was black and wet and somewhere close there was a constant trickle and drip. It was cold. And it was dark.

One of the Welsh archers had found a loaf given as an offering and had divided it amongst his comrades. Each had wolfed down the bread. They had already filled their skins from the holy well and had laughed about how it would stop their flatulence. Raymond did not trust the water within the dank little cave and had avoided drinking. To his mind it was more likely to cause stomach trouble rather than cure it. There were strange devices carved into the stone on all sides of the spring. They were a mixture of animals and human and most were only identifiable as Christian because of the crude crosses that the figures bore. Although only a little sunlight dribbled into the well he could see thousands of scratches on the rock, crosses and suns and lambs and corn sheaves.

'Keep it down,' he reminded the archers, his own voice rebounding dully off the wet walls. He did not know how many of the Welshmen spoke the French tongue, but they did go quiet. While Raymond could understand much of the Welsh language, he still found it difficult to wrap his tongue around the words. For the most part, in Caradog's absence, he and the thirty Welshmen had made do with a mixture of their two languages and hand signals. Caradog had been sent south with thirty archers the afternoon before. He had crossed the river at the head of the herd of the hundred and thirty pilfered cattle. Raymond hoped that on horseback Caradog would make good progress and that he would be back at Dun Domhnall with their vital shipment in a few days.

Raymond and the thirty remaining archers had ridden north along the west bank of the Bearú, camping out on a small island in the midst of the river, a mile north of St Fiachra's Monastery. An army of Ostmen was on the move and Raymond had to find out what they were about. He had imagined all sorts of mischief that might have brought them so far from the coast. None of them were to the benefit of his small bridgehead and so he had decided to discover their plans by any means. His scouts had gone as close to the Ostman camp as possible during the night. The enemy had constructed a wall of thorns and branches at the meeting of a small stream and the river, but the Welshmen had guessed from their fires that there could be as many as two hundred in their number.

Other than the flies which plagued them, the island had been a fine site for their own camp but in the darkness, as Raymond had checked on the picquets, he had suffered a moment of confusion and panic as, in every direction, fires were lit on hilltops. To the south on Brénainn's Hill where they had raided the cattle and on seven peaks in the Black Mountains to the east, they burned brightly against the star-filled sky. He had believed it to be a signal between the tribes of the area, letting them know that there were raiders about. He had almost woken the camp to have them on alert before one Welsh archer had stopped him and told him that it was Lammas. In Striguil the festival was recognised with loaves left on the church altar, but it seemed that the Gael, like the Welsh, celebrated the first harvest a little differently.

Despite his lingering misgivings that his little force had been discovered, he had ordered the horses hobbled on the island and then used a small weir to aid their fording to the eastern bank. Each man had two arrow bags at his hip. Dawn had not yet crept over the horizon as they had made their way through the jumble of undergrowth and trees by the river, heading uphill. After only a few minutes of noisy, frustrating work, they had emerged into a very different landscape to that which they had known on the other side of the Bearú. The woods had disappeared into a land of arable fields heavy with barley and oats and corn. And beyond that, on the brow of a hill, a fort was outlined against the sky.

Even from half a mile away Raymond had been able to make out the thick trunks that surrounded the thatched roofs within. Without a word his men had frozen and ducked back into the cover of the woods, awaiting his orders. He had not believed that he had made camp so close to the fort without someone noticing their presence or raising the alarm. The sun had been rising and Raymond had realised that they would be unable to remain unnoticed in the trees for very long. By the same token, to tarry in the woods any longer was to miss the chance to ambush the Ostmen as they moved eastwards. Raymond had all but decided to pull back across the river when one of the archers, Ieuan, came forward.

'No smoke,' he had whispered in his thick Gwent accent. Raymond must've looked confused, for Ieuan had gripped his bow in the crook of his arm and wobbled his upturned fingers to indicate the flickering flames of a fireside. He had then pointed to the fort and tried again in the French tongue. 'No smoke.'

Raymond had immediately understood. There were none of the telltale signs of fires burning within the thatched houses. The fort was empty. He had been about to lead his men into the fields when to the north movement caught his eye. They came in pairs or small bunches at first, from beyond the bend in the river where the land was higher, too distant in the grey dawn light to make out who they were or their intentions. Raymond had felt the archers retreat further into the undergrowth at the sight of the people in the golden fields.

'Back to river?' Ieuan had asked as he eyed the newcomers.

Raymond had felt his body urge him to flee in that direction. But something had also told him to stay. He had squinted and held up a hand to block the glare of the dawn. The people on the hill looked like they were taking part in a strange dance: their arms had flailed about and they ran about in a manner Raymond had not immediately understood.

'Listen,' he had urged Ieuan. He had turned his left ear forward and strained to hear above the rustle of leaves, the river at their back, and morning birdsong. Ieuan had copied his actions, his brow creased in concentration.

'There! Do you hear it?' Raymond had asked. He had heard the strike of metal on wood, that distinct clip of steel weapon upon shield which he had heard a thousand times before. He turned his head and looked northwards again.

That was when the main body of Ostmen had appeared. They had come in a great shuffling mass of men, their shields facing outwards in every direction. Around them had circled a crowing army of Gaels who bombarded the Ostmen with darts and stones from distance. It was a fighting retreat.

Raymond could've applauded the discipline of the Ostmen. Caught out in the open, miles from their home, they had clung together as they crossed the fields, using their shields to block the missile barrage that came from above. Only the most foolhardy of the Gaels had come within reach of the Ostmen. They had been cut down before the warriors retreated back to the relative safety of the circular shieldwall. Most of the Gael had stayed fully fifty yards from their axes, content to try their luck from distance. Raymond had seen the bodies of the fallen emerge from the cluster of Ostmen as they had lumbered onwards. He had seen the Gael stoop to pick up weapons previously hurled into their enemies' midst. They had thrown them again. He had seen slingers twirling their rope launchers around their heads. He had heard the sickening impact of rock on armour-clad flesh.

The Ostmen's objective had been obvious. The bend in the river and the curve of the hillside took them directly towards the fort on the hillock above Raymond and for a moment he had pondered sending his archers across the fields to take control of the empty stronghold ahead of them. But he had not followed through. It would do no good for his men to become besieged without an obvious escape route or sufficient supplies.

There was no other option for the Ostmen. They had lumbered slowly in the direction of the fort, defending their flanks and leaving the injured for the Gael to kill. Whether the natives were so occupied with attacking the Ostmen, or they lacked any leaders, they did not seem to notice the possible refuge until it was too late. While still half a mile from their destination, the Ostman commander had sent forward a small group of warriors. They powered through the scattered line of Gael to claim the fort and to hold its gates until the main group caught up.

As he had watched the brave men cross the fields, Raymond had realised that soon his raiders would be spotted, either by the Ostmen or the Gael, and so he had commanded them back into the trees. They did not go very far before they had discovered the holy well and had crowded in.

'Keep quiet,' Raymond hissed again, shifting his weight onto his left leg so that he could look up the stone passage. As he had arrived he had marked a discoloured spot on the wall where the rising sun had been touching and now saw that the line of sunlight was well below the spot. 'I'm going up for a look. Stay here,' he ordered and gestured the same with his hands. When one archer made noises suggesting he would follow, Raymond said 'Stay' in Welsh and motioned with his fingers that he would walk around.

The stone steps carved into the floor of the sacred underground site were covered in cold puddles which seeped through his leather shoes, already sodden from the river crossing. The sound of splashes and the slap of his feet echoed around him as he rose to the surface. He peeked out. He could hear jeers and shouting in the distance, the clash of arms. A hawthorn bedecked in pieces of torn linen strips hung over him quivering in the breeze. He crouched and jogged the few metres through the wood to the treeline.

'Ieuan,' he hissed. A double click of a tongue sounded in response and Raymond dropped to his knees, crawling forward to lie beside the sentry. Neither said anything as they stared out over the fields to where a furious battle was taking place before the gates of the fort. The main body of the Ostmen had reached the gates and were still being assailed by projectiles from all sides. Raymond – a quarter of a mile away – could see how the Ostmen had formed into a semi-circular formation around the gates, their colourful shields raised to the sky. Some of those behind them also bore shields but Raymond was confused that more did not attempt to defend themselves. He strained his eyes on the people beyond the shieldwall, those attempting to force their way into the fort. His neck craned forward as if it would help him see more clearly. And then suddenly he saw them.

'They have their families with them.'

Ieuan didn't seem to understand but Raymond could distinctly see women and children as they pushed through the gates and into the small fort. His ears could even pick out screaming, too high-pitched to be adult men. He looked to the north and could see more Gaels streaming over the hillside and fields.

'Damn it,' he said and shook his head. He knew that there was little hope for the Ostmen, even if they did get the gates shut and barricaded inside the fort. He would've been happy to pull back across the river and leave them to their fate if not for the presence of the women and children. What great misfortune had caused the Ostmen to come this far into enemy territory with their families, he wondered.

'What doing?' Ieuan asked in his best French.

Raymond did not turn but climbed up so that he sat on his knees. He extended his left arm and curled his hand into a fist. His right hand went up and then stretched back towards his chest as if he was drawing a bow. He released an imaginary arrow towards the Gael as Ieuan watched him.

The Welshman nodded his head. 'Fight?'

'Fight,' he replied.

It was fully five hundred feet uphill through the field to the wall. The barley had already been harvested, the sheaves piled all around, but Raymond was still sweating profusely and breathing hard by the time his shoulder thumped into stone blocks at the top. Beyond was a field of corn. Up and down the length of the wall, thirty Welshmen ducked into cover, or ran the last few steps. Each panted hard from the sprint. Raymond swiped perspiration from his eyes and rose to look over the low wall.

'They've seen us,' he told Ieuan who knelt at his side. A

small group of warriors had broken away from the main pack and were coming down the hillock towards their position. The Welshman rose to his feet and looked at the group rushing towards them.

'Archers,' he shouted and pointed in their enemies' direction. The Welsh were on their feet but did not draw their bows. The fifty warriors were out of range, given the direction of the wind and the incline of the hill. Ieuan waited for them to close to within a hundred paces before giving the order to draw. It took two flights of arrows to send the two survivors scuttling back up the hill.

'Let's go,' Raymond shouted and leapt over the stone wall in one bound. His feet crushed stalks of corn, before meeting with hard, cracked soil. This time he and the archers did not run but advanced in a long line towards the fort. He imagined that they must look very few to the warriors above. After a minute they found the bodies of those killed by their first arrows. No command was needed for the Welshmen to pause and extract their arrows from the dead, or to finish the wounded using their sidearms.

Raymond came across a beardless boy with an arrow in his neck. He was already gone, his blood feeding the corn stalks. Although not as practiced as the Welshmen Raymond drew his dagger and removed the arrow, lobbing it to the nearest archer to reuse. He then wiped his hands clean on the boy's woollen shirt. Throwing darts and a launcher had spilled out of the boy's hand and Raymond picked them up, before advancing with his comrades. Another group of Gaels had come down the hill to meet them. They began slinging stones and throwing darts when they were a hundred paces away, but all fell short. The archers' response did not and the survivors quickly saw that they were outmatched. They fled, not back towards the fort, but north from where they had first appeared and the others, seeing the effectiveness of the Welshmen's barrage, began peeling away too.

'A few more flights should do it,' Raymond told Ieuan as they came within range of the rampart. There were still a lot of Gaels surrounding the hilltop fort and he instructed Ieuan to take half the troop east while he took the others around the other side.

'Prepare,' he shouted and waited for the archers to extend their arms. 'Loose!'

They were at the same height as the Gael now and a hundred feet away. At that range most of the Welsh archers could knock an apple out a tree. Fifteen men fell and seconds later another group tumbled to the grass. Raymond even added a dart to the arrow storm. It was enough for the Gael who bolted through the fields. Raymond turned to see more pouring around the far side of the fort. After a minute, Ieuan's band appeared from that direction and rejoined with Raymond's men. All were breathing hard from their work. Raymond pointed an arm to the bend in the river and then towards his own eyes. Ieuan understood and barked some orders towards his men who fell in behind him as he jogged northwards. They would keep an eye on the Gael.

Raymond did not follow. He turned and looked at the small fort. It was like the citadel of a castle, but without a high earthen motte beneath it. Warriors crammed along the palisade, shading their eyes from the sun in order to watch him. He took a deep breath and walked towards the closed gates, making a show of throwing his fist-full of darts and its launcher to the ground. He then held his arms out from his sides to show that he intended no harm. He was twenty yards from the gates but he could hear the blubbing of children from inside. He could see a great commotion through the gaps in the timber post wall.

It was several minutes before the gates were hauled open and four figures emerged into the sunshine. All were tall. All were armoured. Three had spears. The lead man looked over both shoulders before edging forwards in Raymond's direction. One of his companions knelt beside one of the many bodies littered around and called for help from those inside when he discovered someone alive. More appeared from inside the fort to help the warrior lug the wounded man inside. Raymond watched as others circled the walls searching for more survivors. He saw one man stab down once into the spine of a Gael who made a bid to crawl away from the battlefield. Raymond turned his attention on the helmeted men who approached. Their leader's long, grey beard reached to his ribs, his eyes small and suspicious.

'I know you,' the man stated as he came to a halt in front of Raymond. 'I saw you at Dun Domhnall, during the battle. You led the foreigners.'

Raymond kept his hands away from the weapons on his belt, but the Ostman rested his upon the pommel of his sword and blade of his axe. The man's voice was even, but Raymond couldn't shake the feeling that the man's gruff French hid anger.

'I am Raymond de Carew. I was captain at Dun Domhnall.' He inclined his head. 'And you? You fought there?'

The man nodded before removing his helmet. He was completely bald underneath. 'I did, at Konungr Ragnall's side. I can't say that I enjoyed the experience.' His massive grey eyebrows almost completely hid his eyes though Raymond suspected he was little more than forty years old. 'I am Jarl Gufraid.'

'From Veðrarfjord?'

Gufraid did not answer. Instead he turned his face towards the river bend to the north and nodded his head in that direction. 'The Gael will be back soon – you might want to think about getting your people back across the river.'

'My men will keep an eye out for them.'

'The Gaels have a festival every year; they trade and swap bulls, sing songs and have wrestling matches. Many tribes take part. Once the survivors get back they will send more warriors to attack us. You should go.'

Raymond nodded. 'We will be gone before they return. What will you and your people do?'

Gufraid rocked from one foot to the other and shook his head. 'That depends on what you want with us.'

'I want nothing from you.'

The Ostman said nothing for several moments. Instead he watched Raymond as if assessing his words for deceit. 'My men would have me take you captive. They think we could use you to barter for safe passage through these lands.'

'That would be quite dishonest given that I just saved your lives.'

'It would,' Gufraid nodded. 'But -'

107

'But you have people who depend on you to keep them safe?' Raymond guessed, peering around Gufraid's shoulder towards the gates of the fort. 'I assure you that I don't make war on children.'

Something changed in Gufraid's demeanour at Raymond's words. He turned away and cleared his throat. A deep breath steadied him again. 'For that you have my thanks, and that of all my folk. We were in a tight spot,' he admitted before switching to the Danish tongue and addressing the men who accompanied him. His two warriors nodded once before walking away. 'And so, as a reward, we'll not capture you today.' A sad smile forced from behind his beard.

'Who were the warriors that attacked you?'

'The Uí Drona and that bastard Donnchadh Ua Riagháin,' spat Gufraid.

'Donnchadh was at Dun Domhnall, allied to the men of Veðrarfjord.' Raymond recalled the moustachioed old man, wrapped in saffron-coloured robes and bedecked in jewellery.

Gufraid ignored Raymond's comment. 'We had to abandon our cattle too.' With effort, Gufraid turned his grimace into another grin. 'But let's forget all that. This is quite an auspicious day! It is not everyone who gets to speak to the ghost of a dead man.' He saw Raymond's confused expression and laughed. 'Konungr Ragnall's son, Sigtrygg, has been telling all Veðrarfjord how he killed *Raymond the Stout* in single combat during the battle for Dun Domhnall.'

'He very nearly did,' Raymond replied, a hand going to the side of his head. 'But thankfully I live to fight another day. I'll catch up with Sigtrygg soon and I'll be sure to mention his mistake.'

'Is that what brings you this far north?'

Raymond shook his head. 'I was hungry,' he said, patting his belly, 'and have grown bored of fishing for my dinner. I heard that the best cattle come from the lands of the Uí Geintaigh so we came north to find some. What brings you upriver? Did Ragnall send you?'

The Ostman grimaced. 'No, more's the pity. Ragnall has been deposed by Sigtrygg.' He stopped suddenly, perhaps realising that he had said too much.

Raymond had spoken to Ragnall of Veðrarfjord only once, just before the battle for Dun Domhnall. He remembered the thin, unpleasant man who had insulted him, calling him 'Strongbow's cowhand'. Ragnall had correctly guessed every detail of Strongbow's plans for conquest of Veðrarfjord, had outlined how he would beat the Normans, and had brought Raymond to the very brink of defeat in battle. Raymond could not believe that a man such as Ragnall could've been outfoxed by the brutish Jarl Sigtrygg.

'Ragnall is dead?'

Gufraid shook his head slowly as he considered his answer. 'Imprisoned. His wife and younger sons are held captive too.'

'Yet you are here in the north, surrounded by enemies rather than safe behind Veðrarfjord's walls?' Raymond looked through the gates of the fort again. A small girl stood in the gateway, staring out at the two men. 'And your people have brought their families with them?'

Gufraid said nothing.

'I cannot imagine what drove you from your home, but I do know that you cannot stay here.' As he spoke, Raymond raised a hand to the northern horizon. Over the fields his archers had reappeared and were trotting through the golden crops in the direction of the fort. The message was clear: enemies were approaching.

Raymond watched Gufraid as he also interpreted the Welshmen's actions. He shouted a warning to his people inside the timber walls. The volume of voices inside increased as a result.

'If you turn south to go back to Veðrarfjord, children or no, you become my enemy,' Raymond cautioned the Ostman. 'It is obvious that you cannot go north. To the east is Diarmait Mac Murchada, and to the west, the Osraighe.'

Gufraid bared his teeth, not in anger but in fear and indecision. 'We cannot go back to Veðrarfjord.'

'Why not?'

He did not reply. In the distance, over the fields, the sound of horns and drums and shouts began.

'I refused Sigtrygg's call for my submission,' Gufraid replied. 'He married the sister of Máel Sechlainn Ua Fhaolain and brought the damned Déisi inside the city walls. If I had appeared before him Sigtrygg would've killed my captains and me. He is Konungr of Veðrarfjord now.'

'So you ran?'

'He murdered another of Ragnall's jarls, a friend of mine. I came north to seek an alliance with Donnchadh Ua Riagháin. I thought that with his help I could expel Sigtrygg from Veðrarfjord. But Sigtrygg had already bought the loyalty of the Uí Drona.'

'And so they attacked you.' Raymond sighed and shook his head. His own family had been ousted from their estates at Cilgerran by the Welsh when he was a boy. Raymond had not been there with his family, but he had heard how his mother had led his younger siblings and servants in a terrifying night-time flight across the Emlyn countryside to safety in Nanhyfer while his father and his few remaining milites had held back the Welsh advance. He imagined his late mother amongst Jarl Gufraid's kin, terrified within the walls of the fort. He pictured tears upon her face and his brothers and sisters huddled around her, dishevelled and frightened, listening to the din of the approaching foe. Raymond's hands tightened into fists. He turned and surveyed the landscape - the fort and the horizon, the fields and the little island where they had camped during the night.

'You know why we are in Ireland,' he told Gufraid. 'My master, the Earl Strongbow, will soon arrive and eject Sigtrygg from Veðrarfjord. It sounds like, for the moment, your aims and his are the same, and -'

Gufraid snorted a sardonic laugh. 'I see where you are going with this. You would have me support a foreign invader of my home city!'

'Has Sigtrygg not already taken Veðrarfjord at the head of a foreign Déisi army?'

The Ostman sucked air through his teeth as he considered Raymond's words. The boom of drums echoed around the landscape and at his back women and children wailed in fear. Wounded men howled in agony.

'My archers will keep your people safe until we cross the river. Then we will escort you southwards. Trygve of

Cluainmín will give your people shelter until Strongbow arrives and then we will fight together to get rid of Sigtrygg and his Déisi. With Sigtrygg dead you can all return home with the friendship of the Earl Strongbow.'

Raymond could see the strain on Gufraid's face as he wrestled with the decision. But time and circumstances were against him. The retreating archers were two bow shots away and closing, and up on the hill above the river, Gaelic warriors had reappeared. There were hundreds of them.

'It seems that I have no other choice,' Gufraid said. 'If I agree to this, I must have your assurance that you will let us resettle within Veðrarfjord. I want your assurance that Ragnall and I will be granted rights in the city by your Lord Strongbow.'

'Agreed – as long as you help me get into the city.'

'I will do my best.' Gufraid grimaced and shouted over his shoulder into the fort. Four men had appeared. They had an array of weaponry about their belts. Gufraid briefly addressed them before pointing at Raymond and then to the bottom of the hill towards the island crossing. The men nodded their heads and then ran back into the fort, barking orders in all directions. 'I will return,' Gufraid said as he too entered the fort.

Ieuan's whistle heralded the return of the Welsh archers. Raymond could see that they were breathing hard from their efforts. They had stopped fifty yards from the fort and Raymond jogged over to them.

'We go?' Ieuan asked and pointed to the river crossing.

Raymond nodded. 'Send ten men now. Tell them to get the horses ready.'

A sharp intake of air from the Welshman alerted Raymond to activity at his back and he turned to see people begin walking out of the fort.

'No!' he shouted as several of the archers began to raise their weapons in defence. He turned back to Ieuan. 'They are coming with us. *With us*,' he stressed and pointed towards the island.

Ieuan looked perturbed by Raymond's words and repeated them as if he had not been able to translate them into his native language. 'With us?'

111

Raymond did not have time to explain. 'Ten men,' he ordered again. 'Tell them to get the horses ready.' He waited while Ieuan reiterated his commands in Welsh and then watched as a band detached from the larger group and made their way back through the fields towards the river in the trees. He watched them vault over the stone wall and disappear into the barley field. Ieuan raised an eyebrow in Raymond's direction and then pointed to the great dark mass of Gaels up on the hillside. They were less than half a mile away.

Raymond nodded. 'I know. I know! We won't be far behind.'

He looked back at the gates of the fort. More and more people – warriors, old men, women and children – were coming through the gates and streaming down the hill through the corn field. Raymond pointed towards the river and shouted for them to follow though he had no idea whether they would understand. He spotted Gufraid kneeling just inside the gates and crossed to him. There were still fifty people inside the fort. Many were wounded. Gufraid was attempting to hoist one man to his feet by an arm wrapped around his shoulders.

'You must get them to go faster. The Gaels are almost upon us.'

Gufraid looked up as if shocked to see the Norman captain. 'The wounded -'

'Will have to be left here,' Raymond completed his sentence.

'Leave them?'

'If you want the rest of your people to live,' he said and nodded. 'We must go now and get across the river.' Gufraid shook his head, but Raymond would not relent. 'If we are caught on this bank we will be massacred.'

'Your archers -'

'Haven't enough arrows to kill them all. We need to get across the river.'

Gufraid gave Raymond a pained look. He disentangled the wounded man's arms from about his neck and turned to face the Norman captain. 'We have thirty who are hurt. There must be something we can do?'

Raymond shook his head. 'I'm sorry. Get those that are

coming to move out.' He heard his name being shouted by Ieuan from outside the fort and began backing through the gates. As he did so he pointed a finger at Gufraid. 'It is time to run. Get to the river!'

Chapter Four

The shingle and sand collapsed beneath his feet as Father Nicholas stepped off the ship's gangplank and onto the beach at Melrfjord. Drizzle fell around him, just as it had for most of the journey from Ireland. It was like being inside a cloud. Nicholas wiped his face on his woollen sleeve. Falling to his knees, he looked to the dreary heavens and offered his thanks to Holy St Non for her guidance on his journey, for bringing him safely back to his homeland.

'Will you join us for a nice mug of ale?' the Welsh archer Bryn asked him as he leapt on the beach. 'There's no better way to celebrate being home again.' He nodded his head at the small town which was crammed between the beach and the high ridge of land.

'Thank you for the offer,' Nicholas said. 'But I must seek news of Strongbow in the castle.'

The Welshman shook his head. 'If its news you want there's no better place than an alehouse to find it.'

Father Nicholas was unconvinced that the sordid talk of sailors would be what he was after. He also knew that the castle was half a mile away – a long walk along a heavy beach in already sodden robes. 'Perhaps it would be sensible to check in the town first. Lead on.'

'The first round is on you, Father,' Bryn laughed, slapping the priest on the shoulder and almost knocking him over. They were joined by Bryn's four companion archers. Each man was jubilant to be back in Wales and joshed and punched at each other like excited oblates.

'*Bhreathnach*,' the Ostman captain shouted from the wide belly of his merchant vessel. 'Be sure to be back before dawn. We leave for Cardiff on the morning tide. If you want ferried to Pembroke, you will need to be aboard.'

'We'll be there,' Nicholas shouted back before scampering

after the archers.

The town of Melrfjord was little more than one street running parallel with the estuary, so much smaller than Waesfjord which they had left behind in the early hours. The houses were small and each contained a shop selling wares that would interest only mariners. Nicholas saw one shop selling thick ropes. Inside was a whole family. They twisted hemp fibres into coils to sell to the merchants. Another abode was filled with women mending a sail. Small empty barrels were on sale further down the street beside a shop selling tar. Melrfjord was midway between the big English towns of Bristol and Gloucester and the Ostman cities on the Irish coast, and had become a frequent haunt for overnighting sailors. The town had no church and no wall. It needed neither, Nicholas supposed. At the first sign of trouble he fancied that every household would take to the safety of the seas in one of the many vessels that littered the estuary's shore.

Nicholas could hear the alehouse before he could see it. The sound was a low rumble of conversation, interspersed with hoots of laughter. Of all the buildings in the town it was the only one that looked permanent. The thatch had recently been replaced, Nicholas noted, and the walls were gleaming white. He could see splotches of limewash on the ground which had not yet been washed away by the rain. It was by far the biggest structure in the town and looked to Nicholas' eye like every other building had sprouted out from it.

'All right, boys, no trouble inside,' Bryn told his fellow archers. 'We're just here for a quite drink, right.' Each man agreed and Nicholas felt his own head nodding along with them.

Bryn ducked under the eaves of the roof and pushed open the door. The swell of noise and smell of ale swept over Nicholas as he followed the Welshmen inside. For all intents and purposes the alehouse was like any lord's hall, perhaps smaller and more crowded, with a lower roof and unadorned by tapestries on the walls, but there were plenty of tables and a raucous noise from every corner. The five Welshmen made directly for the bar at the far end, leaving Nicholas by the door. Three large men sat just inside and studied him with sober eyes before one reached out and slammed the door shut with his foot.

'You after a woman?' one of the men asked. 'Talk to Arno behind the bar. He'll find you one for the right price.'

'I, well, no, that's not to say,' Nicholas stumbled before hurrying after Bryn. On either side were men much like those he had seen in battle against Raymond in Ireland. There were women of ill-repute at each table, laughing loudly and drinking alongside the men. One man snarled at him in a language that he did not understand, and he bumped into another who was missing an eye. The man carried four mugs. Beer sloshed over the rim and down his front.

'My apologies, sir,' Nicholas said as he rounded the irate sailor and made for the bar where Bryn was standing. Nicholas did not speak but swiped a mug from in front of Bryn and hungrily swigged down a gulp of ale.

'Easy there, Father! You need to pace yourself,' the Welsh archer laughed and held up a finger towards the innkeeper for a replacement pot. 'Drink up, lads. It is good to be home.' Each of the archers sank their ale in one. Nicholas gulped down five times to empty his mug. Bryn's hand was in the air straight away, five fingers splayed out in the direction of the grey-haired innkeeper. The man – Arno, Nicholas presumed – soon returned with five drinks and the offer of pies baked just that morning. Bryn forced a second mug of ale into his hands.

'I'd prefer a small tot of wine, if any was available,' Nicholas stammered.

'If you hear of any wine be sure to let me know,' Arno replied. 'Every drop I've got has been drunk by them 'uns up at the priory. We've no free rooms either, not even a place in the barn, before you ask for one, what with all these merchants descending upon us from God knows where.'

Nicholas was going to begin questioning Arno for news, but before he could begin the innkeeper wandered away, muttering angrily and shouting commands at a woman lounging in the corner. Instead, Nicholas followed Bryn. The archer led his friends away from the bar towards a free table in the midst of the inn. Nicholas spotted the one-eyed man with whom he had collided and chose a place on the bench on the far side. It was

116

only when he sat down that Nicholas noticed the smell of urine and filth coming from the dank rushes on the floor. He clapped his hand to his face, but it did no good. His weeks spent on the open sea or out on the windy headland of Dun Domhnall had led him to become accustomed to fresh smells.

'I'm going outside,' he told Bryn. 'I cannot bear the stench in here.'

'Stench? Yes, there is a bit of a reek.' Bryn made no move to leave or follow Nicholas, but took a long swig from his mug and turned his back so that he could listen to one of his fellow archer's stories about a girl from Melrfjord who ate soup made from seaweed.

Father Nicholas made for the exit. One of the big men at the table just inside the door stopped him. His foot shot out to prevent Nicholas from opening the door. The man eyed Nicholas angrily before turning towards the bar and whistling a sharp note. The priest saw Arno give the man a hand signal and the foot slid back under the table.

'Don't forget to come back and settle your bill, Father.'

Nicholas fled through the door. It was still raining softly outside and he pulled up his hood as he crouched under the thatch. Now clear of the inn, he inhaled deeply through his nose. Across the river was a small settlement. Nicholas could see a few fishing boats pulled up on the beach but most of the vessels were big merchantmen. He walked towards the muddy beach, where the river curved northwards and narrowed into a river. Both banks were crammed with ships. There were boats of all kinds, but almost all were longer than fifty feet. Even from his position, and with his landlubber's eye, Nicholas could see that they were empty of cargo. A voice from his left interrupted his study of the ships in Melrfjord's river inlet:

'We'll see about that! Arno and I have a standing arrangement – when I am in Melrfjord he must have a bed for me. That was my only condition and I will throttle him if he cannot live up to it.' The voice was educated and belonged to a tall man who was marching off the beach in the direction of the inn. He had his brown cloak hoisted into his arms in an effort to keep it clear of the beach and clean. Behind him were four warriors. The man flicked a hand at them to signal that he no longer wished for their company.

'Just make sure the horses are recovered from the sea journey,' the man shouted over his shoulder with such authority that Father Nicholas was moved to bow, assuming that he was a nobleman.

'My Lord,' Nicholas mumbled as the man got close.

The man snorted a laugh. 'I'm no lord, but a cleric just arrived in Wales and none too keen on the prospect of staying longer than I must.' He paused to consider Nicholas and pulled down his hood to reveal a head of auburn hair. 'I am talking to a brother priest, yes? Father -'

'Father Nicholas, a clerk to the abbot at Tyndyrn. And you, sir?'

'Hubert Walter,' the man replied.

He had a mischievous smirk, Nicholas thought, not around his mouth but in his eyes.

'I am a chaplain, of a kind, to the Sheriff of Yorkshire, Sir Ranulph de Glanville.' He shook his shoulders, sending rainwater everywhere. 'An extremely damp chaplain! Shall we go into the inn and out of this rain?' he suggested and took two steps in that direction.

'I wouldn't go in there. There is a hideous smell,' Nicholas told him.

'No worse than anywhere else in Wales, I would wager. Have you ever been to St David's, Father Nicholas? They were keeping pigs and cattle in the chancel when last I visited! And the bishop secretly wishes for Canterbury to advance his see to an archdiocese! Can you imagine it? Perhaps he means to have the beasts preach to the Welsh?'

'I have heard that St David's Cathedral is very grand indeed,' Nicholas replied gruffly.

Hubert grinned. 'Perhaps I exaggerate. And indeed good Bishop David FitzGerald may yet improve the standing of the cathedral. Might I trouble you for a mouthful of your ale? It might afford me a better appreciation of Wales and, if not, perhaps its relaxing qualities will make me more amiable company.'

Nicholas had quite forgotten the mug of ale in his hand and offered it to his companion. Hubert sank half the drink in one and then handed it back. Nicholas refused and Hubert drank the rest of the ale in another gulp.

'It's surprisingly good. Well, I bid you a safe journey back to Tyndyrn, Father Nicholas. I must seek a room for the night, if such a thing is possible in this dreary little backwater.'

'There is no room at that inn,' Nicholas shouted at Hubert's back.

The auburn-headed man laughed. 'A very good joke, Father Nicholas.'

'A joke?' Nicholas mumbled as the priest vanished into the building. Hubert was only gone a few minutes before the door to the inn reopened and he emerged with the innkeeper, Arno, on his tail.

'Please, be reasonable, Father. I haven't seen you in four years and you just turn up asking for a room? How was I to know?'

'Yes, of course. How could you possibly have known? Other than the fact that I told you that it would be in these exact circumstances that I would require room and board when we struck our deal and I gave you the retainer.'

'I could not turn down the merchants' money. Please, Father!'

'No,' Hubert insisted. 'All payments will end today, and your nephew, the boy I arranged to study at Rievaulx Abbey? I will be sending word to my friend the abbot as soon as I am able that he is to be dismissed and thrown into the streets to starve.' Hubert ignored Arno's appeals for clemency on behalf of his nephew and strode towards Nicholas. 'I am forced to go upriver to beg a bed from the good brothers at Pill Priory. Might you join me, Father? It is a short walk.'

Nicholas's eyes flicked from Hubert to Arno and back again. 'Of course, but are you serious about the boy -'

'You wish me to reconsider my decision?' Hubert winked once as if letting Nicholas know that he was in on a conspiracy and then turned on Arno. 'You have the good fortune to have met with the favour of kind-hearted Father Nicholas of Tyndyrn this day. I will forgive you on this occasion, Arno. It will not happen again. The next time I have the calamity to find myself in Melrfjord you had better have a room ready for me and the finest wine from Gascony to drink. Do I make myself understood?'

Arno mumbled his thanks and bowed his head. 'I will be ready, Father.'

'Good. You and your nephew have Father Nicholas to thank for my change of heart. What do you say?'

'Thank you, kind Father Nicholas,' the innkeeper said. 'With all my heart, I thank you.'

Nicholas had been caught quite off-guard by the frenetic pace set by Hubert Walter. 'I did nothing,' he muttered.

'Nonsense! You have saved Arno's livelihood and his nephew's immortal soul. I think that it is only right that your friends inside the inn will have three, nay four, rounds of ale on the house. And Arno? You can tell them that it is Father Nicholas who has paid for them.'

Arno nodded and again thanked Father Nicholas.

'Good!' Hubert said and clapped his hands together. 'You can also tell his friends inside that Nicholas will be staying at the priory tonight.' With that Hubert threw his hood over his head and began walking up the street in the direction of the river inlet. 'Come! Let us go.'

Nicholas hurried to catch up. 'Are you sure that there will be beds at the priory, Father? Arno made mention of a large number of people staying there.'

In answer, Hubert produced a document from a leather satchel at his hip. It bore three seals: that of the Sheriff of Yorkshire, the See of Lisieux, and the Royal House of Anjou. 'I am about the King's business. I do not think they will deny me – or any friend of mine – a meal and somewhere to sleep comfortably.' He returned the roll of vellum to his bag. He had not broken step.

They quickly left the town behind and picked up a small path that followed the course of the river. Hubert's long stride never shortened and Nicholas was sweating and uncomfortable due to his efforts to keep up.

'I don't understand,' Nicholas called in Hubert's direction. 'I thought you said that you were chaplain to the Sheriff of Yorkshire?' His question was more in hope of slowing Hubert down than for conversation.

'I am.'

'Forgive me, but I would never have imagined that a chaplain would be entrusted with a king's correspondence.'

Hubert barked a laugh. 'It is not usual, I'm sure. But my role in my uncle's household requires me to take up some other small responsibilities from time to time. It was in the course of those tasks that I agreed to carry a message back to England from Normandy.'

'You were in Normandy?'

'I was.'

'Did you meet the King?'

'I have had that honour, yes.'

'What is he like?'

'The King?' Hubert cleared his throat. 'Oh, he was the very ideal of regal magnificence when last I saw him.'

'Really?'

'Of course! His raiment was glorious, his voice splendid to hear, his munificence -'

'You are making fun of me.'

'No, no! I apologise that you would think so.' Hubert had come to a stop on the path and waited for Nicholas to catch up. He threw his hand onto Nicholas's sweaty shoulder. 'Perhaps I have become tiresome. I have simply been asked too often on my journey about our King. Please forgive me.'

'There is nothing to forgive.'

'Wonderful,' Hubert interrupted and set off again. 'Perhaps I should be quiet for a while and allow you to tell me about your adventures? I have been wondering why a clerk from Tyndyrn would find himself this far west with a body of Welsh archers for protection.'

Nicholas was immediately defensive and would've denied having 'adventures', had he not then recalled his last conversation with Raymond de Carew. He had been instructed to tell the story of the battle for Dun Domhnall often and loudly. Yet he felt reticent to tell the story to Hubert Walter when given the opportunity. His fellow priest was certainly talkative and would no doubt spread the word just as Raymond had requested and amongst the very top rank of the nobility if his claims were true. Something in Hubert's manner prevented

Nicholas from committing to telling him the tale.

'Nicholas?' his companion asked. 'Are you quite all right?'

'I -'

'No, I can see that I have pressed you too closely and have caused you even more distress. I apologise for it. Our Lord above knows that I am afflicted with Eve's compulsion to know everything, to hear all. It is quite obvious that it is a tale to which you have been sworn to silence.'

'No, no! It's quite the opposite,' Nicholas said and collected his thoughts. 'I was merely considering where to begin my telling.' He paused again. 'My ministry has taken me from my home in Cemais to Pembroke, where I was instructed by the constable -'

'Sir Maurice FitzGerald?'

'Yes, Sir Maurice told me that I was to accompany his half-brother, Sir Robert FitzStephen, and a company of warriors to Ireland -'

'That was last summer?'

'Yes,' Nicholas replied. He was surprised that Hubert knew so much of the comings and goings of Dyfed and Wales. 'But on the morning that we were to depart Sir Robert asked me to take news of the death of Tewdwr ap Rhys to his father in Carmarthen. This I did as best I could and then returned to Pembroke. That was where I was when I received a request from the Abbot of Tyndyrn to serve that great house, but I had barely darkened its door before the abbot sent me to Ireland with Raymond de Carew -'

'Raymond?' Hubert barked a laugh and stopped walking to face Nicholas. 'It truly is a small world!'

'You know Raymond?'

'We met briefly in Westminster at the Young King's coronation. Is he in good health?'

Nicholas nodded. 'When last I saw him, yes. He was injured in battle but had almost fully recovered. And it is news of that battle which brings me back to Wales.' Nicholas cleared his throat and waved his hand in the air dramatically. 'His was a glorious victory against an overwhelming army of savage Gaels and demonic Danes,' Nicholas recanted as they continued along the course of the river valley. He outlined the strength of the enemy army and Raymond's heroic actions which brought about victory. For his part, Hubert did not interrupt the telling once. 'And that is the story I will tell when I reach Striguil,' Nicholas concluded. 'It is one which I hope you will tell on your travels too.'

Nicholas and Hubert had at that point been walking for some time and had passed through the fields worked by the brothers of Pill Priory. They had already spied the top of the stone tower at the priory ahead and could hear the chiming of bells for Sext. Ahead, Nicholas glimpsed the small bridge which spanned the stream.

'So, unless I am completely wrong, you would be back in Wales to find Strongbow?' Hubert asked with an amused shake of his head. 'I have been extremely stupid. I can only assume that the mug of ale in Melrfjord was stronger than I reckoned and that my wits have been dulled to the point of a layman's'

'I do not follow.'

Hubert said nothing but extended his long stride as they rounded the last river meander. There, over the stream and fields, beyond the buildings of the priory, he pointed towards the northern horizon. On top of a high bluff there were warriors on guard. Strips of smoke from a hundred small fires were dark against the grey sky but it was a banner that drew Nicholas's eye. The crimson chevrons on the gold field with its three-pronged label loomed above the priory like the absent sun.

Hubert's hand fell onto Nicholas's damp arm. 'We are about the same business,' he said. 'We are both on the hunt for Strongbow. And we have found him.'

Drizzle collected and rolled down the small windows of the chapterhouse. The lead strips holding the warped glass in place could clutch the droplets for only so long. Strongbow watched them gather volume and then suddenly race downwards across the small pane only for the drops to be prevented from continuing on their course by another line of thick grey lead.

'My Lord, are you even listening to me?'

Strongbow turned away from the window to look at the man who had addressed him. The merchant, Peter ap Gwilym, was well-dressed for a ship's captain. He had a long blue cloak

123

lined with gold trim, an unblemished leather belt and red velvet gloves. His clothes made Strongbow's look dull and worn. The earl was glad that he had a cloak about his shoulders, not only to protect him from the clawing cold within Pill Priory, but also from the merchant sailor's judgement. At Peter's back were two clerks who took note of every word that had been uttered during their negotiations. Strongbow's own team was limited to his steward since his son-in-law, Sir Roger de Quincy, had left his side an hour before.

'I am sorry. My mind was elsewhere. I missed the last in your list of demands.'

The merchant looked annoyed at Strongbow's seeming disinterest. 'I was saying that, in the absence of any payment up front, I'll require exclusive rights to all the wool trade out of Dubhlinn. That is only fair for the use of my three vessels. They are dangerous waters.'

'I have already told you that Aylward of Bristol has taken those rights in return for use of his four ships. The Dubhlinn wool trade has already been assigned,' he stressed. Peter turned away to confer with his two clerks. Strongbow sighed and rubbed his eyes with his thumb and forefinger. 'I can still offer you special rights to the wine trade into Veðrarfjord. What do you think of that? You have interests in that business, I am told. It should prove extremely lucrative, but not if I cannot get my army to Ireland.'

'We have been over this!' Peter retorted. 'There is next to no desire for wine in Ireland. I know, for I have tried to sell it to the Ostmen. You may as well be trying to sell papal indulgences to the clergy. The Ostmen are only interested in drinking ale or mead -'

'And as I have tried to explain, you will not be selling the wine to Ostmen once I have taken the city. You will be selling it to Normans of high standing, men of good taste, men who will pay for quality wines from Aquitaine.'

Peter returned to his muted conversation with his clerks and Strongbow slumped deep into his chair. The talks with the merchant captains had lasted two days already and Strongbow was exhausted. The long line of traders who had crammed onto the benches around five of the six walls of the chapterhouse had gradually diminished as deals had been struck or rejected. It would, he mused, have been much worse had no one responded to his appeal for ships. There was simply no more money or lines of finance left for him to use to hire a fleet of his own to ferry his army across the sea. All that was left was to offer speculative trading rights within the cities that he meant to conquer as payment for the traders' assistance. Not that every one of those who had answered his call were simply 'traders'. Some were smugglers and others, he was reliably informed, were little more than pirates. Strongbow didn't care. As long as they upheld their part of the deal he would his. Six captains had already agreed terms, but he still needed Peter ap Gwilym's three ships in order to transport all his army of a thousand men, six hundred horses, armour, weapons and replacement equipment to Ireland. To leave any part behind was to risk defeat and Strongbow had risked enough for the lack of three ships to bring about his ruin.

Peter cleared his throat to draw back Strongbow's attention. 'I don't think that I am going to be able to help you, unless -'

'Unless?'

'Unless you can include the rights to all the birdskins traded in Veðrarfjord and Dubhlinn. That would be in addition to those of the wine trade that we have already agreed. It is a fair deal in return for my ships.'

Strongbow could feel his ire rising at the impertinence of the man. 'You think that is fair?'

'Perhaps *fair* is not the correct word. It is good business.' Peter turned to look at the empty benches in the chapterhouse. The only occupants of the room were two hooded priests who awaited their turn to approach. 'Or you can wait and see if any other captains with three ships turn up to offer their services. Maybe they will, but maybe they won't. Waiting might be more costly to you than it is to me?' Peter ap Gwilym's smile was wide and deliberate.

The earl bit down to stop an outburst from exploding from his lips. His money problems were well known around Wales. Sixteen years before, he had backed to wrong man in the war for England's throne and Henry FitzEmpress had made him pay for that loyalty. Denied position and patronage from the new royal court, he had also been deprived of the greater part of his father's estates in England, Wales and Normandy. He should have been one of the wealthiest men in the kingdom, but under the constraints placed by King Henry his finances had been all but shattered. He simply could not afford one more week sitting around at the priory while his army consumed what little stores were left. Another week of expenditure would mean having to hawk Usk or Goodrich to a moneylender. He simply had nothing else left to sell other than land and castles.

Strongbow slumped further into the chair. 'Very well, Captain. You will have the rights to trade wine to Veðrarfjord and birdskins to Veðrarfjord and Dubhlinn.' He waved a hand for his steward to come forward. 'Take him into the prior's library, Mark. Write up the contract and then bring it back when it is ready for me.'

The merchant shared a quick surprised look with one of his companions before bowing and making for the exit of the chapterhouse. As they did one of the two priests climbed to his feet and closed the great oak doors behind them.

The sound of the lock coming together startled Strongbow from his thoughts. 'If you are here on the behalf of the prior, you can let him know that I am doing everything I can to remedy our situation,' the earl told him. 'I know I said that my army would be here a maximum of three days, but I am certain that it will only be a few-' Strongbow paused when the priest removed his heavy hood to reveal his face. 'I know you. You are that priest, Raymond's friend, the one who I met in Westminster. Gilbert, is it?'

'Hubert, Lord. Hubert Walter. But I would appreciate if you would keep my name and my presence here private,' he said as he turned the large iron key in the lock. 'The King has spies everywhere and it would not do for one to overhear our little talk and report back to him on its content.'

Strongbow sat up straighter. 'Why on earth would the King's agents wish to listen in on one of my conversations?'

Hubert held up his hands and smiled. 'I will tell you everything, but first I should allow my companion to introduce himself. His story will follow my own.'

The second priest climbed to his feet and bowed. 'My Lord.

I am Father Nicholas, the Lord Abbot's clerk, from Tyndyrn. Your captain, Raymond de Carew, asked me to accompany him to Ireland nearly two months past. I've recently returned with news of your army.' He paused and cleared his throat. 'His was a glorious victory against an overwhelming army of -'

'While Nicholas's story is of great importance to you,' Hubert interrupted his fellow priest, 'I assure you that mine is greater still and I beg his patience while I tell you of it.'

Strongbow noted that Father Nicholas sat down with barely a moment of protest. His attention turned to the auburn-headed priest. Hubert had bowed his head and was pensively tapping the ends of his fingers together. They had only met once, a few months before, when Strongbow had appeared before the royal court in Westminster with the hope of securing a licence to leave England from King Henry. Strongbow had seen with his own eyes the reach of Hubert's influence within the king's inner circle of ministers, his network of informers. That Hubert had ventured this deep into Wales rather than trust a courier with a letter made his news important enough, Strongbow presumed. He suddenly felt hot and shed his cloak onto the bench behind him.

'I have ventured a long way to fulfil my pledge to Raymond and help you,' Hubert began. 'I should warn you that once my information is given, I will consider my part completed. If you require my services on any other matter it will require another payment.' He then reached into the satchel at his hip and produced a tightly rolled document. The heavy wax seal dangled and swayed from Hubert's hand. 'I cannot allow you to open this letter and read the contents, although it is addressed to you, Lord.' Hubert held it out for the earl. 'However, I can allow you to inspect the seal.'

Strongbow wiped his sweaty hands on his tunic and leant forward to take the document. The vellum felt smooth and crisp in his hands and he turned it over twice in order to look at the arms pressed into the wax seal. 'The King's royal arms, the See of Lisieux, if I am not mistaken, and, I'm sorry, it looks like the arms of York?'

Hubert nodded and held out his hand for the document's return. '*Yorkshire*, on behalf of my uncle, the sheriff, Sir

Ranulph de Glanville.'

Strongbow did not hand over the letter. 'Yet you say this is for me, sent by the king?'

'It is. And if the seal is broken he will know that you have read it and are therefore aware of the contents.'

'And you are going to tell me why I shouldn't read it?' Strongbow's fingers sought out the central wax seal. He could feel them put pressure on the embossed image. It would only take the slightest effort to break it.

'If you read it then you will be trapped,' Hubert replied.

'I could read it and then burn it. That would do away with any evidence.'

'The outcome would be the same,' the priest warned, 'and the effort unnecessary, for I know exactly what is written inside and have voyaged here to tell you of it.'

Strongbow's fingers moved away from the seal in order for him to point a thin, worn finger at Hubert's chest. 'That would require me to trust that you are telling me the truth of its contents. You might be embroiling me in one of your many court intrigues.'

Hubert did not speak for several seconds. He tapped his fingertips together again. 'I am pleased to hear of your caution even if I assure you that it is not needed today. I had hoped to convince you of my trustworthiness by allowing you to see the document.' Hubert held out his arms from his sides. 'I see that I must hope that the trust Raymond de Carew has put in me is equal to that which you have in him.'

Strongbow snorted a short laugh. 'You have picked an interesting time to bring up such a thing and such a person.'

Hubert's brow furrowed. 'Raymond paid me to help you get an army to Ireland -'

'Raymond paid you to secure a definitive licence for me to take an army to Ireland. I still haven't received one from King Henry – for all I know this letter might contain just that.'

'It does not. But it is on that same business that I am here in person - to make amends for that small,' Hubert paused to search for the correct word, '*deviation* in our plan.'

Strongbow frowned and looked down at the letter again. He studied the three wax seals, one royal, one ecclesiastical, and

128

one bureaucratic. They represented the new power structure under King Henry FitzEmpress. There was no room in his kingdom for the nobility, for the old Norman warrior class. There was no room for men like Strongbow. He felt his teeth bare and his fingertips press down again on the king's seal. It would take only the meekest pressure to find out what the document contained. A sigh escaped from Strongbow's chest and he quickly held the document out for Hubert to take back, the seals intact.

'It was hardly your fault that our plans went awry in Westminster. Raymond must shoulder the majority of the blame. I will trust you. Please tell me what is written inside,' Strongbow said and watched as Hubert visibly relaxed his shoulders. He noted that Father Nicholas shifted uncomfortably at his mention of Raymond.

'Thank you, Lord. Where to begin? Since I saw you last I've been in Brittany and Normandy on my uncle's business. That work found me at Ger Castle near Domfront when the king's retinue arrived. That was what, a week ago? The King had been in the south, at a conference with Thomas Becket.'

'The archbishop? I thought they were all but at war?'

'Pope Alexander wishes for an end to their disagreement and is putting pressure on the king to allow Becket's return to England. In any event, the King has somehow found out about Raymond's landing in Ireland,' he cleared his throat, 'goodness knows how. He knows that he is there on your behalf and he demanded that the Bishop of Lisieux send this document to you.' Hubert paused to return the letter to the safety of his satchel. 'It states, in the clearest of terms, that you are prohibited from leaving Wales, and that you are to disband your army and return to Striguil to await his further orders.'

'*Return to Striguil?*' Strongbow felt his jaw tighten. 'He gave licence to Diarmait Mac Murchada to seek help -'

'I know.'

'And I have tried to seek definitive permission to -'

'I know, Lord.'

Strongbow climbed to his feet and turned his back on Hubert. He stared out the chapterhouse window where more raindrops gathered and slid down the pane. 'If I do as he directs

I will be utterly ruined. I have spent every penny that I have.'
He bowed his head. 'I have accumulated debts. Henry knows
that this will destroy me. Is he possessed of a single ounce of
Christian forgiveness? Have I not served my time for
supporting Stephen de Blois?'

Hubert did not answer.

'The king refuses to give me back my earldom, and he
refuses to let me leave to seek my fortune in Ireland. Damn it
all, he refuses to grant me a warrant to marry! If this is his idea
of justice then I say that he is no king of mine.' Strongbow
suddenly slammed his fist into the dusty sandstone wall. He
immediately regretted it – he had caught the knuckle on his left
hand and had opened a cut. He clutched his injured hand to his
chest and closed his eyes against the pain.

'My Lord, are you quite all right?' Father Nicholas asked.

'I am fine,' Strongbow gasped. He opened his eyes to find a
red mark of blood bright on the beige block of stone before
him. There was more blood seeping between the fingers of his
right hand. The pain had stopped his flow of righteous
resentment against King Henry in its tracks. 'But the truth is
that Henry will surely hear of my leaving. He will declare me
traitor and declare my remaining lands forfeit. He could take
Striguil. He could take my home.'

Hubert interjected. 'With respect, Lord Strongbow, King
Henry has bigger problems than your departure from his
kingdom. If I know Thomas Becket, and I think I do, he will
keep the king busy for the coming years. Henry might not even
remember that you have gone until you have made your fortune
and are able to return.'

Strongbow turned back to face Hubert. He did not detect
any deceit in the priest's face, but he decided not to disclose his
true intentions in Ireland. For Strongbow had more than mere
plunder in mind. He had been promised a wife and the chance
of a throne. He intended to claim both.

'Yes, that is very true,' Strongbow replied. 'That son of his,
Prince Harry, is likely to cause problems for the king from
what I have seen. It is a risk, but I have few options remaining
to me now. If I remain in Wales, the king and my creditors will
bring about my ruin. At least in Ireland I will have a chance of

success. It will be up to me to succeed.'

Hubert reached into his satchel and produced a strip of cloth which he offered to Strongbow. The earl took it and wrapped it around his damaged hand.

'I will travel to York,' Hubert said. 'When I arrive I will write to the Lord Chancellor and tell him that you had already departed Wales before I arrived to deliver the king's ultimatum. It could take me a week to get back to York from here. It could take the same time for my correspondence to reach the king's court in France.'

'You do me a great service, Father Hubert. I will not forget it.'

Hubert smiled. 'Perhaps there is a wealthy bishopric in Ireland that might require a dean?'

'Perhaps there might be.'

'Then the pleasure is mine, Lord Strongbow,' Hubert said with the slightest bow of his auburn head. 'Now, you should really hear Father Nicholas' story of your army in Ireland.'

'That will not be necessary. I know precisely what happened. And I know what Raymond did,' he replied, sending an irate look in Father Nicholas's direction.

'You do?' Nicholas asked.

'I can only but hope that Sir Hervey has remedied the mess that Raymond -' Strongbow was interrupted by two attempts to open the door to the chapterhouse from the outside. The sound was followed by a loud knocking.

'My Lord?' a voice called from the other side. 'The door seems to be locked. Are you all right in there? Earl Richard?'

Hubert drew his hood back onto his head and backed towards the wall as Strongbow crossed the room and unlocked the door to allow his bald steward to re-enter. 'I am fine, thank you, Mark,' he said, beckoning for his servant to follow him back into the chapterhouse. 'I was just hearing an account of our army in Ireland from Father Nicholas here and did not wish to be disturbed.' Strongbow could feel his face gripped by a scowl as Peter ap Gwilym and his retinue of clerks came into the room.

'I would love to hear the priest's version of events,' a voice said from the darkness of the hallway beyond. 'I would be very interested indeed.'

Strongbow watched as Sir Hervey's man, Rechin, entered the room and loomed over Father Nicholas. The priest quaked under the warrior's gaze and Strongbow felt some sympathy for the young man. Rechin was a terrifying person with a deeply lined face and armour that bore as many scars as the man himself. He had arrived in Melrfjord just two days before with news of the bridgehead in Ireland and of his master, Sir Hervey de Montmorency, Strongbow's uncle.

Rechin placed his large, calloused hand on Nicholas's shoulder as he addressed Strongbow. 'I know this one to be Raymond's friend and can only have come back to Wales to speak lies against Sir Hervey and to inflate Raymond's part in the battle just as I have warned he would.'

'First let us conclude our business with the merchants then we can discuss Raymond's shortcomings in command,' Strongbow replied. He turned to his steward. 'You have the contract drawn up?'

'It is ready, Lord.'

'Good.' He turned to Peter. 'And everything is in order?'

'It is. My ships are at your disposal.'

Strongbow smiled and climbed to his feet. 'Then my fleet is complete. Give a copy of the contract to the abbot for safe-keeping,' he told Mark, 'and then follow me up to the camp. We must make our final preparations. We will make sail for Ireland in two days.' He turned to Father Nicholas. 'That is, of course, if Raymond hasn't succeeded in burning my bridgehead to the ground.'

'Father!' Nicholas called to Hubert Walter. 'Wait, please!' he shouted. His voice echoed around the priory cloister, but his fellow priest did not stop. Nicholas increased his pace, hauling his robes into his arms as he cut across the cloister garth, dodging between the apple trees, to intercept Hubert. It did no good. Hubert's rangy gait took him down some steps past the priory cellarium and out of sight.

'Hubert!' Nicholas called again as he tracked him. His leather shoes slapped as he ran down the last few steps. He had just taken a breath to call the priest's name again when a hand

132

shot out from his left and went across his mouth. Another arm hauled him backwards through a doorway and into the cold darkness of the monastery food store.

'I would appreciate if you did not shout my name again,' Hubert spoke very deliberately into Father Nicholas's ear. The pressure across Nicholas's mouth and chest released allowing him to turn around.

'I am sorry, I wasn't thinking. I just saw you steal out of the chapterhouse before Strongbow marched off. You heard what was said in there. I don't know what to do.'

Hubert nodded. 'I'm sympathetic, but I really don't know how I can help.'

Nicholas attempted to come up with an argument to sway Hubert's mind. He ran over the short conversation in the chapterhouse, remembering Strongbow's anger, Rechin's ridicule, and his own spluttering efforts to defend Raymond's conduct during the battle for Dun Domhnall. Each attempt to ascribe reason to Raymond's actions was scorned or swatted away by Rechin. If anything Nicholas felt that he had made things worse for his captain: Raymond's brave foray against the enemy was portrayed as foolhardy, his duel with Jarl Sigtrygg exposed as the rash actions of a novice warrior, and his loss of the outer walls of the fort, and particularly Strongbow's ship, *Waverider*, depicted as evidence of his deplorable captaincy. Rechin even convinced Strongbow that Raymond's tactical use of the cattle herd as a battering ram was nothing more than a stroke of good fortune.

'You can help me convince Strongbow that Rechin's version of events is untrue.'

Hubert sniffed a laugh. 'The problem with Rechin's account is that it is, from what I hear, very close to what actually happened. You've also got to overcome Strongbow's predisposition to agree with the loudest voice in the room.'

'You might've come to my aid. You did say that you're Raymond's friend.'

'And despite that I'm still unsure what I could've done to assist.'

Nicholas looked to the vaulted ceiling. An idea suddenly came to him. 'Strongbow said that he was in your debt. You could offer -'

'No,' Hubert interrupted and held up a finger. 'I know that your heart is in the right place, but the currency I peddle is information, and getting my hands on it relies principally on taking advantage of favours and debts like that which Strongbow offers. If I start wasting them as you would have me do, I will be of no use to my uncle. Do you understand?'

'Surely you obtain some information through friendships too?'

'Not as often as you imagine.'

'I would owe you, as would Raymond,' Nicholas attempted.

Hubert smiled. 'And as helpful as that might be it does not come close to Strongbow being in debt to me.' He put a reassuring hand on Nicholas's shoulder. 'Sometimes you've got to accept when you have been beaten by a better player. My only advice is to go to Strongbow and admit that Raymond has made mistakes, that he will learn from them, and that despite them he has accomplished exactly what he promised: to build a strong bridgehead and collect enough beef to feed Strongbow's army while it assaults the walls of Veðrarfjord.' Hubert's expression changed when Nicholas's gaze drop to the ground. 'What is it?'

'The fort was quite badly damaged in the fire -'

'The fire that Raymond started?'

'Yes. The outer wall hadn't been repaired.'

'That could be problematic. Anything else?'

'The cattle – they had not been recaptured when I left.'

Hubert sighed and shook his head. 'Well, you better make sure to convince Strongbow otherwise, and then hope that Raymond remedies that state of affairs before the earl lands in Ireland. If he arrives and there is nothing to feed his army he won't be able to sustain a siege for very long. And honestly, if Raymond has not been able to accomplish a small feat like fixing a wall then there really is nothing you or I can do for him.'

Nicholas glumly nodded his head.

'Good.' Hubert's hand slipped from Nicholas's shoulder to his hand and he shook it firmly. 'I bid you good fortune,' he said and made for the cellarium doorway.

'Where were you going?'

'I'm going back to Melrfjord.'

'You said that you wished to stay here tonight?'

'There are too many people at Pill Priory, too many eyes that might identify me. I'd prefer to put a few miles between me and Strongbow.'

'You'll sleep aboard your ship?'

Hubert nodded. 'It wouldn't be the first time. The rain is clearing and it is quite warm. We'll depart on the early tide.' He pulled up his hood. 'Good luck, Father Nicholas. Give my best to Raymond when next you see him.' With that Hubert stepped out into the sunlight and looked over each shoulder. Assessing no one to be around, he stepped into the corridor and out of sight.

Nicholas was left alone in the cellarium, his back to the high towers of barrels and dusty sacks of grain. The smell of cooking bread drifted from the nearby priory bakehouse. His stomach growled in hunger. Nicholas had believed that he would merely be delivering news of Raymond's victory and that his message would be enough to urge Strongbow to cross the sea. He had never considered that he would be forced to defend Raymond's reputation, to protect his captain's very future. The thought of confronting the Earl Strongbow again made Nicholas want to run all the way back to Melrfjord, to take ship straight to Tyndyrn and to disappear into the safe ranks of monks at the abbey.

He made for the cellarium door only to stop under its high arch. He did not move but instead stared into the corridor beyond. To go right was to walk back towards the cloister, the priory and to Strongbow. To turn left was to follow Hubert Walter back towards the sea, to take ship and to leave behind the adventure in Ireland. Nicholas looked down the stone-walled corridor in both directions. There was nobody to be seen. The priory was very much like Tyndyrn, if not quite as grand and the stone walls made him think of his life back in the Gwent monastery, of empty corridors and quiet cloisters, of tolling bells, regular meals, and ordered prayers. They made him think of the eight other clerks who assisted the abbot, of their safe existence behind the high stone walls. That was what would be awaiting him should he return to Tyndyrn. He would disappear into the bevy of clerks.

At Dun Domhnall it had been different. He had been needed. He had been relied upon by Raymond and his conrois for his medical skill and spiritual guidance. Of course, he had been hungry and frightened too. He had also been trusted. Nicholas inhaled deeply through his nose and turned right. Hoisting his robes, he jogged up the steps and into the cloister. He knew it could not be long until the Nones prayers began and he hurried towards the chapterhouse to avoid that rush of men.

'My Lord Strongbow, it is imperative that you understand that -' he announced as he burst through the closed oak doors. He stopped talking when he realised that the room was empty of people. 'Thank goodness,' Nicholas gulped. His entry into the room had caused a scattering of paper to blow off the table at the other side of the room and he crossed in that direction in order to fix the mess. As a clerk at Tyndyrn, he knew that he should not have looked at the contents of Strongbow's papers, but he could not help himself. The first one was a list of the names of merchant captains, their vessels and their capacities. He quickly tallied twelve ships as he returned the list to the table top. The next showed Strongbow's expenditure and where he had used his money. The total that had been used to purchase food supplies made Nicholas gasp, but below were more outlays for animal fodder and replacement equipment.

The last document was a list of warriors who had agreed to accompany Strongbow to Ireland. The names d'Evereux, Stafford, Lambert, Rochford, Cafer, and Furlong meant nothing to Nicholas and nor did the numbers alongside their names. It soon dawned on him that they were the type of troops that each captain would bring with him. Most had only ventured two or three milites and some had only promised their own aid and the attendance of one esquire. Nicholas did spot one man named Sinnot who had raised a force of twenty spearmen from his Devonshire estates. There were also impressive contingents from some men of whom Nicholas had heard, good Gwent men: Milo de Cogan would bring ten milites and thirty esquires, a feat matched by Robert FitzBernard, Strongbow's marshal at Striguil. A Somerset landowner named Thomas de

St Aubyn would bring fourteen milites and forty esquires with the proviso that Strongbow arrange the Abbot of Tyndyrn to take his illegitimate son into his care. Nicholas supposed that the David and Adam de la Roche mentioned in the list were of the Flemish family from Dyfed. They had promised the service of seven milites, eight esquires and twenty-one infantrymen. The names of Jean de Clahull and Richard de Maroine were familiar too. The most notable warband came further down the list - Maurice de Prendergast would bring forty horsemen and two hundred crossbowmen to Ireland to fight for Strongbow. Nicholas did a quick tally of the numbers on the document: an army of almost a thousand would cross the sea back to Ireland.

'Impressive,' he murmured as his mind conjured an image of the army of Ragnall of Veðrarfjord as they attacked Dun Domhnall. That enemy horde had been three thousand-strong and had been driven back by the power of Raymond's seventy Welsh archers. If Strongbow brought more of the dangerous marksmen to Ireland he doubted that any army could stop the Norman takeover. Nicholas' finger went back to the top of Strongbow's list as he scanned it again to determine the number of mercenary bowmen in the army. He counted two hundred milites and six hundred men of other ranks, but had to check a second time to make sure that he hadn't made a mistake and missed a large body of archers.

'Only two hundred?' Nicholas whispered as he got the same figure again. 'Two hundred crossbowmen won't be nearly enough to conquer Veðrarfjord.' He scanned the list again but Maurice de Prendergast's was the only archer force that Strongbow had contracted to journey with him to Ireland. Father Nicholas shook his head. Raymond had told him that Strongbow would need to employ at least four hundred archers if his enterprise was to succeed. Nicholas wasn't a military man, but he had seen the effectiveness of arrows on the battlefield and, on their journey back to Wales, he had been instructed in the use of Bryn's bow. He had felt the weapon's power.

Nicholas quickly re-arranged everything back onto the table. He had heard footsteps on the corridor floor. He grabbed a quill from the ink pot and quickly scribbled down the figures and stuffed the sheet of parchment into his sleeve. He had only managed to get all of Strongbow's letters back onto the table when the door creaked open and the earl's steward, Mark, entered the chapterhouse.

'What are you doing in here?' Mark demanded when he saw Nicholas.

'I was awaiting the earl's return,' the priest replied as Mark crossed the room and looked down at Strongbow's correspondence. Finding nothing amiss, he looked suspiciously at Nicholas.

'Earl Richard won't be back for a few hours. He is preparing the army to depart for Ireland.' Mark's eyes flicked towards the door. 'Perhaps you would be more comfortable waiting elsewhere?'

Nicholas smiled innocently and climbed to his feet. 'If you could send someone to find me when he returns,' he warbled and left the room. The priory monks had begun filing out of the church and Nicholas scampered into the midst of the cloister garth to avoid them. They came in tight knots of five or more, each monk or priest indistinguishable from the next. Nicholas imagined what they would be thinking – about their duties, no doubt, or perhaps what they would be having for dinner. Each monk knew that in three hours they would be called to return to the church again for Vespers. They would chant the same prayers as they had the day before. It would be the same for the rest of their lives.

Without bidding the words of the rite came into Nicholas's thoughts: *Deus, in adiutorium meum intende. Domine, ad adiuvandum me festina. Gloria Patri, et Filio, et Spiritui Sancto. Sicut erat in principio, et nunc et semper, et in saecula saeculorum. Amen. Alleluia.*

Nicholas scowled and forced the words from his mind. Instead he pulled the scrap of parchment from inside his sleeve and re-read the figures that he had scribbled down: two hundred milites, six hundred men-at-arms, and two hundred crossbowmen, his note said.

'What would Hubert do?' he mumbled over and over, biting his lip. Nicholas knew that he had failed in his mission. He was supposed to have given tidings of Raymond's great victory, to have improved his captain's standing with Strongbow. Rechin had put paid to that plan. But Nicholas knew that he could still help. His fist closed around the scrap of parchment. He could still prove that the captain could depend on him. It would be difficult, but Nicholas knew that he had to try. He turned his eyes up, to look through the fruit trees to the grey sky above.

'O God, come to my assistance. O Lord, make haste to help me,' he translated the Latin rite into the French tongue. 'I will not be going back to Tyndyrn just yet, my Heavenly Father, as I was instructed to do by the abbot. I fear that I am needed elsewhere and beg your permission to disobey his command.' Nicholas reached under his robes and took hold of the money-pouch secreted inside. He juggled the tiny number of silver coins left at his hip. 'I have a plan to help them, to help Raymond, but I do not know if I can accomplish it on my own,' he whispered. 'Raymond does not know it, but Strongbow has lost faith in him and I fear that unless I do something he will not regain his lord's favour. He is depending on me. I will need your help, Lord, and that of Bryn and, if it is within your power, Hubert Walter too – though I will understand if even you cannot convince him to assist me.'

Nicholas thought about what he would do and then crossed his chest, gripped his eyes shut as if it would add emphasis to his prayer.

'Gloria Patri, et Filio, et Spiritui Sancto. Sicut erat in principio, et nunc et semper, et in saecula saeculorum. Amen. Alleluia.' He kissed his fingers and then opened his fist to look at the piece of parchment inside. He nodded his head and gripped his jaw. 'All right, what is my first step? Back to Melrfjord,' he said and strode towards the covered arcade.

Chapter Five

Raymond could see a silver strip of river and stowed ships' rigging over the timber wall of Cluainmín. The last time he had visited the town had been by the river in Strongbow's ship, *Waverider*, and he thought back over that stay. Having no idea what reception he would receive in the small market town had made him nervous. The foliage-blanketed banks of the river had not helped his feeling of apprehension; the idea that his crew were being watched had put every man on their guard. Thankfully, they had received a friendly welcome from the King of Cluainmín, Trygve, and had left the Ostman longfort laden with bartered goods and animals, and an accord to keep the peace between their peoples.

The approach to the town from the landward side was far more pleasant for Raymond. From horseback he could see over the heads of the long column of Jarl Gufraid's refugees and across the fields for miles in every direction and the sun was shining above him. His scouts had already returned with King Trygve's permission to continue across his territory.

'You are sure that Trygve will not harm my folk?' Gufraid asked again. It had been three days since Raymond had first crossed paths with the jarl in the lands to the north. It had been three days of trekking across country, three days of worry that the Uí Drona would swoop down upon them and finish the job they had started at the fort. With every step bringing them closer to Cluainmín, Raymond could feel his body relax, but he could tell that his new ally was just as anxious as when they had escaped. Gufraid was still in enemy terrain.

'Trygve says that he will protect your people,' replied Raymond. 'And I believe him to be an honourable man.'

Gufraid, like all the Ostmen, was walking and Raymond swung his leg over the side of the saddle and dropped down beside him. Dreigiau didn't break stride as Raymond looped his reins over his head to use as a lead-rope.

'I have heard stories about Trygve in Veðrarfjord. They say he was a thief and a murderer.'

Raymond shrugged. 'I don't know about that. Nor do I know what Trygve will demand in return for helping you.' Raymond lifted his chin in the direction of the town walls. 'But we will find out soon. We are almost there.'

Gufraid nodded his head and sighed. 'What other choice do we have?'

'None,' Raymond said.

The jarl shook his head sadly before shouting something in his own language and plunging into the shuffling column of people that made their way down the small path. In all there were a hundred and fifty Ostmen in their party. Of those, Gufraid reckoned that forty were fighting men while the rest were women, old folk and children. What few possessions Gufraid's exiles had rescued from their homes were either strapped to their backs or huddled in their arms. Everything else had been left on the road.

It was only after they had got the Ostmen across the river and moving southwards that Raymond had discovered that their new allies had almost no provisions. Hundreds of Uí Drona warriors had followed them to the riverbank, but the threat of the Welsh archers had prevented their crossing. Instead the Gaels had been content to shadow their movement, staring across at them through the trees from the far bank of the Bearú. Raymond had known that he could not outrun the Gaels, but had hoped that difficulty in crossing the river - as well as the impending fall of night - would disperse the enemy. It had not and Raymond had been forced to find a refuge for the night. The abbot of St Fiachra's Monastery had not been pleased to see Raymond's return. He had been even less happy to see his church occupied by over a hundred dirty and tired refugees, but his repertoire of curses was only unleashed when Raymond had ordered four of his remaining cows butchered to feed Gufraid's folk that night. The Uí Drona had tested their lines throughout the night, but had not pressed home any attack. By daybreak, when Raymond's column had continued south, there was no sign of the enemy. Despite being lumbered with both the old

141

and the young, they had made good progress and had caught up with Caradog and his cattle train the next evening. The Welshmen had made camp on the eastern bank of the river in the burnt out remains of another monastery and Raymond had ordered his group across to join them. The monastery was the same one that Sir Hervey had visited just a few days before and it still showed signs of that attack. There were new graves on the hillside and blackened stakes where once buildings had stood. What few monks remained had fled into the countryside when they had spotted Caradog's men on the northern horizon, although the townsfolk had remained and had even produced some small foodstuffs to keep on the right side of the Welshmen.

That morning the company had again split. Caradog had taken the cattle and most of the archers southwards along the bank of the river in the direction of Dun Domhnall while Raymond had selected another path which veered east. Eventually, he guessed, it would lead to Cluainmín.

Now, with the town gates in sight, the Norman captain could feel the sun's heat on his back. He adjudged it to be late in the afternoon. With any luck Caradog and his consignment of cattle would be nearing the security of Dun Domhnall. He allowed himself a moment to savour the satisfaction and relief of a completed task. His bridgehead was ready for the arrival of Strongbow, and better, he had almost tripled the amount of cattle that he had gathered previously. He had also successfully held his ground when faced by an overwhelming enemy army, and had delivered a serious wound that had led to the removal of Veðrarfjord's king from power. And with Gufraid by his side he had secured the very best intelligence about how to break into the Ostman city. Raymond imagined the greeting that would accompany Strongbow's arrival at Dun Domhnall. He pictured the earl planting a hug across his shoulders and then raising his arm in salute to show that Raymond de Carew held his greatest favour. Perhaps a knighthood would follow? *Sir Raymond* sounded very nice. In his mind's eye Raymond could see Basilia, Strongbow's daughter, amongst the crowd, watching his glory unfold. She would see his victory and she would remember their last conversation, that he would make

142

her father a king in Ireland. She would remember that he would do it in order to earn her love.

Dreigiau seemed to sense something and bumped his cheek against Raymond's shoulder.

'Good lad,' Raymond told the courser, rubbing his chin.

On either side of the path were fields. The grass had already been cut earlier in the day and slaves were busy raking the dried-out hay into wind-rows and piles to keep it dry through the night. Up on the hills he could see large haystacks already taking form while in a couple of fields he could see that wealthier farmers had constructed roofed buildings to keep the precious fodder dry. Many of the slaves stopped their work to stare at the trundling column that made its way towards the town. Raymond visualised himself as lord of a manor with fields and workers such as these to do his bidding. He pictured himself barking for them to return to their work. He was so wrapped up in his little daydream that he didn't realise that Gufraid had rejoined him.

'Cluainmín is no Veðrarfjord. That is for sure,' Gufraid grumbled, flapping a hand in the direction of the town. 'That wall isn't tall enough by half. It's more like a farmstead than a town.'

'I would imagine that Ragnall said something similar of Dun Domhnall before he lost his army and his kingship upon our walls.' Raymond replied. Not that the jarl was wrong – the timber wall was low, lacking an earthen glacis, and it only defended two sides of the town. The other sides were protected solely by two arms of the river. He had briefly walked around Cluainmín and knew that there were twenty or thirty thatched households inside with gardens, cattle yards and workshops. It was, even in Welsh terms, a small settlement. But Raymond knew Cluainmín's great secret, one that Trygve would kill to protect: the huge silver mine hidden on the far bank of the river.

Gufraid removed his helmet and began wiping beads of sweat from the bald dome of his head. 'I don't think Ragnall will make the mistake of underestimating you again.'

'And nor will you?' Raymond chanced.

The jarl merely shrugged before refocusing his gaze on the

path ahead. 'What's happening? The column is slowing down.'

Raymond nodded his head towards the gates of the town. 'Trygve has sent out his warriors to meet us. We should go and talk to them.' He handed Dreigiau's reins to a nearby boy and walked briskly towards the front of the line of people. Gufraid followed, speaking briefly to several of his warriors as he walked up the length of the column. Without the need of an order, his people had slowed to a halt. As they got closer, Raymond could see a small bunch of nobleman and priests standing around the vast frame of King Trygve of Cluainmín. Men had called Raymond fat since he was a boy, and not without cause. But where Raymond kept his propensity towards plumpness under control by rigorous exercise, Trygve had constructed a litter so that even the bother of walking had been taken away. As a result Trygve was immense, by far the heaviest man that Raymond had ever seen. He lounged on his litter in the sunshine, his long hair and beard heavy with silver trinkets. His bare arms and torso were dark with tattoos, now warped by his ever-more engorged body. Trygve raised his arms in welcome, beaming a great smile in Raymond's direction and saying something in his own tongue.

'He wants to know if you have brought any more Frankish wine for him,' Gufraid translated. 'He says that he had all six casks drunk inside a week.'

Raymond smiled. 'Tell him that my lord, Strongbow of Striguil, will soon make land and will have wine for all those who are his friends. Tell him that he will have so much that he will be able to bathe in wine if he should wish to.' A loud bark of laughter accompanied Gufraid's interpretation.

'Trygve says that it tastes so good that he would still drink it even if it was used for bath water by each of his warriors.'

Laughing, Raymond held his arm out to shake Trygve's arm. 'I must introduce Jarl Gufraid,' he said, pointing at his companion. 'It is his folk that require your protection and permission to live on your land.' He paused to allow Gufraid to translate his words and to make his own introductions. It took several minutes, but Raymond did not interrupt or understand their conversation.

'Trygve agrees to let us remain here,' Gufraid finally

reported. 'However, he wishes to know what we shall eat.'

'You shall have ten cattle to get your people through the first few days. Then you'll have to fish in the river and barter with the townsfolk.'

Trygve seemed pleased with the response and waved a pudgy hand towards the south. Raymond turned in that direction, following the course of the river. There was a large marsh stretching for at least half a mile, but it was in that way that Trygve seemed to be pointing. Whatever he had said had caused a disagreement between the two Ostmen.

'Támh leacht?' Gufraid asked angrily.

'Támh leacht,' Trygve repeated with just as much force, indicating to the south again.

Raymond did not understand, but stepped between the two men with his palms raised. 'What is wrong?' he asked Gufraid.

'He will not allow my people inside the town walls. He says that we can make do with the land over there.' He waved a hand towards the marsh.

'He thinks you can live in a swamp?'

'Beyond that,' Gufraid complained. 'There is a bit of land where they bury those who die of plague.'

Raymond's eyebrows curled into a frown and he turned towards Trygve. '*Taw-Law*?' he attempted and raised his shoulders. Trygve spoke briefly before folding his arms across his wide chest.

'Trygve says that there is a river for water and a natural weir for fishing, but I thought the point of being here was to be safe within the walls of the town,' said Gufraid.

'With any luck you will not be guests here at Cluainmín for very long,' Raymond replied. 'And the more distance between you and the town will mean the less chance of disputes breaking out. You can harvest the reeds from the swamp to use for shelters and hunt in the forest for food -'

Gufraid held up his hand and spoke briefly to Trygve. 'They haven't had plague in the town for six summers.' He closed his eyes and nodded his head. 'We will make do with Trygve's *generosity*.'

Raymond smiled and patted Gufraid on his shoulder. 'Your people are hungry and homeless, but they are alive. It will get

145

better from now on.'

The jarl opened his eyes and Raymond was surprised to see a hint of tears there. Gufraid steadied himself and then spoke briefly to Trygve. The King of Cluainmín laughed heartily and then whistled for his slaves. The six men ran forward and then, with huge effort, hoisted the king and his litter in the air. Trygve shouted again as they turned and lumbered towards the gates of the town.

'Trygve says that my folk are now under his protection,' Gufraid translated, 'just as his people are safeguarded by Raymond *Wine-Giver*. He says that we have a month.' Both men turned their eyes towards the wooden gates as they closed behind Trygve's party. Ten warriors then appeared on the walls of the town, staring down at Raymond and Gufraid. They were now armed with spears and shields.

'Yes, Trygve has been most welcoming,' Raymond said. 'He didn't even ask for anything in return for his help.'

Gufraid eyed the warriors above. 'We should get out of here.'

Raymond nodded his head as both men returned to the column. Gufraid quickly shouted his orders to the hundred and fifty souls. Within a few minutes they were moving south along a path wide enough for only two people abreast. The countryside was soft and green, but before long they had left even the most outlying fields and farmsteads behind and the land became more wooded. Raymond and Dreigiau walked alongside the five Welsh archers at the front of the column. None spoke much French, but Raymond got the feeling that they were happy to be herding the Ostmen rather than cattle as were their kinfolk. Nevertheless, dusk was falling and Raymond was keen to have Gufraid's people settled, rather than spread out across the landscape. They finally completed their half-mile walk and arrived at their camp as the night began to fall. Raymond was standing on the hillside under a large oak, looking down at the marsh and the river beyond it when Gufraid found him.

'At least it is warm,' the Ostman said. 'We can sleep out in the open tonight, and then start on building shelters, gathering water and fishing tomorrow.'

146

Raymond nodded his head. 'I'll leave at first light. I'll send back men with the cattle as I promised as well as any materials that I can spare; saws, buckets and barrels, that sort of thing.'

'Thank you.'

'A small piece of advice – keep away from the eastern bank of the river. Don't ask why, but I assure you that Trygve will have posted warriors over there. If you want to keep your people safe, tell them to keep to this side.'

Gufraid cocked an eyebrow but asked no more. There was still an air of tension about the Ostman jarl, Raymond thought. He wanted to put it down to the turbulence of the last few days, but something told him that there was more to it. Gufraid seemed on the verge of speaking, to ask something of him, but the words did not seem to come. He shifted his weight from foot to foot as Raymond let the silence between them stretch.

'When your Lord Strongbow comes, what will his plans be for Veðrarfjord?' he finally asked.

'He will capture the city and rule it.' Raymond shrugged his shoulders. 'Diarmait Mac Murchada promised him land and a wife and the throne of Laighin after him. Veðrarfjord will probably become his capital.'

Gufraid sucked on his teeth. 'And the folk who live there now?'

'They will be allowed to go about their lives as they have before,' he turned to look at the jarl, 'if they bow to Strongbow's laws and live in peace with him. What plans do you think Sigtrygg has for the city, for her people?'

The jarl shook his head slowly. 'I don't think that he is the sort of man to make plans. Sigtrygg wants the world to see his greatness, nothing more.'

Raymond chuckled. 'I never thought that I would see similarities between Strongbow and Sigtrygg.'

The Ostman inhaled deeply through his nose. 'And you are sure that if your Earl Strongbow is successful he will allow Ragnall and me, my people, to settle in Veðrarfjord? Can you promise that we will be granted rights as freemen under your lord?'

'He will need people he can trust. He will need people to trade, so yes, I can promise that.'

Gufraid turned away and looked back towards the disorderly camp that was beginning to take shape on the hillside. Small fires dotted the field, ten or so strips of smoke drifting north on the small wind, as his folk prepared whatever food they had saved.

His long grey beard rubbed against his chest as he shook his head. 'Then the best I can do is to ensure that as few of the people left in Veðrarfjord perish. The best way to do that is to make sure that Sigtrygg loses this war as quickly as possible.'

'What do you have in mind?'

Gufraid lifted his helmet and placed it back on his bald head. 'That we cross into Veðrarfjord territory tomorrow at nightfall and bring the war to Sigtrygg's allies.'

The first sign that all was not well was the fiery corona that glowered around the edge of the southern hills. The Veðrarfjord sentries were either asleep or had thought it to be the effect of the rising sun, rather than a hall burning. It was only an hour later, when the dawn had truly broken, and the thick black cloud of smoke was clear on the red southern sky, that they had finally found the nerve to rouse Sigtrygg from his sleep. His new wife, Máel Sechlainn Ua Fhaolain's sister, Sadhbh, had squealed in fright as Amlaith had bundled his way into Sigtrygg's quarters in Ragnall's Hall and announced that there was trouble to the south.

'Shut up,' Sigtrygg had growled at his wife as he had leapt from under the wool blankets and swiped a cloak from a nearby table. He threw it over his shoulder and demanded more news from *River-Wolf*'s ship-master.

'A few miles away, a fire,' he had shrugged.

'Is it the foreigners? Is it Strongbow?'

Amlaith shook his head. 'I don't know. We need to find out. You could send the Déisi?'

Sigtrygg splashed water on his face and then shook his head violently, as much to get his mind free of the dullness of sleep as to remove the excess moisture. He found it difficult to believe that an army under Strongbow could have landed anywhere in his territory without him hearing about it or a warning being sent. He had loyal men watching every landing

148

site on the coast and his brother-in-law's people, the Déisi, guarded all the western approaches to the city.

'I will go myself,' Sigtrygg told Amlaith. 'Tell Máel Sechlainn that he will send fifty of his men with me.'

'It could be a ruse to get you out in the open.'

Sigtrygg ran his hand over his braided beard. 'It almost certainly is a ruse. But I can't allow it to happen without a response. Get the Déisi ready to move out.'

Amlaith stole a last glance at Sigtrygg's pretty young wife and then backed out of the room.

'It's the Grey Foreigners, isn't it?' Sadhbh stated. 'The Liathgall have come for us.'

Sigtrygg pulled on his trews and a shirt before running a comb through his ginger hair. 'More likely it is a rebel sect of your brother's folk. They smell an easy target like a dog smells a badger den. We'll make them pay,' he told her as he tipped his mail shirt over his head. It tumbled over his shoulders as he bounced up and down. He secured the armour with a stout leather belt. 'Make sure you have some food ready for my return,' Sigtrygg said as he made for the door.

His hall was cold, the embers of the fire still smoking in the hearth. It was also empty other than two young boys who sat at a table eating porridge. Sigtrygg paused only to secure his weapons to his belt and to find his shield and an axe behind the dais.

'Where is Orm?' Sigtrygg demanded of the boys. 'He is supposed to be watching you two.' Both bowed their heads towards their bowls. Ragnall Óg and Óttar were his half-brothers and, like their father, were prisoners. Neither was old enough to hold a spear or axe and so Sigtrygg had appointed a guardian for the boys to allow them some freedom. Their father was afforded no such allowance. Ragnall was confined to the upper rooms of the Rögnvald's Tower, secure from those in the city who might try to free him and unite the factions behind the former king in order to depose Sigtrygg.

'I asked you a question,' Sigtrygg snarled as he dropped his axe onto the table and grabbed a hold of Óttar's shirt. The boy squealed and began to cry, spitting a mouthful of porridge all over the table in front of him. Sigtrygg released his grip and stepped back from the mess and the tears. Behind him the door opened and Jarl Orm stepped into the hall.

'You were told not to leave these prisoners alone,' Sigtrygg accused.

If Orm was shocked by the outburst he didn't show it. He was a young man whose father and two elder brothers had died in battle with the Normans at Dun Domhnall. Although the youngest of all the Veðrarfjord jarls, his family had been amongst the richest, holding a large estate at Áth Skipir on the south coast as well as an impressive fishing fleet. He was wealthy and he was confident.

'Your man Amlaith said there is trouble to the south,' Jarl Orm replied. 'I knew that Ragnall Óg and Óttar would be good boys and would not run off if I went to see for myself. I don't think anyone would dare steal them from your hall, Sigtrygg.' Orm's eyes flicked to Sigtrygg's cache of weapons at his side. 'Boys, come here,' he said quietly but firmly.

Sigtrygg's hand returned to Óttar's shoulder, holding the boy in his seat. 'I gave these boys into your keeping to show you how much I value an alliance between our families. Was I wrong to trust you with them?' Sigtrygg stared at Orm. There was far more to their arrangement and both men knew it. Sigtrygg did not trust Orm or any of his people, but the price of their co-operation had been this deal and there were benefits for Sigtrygg too. Keeping the two boys hostage meant that Orm was himself forced to live within the city walls, and had to split his warriors between his own manors far to the south and those who remained at his side in Veðrarfjord. Possession of Ragnall's sons had weakened Orm.

'Your brothers are perfectly safe with me,' the younger man confirmed. 'What I need to find out now is if my estates are safe.' Jarl Orm's eyes dropped to meet those of Sigtrygg's brothers. 'Boys, come here,' he repeated. Neither moved as Sigtrygg's large hand remained planted on the younger boy's shoulder. The elder, Ragnall Óg, began to weep. Orm's gaze returned to meet Sigtrygg's small, angry eyes. 'If I cannot protect my own folk then I am no jarl, and nor should I be if the old and the young,' he looked deliberately at the two boys, 'are threatened by an enemy and I am not there to protect them.'

Sigtrygg seemed to consider the jarl's words and suddenly released his hold on Óttar. Both boys fled to Orm's side.

'You are right, of course,' Sigtrygg said. 'We will go south together and see if we cannot intercept these raiders.'

Orm nodded. 'And the boys?'

'They must stay in the city where they are safest. I will have Sadhbh watch them.'

Jarl Orm nodded his head. 'I already have my warriors ready to march south.'

'Good,' Sigtrygg stated as he hefted his axe. Both Ragnall Óg and Óttar cowered behind Orm as he stomped past them and towards the door. He paused before stepping out of the hall and into the street. 'Your father would be very disappointed in how you have turned out,' he said, turning his eyes on Orm.

It was still early but Veðrarfjord was already awake. He could hear the sound of animals and humans and the river as he crossed the king's compound towards the rest of the city. Above the thatched roofs he could see St Olav's Church and it was in that direction that he walked. Without need of command, a troop of his warriors descended upon him, protecting him from all sides. As they passed the church they could hear the monks' morning prayers being sung inside. They passed shops and homes where men called out for news about the plume of smoke pumping skyward from beyond the southern horizon. Sigtrygg ignored them all.

It only took a few minutes walking to take Sigtrygg to the southern point of Veðrarfjord. The climb up the earthen glacis was punishing in his armour, but once he had started Sigtrygg refused to pause to catch his breath. He hauled his body up a ladder and onto the palisade on the wall. A final effort took him onto the barbican above the western gates. Swiping sweat from his brow, Sigtrygg stared over the countryside. A small plateau of land arose a few hundred paces from the walls. The area was crowded with poorer houses, those belonging to people who could not afford the grandeur of living within the city, but wished for its protection and the economic opportunities that the longfort offered. Sigtrygg stared down at the hovels. Some were little more than huts, but others were far more significant and were built right up against the foot of the main defences of

Veðrarfjord.

'River rats,' Sigtrygg growled as he turned his eyes to the blue morning sky. A great funnel of black smoke was still visible. Sigtrygg judged the source to be no more than a few miles away. He could feel his anger rising that anyone would have the audacity to come so close to Veðrarfjord and do such damage. Sigtrygg promised that there would be repercussions for that insult to his kingship and power.

A shout from below let Sigtrygg know that Máel Sechlainn Ua Fhaolain and his small body of Déisi warriors were ready. He could see his brother-in-law's saffron-coloured clothes and long hair and began descending from the barbican to meet him.

'There is trouble,' he told Máel Sechlainn. 'Get your men headed south and find out who has attacked us. I'll follow with more troops.'

Máel Sechlainn nodded his head. 'I am getting sick of being cooped up in this filthy city of yours anyway,' he joked. 'I will never understand how you Dubhgall live like this. It is almost like being a farm beast.'

The King of the Déisi did not give Sigtrygg the chance to reply to his insult, instead raising his spear and crying out for his men to follow him. They jogged under the barbican and out into the country beyond. It took longer for Orm to assemble his warband and by the time he did so the Déisi had already disappeared from view down the river valley. Sigtrygg's group followed as quickly as they were able. Unlike the Gaels, they were weighed down by armour and shields and were already sweating under thick woollen gambesons when they came across the first people fleeing away from the raiders. Young men came first, carrying what they could, and behind them were their families. A long line of refugees from Dubháth stretched out down the river valley. Sigtrygg did not allow them to stop but told them to continue to the safety of the city.

'They came in the night,' an older man told his king. 'The manor house was on fire before we even knew we were under attack. They threw a dead sheep into the well. We couldn't stop them,' the man told Sigtrygg. 'There is nothing left.'

Sigtrygg cursed and sent the man on his way. The manor at Dubháth was an estate from which the King of Veðrarfjord could derive food and wealth. Weeks before, Sigtrygg had ordered most of the fighting men from Dubháth to bring whatever had been harvested and join him in the city. He was glad for that foresight for it had saved most of the provisions, even if it had robbed the freemen of the manor of any hope of defending what was left.

Their progress was slowed by having to circumnavigate a wide, soggy bog. They climbed up onto a ridge from where they were able to approach without the same threat of ambush as they would have in the woods in the valley floor. From above, Sigtrygg could also see the Déisi milling around in the ruins of the village.

'They came from the west,' Máel Sechlainn told Sigtrygg, his hand flapped in the direction of a wooded hillside. 'The wind was from the south and they attacked before first light.'

The roof of the manor house had already collapsed and the thatch had burned brightly enough to cause the wooden walls to alight. One building had suffered only minor damage. Sigtrygg could see the torch that had been flung onto the roof had been suffocated by the dirty thatch.

'They had no wall and no chance,' Orm stated as he joined Máel Sechlainn and Sigtrygg.

'We found dead men for a hundred paces into the wood,' Máel Sechlainn told them. 'They did not chase them far.'

Sigtrygg sniffed the air. 'Is that pig meat that I smell?'

Orm nodded. 'They speared the pigs and threw the carcasses into the hall. That's why it burns so hot. The rest of the animals scattered.'

'These were not cattle thieves,' Máel Sechlainn stated.

Orm was kneeling beside one of the two bodies in the village. 'That was caused by an axe,' he said, pointing at the horrific, gaping wound on the man's chest.

Sigtrygg hissed, 'Gufraid.'

A shout interrupted the three men's conference. Máel Sechlainn was on his feet and running in the direction of the lookout, leaping nimbly over an upturned cart. Sigtrygg watched him disappear beyond another smouldering wreck of a house and followed with Orm close behind. He did not need Máel Sechlainn's man to tell him why the warning had come.

Beyond another hillock Sigtrygg could see more smoke rising towards the sky.

'Baile an Gharráin?' Orm suggested.

'Get the men ready to move out.' Sigtrygg stated. 'They are only a few miles away.'

Máel Sechlainn's hand fell on his arm. 'Wait,' he said. 'Whoever it is, they are trying to draw us away from the city.'

'It's Gufraid,' Sigtrygg insisted.

'Whoever it is, his next stop will be Áth Skipir,' Jarl Orm said. 'We need to catch up and destroy them before they get there.'

'They will already be gone before we get there,' Máel Sechlainn told them. 'They're trying to draw us away from Veðrarfjord.'

Jarl Orm was a head shorter than the King of the Déisi but he was not daunted. 'I will protect my home,' he stated bluntly, and whistled loudly.

Máel Sechlainn didn't drop his gaze until he heard the jangle of mail and thump of many feet come from the direction of the village. It was Orm's men come to answer their master's call. Máel Sechlainn took an involuntary step back from the young jarl.

'We will protect my home,' Orm repeated, 'and then we will return to Veðrarfjord to protect yours, Sigtrygg.' He did not await permission or an answer but jogged away, followed by his fifty warriors.

'You still think it is Gufraid?' asked Máel Sechlainn.

'I know it is him,' Sigtrygg spat.

'What reason would he have to draw us away from Veðrarfjord?'

'The prisoners,' Sigtrygg exclaimed. 'He thinks that he can walk straight into my city, free my prisoners. I'll be damned to hell for all eternity before I allow that to happen. Do you hear me?' he exclaimed at the sky. 'To hell!'

Máel Sechlainn shook his head. 'We can't allow your father to get free. The whole city could rise against us.'

Sigtrygg hissed. 'Gufraid might already be marching on Veðrarfjord. There is a valley to the east that would bring them out near the Siúire. That's where they'll go.'

'Then that's where we will go. Orm can chase him northwards while we make plans for our own ambush.'

Sigtrygg smiled. 'We'll cut them down them at Gunnarr's Place.'

Raymond hauled himself out of the stream and onto the bank. He took care to avoid the nettles and grabbed hold of a fistful of grass, using it to help him free his lower half from the clawing grip of the brown water. He was soaked to the skin and panting and had to crawl up the last few steps to where the land levelled out. After a few seconds' searching in the longer grass he found the place his weapons had landed and fixed them back to his belt. Raymond shook his shoulders and poked a finger into his right ear to clear the discomforting water that sloshed around inside his head. The stream had proved a much greater challenge than he had thought it would and in several sections he had almost lost his footing as he had crossed.

Wiping the remaining river water from his face, Raymond fixed his eyes on the tree line and ran forward, crouching as low as he could while inspecting the landscape to his left and right for possible threats. His sword bounced on his left thigh while the darts bunched at his spine hopped and clattered with the provisions in the bag around his neck. He held them all down as best he could with his left to prevent any more noise than was unavoidable. The wood was heavy with foliage and caused Raymond to slow down and pick his path. The spear in his hand proved useful as a tool to rip the heaviest bramble and ferns aside, but his eyes remained on the woods ahead. He had not gone far when Ieuan caught up with him. The tall Welshman was just as wet as Raymond and was still covered in black soot from the burning embers of their last target. Ieuan did not speak as he followed his captain further into the thicket with an arrow nocked upon his bow. They were going uphill again and soon came to a small clearing where they came to a halt. They had come over the crest and looked down onto a plain filled with forests.

'Smell,' Raymond whispered to his companion, pointing to his nose and underlining his words with two loud sniffs.

Ieuan copied his actions. 'Môr. The sea.'

Raymond nodded and pointed his spear back in the direction of the river. 'Get the rest to come up. I think that it's all clear.' The bearded archer melted back into the trees without words. Raymond stabbed his weapon into the turf and wringed more river water from his sleeves. A shiver of cold wrapped itself around his chest and he stepped out into the bright sunshine. He immediately felt warmth upon his face and closed his eyes to enjoy the brief rest. He had not slept since the day before and tiredness was starting to get the better of him. He yawned widely and fished out some of the twice-baked bread. He tore a mouthful away with effort and returned the remainder to his bag. To the north he could see the Black Mountains, tiny on the distant horizon, but a comforting marker for Raymond to gauge his whereabouts. The late morning sunshine was strong and he had to raise his hand to cover his eyes. A sparkle of sunlight on open water caught his attention, no more than a mile ahead. The estuary was the divider between Ostman territory and the peninsula of Siol Bhroin where Raymond and his advance force had built Dun Domhnall. He looked at the mountains to the north and adjudged that where he stood was little more than six miles from the Norman fort. It was less to the walls of Veðrarfjord in the opposite direction.

The beach where Trygve's crew had landed his small band of raiders was on the sea estuary ahead. Raymond prayed that the crew would return as they said they would or the twenty Ostmen and fifteen Welsh archers would be trapped on the wrong side of the water. Gufraid had dismissed his concerns, just as he had every worry that Raymond had brought up since their landing at dusk the day before. The Ostman had guided them through the unfamiliar territory in the darkness with uncanny ease and without even the threat of discovery. Their attack on the two manors had been without problems too, causing maximum terror and damage to property. The only ones to perish were the folk who did not flee but put up a fight. He was sure that the survivors would not stop running until they came to Veðrarfjord's walls. They would add to the mouths feeding upon Sigtrygg's stores of food. There, they would spread stories of Norman power and guile amongst the people. And a frightened people were a people half beaten. In all, the raid had been a complete success. Yet Raymond still felt anxious.

Gufraid was the reason for his unease. It had started soon after his people had made camp on Trygve's land, though Raymond had not then been fully aware of it then. He had dismissed his every instinct that Gufraid was hiding something from him. He blamed his own terror at the thought of crossing into enemy territory, the lasting effects of his head injury, anything other than question Gufraid. The jarl's optimism had been infectious, as was the energy with which he took to the plan. It had been Gufraid who had convinced one of Trygve's captains to transport them to the beach, Gufraid who had convinced Raymond to launch the assault so quickly after the exertions of their cattle raid in the Black Mountains. Only after they had made land in Ostman territory had Gufraid's recklessness become all too apparent. Even then it felt more like enthusiasm, a desire to push on no matter what. His leadership had got their small band off the dunes and through four miles of tough terrain in the darkness of the night before. It had got them past wary shepherds and past the sentinels on the walls of outlying Ostman farms. He had seemed fearless to the point of madness. What had caused the change in behaviour, Raymond did not know, but if anything it had become more apparent since they had torched the second manor a few hours before.

'On, on,' had been Gufraid's maxim whenever anyone in their warband had called for respite from his punishing pace.

Raymond had even caught the cagey and fretful glances between Gufraid's own men at their jarl's decisions. That, above everything else, told him that this was not Gufraid's usual manner. His ally's abandonment of caution caused Raymond to change too. He had taken on all the scouting missions, hoping to make up for Gufraid's risks by edging ahead of their warband. If Gufraid had noticed his efforts he had made no comment on them. The jarl's only concession was to abandon his plan to attack a manor belonging to an Ostman called Gunnarr as it was too close to the city. He had another target in mind. One which he claimed would be less of a risk.

Several minutes had passed since Ieuan had left him, and

Raymond looked despairingly back through the trees for the rest of his company.

'Now you decide to take a break?' Raymond murmured and shook his head at the alarming behaviour of his ally. With one final look at the sparkling estuary he stomped back into the trees, snatching up his spear as he went. His and Ieuan's path was easy to find and he followed it back towards the stream, practicing what he would say to reprimand Gufraid as soon as he found him again. He was already going downhill and picking up speed when he caught sight of daylight beyond the edge of the woods. So when the Welsh archer appeared from his side it almost made him cry out in fright.

'What -' he began before the panicked look in the Welshman's eyes caused him to quieten and lower down onto his knees. The bowman put a single finger to his lips and then waved for Raymond to follow him. They shuffled forward to the treeline. There, Ieuan lay in the shadows, staring downhill towards the stream. On either side of the Welshman were his archers. Ieuan did not turn to register Raymond's presence but continued to stare out into the open landscape beyond. Raymond lay down beside him and followed the direction of Ieuan's gaze.

'Holy Trinity save us,' he mumbled.

For on the far side of the stream a large body of Gaels had appeared on the horizon above a hedge of yellow broom. Worse, despite all his efforts to keep the company moving forward, Gufraid had not yet got his twenty warriors across the stream. Instead they sat in the shallows, hidden for the moment from the Gaels by the high clay river bank at their backs. The enemy was less than a hundred paces away at the brow of the hill.

'What now?' Ieuan whispered in his abrupt French.

Raymond did not know. Gufraid's men could not move and nor could they see the enemy on the ridge above them. Clearly, they knew the enemy were close. Raymond and the Welshmen could not emerge from their hiding place lest they make the Gaels aware of their presence and draw them to the waterside. Twenty cold, wet and sleep-deprived Ostmen would not last long against the fifty or so in the Gaelic warband and nor would their evacuation be easy if the enemy tracked them to the coast.

'We wait,' he told Ieuan in a low voice.

But will Gufraid stay hidden, Raymond wondered. He thought back over the hours since they had hit the beach, the Ostman's increasing impetuousness in command.

'Stay where you are,' Raymond mumbled in the direction of the huddled Ostmen, urging Gufraid to understand his predicament and to remain calm.

Movement up on the hillside caught Raymond's eye and he refocused on the people on the ridge above. The vast frame of Sigtrygg Mac Giolla Mhuire could not be mistaken for anyone else, even from two hundred paces away. He was by far the largest man that Raymond had ever seen and he was immediately transported back to their fight between the double fortifications of Dun Domhnall. His temples began to thud. The only reason he had survived their duel was due to the timely intervention of the Welsh archers and his esquire's bravery. He should've died under the giant Ostman's frenzied attack. With effort, he slowed his breathing and stared across the valley at Sigtrygg. His enemy had one hand to his ginger brow and was surveying the woods in which Raymond and his men were secreted.

'Don't move,' Raymond hissed to the Welshmen. Ieuan translated it into his native tongue with - he was sure - the added emphasis of multiple curse words.

Sigtrygg's inspection of the woodland seemed to last for ever, so long that Raymond was certain that he would soon send his men across the stream. If that happened Gufraid was doomed.

'Please don't move,' Raymond mumbled again. This time his words were aimed at the Ostmen in the stream. 'Stay still, you damned fool. Do not break cover.'

His temples thumped and he had to close his eyes in an effort to ease the pain that had suddenly arisen behind his eyes. Even with his eyes closer the sunshine glare on the yellow broom seared into his brain. He only opened them as Ieuan's hand dropped onto his sleeve in warning. The distance to the ridge was too far for Raymond to hear the words that Sigtrygg shouted to his warriors, but it was clear that they were readying to move out. The Gaels clambered to their feet and hoisted their weaponry onto their shoulders. Raymond's fists gripped tufts of grass and wildflowers. There was nothing he could do. If Sigtrygg ordered his men towards the stream, he would have to leave him to die. A fighting retreat to the beach would be almost impossible in the woods where the archers' range and effectiveness would be reduced to little more than twenty paces; to a beach, he remembered, upon which he did not trust that a ship would be waiting. He could merely watch, though the throb in his temples made it almost impossible to keep his eyes fixed on the horizon. A rasp of air shot from the top of his lungs has he saw the Gaels finally turn and disappear behind the broom hedge. They were going back towards Veðrarfjord! A murmur of relief started amongst the archers until Ieuan threatened them to silence again. Up on the ridge opposite, Sigtrygg still stood, watching the part of the woods where they were hidden. In the trees above, Raymond could hear birds taking to flight and he wondered if that was what had caused Sigtrygg to remain. If he did suspect anything, he did not remain long, but left the ridge to follow his allies.

Raymond finally felt his fingers unwind from the grass and his breathing return to normal. After a few minutes he licked his lips and rose to his feet. He held out a palm to indicate that the Welshmen should stay where they were. Raymond then emerged from the dark of the woods and ran down into the valley. He almost fell on a number of occasions because his eyes were fixed on the broom hedge above rather than the uneven ground beneath his feet. No one reappeared on the horizon.

The twenty Ostmen were in a sorry state. They had been up to their chests in water for quite some time when Raymond came across them. Most were shaking from the cold as they huddled in the darkness of the overhanging river bank. Twenty sets of eyes looked up in relief as Raymond appeared on the eastern bank and put a finger to his lips before beckoning for them to cross. He was sure that the racket made by their dripping clothes and awkward, frigid bodies was sure to draw the Gaels back, but it seemed that one saint from the Holy

160

pantheon was with them that day and the enemy did not return. Most of the Ostmen were so cold that they needed help to climb the bank and Raymond was sweating by the time he hoisted the last man out of the water and sent them uphill into the woods. Ieuan had the good sense to keep the Ostmen moving and Raymond found them sitting in the sunshine in the clearing on the far side of the hill. The Welshman mimed that he had sent his archers ahead to scout the land ahead for any further dangers.

'No forget,' he said forcefully, pointing to his own chest, as he vanished back into the woods to watch the land behind in case of the enemy's return.

Raymond dropped down beside Gufraid who was still shivering and clutched his arms to his wide chest. Steam rose from his bald head as the sun shone on it. Raymond considered that a good sign.

'I thought we were caught.' The jarl's teeth chattered. 'I couldn't even move to see if they were still up on the ridge.' Gufraid buried his head in his elbow to quieten the cough which erupted from his chest. When he reappeared he was sniffing uncontrollably. 'I couldn't have endured the cold for much longer.'

'We got away, that's what matters. It has been a successful raid,' Raymond told him. 'When we return with Strongbow we will be -'

'"Return with Strongbow?"' Gufraid looked up. 'What do you mean? We still have one more manor to attack.'

Raymond smiled encouragingly and flapped a hand at the sodden company of axemen. 'We have done well. There is no point in risking our lives needlessly. Every Ostman in the region will know that there is trouble afoot. The whole lot of them will be falling back on the city for protection. It is time to go home.'

'No! We cannot leave yet,' Gufraid insisted. Raymond saw the flare of energy, the hot-headedness of the last few days return to the jarl's face. 'We have one more target!'

'I don't understand. Why would we -'

'We need to attack Fiodh-Ard Liag now,' Gufraid said and reached out to grab Raymond by his arm. 'We must go on. On!

If Sigtrygg suspects it was me who -' His eyes darted from side to side as he sought the words to make Raymond bow to his will. They did not come to him and Gufraid sank back to the ground, his hand releasing its hold on Raymond's forearm. 'If Sigtrygg thinks I had anything to do with this raid he will kill my boys,' he finally admitted.

Raymond watched as his ally visible slumped, his head bowing, his spine curved. The energy that he had expended to get the small band of raiders to the hillside had finally caught up with Gufraid. Raymond said nothing for several seconds, but looked over each shoulder to make sure that none of their company had heard Gufraid's admission or seen his reaction to it. Most still had their heads down, rubbing their arms and trunks or wringing water from their long hair and clothes. He turned back to his ally.

'You should've told me that he held your children prisoner,' he whispered.

'I didn't know if you would care.'

'I care because it might affect our agreement. I held up my side. I got your people to safety. Now I find out that you might turn on us at any moment.'

'I would never -'

'I'm not a father ...' Raymond began before spluttering to a halt. An image of Alice of Abergavenny had stormed into his mind's eye and he struggled to force it away. 'I am not a father, but I can imagine that there's nothing that a parent wouldn't do to make sure their children are safe from harm. If Sigtrygg put a knife to your sons' throats and told you to turn on us, you would without a second thought.'

Gufraid did not stir, but Raymond could feel that his warriors were starting to become aware of their conversation. Raymond was suddenly very aware that with the Welsh archers out scouting the land ahead he was alone with the Ostmen on the hillside.

'What is the name of this manor?'

'Fiodh-Ard Liag,' Gufraid repeated. 'It is no more than a mile north of here, and defended by perhaps twenty men.'

Raymond sighed. The image of Alice refused to leave his mind. He had barely had time to consider what her pregnancy

162

would mean since she had told him of it. But Gufraid's unhappy circumstances caused him to think back to the day when they had searched the woods of Siol Bhroin for alder bark and foxgloves, and her confession that she was carrying a child. All the shameful thoughts that he had considered came back to him: that he might not be the father, that it might be Prince Harry; that she had betrayed him before and might do so again; that a bastard was a disgrace that might ruin what few hopes he had of marrying Basilia, of leading Strongbow's army to victory. That day in the woods Alice had accused him of lacking ruthlessness, of an inability to make the hard choices that would make him a success in Ireland. She had all but dared him to deny paternity of her unborn child. Alice knew him too well, he realised, and when it came to it, he was not cold-blooded enough to condemn her and the infant to a life of ignominy and deprivation. He wondered if he was ruthless enough to make the tough choice now.

He looked at Gufraid's sad figure. The jarl was a brave man, a leader of warriors, but he stared up at Raymond from his knees. He was shivering and pathetic. It had only been minutes before that Raymond had been anticipating that he would have to abandon Gufraid and his men to their deaths at the hands of Sigtrygg and his Gaelic warband. Despite Alice's accusations, he knew that he did have the capacity to make hard choices, but did that make them the right ones? His raid of Ostman territory had been a great success and what he should do was to make all haste to get back to safety in Dun Domhnall.

Raymond turned his eyes to the sky.

'Damn it,' he muttered and held out his hand to help Gufraid back to his feet.

Alice of Abergavenny held up the finished surcoat and sighed contentedly. She had mixed in crushed foxglove and nettles to the mix and it had given the yellow marigold, cow parsley and St John's Wort dye a shine which had carried across to the finished garment just as she had hoped. It was imbued with warmth and in the late afternoon sunshine the surcoat sparkled like gold. She had to squint to keep looking at it. The splits in

163

the lower half opened and closed in the small wind off the ocean. She spotted a small frayed end of thread and she carefully folded the heavy cloth across her left arm so that she could fix it. She had not had enough fabric to make the surcoat into one of the full-length pieces that the noblemen at King Henry's court in Westminster had been wearing, but it would suit Raymond's frame, she decided, reaching to the knee. Unlike those she had seen in England, she had designed four splits in the lower half of Raymond's surcoat to aid movement and had reinforced them with leather hems. What little bit of fabric she had saved had been made into a small pennant bearing the new arms for Raymond's lance.

She had enjoyed designing the three black lions for the front of the surcoat and had spent a great deal of time in consideration of which manner to depict them. She had finally decided against a single rampant lion and had instead made three black lions that would stride across Raymond's chest with one paw ready to attack. Her design spoke of valour and courage as well as stability and wariness. They were, she decided, the best traits of a warlord – daring yes, but the good sense to do so from a place of balance, power and security. She had added what remained of the foxglove and nettle concoction to the black dye made from oak apples, iris root and alder bark and it had added a certain lustre to the mixture that she had not expected. Alice had required a steady hand to cut the three lions from the linen, but she felt that her small mistakes would not be noticed by anyone other than herself. She unfolded the garment a second time to enjoy its beauty. She allowed herself a moment of pride at the product of her artistry.

She had left the fort several hours before, bound for the little secluded cove on the eastern side of the peninsula. Its steep sides and heavy brush kept the men of Dun Domhnall away and allowed Alice a degree of privacy. She had told William de Vale and Fulk to remain behind but she was absolutely sure that they would have disobeyed and were hidden somewhere above, keeping watch over her as Raymond had commanded. Not that their vigilance was particularly required. Since they had left on their cattle raid the milites had for the most part left her to her own devices. The sullenness that had been directed towards Raymond had transformed into outrage at his departure. The milites' resentment was then directed at Alice, William and Fulk, and in those initial few hours of his absence she had been worried that their fury might lead to violence against their little group. However, sobriety soon returned and by that evening the two factions had descended into an uneasy truce. The milites even began working on the wall as Raymond had suggested and that had kept them busy for several days. Alice, William and Fulk had stayed out on the eastern cape, as far away as they could be from the milites. Sir Hervey had not helped with the work, stating loudly that the labour was unnecessary since his nephew, the earl, would soon arrive and they would join his great army in their attack on Veðrarfjord. Thankfully, Sir Hervey seemed content to remain alone in his hut away from everyone.

The return of the Welshmen at the head of the hundred and thirty-strong cattle train had come as something of a relief too. With them had come the milites' coursers and Raymond's cavalrymen had spent almost a day brushing their coats and cleaning their tack, complaining about the Welshmen's lack of care for the animals while they were in the north. The milites had not given the coursers any time to recover of course, but had insisted upon taking them out the next morning. Walter de Bloet had organised the Norman horsemen into teams and they had driven the cattle out of the fort and into the countryside to get fresh fodder and access to the river for water. The Welsh bowmen had made no argument and nor had Alice. With the absence of the milites she had the freedom of Dun Domhnall returned to her. Raymond's absence had been worrying but Caradog had insisted that it would not be long before he returned to the fort. On that first night back, Caradog had told all the story of their raid in the lands of the north, of the Ostmen and the Black Mountains.

Caradog had also shown the pages and the esquires how to milk the cows. As the sons of fighting men they had little knowledge of farming, and the Welshmen had laughed at their early attempts at the task. They had soon got competent enough for Caradog to declare it the boys' primary responsibility. Each morning before dawn they rose to collect the milk before the milites drove the cattle out of the fortifications. Caradog had even made some passably flavoursome cheese from the milk, forcing the little pages to drink the excess whey in order to build up their muscles, and laughing at their attempts to guzzle as much of the liquid without feeling sick.

It had been Fulk who had let slip to Alice that Raymond had briefly returned to Dun Domhnall three days earlier. He had arrived with the dawn and had gone back northwards before Alice or the majority of the garrison had awoken. He had stayed only long enough to collect ten cows and a handful of Welsh archers, and then he had left again. Where was his destination, or his reasons, he had not disclosed to Fulk. Nor had he left a message stating how long he would be gone.

Alice was still annoyed at that. If she was to be any help to his cause she had to know what Raymond was doing. She again tried to dismiss her concerns, for it was likely that he was simply enjoying Trygve's company in Cluainmín. Perhaps he was trading the ten cattle for wine or beer? She knew that Sir Hervey and the milites had drunk the fort dry in Raymond's absence and being able to treat the earl – particularly when Sir Hervey could not – might be an easy way to maintain Strongbow's favour. Since Father Nicholas' departure, it had become rather difficult to remember which day it was, but Alice was certain that the Feast of St Bartholomew would take place in the next few days. It would be the perfect opportunity to show off Raymond's success in Ireland, Alice decided. If only Strongbow got his act together and crossed the sea. If her time-keeping was correct, only a week remained in the month of August, and soon the summer fighting season would be at an end. Perhaps she did not understand fully the campaigns of warriors, but she did wonder how Raymond's lord could hope to accomplish his conquest before the autumn season began. Every passing day decreased the likelihood of Strongbow's crossing to Ireland and increased the prospect of another attack on Dun Domhnall by the recovered Ostmen of Veðrarfjord. The enemy would be more wary of the archers, she was sure, and Raymond's ploy with the cattle could not be played a second time.

She hoisted the new surcoat and stared at it again. A frown spread across Alice's face as she wondered if Raymond would need the garment any time soon. Its primary use was to mark out a man in battle. In his world a man could rise rapidly thanks to his skill and strength with a sword, but he could not do that if he merely sat out on a headland awaiting his master's arrival.

A rustle of dry branches and leaves, a scattering of stones, coming from above, was enough to rouse Alice from her thoughts. She looked up to see William de Vale hanging by a hand from a wizened tree perched on the steep bank.

'You need to come and see this,' William said excitedly, all pretence of remaining unseen forgotten. He did not await her answer but began scrambling his way back to the top of the cove. She caught a glimpse of Fulk at the top waving his hands for William to hurry.

'Raymond?' she whispered and climbed to her feet, dusting off the little bits of detritus that had become attached to her skirts. Alice looped the precious surcoat around her neck and walked across to the little hidden pathway which she had cut. It was steep and required her to stoop low at several points to make sure the surcoat did not snag on the roof of brambles which enclosed the path on all sides. It took several minutes' effort to get to the top and by the time she did Alice was sweating. Although the sun was in the western sky, she could see the outline of Fulk and William already at the little track running north-south down the middle of the headland. Their bouncing shadows stretched back towards her on the cattle-trodden grassland. She searched the skyline but could not see any sign of Raymond's party.

Alice hoisted her skirts and began to follow the page and esquire. It took her several minutes to make it to the track, and neither Fulk nor William had waited for her to arrive. The day was still hot and she took a few moments to gather her breath, fanning her face with the corner of the new surcoat. That was when she saw them in the distance. A fleet of ships had entered the estuary and were bound for Dun Domhnall.

Alice began running.

Gufraid called the hill Meannán.

He said that a hero of the Gaels was buried at its core, that the hero's father, a great champion himself, had built it thousands of years before using his superhuman strength, gouging the earth with his bare hands. Into that void had flowed the river. Raymond could almost believe that part, for the hill did resemble one of the ancient burial mounds he had seen in Wales, rising unnaturally from the river plain to a pinnacle of five hundred feet. What he could not believe was Gufraid's other story. He said that the hero buried within the hill kept watch over Ireland and would rise again to bring the fight to any invader of her sovereign soil.

Raymond stamped a foot on the ground. 'Hey! We are already here. Better get your weapons ready if you are to catch us.'

'Maybe it is the father who is buried here,' Gufraid said glumly. 'The Gaels have so many stories. It is difficult to keep track of them all.'

Whether or not they were about to be confronted by a corpse-warrior from his resting place beneath, Raymond did commend the hero for picking a brilliant spot for his lonely lookout. He could see for miles in every direction from the rocky outcropping at the top of Meannán. The Black Mountains were a blur in the distance while to the south he could see all the way to the sea. The small islands close to Dun Domhnall were even in view over the hazy landscape below.

'And Trygve's crew? Where are they?'

Gufraid climbed to his feet and pointed northwards to where the three arms of the brown river met. 'There is a creek to the south of that big island.'

'Where will they meet us?'

'At a marsh north of Fiodh-Ard Liag. They will make land at the eastern edge at high tide.'

Raymond shook his head as he stared downhill at the reeds and mud. The tide was turning, but the marsh looked nigh impassable as it baked in the low afternoon sunshine. Their raiding party would have to make their way through woods first, down a steep incline, and then they would face the possible hazard of the grey, mucky beach. 'There are many things that could go wrong.'

'You know that I must try,' Gufraid countered.

'It is your sons' lives that you are risking should we fail.'

'And it is your decision not to wait for darkness to attack them.'

Raymond sighed. He had always been told to avoid a night attack at all costs. His father had told him when he was little more than an infant at Carew Castle. Sir William de Bloet, to whom he had been apprenticed as an esquire, had told him. Even Strongbow had warned against them. 'It was a miracle that we got across Ostman territory unscathed last night. I won't risk an operation in the darkness being a success a second time.'

Gufraid scowled and turned to face the west. He did not blink as the sun shone straight into his eyes. He stared down at the manor on the plain below.

'Who is the lord of Fiodh-Ard Liag?' asked Raymond as he joined his ally.

'Háimar,' he replied. 'A jumped-up little fart of a man. I hear he calls himself *Jarl* Háimar now.'

'How many men can he raise from his estate?'

'Twenty or so, at a push.'

With his fifteen archers, Raymond did not consider that much of a challenge. 'He will see us coming from a mile off,' he warned. Háimar's manor house was built with its back to the river and the plain around it was covered in low lying fields with few hiding places. A high ridge of land running down from Meannán guarded the manor's eastern extreme and would, Raymond did not doubt, hide several lookouts that would alert the manor of any impending attack. He could see masts and ship's rigging in a small creek to the south of Fiodh-Ard Liag. Háimar's folk would be able to escape before Raymond could bring his archer's within range of his walls.

'I can see why Sigtrygg would think your sons would be safe here.'

Gufraid bowed his head. 'It is hopeless then.'

Raymond put his hand on the Ostman's shoulder. 'For you family's sake, I hope not.' He concentrated on the small manor. 'I still don't fully understand why Sigtrygg would send your sons to Háimar.'

'To secure their alliance? Important hostages mean added importance for their keeper. I suspect Háimar desires to rise above his station.'

Raymond's eyes narrowed. 'Ambition eats money. You say that Háimar isn't wealthy?'

'He is a farmer and his folk are Fionngall,' Gufraid stated as if that were enough.

'Meaning?'

'Meaning they have limited trading rights in the city in comparison to we Dubhgall, the Danish folk. The Fionngall are Norse.'

'I didn't think there were any divisions amongst the Ostmen.'

Gufraid sniffed. 'We conquered the Fionngall long ago, and they have adopted our ways, accepted our laws. So we let them live in Veðrarfjord. Some, like Háimar, still have farms. Raising crops is just about all they are good for. They certainly shouldn't be calling themselves jarls.'

Raymond nodded. 'Farmers who wish to be jarls need money and lots of it. What is the quickest way for your people to get rich?'

'To get rich?' Gufraid looked to the sky. 'Raiding, I suppose. No, the slave trade.'

'Slaves,' Raymond murmured, ruminating over the word.

'Do you think Háimar might be bribed?' asked Gufraid after several moments of silence.

Raymond shook his head slowly. 'I have a better idea than that. First, we must cut down a tree – a really big one.'

The six men were sweating as they shuffled in a line down the pathway. The rough bark of the pine trunk had begun to rub as it bumped up and down on their shoulders. They gritted their teeth and kept moving forward.

'Keep your heads down,' Raymond whispered. He was glad that he was at the very back of the shambling group. Being shorter than the Welshmen meant that the tree trunk had not been pressing down on his neck since they had come off the hillside. One of the smaller branches had not been cut cleanly away and it had gnawed painfully at his flesh during the descent from the pinnacle of Meannán. His hands, although seemingly bound over the top of the pine tree, were not really secure and he could remove his fetters at any time. At his spine were five arrows which rubbed uncomfortably against the nape of his neck and top of his backside.

To each side were Ostmen, ten in total. Gufraid had said that to send more would raise suspicion, but they looked very few as they slowly made their way towards Fiodh-Ard Liag. At least their allies were armed, he thought. Ahead of him, Welsh voices began arguing and before he could mutter a warning, Gufraid's man, Grím, stepped forward and slapped one across the back of the head, barking an order in his own tongue. Raymond's eyes flicked to the group of at least fifteen awaiting their arrival, but Grím's sudden violence seemed to have helped with the illusion that he was a slaver and they were his merchandise. Thankfully having spent over a week raiding, the Welshmen and Raymond looked dirty and downtrodden enough that they might be mistaken for slaves.

Raymond almost cried out in pain as the step of the men in front suddenly synchronised and their load plummeted onto the top of his shoulder.

'Keep it smooth,' he hissed, 'unless you want to give the game away and actually get sold into slavery?' The pain was awful, but his first concern was for the bow hidden in a channel cut in the top of the pine trunk. His fingers sought the smooth yew pressed into the gap and he sighed shallowly when he found the weapon still resting snugly in the groove. It was sticky with sap in the channel and he suspected that was the reason the bow had not leapt from its hiding place.

There were fields either side being worked by slaves, making hay or tending to animals. The rest were heavy with oats, barley and rye. Fiodh-Ard Liag was, to Raymond's mind, only a little smaller in scale to Trygve's town at Cluainmín and the equal of Strongbow's chief tenants' enterprises in Netherwent. It was certainly greater than any upland manor with which Strongbow might have rewarded Raymond at the end of his service had they remained in Striguil. It was safer too, given its proximity to Veðrarfjord. It was far from the poor farm that Gufraid had described.

A hail from the group ahead brought the manacled men to a halt. A short man with long brown hair stepped forward and raised a hand in greeting. Gufraid, being worried that he might be recognised, was hidden somewhere to the north, keeping an eye on proceedings. He would bring the rest of the raiders forward when Raymond and Grím launched their plan. Judging by Gufraid's description, the short man was Háimar, Jarl of Fiodh-Ard Liag. Raymond could see earrings bouncing around beneath his long hair, and could see tattoos on his forearms. He could not understand the conversation between Grím and Háimar and instead he glanced at the walls of the manor. The defences were only head high and made out of wide timber posts. The manor did not even have a ditch around it. Five warriors stood to either side of the gate, watching everything that went on. Raymond rearranged his grip on the pine trunk so that he could see the little creek just south of the manor. Three ships were tied to the wharf, their rigging stowed high on single masts. They were small, but Raymond fancied that they would be big enough for all his raiders.

To Raymond's right Grím and Háimar still spoke and he breathed a sigh of relief that his assumption about the jarl's finances had been correct. Háimar could not give up on a ready chance of making money. The story that they had concocted was that Grím was a trader out of Hlymrik on his way home from Wales when he had discovered plague amongst his crew. Fearing that his cargo would succumb to the illness, he had decided to sell them cheaply before continuing west. Raymond was pleased to see that Grím was clever enough to barter with Háimar rather than to accept the first price and raise any doubts over the veracity of his story. Raymond was so rapt by Grím's performance that he did not realise that another Ostman had been going along the line of Welsh archers examining them for signs of plague or other defects. The first he realised was when a rough hand grabbed him by the cheeks and forced him to open his mouth. The bearded man growled something as Raymond moved to protest. He then grabbed his bicep before giving a signal to Háimar that the slaves were of good quality. Raymond spat on the ground and rearranged his shoulders. His billowing shirt hid the arrows but had the Ostman laid a hand on his back their ruse would've certainly been discovered.

He turned his attention back towards Grím and Háimar. Their haggling seemed to be reaching a head. Jarl Háimar waved a hand at the wall and that was the signal for the gates to the manor to open and several people to emerge carrying skins and pulling two carts. Raymond could see grain and firewood in the first, and could smell fish in barrels in the second. A huge dog was tied to the side of the lead cart and it strained against the rope in the direction of the enticing smell coming up behind. It was a good haul, but not nearly enough for six slaves. Grím obviously thought the same and he began arguing with Háimar. At one stage he even turned and shared a joke with his fellow Ostmen. Each laughed heartily. As a response the gates of the manor opened again and six sheep were herded out, causing the great hound to go mad and almost knock over the cart.

In the disorder, the Ostmen of Fiodh-Ard Liag had forgotten to close the gates of their manor and Raymond ogled the gap in the defences. He made eye-contact with the Gufraid's man to his left and then turned back to see that Grím and Háimar had finally reached agreement and were shaking hands and smiling at each other.

Raymond sucked in a lungful of air and bellowed, 'Ieuan!'

Several things happened at once. The people of Fiodh-Ard Liag froze and looked in the direction of the noise and then turned back as Háimar yelled out in pain and collapsed on the pathway. Blood poured from his nose, broken thanks to a blow from Grím's forehead. Gufraid's man put a big foot on Háimar's chest and punched down twice. Háimar's men's attempt to form up was upset by the folk fleeing past them towards the gates and before they knew it, Grím and his men were charging directly at them. Screams and shouting resonated on the timber wall of the manor.

Raymond unlooped the restraints from his arms and stepped away from the pine trunk. Two other men copied his actions, like him removing the bunch of arrows from their backs and tossing them into a pile.

'Ieuan?' Raymond called and pointed to the bowstave hidden in the timber, but the Welshman was already removing the weapon. He grimaced when he discovered the sap all over his hands, but wasted no time in removing the bowstring from around his middle and attaching it to the lower nock. His arm muscles bulged as he bent the yew and fastened the other end. Ieuan gasped with the effort and gave the weapon a preliminary haul.

'The men on the gate first,' Raymond called and pointed towards the wall.

Ieuan did not respond with words but dashed over to the bundle of arrows, scooping them up in one fluid movement. He came to a stop beside the unconscious figure of Háimar. Seconds later, one of the men guarding the gates fell backwards with an arrow in his chest. And then another cried out as he tumbled backwards off the wall and out of sight. At a range of fifty paces, Ieuan could puncture the best mail ever made. The men on the wall were wearing no armour and the power of Ieuan's bow knocked them right off their feet. A third man appeared in the gateway and attempted to haul one door closed. He went down by Ieuan's hand, dust flaring around him as he crashed to the ground.

Raymond put four fingers in his mouth and whistled three times as loudly as he could. If Gufraid was not already aware of the attack, he would be now. Raymond knew that even at full pace it would take some time for the other group to get to the walls of Fiodh-Ard Liag. They could not allow Háimar's men to recover from the initial shock. He ran over and quickly ransacked Háimar's belt of his dagger and hand-axe, tossing them to two of the Welshmen.

'Now the warriors,' he told Ieuan.

The archer turned his deadly aim on the small fight going on before the gates. The Fiodh-Ard Liag men had recovered and were retreating in good order towards the manor wall. Grím's men were doing their best, but they were outnumbered and even the addition of two Welshmen to the fight could not help. Ieuan's intervention changed all that. In less than ten seconds, three men were down and he killed another two as Háimar's men turned and ran for the gates. Grím screeched for his men to follow and they were joined by three more Welshmen who had pilfered weapons from Ieuan's victims.

A shout of surprise came from Raymond's left and he ducked just in time to avoid being struck in his undefended head by an arrow coming from the wall of Fiodh-Ard Liag. Three boys with hunting bows had appeared and were shooting wildly at the attackers. Raymond felt Ieuan's arm wrap around him and bodily force him across to the cover of a hedge just as another flight of arrows skidded across the pathway.

'Thank you,' the Norman captain called as his back thumped into the ground. He saw that Háimar was still lying on the path and he quickly ran out into the open to haul him into cover. The jarl stirred and grimaced as Raymond turned him onto his front to prevent him from choking on his own blood. Another two arrows crashed through the hedge above Raymond. He could see that the intercession of the archers inside the manor had also stopped the assault on Fiodh-Ard Liag. One of Grím's men was down and the rest had run for cover behind the two handcarts. One of the Welshmen reached around to untie the rope holding the dog. The animal was unhurt and immediately dashed out of harm's way once set free.

Raymond could hear a distinct scraping sound and glanced down the path to see the gates of the manor being closed. He muttered a curse word and looked north over the fields through a small gap in the hedge. He could see people on the hill but the distance was too great and he could not make out if they were Gufraid's group or slaves working the fields. His attack had stalled and unless he could get it moving again the chances of taking the manor were slim.

At his side, Ieuan suddenly climbed to his feet and shot off an arrow. He knelt down immediately and merely said 'two' in the Welsh tongue before crawling further up the hedge. Raymond grabbed Háimar's shoulders and followed. A few moments later there was a clatter and thump as arrows began punching through the branches where they had been crouching. Ieuan was doing his part. By the time Raymond had lugged Háimar to his new spot, another of the boy-bowmen was downed. Their skill shooting at rabbits was simply no match for Ieuan's expertise honed across a lifetime of warfare. Not that the last boy was willing to give up. He continued to trade shots with the older Welshman in defence of his home. Ieuan's shake of his head was as much in admiration of the boy's tenacity as it was frustration that he could not defeat his opponent.

Raymond wasn't willing to wait any longer. He could hear panicked orders inside the walls of the town and knew that Háimar's folk were preparing their defences as best they could to meet their renewed assault. The longer he gave them to organise, the worse it would be. He steeled himself and then ran along the course of the hedge towards the gates. He knew the archer would see him, but no arrow lanced through the early evening sky to strike him. Skidding to a halt behind the first cart, he beckoned towards three Welshmen to follow and then pointed towards the large pine trunk lying abandoned a few paces away. They did not move and he mimed swinging the tree trunk, pointing at the gate to Fiodh-Ard Liag.

'Battering ram,' he said, simulating the swinging action again.

The Welshmen swapped nervous glances before warily moving out from behind the cart and following Raymond into the open. There was a puff of dust on the path beside Raymond's left foot where an arrow collided with the ground. It was followed by a high-pitched yelp from the wall of the manor and a cheer of success from Ieuan. Raymond could see the Welshman running towards him.

'Got him,' he cried as he reached his kinsmen. In his hands were his three remaining arrows and his bow.

Raymond stooped and grabbed one of the fetters which had been used to tie him and the Welshmen to the pine trunk. He looped it around the bottom of the tree and waited for the three archers to copy. The trunk was much heavier to hold underarm than it had been on their shoulders, but they managed to lift it and shuffle towards the gates.

The first spear thrown from the wall missed Raymond by a few feet. The next one caught the man behind him on the forearm. It sliced upon a long wound, but the Welshman did not stop, even when more debris began pouring down upon the four men. Ieuan revenged the wounded man by killing the defender with an arrow to his neck, but he wasted the next by shooting before he was properly ready. He had one arrow left and Raymond could see that he was holding off using it.

Raymond had begun chanting a rhythm for the men to follow as they approached the gates. It marked out the tempo of their feet and their arms began to swing the pine trunk in time too. 'One,-two, one-two,' he called, stopping only when an empty barrel bounced next to him and banged into his shoulder. 'One-two, one-two,' he cried again as the first strike bit home into the gates of Fiodh-Ard Liag. The second blow tore bark and sapwood away. A third opened a hole in the gates.

He spotted a man appear just to his right with a spear raised to throw and Raymond held his breath for there was nothing he could do other than hope that he missed his target. As the man braced to throw his body jerked backwards. Ieuan's last arrow punched into his chest. The spearman disappeared, only to be replaced by a woman who lobbed an eating knife at Raymond's crew. It stabbed the Welshman second from the front of the battering ram in the shoulder. He cried out in pain and fell to his knees.

'Get out,' Raymond called in his direction. 'Run!' he added before calling out the tempo again.

The battering ram crashed home. More pale wood skittered free and Raymond could see daylight on the far side. 'One-two, one-two,' he shouted, but he could already feel his arms fading. His voice was too, the pace getting slower as he breathed more shallowly.

Another shower of rocks and weapons clattered on the pine trunk. A fist-sized stone caught Raymond in the chest and a piece of turf thumped into his thigh. The man in front of him was not so lucky: a large branch crashed down onto his head. He went to his knees immediately, slumping across the middle of the battering ram. The rhythm of the battering ram stopped as his weight bore down on Raymond's and his last companion's arms. Both groaned in pain and attempted to dislodge the man.

'Get off,' Raymond appealed as the injured Welshman finally slid to the ground. He breathed heavily and looked quickly to his left and right. A man stood above him, a hand-axe raised above his shoulder ready to launch. Raymond knew that he was the target and could see the anger in the man's eyes. He was less than ten paces away. If he dropped the battering ram and ran Raymond knew that he might make it. To stay was to die.

'One-two,' Raymond called as he yanked the pine trunk backwards and then threw it forwards with all his might. Whether it was his sudden movement, or the reverberations from the strike that caused him to stumble, Raymond could not tell, but the axe remained in the man's hand. And, in a glorious piece of timing, that was when Gufraid and the second group arrived at the gates.

'Shoot,' Gufraid shouted.

The whack of arrowheads striking timber deafened Raymond. He could see the man at the front of the battering ram duck down and raise his shoulder to cover his ears. Anyone who might have thrown stones or weapons had dived for cover.

'One,' Raymond yelled as he again got the pine trunk moving. 'Two,' he roared as it crunched into the gates. 'Come on, break!'

Suddenly, Grím's purple shirt appeared in front of him, and he was followed by another Ostman. The weight bearing down on his forearm lessened. The impact of the battering ram got louder and then, with Grím shouting out the commands, the gate suddenly burst off its hinges. Grím and his companion didn't wait, but dropped their grip on the battering ram and aimed a few well-placed kicks to open the gates further. He wasn't a big man, but Grím quickly dealt with the obstruction.

Raymond had never been part of a charging Ostman attack, but he had faced one and he shouted for space as he hauled the pine trunk out of their way just before Gufraid and his men ran past him and into the manor. His shoulder was in agony as he disentangled his arm from the battering ram. He could see that his surviving companion was in a similar condition. Ieuan appeared to be tending to the man who had fallen before the gates and Raymond left him to his business. A couple of the late arrivals were going through the belongings in the cart and Raymond directed the archers to pack the skins and food into one of the small vessels tied to the wharf.

Crossing the path, he found Jarl Háimar sitting up with his back to the hedge. He was being watched by another bowman. He had no idea if the Ostman could speak the French tongue, but the threat of the Welsh archer seemed to encourage the jarl to comply with Raymond's direction. He forced Háimar back towards his manor.

'They have barricaded themselves in the great hall,' Gufraid told him as he drew close, flashing a thumb at the large wooden building ahead. He turned his eyes on Háimar. 'And they still have my boys.'

Raymond took hold of Háimar's shirt and shunted him towards Gufraid, wincing at the pain in his shoulder. 'Go and get your children back. There is no need for further violence. Tell them that we'll go as soon as they are handed over.'

Gufraid nodded and force-marched Háimar towards his own hall. Raymond could see the sparkle of the evening sun on a blade at his throat. He could not understand Gufraid's words, but he could hear the emotion in his voice. There was a brief back and forth between Gufraid and someone inside the hall. Soon, the door of the great hall opened and three haggard-looking young men emerged. Gufraid waited until they were almost level with him before releasing Háimar. The small jarl walked back to the hall with as much dignity as he could muster and then stood in the hall doorway, staring out.

Raymond called for the Ostmen to lead the way and then Ieuan and he marched out through the gates alongside the Welsh archers. Everything except the dog had been piled into the small boat, but they had to throw the grain onto the mucky beach to make enough room for all of Gufraid and Raymond's party.

With his jarl occupied with his three sons, Grím took command of the vessel and proved an able replacement. The small creek was already filled with water and the eight oarsmen were enough to pull the boat into the midst of the River Siúire. They unfurled the sail and, with the sinking sun behind them and a fair wind coming from the south, Grím pointed the bows towards Siol Bhroin.

The ship was called *Seagull*, *Mæw* in the Saxon tongue. Her

179

captain, Aylward, was a man of Bristol and of that folk.

'She's usually used for coastal work, so she's in her element in these waters,' Aylward promised Strongbow. 'She can get you into any port, *Seagull* can,' he said, digging his elbow into Strongbow's ribs again, 'if you know what I mean.'

Strongbow really didn't, but he smiled politely again as Aylward made another attempt at innuendo.

'Knows what's what and what goes where, does ol' *Seagull*.' The Saxon's elbow bumped Strongbow's ribs again. 'And remember: if you ever need my ships again, you only have to ask, Lord. You'd not want to be going elsewhere for transport. The FitzHarding men might hear about this little enterprise otherwise. They'd go straight to King Henry with it and you wouldn't want that, no? Not me, I'm your man in Bristol.'

'I will keep you in mind,' Strongbow replied curtly and moved away from the steering oar to the other side of the ship. The rest of the fleet were further out to sea than *Seagull* and had successfully negotiated the two small islands that guarded the bay. The wind was coming from the south-west and one of Aylward's men tugged on the sheets to keep the sail at its most effective angle.

'Because obviously you are going to be needing access to shipping,' Aylward continued. 'And I can do it cheap because now we have a relationship.'

Strongbow turned to see that Aylward had followed him and had given control of the vessel to another man. He shooed away a sailor on the port side and took his place, fiddling with the braces, unwinding them from the wooden stay and then tying them up again.

'I'm just saying: I know those FitzHarding men. I grew up working their boats. Devious bastards,' he said.

'Wasn't FitzHarding also called *Robert the Devout*? It seems incongruous that a man known as being so good to the church would also be as difficult as you suggest.'

Aylward didn't miss a beat. 'But why was he being so pious? That's what you have to ask yourself, Lord: what crimes are they trying to atone for? I'm telling you, they would cheat you sure as they would look at you! That goes for the son,

Maurice, and Old Robert, God rest his soul and all that.' Aylward quickly crossed his chest before continuing on with another anecdote about the time before he had struck out on his own as a merchant, of the double-dealing FitzHardings and their many misdeeds.

Strongbow turned his body so that he could look at Ireland over the rolling sea. The land looked no different from Wales which they had left early that same morning. It was the same green and browns and yellows, the sea still munched white at its shore. That gave him heart and calmed his nerves somewhat. Strongbow jumped as Aylward suddenly broke off from his story in order to yell across at the new steersman.

'Bring her south, Algar. Now where was I? Oh yes, so old Robert FitzHarding sells the same stone to the Cistercians twice!' Aylward laughed heartily before launching into another tale from his past.

Scowling, Strongbow returned to his vigil. The headland was still half a mile away, but he made out a few tiny figures and huts before *Seagull* plunged back downwards and the fort was lost from sight. In the belly of the ship he could see more warriors staring over the side, attempting to catch a glimpse of the new land. Others comforted the hobbled horses in their little stalls promising them, no doubt, that their long-awaited dinner would soon be served and the dreadful sea journey complete. Unlike the other vessels, *Seagull* was not so tightly packed, having left room to carry Raymond's conrois, esquires and horses to their new destination. The sixty men on board were principally made up of the retinues led by Jean de Clahull and Richard de Maroine. Both knights were prepared to stay in Ireland as long as it took to capture Veðrarfjord – as long, that was, as they were not called to attend upon King Henry or their suzerain lord. Both were men of property, holding lands from the Earl of Gloucester. Both wanted more, and Strongbow had promised them it.

Seagull mounted the peak of another wave giving Strongbow another view of Raymond's fort. He could see the wide green expanse and fancied that he had caught a glance of the wall that Rechin, Sir Hervey's man, had told him had been constructed. What he could not see were any cattle. The ship

181

tipped and his sightline was blocked by the grey ocean before he could concentrate his gaze on any part of the fortifications. At the apex of the next wave, he tried again. This time he was certain. There were no cattle within the walls of Raymond's bridgehead.

'Rechin!' he shouted, cutting off Aylward mid-story. 'Rechin,' he called again. The untidy warrior's head appeared about halfway up the deck. He gingerly got to his feet, reaching up to use the sail to steady his weight. Several of Aylward's sailors yelled out in harmony in the English tongue to get him to leave it alone. Rechin had already lurched across to the mast and hung onto that before making a dash to the port side of *Seagull* through the lines of men and horses.

'Lord?'

Strongbow did not turn. 'You came to me at Pill Priory and told me that Raymond had failed in his duty. You said that Sir Hervey had taken command of the bridgehead in Ireland. Is that correct?'

Rechin glanced at the shoreline, still a quarter-mile away. 'I did, but -'

'Then why can I see no cattle in the fort? Does my uncle not realise that was the whole reason for sending my best troops ahead to Ireland?' Strongbow twisted on his heel and stared at Rechin. 'I like to think that I am a fair and even-tempered man, but this really is pushing me to my limits. Where are the cattle that I was promised?'

Rechin was not used to seeing this side of Strongbow. He had only ever seen the worried old man, locked away in the priory staring at sheaves of paper and counting out coins. He looked to Aylward for assistance, but the merchant sailor had skulked away and had taken back the helm.

'I don't … that is, I'm not a farmer. However, I would suggest -'

'Where are my cattle?' Strongbow roared. He had not felt a fury like it since his abysmal treatment by King Henry at court in Westminster. His whole campaign, nay, his whole future, relied on his captains collecting enough food to feed their army while they besieged Veðrarfjord. If this had not been done his fleet may as well turn back towards Wales! He had raised an army and brought himself to the brink of financial ruin and all Raymond and Sir Hervey had to do in the same time was to corral a few cattle into the fort.

'Perhaps Raymond has awoken and taken back command?' Rechin continued. 'I've been gone for almost a week and I know Sir Hervey wouldn't let you down, Lord. Yes, it is probably Raymond's fault. He was the one that lost the cattle in the first place. It must be him.'

Strongbow sighed angrily and dismissed Rechin with a wave of his hand. 'Useless,' he moaned, loud enough for Sir Hervey's man to hear it. He turned back towards the sea. The other eleven vessels in his fleet were still far out to sea, but had cleared the danger of the islands. As ordered they would continue to their new landing place, a beach in Ostman territory selected by Sir Hervey. It was, Rechin had reported, the perfect site for disembarking their horses and the few supplies left over from their camp in Wales. 'Much better than Dun Domhnall,' he had added. It was there that Strongbow would journey once he got the answers he needed. Behind him, Aylward shouted something in the English tongue to his crewmen.

'We're going about, Lord,' Aylward warned, switching to French and pulling the steering board to his chest. *Seagull* dipped her shoulder and turned in a wide circle. Aylward straightened her up as her bows pointed into the wind and then began issuing orders again.

The sail flapped wildly above the ship and Strongbow could see the horses were getting frightened. He was about to say something to Aylward when the merchant beckoned for him to join him on the starboard side.

'Keep her pointed into the wind,' he said, then left to assist his crewmen.

Strongbow grabbed the steering board and immediately felt the tug of the water against *Seagull*'s bows. He had never piloted a ship before, not even his own *Waverider*, and, despite his fury, he felt the sudden elation and responsibility of being in control. He stole a glimpse and saw the crew struggling with the sail. They had lowered the yard but the close confines made it difficult to stow it properly. Men looped ropes and tied knots as Aylward shouted commands and urged them to hurry.

183

Strongbow looked over the stern of *Seagull* and was troubled to see just how close she was to the black cliffs of Dun Domhnall. He fought the desire to change the ship's course and kept her pointed into the wind as best he could. Finally, after many minutes working at it, the stowed sail was hauled back up the mast and out of the way.

'Beg your pardon, but I had better take us in,' Aylward announced as he rejoined Strongbow and placed his right hand on the steering board.

Strongbow stepped away and watched as Aylward expertly used the current and the effect of the wind on the hull to guide the ship around the eastern cape and onto the small beach below Raymond's fort. Protected from the breeze, he looked up to see a number of men on the rocky outcropping. Welshmen, Strongbow realised. His first impulse at the sight of them was animosity and worry that they might begin shooting arrows at the men packed into the ship. They were Raymond's men and he felt his eyes narrow in suspicion at the sight of them.

'Don't let anyone disembark,' he ordered Aylward. 'And get a gangplank out. We will have men, horses and supplies to get aboard.' Strongbow did not wait for a response but marched down the length of the ship. Several crewmen had already leapt onto the sand from the bows and had run lines up the cliffs ahead to secure *Seagull* ashore. At the bows Strongbow paused, his two hands gripping the sheer-strake, his body tensed to swing over the side.

One more step and I will be in Ireland, he thought. *One more move and King Henry will be able to declare me traitor.*

Strongbow stared at the sandy beach and wondered if it was too late to pull back from the brink. Scabs covered the knuckles of his lacerated left hand, but in his exertions to keep *Seagull* pointed into the wind, several had reopened. Ruby red blood poured down his fingers to drip into the ocean which lapped against the beach. He watched the droplets disappear and thought of his father. He recalled the stories and songs about his grandfather and great-grandfather. His sires were conquerors. Strongbow ached to replicate their success, to have his name placed alongside theirs. One day he would have to meet them in the hereafter and he wanted be able to say 'in life, these were my deeds' and have them look on in pride. He wanted his father to admit that he was worthy of his name. He had been denied the opportunity for his whole adult life. He would not waste it. Strongbow threw his legs over the side and dropped down into the surf. He immediately plunged into the shadow cast by the cliffs by the setting sun. Strongbow could see a small path cut into the cliffside and he walked in that direction. The climb was gruelling but short, and the wind immediately increased as he reached the top. Ahead, the Norman earthworks, crowned with a timber fortification, looked impressive and as Strongbow collected his breath, a small group of horsemen emerged from the gates and began trotting towards him. They were led by Sir Hervey. He could see the hoops of his green, white and red surcoat out in front, his oily long hair bouncing on his thin shoulders.

'Nephew!' Sir Hervey called as he brought his courser to a halt.

Strongbow nodded his head in greeting and waited for Sir Hervey to climb down from the saddle. He could hear his uncle's knees creak as he lowered himself to the ground. The earl did not recognise the two men with Sir Hervey, but beyond the small group he did spot the distant figure of William de Vale, one of Raymond's esquires, on foot as he came along the open grassland towards them. There were two more figures with William. One was a woman.

'Welcome, Nephew,' Sir Hervey tried again, noticing Strongbow's stiff manner. 'Our campaign can truly begin now that you have arrived to lead us. A celebratory drink?' He waved a hand at his men. One produced a skin and began clambering down from the saddle.

Strongbow frowned. 'That will not be necessary. Tell me, please, that you have managed to achieve your objective. Tell me you have collected enough cattle to feed my army.'

'A hundred and thirty head will return to the fort before sundown.' Sir Hervey looked confused at the earl's question.

Strongbow's hands went to his knees and he breathed out. 'Thank you, Uncle. You have no idea how relieving it is to hear that.' Strongbow straightened up and looked to the sky. His lips mumbled a prayer to St Peter. 'Raymond is with them, I presume?'

'Raymond? Hah!' Sir Hervey laughed and shook his head. 'I hope Rechin told you all about his antics in your absence?'

'He did, Uncle.' Strongbow replied as a very sweaty William de Vale jogged the last few steps to come to a halt before him and salute. 'Master William?'

The young man struggled to speak and held a hand up in an appeal for a moment to recover his breath. Strongbow noted his uncle's reaction to William's arrival. He sent a sharp look towards his ragged warrior and then nodded in William's direction. Sir Hervey's man moved over towards William, placing a hand on his chest, and pushing him away.

'The earl doesn't wish to be disturbed by the likes of you,' Sir Hervey wheezed.

'But Raymond told me I had to pass on his greetings to the earl,' William replied. Sir Hervey's man pushed him again. William knocked his hand aside and squared up to him.

'Try that again and I'll break your jaw,' he warned.

Sir Hervey squawked again. 'You shouldn't trouble yourself with his sort, Nephew. He has been around Raymond for much too long and, as you can see, has gone quite wild.' He turned his eyes on William. 'You even took Raymond's coin, didn't you boy? Meaning that you no longer are in the earl's service. What possible right could you have to speak to my nephew?'

'I really don't have time for this nonsense,' Strongbow growled and turned towards his former esquire. 'William, whatever message Raymond wishes or wished you pass on can wait for him to say it to me himself.' His eyes flicked to the other two figures that had trailed William. Both looked winded from running across the headland in his wake. He recognised the woman, Alice the Bastard of Abergavenny, who had caused so many problems for him earlier in the summer. She was Raymond's lover and Strongbow felt a pang of arousal as she turned her angry eyes on him. 'In the meantime perhaps you can tell me where he is, eh?' he demanded. 'Where is Raymond?'

It was Alice who answered. 'He will return soon, Lord. He is abroad on your -'

'We don't know where he is,' Sir Hervey interrupted. 'He

left more than a week ago with the Welshmen and has not returned.'

'He was raiding,' exclaimed William. 'He was trying to -'

'Raiding, yes,' Sir Hervey continued. 'He really has gone native, Nephew. He has been off on his own errands again. I don't know from where he is getting his orders, but I cannot believe they are the ones given to him by you. You would not condone theft and mayhem. Perhaps he is taking his orders from his tame Welshman, Caradog, or maybe it is from an even less qualified source?' Sir Hervey turned his eyes on Alice, coughing gently and inclining his head in her direction.

William de Vale caught the look and stepped forward. 'Raymond is about your business, Lord. He has been since he arrived in Ireland. He built these fortifications -'

'Which I had to rebuild only this week since they proved entirely defective,' interjected Sir Hervey.

'And he defeated the enemy -'

Sir Hervey guffawed. 'Despite making every stupid, foolhardy decision possible! He almost burned down the entire fort and your army with it, Nephew. I was forced to take command and oversee things, to make sure that this bridgehead – your bridgehead – was secure, well-defended and ready for your arrival. You can ask any of your trusted milites the name of the real captain at Dun Domhnall, Nephew.' He turned his eyes on Raymond's friends. 'You can ask them the name of the victor over the horde of Veðrarfjord. None will say Raymond. I can assure you of that.'

William, Alice and the young man with them erupted. Such was their anger that only a few words and almost none of their arguments could be heard clearly by Strongbow. Sir Hervey added to the din with counter-allegations of his own. Worse, William de Vale attempted to move closer and was wrestled to the ground by Sir Hervey's man. Dust kicked up around them as they scuffled on the sandy ground.

'Stop that and be quiet!' Strongbow roared, bringing the racket to a halt. 'I don't have time for this. I only care that we have supplies and we have an army. Now we must combine the two at our new camp. Sir Hervey,' he snapped. 'You will take command of the conrois since their former captain has deserted his post.' William de Vale began to argue but Strongbow raised his hand to silence him. 'No! Raymond has proven a great disappointment, particularly since it was on his counsel that I continued my plans to collect my army. I trusted him! Yet now I find he is off gallivanting to God knows where?' The earl shook his head. 'Those are not the actions of a captain, but of a bandit! And I cannot trust him to lead my troops into battle until he changes his ways.'

Sir Hervey cackled. 'You are right, Nephew. I will lead your men to glory, in your name -'

'You will do better than that, Uncle. You will send your man to hurry the milites and the cattle back here and then you will lead the warriors onto the beach, along with every person sworn to my service. They will make ready every horse. They will gather all the weaponry, all the armour, and stow it aboard *Seagull*. I want to be ready to sail as soon as possible. For before the sun sets we sail for Veðrarfjord territory. Do you understand?'

Sir Hervey smiled. 'I do, Nephew. We are finally going to war.'

'We are.' Strongbow watched as Sir Hervey gave his orders and the man climbed back into the saddle and began riding northwards. 'Good. Now go and make your other preparations, Uncle. Master William, come here!' he added, dismissing Sir Hervey.

The young man glanced at Sir Hervey as he approached. The old knight stared back at him as he climbed onto his horse's back and walked back towards the fortifications.

'Lord Strongbow?'

'Is it true what Sir Hervey said? Are you Raymond's man now?'

'I am, Lord. And I must tell you that what Sir Hervey said was -'

'It is too late for that,' Strongbow snapped. '*Now the wine is drawn, it must be drunk.* Isn't that one of Raymond's favourite sayings? Well, he must learn that there are consequences to his actions. And you must too, since you have chosen his service over mine, the man who paid to have trained you from a boy.'

'My Lord, I thought -'

Strongbow held up a hand. 'No. All I require of you is to deliver this message to Raymond when he finally decides to return. Tell him that his conduct here in Ireland has proven a very great disappointment to me.' Strongbow's eyes flicked towards Alice of Abergavenny. 'Tell him that unless he gets the cattle train to Veðrarfjord I will dismiss him from my service. Since *I* have not paid the Welsh bowmen to be here, and I have no more room for them on my ship, they can remain to help him, as can you,' his eyes flicked to Alice, 'and your friends. If Raymond proves he can handle being a cattle drover at least I will have a use for him in the future.' Strongbow shook his head and sighed. 'I don't like saying these things, you understand, but Raymond must appreciate my position.' He looked at Alice again and felt his expression change again. 'Tell him that I will accept no more excuses.' With that Strongbow stepped back onto the path carved into the cliff and made his way back to *Seagull* to await his conrois.

Rechin was waiting for him. 'Orders, Lord?'

'Everything is in hand.'

'I should return to Sir Hervey then,' he said and, without awaiting Strongbow's leave, took a few steps up the beach in the direction of Dun Domhnall.

'Wait. Do you know how to get to Fearna?'

'Diarmait Mac Murchada's home?' Rechin asked. 'A hard ride maybe half a day to the north. I can find it.'

'Then I have a task for you.'

Chapter Six

Daybreak came as a welcome sight for the sixteen men who trudged south towards the fort. Immediately, they could feel warmth return to their hands and chests. They were unshaven and exhausted from their exertions and some still bore injuries as lasting reminders of their time raiding alongside Raymond and Jarl Gufraid. They hardly spoke. When they did it was only about a desire to sleep.

'Can you believe it has been two weeks since we left to go into the Black Mountains?' Raymond asked as he caught his first sight of the wall of Dun Domhnall. Ieuan smiled rather than attempt a response. The Welshman had two glossy marten skins draped around his neck. Each of the archers had been given a cut of the haul stolen from Fiodh-Ard Liag when they had made land the evening before. Gufraid, in his wisdom, had demanded only the foodstuffs for the Ostmen's share. His warriors had made no argument as they had packed it into their arms and made for Cluainmín and their hungry families. With them had gone Gufraid's three sons, Blácaire, Oistin and Bárid, rescued from their imprisonment. They had been neglected by Jarl Háimar, of that there was little doubt. Gufraid was furious at their condition. He seethed with anger. It was not the way of their people to treat hostages so. As he had left on an eastern path, Jarl Gufraid had reaffirmed his pledge to Raymond.

'I will help you take Veðrarfjord,' he had said and stared at his three boys. 'I will bring forty warriors and if the moment comes when Sigtrygg is at our mercy, I want to be the one to kill him.'

'Be sure to be ready,' Raymond had warned. 'The Earl Strongbow could arrive at any moment. I will send a message to you when it is time.'

Raymond and his Welshmen had considered sailing home in the small vessel in which they had made their getaway from

190

Fiodh-Ard Liag. However, no one had felt so experienced that he might pilot the boat down the unfamiliar waterway, and certainly not at sea. So instead they had dragged her ashore at a little cove on the big island and had hidden her under some branches. Raymond had suggested remaining overnight on the island, but Ieuan had convinced him to keep on going. He feared that the Ostmen might pursue them in their remaining two vessels and attack them during the small hours of the morning.

Ahead Raymond looked at the line of silent bowmen on the march. Their shoulders looked huge with the skins draped across them. One had a wolfskin, others had huge sheepskins, and one even had found an otter hide. The younger archers had made do with what their fellows had said were marten skins. Raymond had not the heart to tell them that they were almost certainly taken from cats. That he was able to reward the archers, if only in a small way, was of a great relief to him. The Welshmen had been by his side since he had arrived in Ireland, had shared his every danger, and deserved some recompense for their efforts. He only wished that he had some way to reward the remaining bowmen still garrisoned in Dun Domhnall.

Their journey south through the woods of Siol Bhroin had been uneventful and the moon had been bright enough to allow them to travel safely throughout the night. They had timed their arrival at the causeway across the river estuary to perfection, crossing just before dawn at low tide. As they had traipsed along the path, a mile to go to home, the peninsula had come to life. Birds and insects had begun to hum and sing in the sunlight. Dew-drooped ferns had unwound, charting a course through the twist of briars, and flowers had opened to release their scents into the air. The scene to the east over the sea was splendid for those awake enough to take in the dawn, though there were few of those among the men.

Raymond kept his eyes fixed on a line of shadow, cast by the sun, which slashed across the middle of the fortifications. There was half a mile between him and his bed. His tiredness multiplied with every step. The moan of cattle out on the headland fort startled him, but only momentarily. Like a drunken esquire seeking to avoid detection, he concentrated on the simple movements, keeping his eyelids open and his step clear of the ground so that he did not fall over. His stomach growled with hunger. Raymond was close enough now to see that the barbican above the gates was empty of sentinels. He was close enough to hear the waves on the rocks on the headland's back. There were more cattle calls coming from within the walls.

'They want to be milked,' Ieuan mumbled at his side.

Raymond had no real knowledge of cattle, but he nodded his head like he agreed with Ieuan's assessment. 'Sounds like,' he muttered.

The last quarter mile down the dry path seemed interminable to Raymond. The fort walls seemed to remain equally far away until he was right below them, in the cold shadow cast by the rising sun. He was the last to the walls and by then the leading men had already shouted to rouse the two Welshmen on guard duty on the barbican. The gates had barely begun to creak open as the raiders began to pour inside, pausing only to respond to the guard's welcome. The long walk between the inner and outer fortifications was a blur to Raymond. He didn't even notice the repairs made to the wall in his absence. His only lasting memory was of the sudden cold and the grey line of archers ahead of him in the semi-darkness. Then, turning through the inner gates, it was suddenly warm again and there was trampled grass under his feet rather than a cold mixture of mud and woodchips. To his right there was a great deal of activity. Men shouted orders to each other and there were moving cattle. The animals were strewn out across the entire western side of the headland.

'Raymond!' the voice of William de Vale rang out above the hullabaloo.

'Hello,' Raymond replied. William was in the saddle of his courser, lightly armed, and ready to spend a few nights in the field if the load of food in his pack were anything to go by.

'You have come back! We were just about to leave the fort to begin searching for you,' William said. He slipped off and onto the ground. His esquire, Fulk, did the same. 'I can't say that I was enamoured of the prospect of several days in the

192

saddle. But at least you are here now.'

Ieuan and the Welsh archers had not stopped to chat but had passed the remains of the marshalsea, making for the promontory fort and their quarters. Raymond ached to follow. He wanted nothing more than to collapse in a bed and sleep for a week.

'Is everything in order?' he asked instead. 'The cattle look healthy. Is there anything else to report?'

It was Alice of Abergavenny who responded. 'Yes, Raymond. I'm afraid that there is much we need to discuss.' Alice was also dressed for travelling, wearing a pair of leather trews that she must have made. Like William and Fulk, she had her black gelding, Rufus, saddled and laden with supplies. 'And it cannot wait,' she added.

Raymond ran his two hands over his face, rubbing the sleep from his eyes as best he could. 'Tell me.'

'Strongbow is in Ireland,' she stated plainly. 'He is gone ahead to face the Ostmen of Veðrarfjord,' she added when he began looking for signs of the fleet on the beach below.

'He was here?' Raymond asked. He was confused by Alice's words and looked up onto the inner wall and over towards the herd of cattle. 'And he left again? He left without the archers and the cattle, without even waiting to speak to me? Where did he go? I don't understand -'

'Raymond!' snapped Alice. 'You must pull yourself together and get ready to move north again.'

'Move north?' He could not believe what Alice was saying. He needed to sleep. Even a few hours would make all the difference. It was as if she didn't understand the efforts that he had put in over the last days and weeks. He looked up at the promontory defences. His fifteen companions were almost at the wall, almost at their quarters. The sunlight was draining as it shone in his eyes. 'I cannot go north again.'

'You will go north, or you will lose everything,' Alice replied angrily. 'I will not allow that to happen.' She turned towards Fulk. 'Your master needs his horse,' she shouted. The burly esquire nodded his head and dashed off.

'Lord Strongbow landed his army in Ostman territory before sundown yesterday,' William de Vale told him. 'Only one ship called here. They picked up Sir Hervey and the rest of the conrois -'

'And you are no longer their captain,' Alice finished his sentence.

'What?' Her words had shaken Raymond. He looked at her, seeking a hint of a jest on her face. There was none. 'Strongbow wouldn't have done that.' He turned towards William. 'He wouldn't have replaced me.'

'He did, Raymond,' his miles confirmed. 'He gave command of the conrois to Sir Hervey.'

Raymond could not believe it. Strongbow had discarded him? 'But I defeated Ragnall of Veðrarfjord in battle,' he said. 'Did you tell him that when he was here?'

William nodded his head. 'We both did. But Sir Hervey twisted our words, and the earl believed him. Sir Hervey is his uncle, his family, after all.'

The fatigue that Raymond had been feeling left his body. 'So what would my lord have me do now? Does he wish me to serve under Sir Hervey?' He watched as William's eyes dropped to the ground rather than answer. Instead he turned to Alice.

'He said that unless you get the cattle train to Veðrarfjord he will dismiss you from his service.'

'Dismiss me?' Raymond hissed. He could feel the fury surge through him. 'After all I have done for him? First he takes away my command, and then he decides that he will make me into his cattle drover?' Raymond immediately remembered how Konungr Ragnall of Veðrarfjord had mocked him as 'Strongbow's cowhand' before the battle for Dun Domhnall. Now his own lord taunted him with the same name. It was a role fit for a serf, not a warrior, and certainly not a captain. Raymond could feel his face burning in embarrassment. He could imagine the milites, his oldest friends, ridiculing him. It was bad enough that they called him Raymond the Fat, but to call him by the demeaning title of *cowhand* was worse again.

'Calm down, Raymond,' Alice said.

'Calm down? I will do no such thing.' He had been expecting to be rewarded for his efforts in Ireland, not to be left on the verge of disgrace. He had expected Strongbow to meet him and to publically congratulate him, to give him command of his army during their attack on Veðrarfjord.

'You must think! Do not allow your emotions to run amok.'

Raymond turned on Alice. 'You said to get the cattle back. I did it. You said to bring the conrois to heel. I tried. You said to get them to fix the wall and it is fixed. I made allies, dug trenches, won victories, took injuries, recovered, and look what it got me – nothing! Dear God, I killed those prisoners!' He looked out over the cattle herd. They mewed and moaned as the Welshman saw to their food and morning milking. 'Despite all that, Strongbow dropped me as if I meant nothing to him at all. So tell me: what do I do now?'

Looping Rufus's reins around her hand, Alice crossed to his side. 'You can regain his favour, Raymond. You can still become his constable at Veðrarfjord.' He did not reply. 'And you still have me.'

He laughed sarcastically at that and stepped away from her. 'Maybe I need to think if I really want to serve a man like him? I do have *real* family in Ireland. I could go to Waesfjord and declare for my uncles, Maurice FitzGerald and Robert FitzStephen. I am sure that they would want my sword.'

'Would they not already have favoured commanders, men with retinues of their own to whom they will already have granted estates and positions?'

'Of course, but I am their nephew.'

'You're saying that they should forget the men who have served them up to now?'

'No, of course not -'

'Oh, I see. Your uncles have no sons?'

'Both have.' He looked expectantly at Alice but she said nothing. 'My Uncle Maurice actually has six sons.' Raymond shook his head. 'There may be no room for me on their lands, but my uncles would help me conquer my own estate. Perhaps when Strongbow fails to take Veðrarfjord, they might assist me to claim the city.' Even to his own ears, he sounded more hopeful than certain. It would take many more men than his uncles' small army to capture a city of Veðrarfjord's size and power.

'What of the Welsh archers?' she asked, flapping a hand towards the cattle herd.

'They'll come too. I'm sure Maurice and Robert would learn to trust them as I have.'

'And Strongbow's men? They are relying on you to bring the cattle. They will have nothing to eat if you go to Waesfjord.'

'Damn it all, Alice. Are you on my side at all?'

William responded before Alice could. 'She's right, Raymond. I know you had a falling out with the conrois, but they are still our friends. I wouldn't want Borard or Dafydd FitzHywell or any of them to suffer because we abandoned them.' He screwed up his face. 'If it was only Walter de Bloet and Asclettin I might think otherwise, of course.'

'There are also the esquires and pages to think of,' Alice continued. 'They are just boys, but they came to Ireland with you.'

Raymond sighed. It used to be so easy to be in command. Back in Wales he had led a conrois of ten milites, men he had known his whole life, men he could trust. They would ride off into the hills on Strongbow's behalf. They would fight and win. They would share jokes and, when they got paid, drink together. Now, everything seemed so complicated. He had thought that his friends would follow him no matter what, just as Charlemagne's Paladins had followed Roland into the Pass of Roncesvalles. Raymond's mind drifted back to the massacre of the Ostmen. He thought of the milites' accusations against him, of his own anger. He had let his desire to earn Strongbow's favour, to prove that he was a leader of men, come between him and the conrois. That had allowed Sir Hervey de Montmorency to weasel his way in.

It's my fault, Raymond thought.

And it got worse: his impulse had been to abandon his command and to run off to his uncles' side, to let them take over responsibility for him rather than work to regain the trust of the conrois. That realisation made Raymond's skin crawl. He thought himself the most steadfast, the most honourable man, but at the first sign of a challenge to his command he had considered fleeing, to abandon all those for whom he should have been accountable. That was not the instinct of a captain of great renown, he knew. It was little wonder that Strongbow had discarded him and put him in charge of animals instead of warriors.

'*Roland, it is thou who hast wrought it all,*' he murmured and bowed his head.

'*Valour and madness are oft allied,*' Alice took up the song, reciting Olivier's famous lines. '*Better discretion than daring pride*. I think that is the next stanza? I do not know the words as well as you, of course.'

Raymond nodded his head. 'So, *Olivier,*' he turned to look at Alice, 'Are you suggesting that I should swallow my "daring pride" and just accept Strongbow's slight against me? Should I meekly lead this brave troop of cattle to the city and sit out all the fighting? Or would you simply have me grovel to Strongbow.' He hated that he had said it as soon as the comment had emerged from his mouth. However, Alice did not give any sense that she was hurt by his words.

'No, I would never say that,' she replied. 'I would only ask where the rewards for your efforts would be greatest. Is it at Waesfjord or at Veðrarfjord? I would only ask where it would be most likely that you will be needed.' She pursed her lips. 'I would ask where it would be that your advice will be heard and heeded.'

Despite his anger, he considered her words. Robert FitzStephen and Maurice FitzGerald were both military men who had fought many campaigns. It hurt him to realise that his kinsmen would never rely on him as a general. He could lead their charges, capture forts, bleed for them, but he would never rise above the rank of miles. Strongbow, on the other hand, had only ever been to war once, and that had been years before as a young man. He had never commanded men in battle. With no other lords sworn to his service, Raymond knew that Strongbow would fall back on the advice of Sir Hervey de Montmorency. That gave him pause for thought. He knew that Strongbow's uncle was no commander. He had proven that at Dun Domhnall. Sir Hervey would put all his friends in danger. Raymond could not allow his voice to be the only one that Strongbow heard. And the earl himself? Raymond's very best memories were not of his mother and father, or of his siblings. When he thought back, he remembered his first days as a page to the Dowager Countess Isabel at Striguil, and of being introduced to her gangly, auburn-headed son. He remembered his pride when, as a ten-year old, he had first attended upon that same son, his lord, the Earl of Pembroke, at a feast and how the earl had given him a mug of wine. His most abiding memories were not of his birthplace at Carew Castle, they were learning to fight under Sir Reginald de Bloet's instruction. He pictured Borard and Asclettin and Denis as boys out on the bailey of Striguil Castle with the picturesque cliffs dropping dramatically down towards the Afon Gwy. He may have claimed to Alice that Robert FitzStephen and Maurice FitzGerald were his family, but in truth, he barely knew them either. He had met Robert for the first time only a year before. Like his mother and father, they lived in the far west, in the frontier country called Little England beyond Wales, a week's ride from Striguil. Raymond de Carew suddenly recognised that the person he had known longest, the person who occupied most of his memories was the Earl Strongbow. If anyone in this world was his family it was him. If he should call anyone his brothers, it was the conrois.

Raymond breathed in slowly. 'Damn it all,' he said and addressed William de Vale. 'Find Caradog and tell him that I need him.' He turned back to Alice and opened his mouth to speak.

Alice raised a hand to stop him. 'I know. We are going north.'

'No, no, no!' old Walter de Ridlesford shouted. 'What we should do is march straight up the coast, throw our ladders against their walls and tear these savages to pieces.'

'I've always known you to be a fool, Walter. But I never thought you to be a hothead,' Jean de Clahull retorted. 'We need to be patient and capture their outlying forts. Then we can encircle the city from all sides, and close the noose around their necks.'

Strongbow ran a hand down his long face as Walter shouted insults back at Jean, cursing his timidity and lack of spine. The barons had been arguing for an hour and were no closer to a consensus than when they had begun. Walter led the group who wished to form the army into a column and march on Veðrarfjord immediately. Strongbow's uncle, Sir Hervey, and Robert FitzBernard were of like mind, but Jean de Clahull and Richard de Maroine were equally set upon a slow squeeze of the city, sending smaller groups out to seize all the outlying manors and forts before moving on the city to impose a siege.

'Is there anything to be said for sending emissaries to their king - Ragnall is it? - and seeking his surrender?' Sir Robert de Bermingham was a man from Warwickshire, who had shown up to Pill Priory quite unexpectedly with ten milites ready to cross to Ireland. He was the only one of their number not from Wales or Devon, and was not known to any of the other barons. His well-armed retinue afforded him a place at the war council, however.

'It's your head, Robert,' Jean de Clahull joked, 'but if you trade words with a damned Dane you run the risk of having it lopped off.' Many of the barons laughed with him. 'While you are off doing that the rest of us should each take our milites and attack their farms and manors -'

Walter de Ridlesford groaned. 'What is the point of that?' he asked for the fifth time in as many minutes. 'We should break camp now and make for the city. I don't understand the need for any more waiting around.'

Strongbow watched as their argument commenced again. Ralph de Bloet buried his head in his hands as Jean and Walter's parties shouted at each other. The Flemish cousins, Adam and David de la Roche, even got up and left the tent in frustration. Maurice de Prendergast had not even appeared for the second sitting of the war council. Strongbow had tried to mediate between the two parties at a gathering after they had made their landing at dusk the evening before. Neither had been willing to concede any point or find common ground about how to proceed with the campaign. In the end, the only way that he had been able to get his barons to leave his tent and allow him to sleep was by promising to meet again at dawn and ordering each of them to lead out scouting parties. Thankfully, given their inability to agree, none had come across any military threat to their amphibious landing in Ireland.

It had only taken their appearance in the estuary for the few natives to flee the village with those belongings that they could carry. Otherwise their landing had been unremarkable. Strongbow had thanked St Peter and St Christopher for their small mercies on that count as well as for the foresight which had been given to Sir Hervey. The beach had proven the perfect site to land his army. It was five miles upriver from the sea on a little headland. Above it, a rocky escarpment gave perfect cover for the camp and a place to keep watch inland and over the waterway at their backs. Should the worst happen and an enemy army approach, his ships could easily escape across the estuary to another beach on Siol Bhroin. Strongbow's uncle had called it Dun Conán. Richard de Maroine and Jean de Clahull had been the first ashore and so they had occupied the few ramshackle buildings in the village. The rest of the army had either slept aboard ship, rolling in the tide, or had set up tents. Those who had not been sent scouting had busied themselves with preparing food or seeing to the needs of their horses.

What little sleep Strongbow had managed had been interrupted with dreams of sea monsters and shipwrecks. Twice he had to get up and relieve his bladder. He felt old. Sleeping on the rough seaside grass had not helped. His back was uncomfortable and he could feel the pull of old injuries down the backs of his legs. As he watched Jean and Walter argue, Strongbow rolled his heels on the ground, stretching his calves, hoping to alleviate the pain. One way or another he would soon be back in the saddle and he could not let any of his barons or warriors see any weakness. This was not the time for doubts.

'Nephew?' Sir Hervey de Montmorency's hot breath hit his ear. It made him wince. 'You need to make a decision. These fools will never agree with each other.'

Strongbow cleared his throat and held up his hands. He was taller than all those assembled by a head, but he found no confidence in that fact. The barons under his command were veterans of Henry FitzEmpress's wars in France and Wales. They were tough and capable and desirous of swift success. All their eyes turned towards him.

'Men, I have heard some really excellent points about how to proceed with the campaign here in Ireland. Really, there have been some excellent ideas.' Strongbow could hear his own voice and hated how weak it sounded. He cleared his throat again. 'Seemingly, there are two options before us. To march directly on the city -'

Strongbow's words were immediately drowned out by shouting, both in favour and in opposition to that possibility, until Milo de Cogan shouted for quiet.

Milo was not a big man, nor was he given to outbursts, but his frustrations had finally got the better with him: 'Shut up the lot of you or, so help me God, I will tear the tongues out of every single one of your heads and cook them for my milites to eat.'

The threat proved enough to quieten the tent again and Strongbow was able to continue. 'The other choice is to seek out and destroy all the outlying forts that will, no doubt, block our route to Veðrarfjord.'

Before another outburst could interrupt, Milo stepped forward. 'I'd just like to know one thing before we make a decision, Lord Strongbow. Where is Raymond? He's been over here in Ireland longer than anyone. His advice and expertise might give us a better idea of what to do.'

'Hah,' Sir Hervey coughed. 'I've been in this land longer than Raymond. Wasn't I the one to select this landing place for the army?'

Milo sniffed and stared at Sir Hervey. 'All right then. If I were to head north from here, who would own the first manor that I would come to? Where are the other chief fortresses in this area? How far is it to Veðrarfjord's walls? How many men are the enemy likely to have in the field? Will they attack us using ships? Or will they remain behind their fortifications? Are the city walls timber or stone? Are there any lords amongst the Danes who might be induced to help our cause?' Milo paused for Sir Hervey to reply. 'I have more queries, but if you can answer those it should suffice for now.'

Sir Hervey did not speak, merely staring at the ungainly-looking Milo who had delivered such a long list of pertinent questions to which he obviously had no answers.

201

Strongbow held up his hands and stepped in front of his uncle. 'All very good questions, I am sure, and we will discover the answers as we move forward. To answer your first, Raymond will join us presently with a large herd of cattle which he gathered over the last few months for us to -'

'Cattle? Good news, because my men are already running out of things to eat,' Ralph de Bloet announced. His declaration was followed by similar comments from all the other barons.

Strongbow smiled despite his alarm. He had hoped that his warriors' supplies would last them longer than the first morning of the campaign. 'It is good that I have left such an able captain with so important a task.' At the base of his spine, Strongbow's fingers wrapped around each other like adders in a nest. He forced his smile to widen across his face.

'So what is your decision?' demanded Walter de Ridlesford.

'What's that?'

'Do we march on Veðrarfjord?'

'Well, as you know both plans have their merits.' Strongbow looked to Milo who said nothing, but stared at him with unwavering eyes. 'Of course, a decision must, in the end, be made,' he turned towards Jean de Clahull, and then to Sir Hervey, his uncle. 'To wait any longer would be utter folly on all our parts.' He breathed in deeply as Sir Hervey curtly nodded his head. 'And so, having heard all parties, my decision – and it was a difficult one – is that we must,' he paused, 'keep going forward.'

For a moment no-one said anything. Each tried to entangle the meaning of their commander's orders. Milo de Cogan frowned and shook his head while Jean de Clahull nodded his and mumbled his support for the plan, convinced, it seemed, that Strongbow had chosen his strategy. It was Walter de Ridlesford who seemed to understand first that their commander was prevaricating. He sighed and crossed to the flap of the tent, throwing it open so that the early morning sunlight poured inside.

'Tell the men to break camp,' he shouted for all to hear. 'The Earl Strongbow orders that we march on Veðrarfjord immediately! We are going forward.'

Smoke still lingered around the city. They had not waited for a sea breeze to blow from the east and waft it away from their walls. The enemy were on the march. They would besiege Veðrarfjord. And so Sigtrygg had burned down Irishtown.

Warriors – both Ostman and Gael – had emerged from the gates of the city bearing torches. The folk living outside the walls were the poorest of people, mostly Gaels but also Ostman families of such little note that they could not afford the safety of a house inside the walls. They were given only a few moments to save their most precious belongings, to drive their animals clear, before the first houses were set ablaze. Brands and torches were launched into thatch. Hot coals were tipped onto bedding. Doors were ripped from their hinges and broken up to feed the flames. It had been a hot summer. Thatched roofs and wattle walls did not take much to catch flame, but the Ostmen had ripped great rents through the daub walls using their axes, letting more air in. The fires roared. Terrified screaming and crying had echoed throughout the night, the moan of animals and men's anger.

And Sigtrygg's men were not finished there. They had emerged into the fields beyond like demons and had climbed the hills spilling buckets of pitch amongst the crops. Fires had raged and died quickly, but they had left great patches of black and the noxious smell of burnt grain. Even as the people had fled northwards they had gagged and spluttered until they were clear of the smoke-bank.

The fires had died in the night, its red glow fading like a second setting of the sun. Daybreak had uncovered the full horror of the warriors' work. A thousand fires smoked and smouldered amongst the fractured timber limbs and collapsed housing in Irishtown. The fields still reeked. It was through that hellish landscape that the enemy marched.

'We could sally out. We could hit them as they are moving.' Jarl Háimar sounded nervous.

Sigtrygg did not reply. He did nothing to assuage his jarl's fears. He didn't even look at him. It took all his effort not to lambast the fool for his opinions, for his loss of Gufraid's sons, for his Fionngall heritage. Sigtrygg kept his eyes on the enemy. From where he stood on the western wall of Veðrarfjord, the line of grey figures looked ghostly, surrounded by smoke, like the dead parading their way to the otherworld. When they had appeared from beyond the marshlands to the south, the warriors on the walls had blown horns and waved banners, chanting insults and defiance at those who threatened their city's independence. The foreigners had not responded. It was as if the hatred spat at them from the walls did not worry them one jot. Soon, the Ostmen's shouts had died down too and, but for the odd whinny of horses, the enemy had remained silent as the marched past the walls, their banners furled, showing off the full might of their army.

'I count a thousand,' Máel Sechlainn Ua Fhaolain said. 'They've brought a lot of horses with them. We shouldn't take our army out of the city.' Sigtrygg's new brother-in-law, the King of the Déisi, was, as always, surrounded by his derb-fine, his priests, his ollamhs, and his brehons. It was obviously too early for his poets and harpers to be at their king's side.

'Their horses will be of no use against our walls,' Sigtrygg agreed. He leaned forward to rest his elbow on top of the timber post wall. He looked downwards to the ground, twenty feet below. The stone glacis, topped by its wooden palisade, was far more impressive than the defences that the foreigners had constructed at Dun Domhnall. 'And nor will their arrows,' he added as he watched the last of the Normans cross the stream and begin climbing up onto the small plateau to the west. A fortified manor house, Brickin's Place, was up there. Defended by a small palisade and ditch, it was no doubt where the enemy would make their camp.

He cursed the temerity of Strongbow. The haughty lord would be humbled for this show of strength before the very walls of Veðrarfjord! Sigtrygg promised that he would cut him down to size just as he had Raymond the Fat. He remembered capturing the outer walls of the foreigners' fort, his duel with the Norman captain, almost a month before. The memory made his blood sing in his limbs. He knew that staying behind the walls was his only choice, but he could feel his heart beating in his chest, sending the urge to attack around his body, to lead his warriors out of the gates and engage the enemy in the burning remains of Irishtown. A glorious victory over the invaders would be sung about for generations. His victory over the aggressors would make him a hero. He pictured throwing Strongbow's body down on the ground before his father, Ragnall. He imagined the envious look on his face as he climbed onto the dais in Ragnall's Hall, the shouts of acclaim echoing all around him. A victory over Strongbow would secure his throne.

'Give it a week sitting up there on that hill and sickness will invade their camp,' Máel Sechlainn said. 'I've seen it before. A week and they will be shitting water.'

'Give them a week?' Sigtrygg asked of the King of the Déisi, hearing his hope of an attack disappear.

'They don't have any cattle with them. Give it two days and they will be hungry,' suggested Jarl Háimar.

'Unless they get into Veðrarfjord. Then they will eat heartily,' Máel Sechlainn replied.

'They will not get into the city,' Sigtrygg growled.

Máel Sechlainn nodded. 'But they will try.' He wrapped his saffron shirt around his left forearm and looked to the hillside. 'And they will try soon, I would wager.'

'Where will the attack fall?' asked Háimar.

Sigtrygg stamped his foot on the wooden allure at the top of the wall. 'They will attack here in the west. The river defends us to the north, the marshland to the east. This is the only place that they can possibly attack us.'

'They will unleash an arrow storm on us, then these *Liathgall* will come with ladders to scale the defences.'

Sigtrygg felt a shiver surge down his shoulders. Gaels like Máel Sechlainn called the Ostmen of Veðrarfjord *Dubhgall*, the Dark Foreigners. Sigtrygg had always revelled in that name, loving the chilling resonance of the word. It was unsurprising that they had already given the Normans a nickname: *Liathgall* – the word rolled around Sigtrygg's mind, the Grey Foreigners. It conjured an image in his mind of wraiths from his worst nightmares, of an unstoppable army, ghoulish and otherworldly, wrapped in spells and smoke as they flew across the land to haunt and kill the living.

'*Liathgall*? That's not what we should call them. With those grey scales we should call them the *Iascgall*,' Sigtrygg

205

boomed, looking for support for his joke. Háimar laughed nervously.

'Fish Foreigners?' Máel Sechlainn repeated. 'Yes, that's very funny, Brother. And fitting, for they are slippery like fish, as well you know. We should not underestimate them again.'

'Meaning?'

'Meaning that we have enough warriors to defend all three walls of the city,' he replied. 'We should make sure to do so. You have heard the same tales as I have – when Waesfjord fell they attacked all sides of the town at once.'

'Veðrarfjord's walls are taller than Waesfjord's,' Sigtrygg countered. 'The marshland and river -'

'Might stop your people from attacking there,' Máel Sechlainn interrupted, 'but I don't know if it will stop these foreigners.' The King of the Déisi inhaled slowly. 'You were at Dun Domhnall. Even before we got to the fort we were licking our wounds. They attacked us with horses, arrows, that damned cattle charge. What might they have to unleash upon us now?'

'You are scared,' Jarl Háimar accused.

Máel Sechlainn did not rise to the bait and prevented his derb-fine from reacting angrily too. He stepped back to see around Sigtrygg's massive frame. 'I am not scared, but I would imagine that to the idiot, caution and consideration may indeed look like fear. Perhaps if you had exercised either quality you would not have lost Gufraid's sons?' Háimar stammered angrily and impotently as Máel Sechlainn continued to outline his thinking to Sigtrygg: 'I have a thousand warriors. You have six hundred and, what, three hundred more boys and old men ready to help where they can?'

Sigtrygg felt an admonishment in Máel Sechlainn's words and he took a half-step closer, turning his massive body towards his ally. 'More than enough to send Strongbow running back to Wales.'

'And we have to man, what, three hundred paces on the west wall?' Máel Sechlainn had turned to a Brehon, who confirmed his estimate with a nod.

'Where the attack will certainly fall,' Sigtrygg insisted.

'And the same again on the east and north walls.' Máel Sechlainn tapped his fingertips on the top of the wall. 'We will send a hundred of your warriors and two hundred of mine, and all your boys and old folk, to man the north and east walls. That will leave our best to face the enemy here in the west. If, that is, you can trust your people?'

Sigtrygg seethed. He had known a rebuke was coming. Since the raids on the outlying manors there had been a steady stream of refugees seeking shelter within the city walls. The tight confines within Veðrarfjord had suddenly seemed worse than ever as hundreds had passed through the city gates. Sigtrygg had attempted to stop the flow, but no matter his threats somehow they still got in with their animals and whatever wealth they could carry. The hot summer weather and sudden demand on food had raised tensions. Prices had soared. Rioting had followed. Sigtrygg was sure that it had been the heads of other families that had instigated the trouble and had sent the Déisi to deal with them. Most had claimed innocence. Máel Sechlainn had killed them anyway. It was only afterwards that Sigtrygg had discovered the true ringleader of the unrest when Bishop Tostig's men had made an attempt to free Ragnall from his imprisonment in the tower at the north-east corner of the city. Named after the city's founder, Rögnvald's Tower had become Sigtrygg's stronghold. He had packed everything of value into its wooden walls – his silver and his hostages – and had placed his most trusted men as its guards. It had been a stiff fight, but Sigtrygg's men had been able to barricade themselves in and see off the danger of the bishop's attack. Máel Sechlainn had caught the rebel bishop as he tried to flee the city across the marshlands in the night, and had suggested hanging him. Sigtrygg had been tempted to skin the traitor alive - it being the Eve of the Feast of St Bartholomew, it seemed like a just punishment. He knew though that doing so would only turn more of the people against him. Instead, he had imprisoned the bishop with his father in Rögnvald's Tower and told the townsfolk that their spiritual leader was needed to minister directly to the former konungr in the time of great peril. Máel Sechlainn had torn down the bishop's palace on Olav Street anyway.

'I trust that people are more scared of the enemy than me,' Sigtrygg told Máel Sechlainn.

The King of the Déisi shook his head. 'That is not ideal either.'

Up on the hillside a horn sounded. Sigtrygg and Máel Sechlainn's eyes darted to the western horizon. The single horn was joined by more dull blares. Above the smoke a single man appeared and unfurled a banner. He was less than five hundred paces from the wall. Every warrior could see him as a slight gust lifted the banner to show the gold and crimson arrow head coat of arms. The war for Veðrarfjord had begun. Strongbow was poised to attack.

'They are coming,' Sigtrygg bellowed. 'Make ready to repel invaders!'

Strongbow's day had begun with a conference on the beach on the estuary. He hoped it would end with the conquest of a city. He could not believe that only two nights before he had been standing on the shingle beach at Melrfjord in Wales, trying to convince lowly merchant captains of better ways to safely transport his ladders across the sea. He remembered the bickering, the increasing fury that the men did not simply obey his commands. That would all change once Veðrarfjord was his. Strongbow was on the verge of greatness.

All around him men prepared for battle. Esquires and pages helped their lords squeeze into gambesons and mail hauberks. Thomas Cantwell's coif rattled and shimmered as he pulled it onto his head nearby. His younger brother, Hugh, was at his side, buckling his sword belt around his middle. Thomas jumped up and down and shook his arms to make sure that the armour was sitting correctly and would not obstruct him. Like most of his warriors, neither Cantwell had mail gloves or stockings. Many had no mail of any kind and had covered their wool and linen gambesons with tough leather coats. Strongbow wondered if all the warriors were, like he, sweating profusely. He held a hand up to block the sun in the cloudless sky.

'Sir?'

His esquire, Michael de Barnewell, was standing by with his surcoat and spangenhelm. The boy offered the linen shirt to him first.

'Ah, yes. Thank you, Michael,' Strongbow said and placed

it over his head. Only two or three other lords wore surcoats emblazoned with their arms, he noted. His had been made by his half-sister, Isabel, during Stephen's reign, over twenty years before. He had worn it when he had marched to York beside the king, the year that Henry FitzEmpress had invaded England and had sought the help of the Scots to capture the north. Strongbow had been a young man then, eighteen years old and an esteemed baron at King Stephen's court. Henry FitzEmpress had been the rebel in those heavenly days. It had been Henry FitzEmpress who had been forced to flee England. They remained Strongbow's happiest memories.

He tried to think when last he had worn the surcoat. He stretched his mind back. It might have been at Easter in 1152, when Archbishop Theobald had refused to crown the king's son, Eustace. It had been a rather undignified moment which Strongbow preferred to forget. Might he have worn the surcoat at Malmesbury? Or when King Stephen had met Henry at Winchester a year later? It had been cold that day, that he did remember, and he had shivered as he had watched his name being added as a witness to the charter. He had believed that he was bringing peace to the kingdom, a peace that had evaded the land for almost fifteen years. Goodly King Stephen had convinced him of that. Bishop Henry and Archbishop Theobald had said so. The truth was that he had signed a warrant for his own death. The only difference was that Henry FitzEmpress believed in making his execution last a lifetime.

'Your helm, Lord Richard?'

Strongbow smiled and accepted his spangenhelm from his esquire. He slotted the iron and steel helmet on his head and breathed deeply. The wall of Veðrarfjord was less than half a mile away, down the slope and through the smoking ruin of Irishtown, outside the walls. It was time.

'Michael, my sword, please.'

His esquire knelt at the small pile of gear that he had brought down from the camp at the top of the hill. Strongbow raised his arms so that the boy could strap the side arm around his middle. The weight of the mail lifted off his shoulders and onto his arms, but the addition of a belt helped a little. He pulled the weapon halfway out of its scabbard. The edge was

209

sharp and he congratulated Michael on such excellent work. The sword had been his father's but he dared not dwell on that fact less he lose all confidence. Michael returned with a dagger and a mace which he made secure on Strongbow's belt. As he did so, the earl glanced across at the Cantwell brothers. They were drinking wine from a skin and were laughing and joking. He could see that neither had called for their lances but they did have shields across their backs.

'Shield, Michael.'

The boy had obviously spent some time repainting the little-used shield, for the crimson chevrons and blue three-pronged label across the top shone. Yellow paints were a little bit more difficult to find, it seemed, for the gold field remained slightly faded. Strongbow smiled at the boy's eagerness and promised him a reward for his good work as he looped the leather guige over his shoulder and moved the leaf-shaped shield to his back.

'Really, Lord Richard? A reward? Could I have a new saddle, or, maybe, a horse of my own? I know that Sir Richard de Maroine has a courser that he wants to sell. It bit him on the shoulder during the crossing from Wales. Milo de Cogan says that it is a particularly good one, and very reasonably priced. He said he would take Sir Richard's arm off for it, but I think he might have been joking. I know that I could get her going better than Sir Richard, I just know it.'

Strongbow laughed at his esquire's eagerness. The truth was he was delighted to be talking about anything other than what was to come. His last experience of fighting had been against Danes in the streets of Westminster, savages with axes and circular shields coming through the smoke, and the memory of killing one of them still awoke him in the night. Before that it had been at Wallingford with King Stephen, when Roger of Hereford had attempted to break out of the besieged castle. Two street brawls were the sum of his martial experience. And now he was faced with scaling the walls of a Danish city.

'I must do my part, I must do my part,' he murmured and closed his eyes.

'Lord?' Michael asked.

'We must all do our part today, Michael,' Strongbow said and forced a smile onto his face. The boy nodded seriously.

210

To his right Strongbow could see his uncle, Sir Hervey de Montmorency, calling for the milites to form up and get ready to advance. He could put it off no longer and followed the Cantwell brothers across to where Sir Hervey had collected his eight milites. He nodded to Ascellin FitzEustace and Denis d'Auton. Both returned the gesture, but neither moved to join him. At their backs were more men that he recognised: Gilbert de Borard, Thurstin Hore, and Amaury de Lyvet. All were heavily armed and Strongbow suddenly felt very silly to have thought that he could be stand alongside these men in battle. They were half his age and veterans of battle. They looked confident and strong. He glanced down at his gaudy surcoat and wished that he had never put it on.

It was already late in the afternoon, but his barons had agreed to make an immediate assault on the city. Strongbow had been expecting a flat refusal after the long march across Ostman territory, or a similar scenario to what had happen at their beach conference. But the barons proved keen to test the walls of Veðrarfjord. That was when he had deferred command for the attack to Sir Hervey. He was convinced that it was the correct appointment. Sir Hervey had decided on a straight-forward plan to claim the city. Six hundred men, led by two hundred dismounted milites, would attack the west wall of Veðrarfjord. Twenty ladders would be used to scale the walls and overwhelm the defenders. Milo de Cogan was the only voice of opposition, and even then his suggestion was only that one of their number might lead a diversionary attack on the north wall to draw some warriors away. Strongbow had thought it a sensible idea but Sir Hervey would not hear of their forces being divided and when Milo had not pressed his point, Strongbow had given his backing to his uncle's plan. Maurice de Prendergast had not waited for orders from Sir Hervey but had identified a point where his two hundred Flemish crossbowmen would take up position. They would shoot over the attacking milites' heads, giving them cover to close on the wall. After that, he had said, it would be up to the men on the ladders to push through the assault.

'Men,' Sir Hervey shouted. He broke down coughing but recovered and started again. 'Men, we are going to take the city. Milites to the front. Your captains know my orders, so pick up the ladders and get going.'

Strongbow took a half step forward to add a few more words to Sir Hervey's, but the milites had already started moving towards the ladders and he lost his nerve. Instead, Strongbow followed the Cantwells. The brothers had joined the back of the group containing the Striguil conrois, and Strongbow decided that was the best place for him too.

'Lord Richard,' he heard Michael de Barnewell squeak. A few of the warriors around him also noticed the boy's high-pitched voice and mocked him by repeating his words. Strongbow felt his own ears burn in embarrassment.

'Michael! Over here,' he called through clenched teeth.

The boy had his lance over his shoulder and offered it to his master. 'I didn't know if you had forgotten it or would need it so I came to find you.'

'I don't want it,' he said. 'I won't be able to use it when I'm,' he sought the correct phrase, 'when I am climbing the …' He glanced at the wall of Veðrarfjord. It was still two bow shots away, but it looked intimidatingly tall. There were hundreds of figures on top. They were warriors from his worst nightmares and they would try to kill him. The sun was in their eyes but they would certainly see the attackers coming forward. Strongbow suddenly felt the enormity of the task ahead. His bowels felt loose and his breath short in his chest.

'My Lord, are you quite all right?'

'Yes, I am fine, thank you.' Strongbow struggled to even say those words. The esquire leant forward and handed his master a skin. The water was cool and sloshed down Strongbow's parched throat. 'I don't require anything more, Michael. You need to get back up to the camp. Make sure that everything is packed up and ready to move into the city tonight.'

Michael nodded his head. 'Good luck, my Lord,' he said and then scampered off.

Strongbow drank again and gasped at the relief. He could see that several bands of warriors were walking downhill with ladders over their shoulders. They were silent for the most part. Those on the wall were not. They screamed insults and abuse over the smoking ruin of Irishtown. Arrows flew from the rampart but fell well short. Even buried beneath a gambeson cap, mail and helmet, he could hear the drum of spear-shafts on shields in time with the singing. Even from four hundred yards away he could hear the stomp of feet on the timber allure. He could see dust tumbling from the wall as the packed ranks of Ostmen stirred their folk into a battle frenzy.

To his left he could see that Maurice de Prendergast had his crossbowmen out in front of the milites on a projection from the hill. It seemed impossible for the Flemings to shoot so far, but as he watched their captain nocked a bolt and then sent it flying. Strongbow lost it against the sky, but Prendergast seemed satisfied with the result for he began ordering his two hundred bowmen into a line formation.

Ahead, his group had come to a halt. Strongbow turned and saw that there were still several more groups carrying ladders down to their position. He could see the lightly armoured men who served David and Adam de la Roche, and the bright blue of Robert de Bermingham's surcoat. He swallowed another slug of water and wished that it was wine.

'I must do my part,' he mumbled and pushed through the warriors to where the Cantwells were taking their turn carrying the ladder. Tapping Hugh Cantwell on the shoulder, he asked, 'Might I help with that?'

'You'd like to carry the ladder?' Hugh looked shocked and sought advice from his brother about how to respond. Getting no answer he relented and allowed Strongbow to put the bottom rung of the ladder onto his shoulder. He immediately felt happier and offered his skin of water to the men on either side of him. Each raised his hands to refuse and Strongbow noted a hint of suspicion from the Striguil milites. He was still trying to imagine why they might be annoyed at his presence when Sir Hervey appeared on horseback before the army and signalled the attack.

'Let's go!' he heard Thomas Cantwell shout a split second before a roar of anger erupted from all the men around him. Strongbow felt himself lurch forward as the bottom rung on the ladder, pulled by Cantwell, hauled him forwards. It was all he could do to stay upright. To either side there were warriors

213

running downhill towards the walls.

'St Peter save me!' Strongbow called as he slipped and reeled and ran. His water skin was lost underfoot after only a few steps, and his sword almost tripped him twice before he reached across with his right hand to hold it away from his legs. His spangenhelm jumped around uncomfortably on his head, disrupting his sight. The wall ahead was a bouncing blur of black ash, brown timber and blue sky. What little he could see quickly disappeared by the sweat pouring into his eyes.

'Cantwell!' Strongbow called. 'I require a moment to stop!' He knew that the man at the far end of the ladder would never hear him. The racket of shouting from the attacking army lasted only a few seconds as the men soon were breathing hard from their efforts, but their cries were taken up by those on the wall. They shouted and raged and sang their songs of defiance, calling for their ancestors to grant them strength, and for their sons to match their boldness in battle.

Strongbow could hear the change in their song as the first flights of Prendergast's crossbow bolts began to fall on the wall of Veðrarfjord. Insolence was overtaken by injury. Anger was silenced by sudden terror.

'Keep going,' he heard someone shout close to his ear. He half-turned but could not see who was at his side. The wall was less than two hundred paces away. That was when the Ostmen unleashed their bombardment. It began slowly. A man to Strongbow's left fell, and then one ahead, running alongside Thomas Cantwell. Then he saw the first arrows standing proud in the ground, shot from the walls of the city. The Ostmen's hunters were no match for Prendergast's two hundred professional crossbowmen and they were forced to hide behind the wall out of reach of the waves of bolts.

Instead of grass, Strongbow noticed that they had entered a field which had been burned. Black ash covered everything. Strongbow put his hand to his face to block the stench rising from the crumbling stalks of barley, but Cantwell kept going despite the slick underfoot conditions. Strongbow gulped down another lungful of dust-ridden air and concentrated on chanting in time with the stomp of his feet: 'Must do my part, must do my part.'

He could feel Cantwell angling a little bit to the left and Strongbow raised his head to see that they were almost upon the burnt-out remains of the town outside the walls. His lungs were burning and he wanted nothing more than to stop, but Cantwell's strength at the far end of the ladder kept forcing him onwards. Strongbow could still see smoke drifting from blackened and scorched wooden struts. They poked out of fallen-down buildings like broken bones in a fracture. Ash from thatch fires was kicked up by the feet of the men ahead, and the sun blinded them. Very quickly Strongbow found that he could see nothing at all. Even Cantwell disappeared into the fog. The earl licked the acrid taste from his lips and concentrated on the point where the frame of the ladder vanished into the smoke. Every now and then one of his warriors or a burnt out building would appear into view before disappearing again. The city had also vanished, but Strongbow could still hear shouts and anger ahead.

The first sign that they were nearing the foot of the defences was when he felt the far end of the ladder leap in the air.

'Ditch!' he heard Cantwell shout, and not a moment too soon. Strongbow only just managed to clear the flooded fosse in a single bound before the far end of the ladder started angling upwards. Strongbow unlooped his arm and kept pushing the rungs forward. He emerged from the ash cloud to find Thomas Cantwell hoisting the ladder upwards. At his back was the stone glacis of Veðrarfjord. And above, the wooden wall.

'Get that ladder up!' Cantwell shouted hoarsely.

Strongbow could feel that the top of the ladder had become stuck. He grunted with effort and gave it shunt from side to side. It came free. Strongbow pushed upwards until he joined Cantwell at the foot of the wall. Twenty other warriors had their backs pressed to the wall. The younger man offered no congratulations. Instead he reached around the vertical ladder and grabbed Strongbow by the shoulder, hauling him into the wall. The earl's shoulder smashed into the stone glacis and he called out in pain and anger at such treatment. A few moments later, masonry and heavy pieces of wood began raining down from above. One large brick sank into the soil right where

Strongbow had been standing.

'The Flemings have had to stop shooting,' Cantwell shouted into Strongbow's ear. 'They don't want to kill us! Whatever you do, my Lord, don't look up. Let your helmet take the hit rather than your face. Do you understand?'

Strongbow nodded and coughed. The ash was viscous and clotted in his mouth.

'Hold the ladder steady,' Cantwell shouted in Strongbow's direction before turning to the men on either side of him. 'This is it,' he shouted and pulled a short hand-axe from his belt. 'Follow me!'

Strongbow barely had a chance to grab a hold on the inside of the ladder before Cantwell and his brother had begun climbing. They were followed by Borard and Amaury. Then Dafydd FitzHywell was climbing. The ladder bounced around in his hands and ash clogged his eyes and mouth. Sweat poured from his brow but he dared not remove his hands to swipe it away. The shouting and clash of arms was incredible above him, steel striking wood and the sickening dull thwack of torn flesh. Strongbow cried out as Asclettin stood on the fingers of his left hand.

After them, no more men could climb onto the ladder and the men ran off to see if they could find another place to scale the wall. Strongbow resisted the desire to look up. Debris still fell all around him. Thankfully, the ash had begun to settle again and, here and there, it provided him with little windows to view the attack. Hundreds of men were on the ladders. He could see the flashes of sunlight striking blades at the tops of the wall. The loudest shouts came from those halfway up the ladders. They could not get within reach to fight, but they shouted on encouragement to those who were.

Strongbow tried to block out the cacophony of noise. Through the rungs of the ladder he could see the hillside. He could see figures running through the fields to get to the battle site. They were crossbowmen. He could see Sir Hervey on his horse, watching the walls from a hundred yards away. As the bowmen passed him he seemed to issue new orders. Strongbow did not see the result before they all disappeared behind a passing cloud of ash.

A burning bale of hay tumbled over the wall and landed at the foot of a ladder three down from Strongbow's position. The earl winced as it slammed to the ground. The man holding the ladder steady stepped out and kicked it until it rolled away. He turned to shout something up at his comrades when a scream sounded from above and another warrior fell from the top of the ladder and crashed into him. Strongbow jumped at the shocking collision. He desperately wanted to look up and see how his men were getting on, but he dared not do it. Instead he muttered an appeal to St Peter for his help and began praying. He had barely started when Thomas Cantwell fell and crashed into the ground beside him.

'St Peter save me!' Strongbow shouted and stepped to Cantwell's side. The miles was in great pain. He had fallen all of thirty feet onto his back. His shield had taken most of the impact, but his head had whipped back with great force. Strongbow gripped the injured warrior's shoulder.

'It will be all right,' he told Cantwell. He took a deep breath and looked upwards. 'It will be all right,' he repeated again and again.

Raymond awoke and sat up. He did not know where he was. There were trees all around him and the slumped figures of Welsh archers in the shadows. He swiped at his eyes and looked around the slope of the hill. There were no fires nearby. Everything was unfamiliar. The sun was straight ahead, almost dipping behind the low peak to the west, casting a red-yellow light over the island. He had been dreaming of birds and arrows again, of the dark-haired woman, but he could remember no detail. A headache threatened to rise again.

He could hear voices below him and carefully climbed to his feet, picking a course through the sleeping Welshmen. It was a strange scene, like some enchantment had been placed over the archers. He had heard stories of such things happening in Wales, of course, where wood-witches and wizards were known to practice strange heathen arts, and he supposed that in Ireland it might be the same. As he descended through the trees Raymond caught sight of the River Bearú sliding past. The far bank of the river was as heavily forested as the one upon which he stood, but he could see a mucky little marshland landing site and he recalled where he was and why he was there. As if she was privy to his thoughts, a nearby cow called loudly. Her moan was taken up by five more cattle and then the whole hillside was swaying with their calls. Above he could hear flocking birds readying to nest and adding to the racket.

Raymond paused and stretched his back. The journey north with the cattle train had taken all day, had been a bit of a blur for him and also, he presumed, for the fifteen archers who had accompanied him on the raid into Ostman territory. Jarl Gufraid – a different man since his sons had been rescued from their imprisonment – had stepped into command, setting all the scouts and sentries as well as keeping the cattle moving forward through the woods of Siol Bhroin. It had been enough for Raymond to keep his feet from tangling beneath him as he walked northwards to the island, journeying the same paths that he had the night before. He had snatched a few minutes' sleep here and there, but he still felt lightheaded from its lack over the last three days. He blinked tiredness from his eyes and continued downhill towards the sound of cattle.

William de Vale was stationed above the beach and greeted Raymond with wide a smile. 'They are almost ready to attempt a crossing,' he announced. 'They took Fulk to help. I think he impressed the Welsh boys with his knowledge of cows.'

Raymond looked past William towards the river. He could see the cattle being herded onto the sand. Behind them came a mixture of Welshmen and Gufraid's folk, shouting and hollering and waving sticks and spears in the air to keep the beasts moving forward. A little further down the beach was a silent group of more people. They had been posted there to make sure the cattle did not run off down the beach rather than in the direction that Caradog wished them to go. He could see Alice's long fair hair amongst their number.

'I'm here to make sure that none of the cows escape up this way,' William said. 'I could use a bit of help,' he added and glanced uphill in the direction of the sleeping bowmen.

'They'll have to wake up soon anyway. Go and get them. I'll stay here.'

William disappeared and Raymond concentrated his gaze

on the activity going on around the little ship in the shallows. The sail was stowed and he could see by the footprints on the sand that the oarsmen had hauled the ship around so that the bows were pointed towards the river. The Ostmen stood alongside her and were staring back at the stern where Gufraid was tying a rope around the neck of a heifer. She was not happy with that arrangement. Even with his untrained eye, Raymond could see as much, but Gufraid kept to his task despite her efforts to break free of his grasp.

'Hurry up,' he mumbled. The herd was closing on Gufraid's position as were the line of people from the far end of the beach.

Finally, Gufraid shouted his orders and the oarsmen heaved the ship into the river. He could see the large figure of Grím yelling instructions. It took them several pushes to get the boat floating as the heifer tied to the stern continued to fight against them. Raymond could see the taut rope had been tied to the back of the ship. Gufraid and another man cajoled the heifer into the small grey shallows, but it looked like an impossible task to Raymond. For several seconds it looked like Grím's oarsmen must be dragged back onto the beach by the joint efforts of the current and heifer. However, just as it seemed most hopeless Raymond saw the rope go slack and the heifer plough into the water up to her middle along with Gufraid at her side. The oarsmen wasted no time in leaping aboard and getting the oars out and paddling. Jarl Gufraid let go of the heifer's harness and waded back to the shore just in time to avoid being trampled by the herd of cattle coming directly at him. In the water, the heifer bellowed and swam and was dragged towards the far bank by the little ship and the lead cattle, hearing her calls, plunged into the river without pause. All but a few of the animals followed them into the watercourse. The line of warriors with Alice closed in around those stray few and began shouting and hooting, scaring the remaining cattle towards the crossing. Raymond watched as all the cattle swam across the water, their massive shoulders powering them across the gulf without issue. Even the little calves were able to swim in the older cows' wake. Raymond could've applauded the skill and timing with which Caradog and Gufraid had performed the manoeuvre. Had he done the same with a conrois of horsemen, it would've been impressive, but with silly and obdurate beasts like the cattle it was even more remarkable.

'They got across?' William said as he rejoined Raymond on the little knoll by the beach. At his back were fifteen weary Welshmen, too tired to even put up a fight against being woken again.

'They made it.' Raymond watched as the ship made land on the far bank, only a hundred and fifty paces away. There was a sudden rise in the land on the opposite shore and it was from that direction that some of Caradog's Welsh bowmen appeared from the woods. As the cattle came ashore they corralled the herd on the muddy marshland, preventing them from disappearing into the forest above.

'Well, we may as well get ready for our turn to cross,' William stated to the archers. 'Come on, let's go,' he announced and Raymond was pleased to see that the fifteen men, including Ieuan, followed without argument.

He joined the back of the exhausted group as they descended towards the beach. They followed the footprints left by the drovers across the sand and by the time they came to the river the ship was already on its way back across. To the north Raymond could see the long shoulder of Brénainn's Hill, perhaps ten miles away.

Alice of Abergavenny came and joined Raymond and William. She took his arm and stood at his side to shelter from the stiff breeze that lanced up the river's course. Her hair whipped around his chest and face.

'Gufraid says it is the land of the Uí Dheaghaidh, whoever they are,' she said and indicated across the river. 'He doesn't think there will be any trouble from them, but he ferried half the archers across to make sure.'

Her words seemed distant to Raymond's drowsy mind and he had to ask her to repeat what she had said. He looked at Ieuan's men who had all sat down on the beach. 'We'll camp on the far bank tonight and then push on at first light.'

Alice nodded. 'Gufraid has already made arrangements for the camp. He sent scouts inland.'

Her words somewhat upset Raymond, but he bit his tongue. The jarl and his forty warriors had intercepted them on their journey northwards. Despite suffering the same privations that had Raymond, Gufraid had returned to his side reenergised and, along with Caradog, had been the real leader of their company. He had selected the crossing point, and had retrieved the vessel that they had stolen from Fiodh-Ard Liag from its hiding place at the southern end of the island. The jarl had even decided upon their next move.

'There is an island just downriver from Veðrarfjord,' Alice told him. 'There is a ford to get from the north bank of the River Siúire to the island. Gufraid says that we will use it to cross into Ostman territory. Gufraid says that we will be at Lord Strongbow's side by midday tomorrow.'

'"Gufraid says, Gufraid says". Since when has he been in command?'

Alice let go of his arm. 'You should be thankful that Gufraid was on hand to help you. Otherwise we would not have the cattle across the water.' She turned away as the hiss of wooden hull on sliding sand sounded at the river's edge. Grím had returned, ready to ferry those remaining on the eastern shore across. Several Ostmen moved to board the ship until Alice shouted for them to stop. She crossed to Grím and spoke briefly to him, in what language Raymond did not know. Her hand shot out to point at him.

'The archers must go first,' she said loudly in French, turning her eyes on Raymond. 'They are more in need of rest and recovery than anyone else.'

Thomas Cantwell screeched as Strongbow lost his grip on his shoulders. He thumped to the ground and lay there clutching his head with his good arm. The other was contorted into a bizarre shape at the elbow.

'Hold on!' Strongbow shouted and grabbed the collar of his gambeson. 'We're nearly there.' He could feel sweat pouring down Cantwell's neck as he began hauling him again. It was only a few steps to the ladder and what little cover it provided. He propped the miles up against the stone glacis of Veðrarfjord. Debris still fell from above. The noise of battle still raged at the top of the wall. Droplets of perspiration dripped off the end of Strongbow's nose as he fought the urge to remove his spangenhelm. Up and down the length of the wall he could see bodies prone on the ground. Other men were limping back towards the hill through the burnt-out Irishtown. One man was limp in the arms of two milites. Even from Strongbow's position he could see the trail of blood left behind.

A shout of pain emerged from Cantwell, forcing Strongbow to turn. The miles nursed his injured right arm in his left, but the earl could see that the elbow was dislocated. It was certainly beyond his capability to fix.

'Can you make it back to the camp?' Strongbow asked. 'You need to get someone to see to that arm.'

'I need to make sure that Hugh is all right,' Cantwell moaned before looking upwards. 'Hugh?' he cried. 'Hugh – are you well?' There was no answer and Cantwell cursed as he levered himself back to his feet. 'Where's my damned sword?'

'I don't know,' Strongbow replied before realising what Cantwell meant to do. 'You cannot go back up the ladder, Cantwell! You won't be able to hold on.'

Cantwell grimaced and pushed past Strongbow. Immediately he was struck by a spear thrown from above. Thankfully his shield – slung across his back – took the impact. It did not stop Cantwell screaming out as the rim of the shield slammed into his injured arm.

'Get back here, you dullard!' Strongbow ordered and grabbed him.

To their right a ladder collapsed in a shower of splintered wood, sending four men tumbling to the ground. A cheer went up on the wall above. Those men at the bottom were able to jump clear, but those above were not so lucky. Two slammed into the ground on top of each other while a third was left dangling from the outside of the wall. He held on for several seconds but the weight of his armour was too great and, with a squawk, he fell, dropping twenty feet onto the stone glacis. He did not get up again.

Above Strongbow the ladder began to quake and creak as two warriors retreated down to the ground. The first was young Dafydd FitzHywell. 'This is madness!' he announced as he slammed his back to the glacis.

'Have we made any progress?'

'None,' Asclettin FitzEustace replied as he joined the group sheltering beneath the ladder. He crouched beside Strongbow. 'There are too many men defending the wall. There is no space to swing a sword.'

'Is Hugh alive?' Cantwell asked and winced as about surge of pain went through his arm.

'He is, but he's tiring. We need to get him down. The Ostmen aren't for budging today.'

'Sir Hervey said that we would easily be able to overwhelm them!' Strongbow replied.

'He is welcome to try if he wants,' Dafydd mumbled and jerked a thumb at the earl's uncle. Sir Hervey was still on his horse, a hundred paces from the wall, beyond the burned town, shouting at some of the injured men who were retreating.

Strongbow didn't reprove Dafydd for his comment. Instead he glanced upwards. All he could see was the occasional flash of sunlight on steel, the soles of boots, and the sway of gambeson skirts. He breathed deeply. 'We need to tell Amaury to come down. Tell him to bring Hugh and Borard too.' Asclettin and Dafydd swapped a look. 'Bring them down,' the earl insisted.

The older man nodded his head and in response Dafydd stepped back into the shower of debris being thrown from the walls, putting his hand to the side of his mouth to repeat the orders. The ladder began to bounce as all four men retreated to the foot of the wall. Strongbow wisely lowered the ladder so that it was out of reach and could not be damaged by those at the top.

'What the hell is going on?' Hugh Cantwell demanded when he reached the bottom. 'Are we retreating?' His face was covered in blood except where rivulets of sweat had run from beneath his helmet. Strongbow could not tell if the blood was his or someone else's.

'We are not retreating yet.' Strongbow had to shout to make his voice heard. 'Hugh, you will get your brother back to camp. He is badly hurt and needs attention. Asclettin, you will go to Sir Hervey and tell him that he is to signal the withdrawal.

Make sure he understands that I sent you,' Strongbow emphasised. 'He must get Prendergast's crossbowmen to cover us as we pull back.' He inhaled deeply. 'Borard, you will hold the ladder steady. Dafydd and Amaury, follow me!'

Without waiting for anyone to stop him, Strongbow hoisted the ladder upwards again and then leapt onto the first rung to begin climbing. 'I must do my part,' he repeated over and over again as he pumped his legs. He stole a glance to his left. Hundreds of men were stationary on ladders up and down the west wall of Veðrarfjord. More were immobile on the ground, hunkered with their backs to the stone glacis at the foot of the defences. Smoke and sunlight obscured his view, but he could see airborne weaponry and warriors. The tumult of battle was overpowering. Insults and screaming were hurled in either direction, the disjointed song of steel clashing with steel and wood.

He was more than halfway up when he heard Amaury de Lyvet's warning: 'Lord, your shield!'

Strongbow stopped as the sudden realisation hit. He was exposed. He could see it was already too late. At the top of the ladder was a bearded man and as they locked eyes, he hefted a wine barrel on his shoulder. Strongbow could see the delight in the man's eyes, the animal madness as he bared his teeth and made ready to throw. *There is nowhere to go*, Strongbow thought. He could feel the panic spreading as he clung to the ladder, paralysed by visions of Cantwell's broken body on the ground. *There is nowhere to go*! The man hoisted the barrel above his head. The earl pressed his body to the rungs and urged his eyes to close, but they would not respond. He was aware of Amaury shouting another warning, but all he could hear was his internal voice shouting. *There is nowhere to go*, it repeated again and again. The words infuriated Strongbow. He thought of his father. He pictured Henry FitzEmpress up on his dais in his crown and finery.

'I am going somewhere!' he yelled and took a step upwards. 'I am going to succeed,' he exclaimed again as his hands reached up the ladder. He attempted to draw his sword, screaming incoherently.

That was when the Ostman launched his missile.

Had it hit Strongbow it would likely have killed him, but in his effort to draw his sidearm he had leaned back, hanging to the ladder by his left hand. Amaury shouted as the barrel crashed into his shield and deflected away to smash on the ground. Black liquid spilled out and was ignited by the remains of the burning bale. Strongbow could hear Borard's surprise at the sudden outbreak of the fire as he hung by his left hand and stared at the flames.

'Keep going!' Amaury and Dafydd shouted.

The ladder shook as the earl righted himself on the ladder and licked his parched lips. 'Keep going,' he muttered and began climbing again. With every step his voice got louder so that by the time he got to the top he was shouting the words: 'Keep going!'

A face appeared above the timber palisade and Strongbow lashed out with his sword. The man was moustachioed and had his hair tied back in three bunches. He jerked aside as Strongbow made his attempt and then reappeared with an upturned spear. He snarled as he stabbed downwards. The earl managed to deflect the first attempt, but dropped his sword as the man punched down again into his chest. His mail took most of the impact and his helmet the next, but Strongbow knew that soon he would either be badly injured or thrown from the ladder. The Gael lunged again and Strongbow, without a weapon, grabbed hold of the spear-shaft, pulling downwards as hard as he might. His opponent let go rather than be hauled over the top of the palisade. Strongbow dextrously reversed the spear in his fingers and began wildly slashing at the top of the wall as he climbed.

'Yes, Lord Strongbow!' he heard Dafydd scream elatedly. 'Strongbow, Strongbow!'

The earl could feel the rungs sticky beneath his hands and looked down to see the bloody limit of the Cantwell brothers' fight. He snarled and climbed above it, still slashing at the pinnacle of the wall with his stolen spear and shouting. He reached up and curled his fingers around the top of the wall. He was going to be the first man into the city! Strongbow could already taste victory.

'Keep going,' he chanted and took a deep breath, readying

225

his arms to hoist him inside the walls of Veðrarfjord.

A large hand shot out and grabbed the shaft of Strongbow's spear, holding it fast. Strongbow attempted to pull it clear, but the man's hold was firm. His enemy's face appeared over the top of the wall. Even beneath the mail hauberk and helmet, he recognised the man. His huge frame and red, braided beard which hung like tusks beside his mouth were unmistakable. It was the man who had attacked Strongbow's conrois in the inn at Westminster two months before.

It was Sigtrygg.

The Earl Strongbow let go of the ladder and tugged downwards on the spear again. But his two arms did not prove enough to dislodge it from his enemy's one-hand hold. Sigtrygg was simply too strong. The Ostman grinned widely and, still staring down at Strongbow, raised an axe to shoulder height. Strongbow could see the arc of the strike and let go of the spear and ducked. He heard the axe blade bite and felt the woodchips dot against his helm.

'Get out of there,' Amaury shouted and tugged at his heel.

Strongbow looked up to see Sigtrygg extricate the axe and raised it above his head again. His left hand was clinging to the ladder and rather than brave another attempt by the massive Ostman, Strongbow flung himself sideways so that he dangled beneath the rungs with his back to the wall. His mail was a dead weight on his shoulders and waist, but he was out of reach of Sigtrygg's axe. He looked past his feet at the top of Borard's head. It was just a few feet beneath him. Strongbow called out a warning and let go of his hold. The collision of his buttocks with the top of the stone glacis was agonising, even with his shield and gambeson taking part of the sting out of the impact. He groaned as his face and chest collided with the inside of the ladder close to Dafydd's knees, before spilling to the right and onto the ground beside Borard. Winded and sore, he lay on the ground until he felt Borard's hands grasp his surcoat and lift him into the cover of the wall. Things suddenly went very dark as Strongbow fought for a breath.

'You are all right, Lord,' he heard Borard shouting. 'Open your eyes.'

Strongbow did as he was told and saw that the miles had his

shield covering them both from all manner of weapons and stones that were being thrown from the wall.

'Sir Hervey is shouting for the retreat,' Borard yelled as he forced his fallen sword back into his grasp. 'Can you run?'

The earl nodded his head and pulled the man in close. 'Make sure all the ladders are taken with us. I cannot afford to buy more,' he wheezed.

Borard smiled and helped Strongbow to his feet. 'Get your shield up and get ready to run,' he told the earl. At his side, Amaury and Dafydd appeared with their shields protecting their heads. Debris crashed into their upturned shields.

'Ready?' Amaury asked as he took hold of the bottom of the ladder.

Dafydd was ready to take the other end and nodded his head. Strongbow took a deep breath and gestured that he too was ready to make the dash clear of the wall.

Up and down the length of the wall, men were fleeing. The rapturous cheer from the Ostmen was loud and somewhere amongst their number a set of pipes began playing. Men sang along, no doubt about the valour and daring of their folk, and the pathetic attempts of their enemy.

'Then go,' Borard shouted.

Strongbow gathered his breath and followed Borard. A spear crashed into his shield. The ferocity of the throw was such that the spear tip punched through the willow boards and almost caused him to stumble. He half-turned to see Jarl Sigtrygg standing tall on the wall, cheering with his people.

'Keep going!' the earl shouted at Borard, Amaury and Dafydd. 'Keep going.'

The first cow splashed into the ford without breaking stride, the silty bottom and cool stream feeling as pleasant to her as it certainly had to Raymond. The march down the River Bearú had been into blazing sunshine and the quick dip in the river had proven most welcome. He had forded the river with the first group of archers. Up to their middles in water, they had been almost blind due to the sparkle of the high midday sun. Not that they needed to be too cautious about an attack. Gufraid's son, Blácaire, had already taken the ship down the

227

Bearú and into the River Siúire, landing on the island and making a thorough reconnaissance. Grím had been waiting at the northern side of the ford for the cattle train to catch up and had reported to his jarl that the two Ostman forts on the island were deserted.

It was a short arrow shot from the north bank of the river to the island and Raymond covered it in a few minutes. Inevitably, the cattle took longer. The Welshmen kept them moving forward with shouts and prods of bowstave, but their main aim was not speed. The river was low, but the sliding underfoot conditions and heavy flow still made it treacherous and they did not wish to lose any of the young heifers or calves to its murderous grasp. A day before Raymond might have lost his temper with the men but a full night's sleep had gone a long way to rejuvenating him. Even the short walk in the morning sunshine had helped and he could see that it was the same for Ieuan and his men. Their chatter had barely let up the whole way south.

At the back of the column came Alice, Fulk, William and Gufraid's warriors. All three were mounted. William had transferred to Dreigiau. The tough little courser was less cooperative than his own mare and he feared that without a rider Dreigiau might refuse to cross the water. Fulk had a second horse to manage, one carrying food and equipment, but he seemed well in control. It was Alice that Raymond watched. He had used her horse's natural aversion to open water to help break him only a few weeks before. However, he need not have worried. Following a momentary pause at the water's side, Alice clipped her heels to Rufus's black flanks and he followed William and Fulk into the water behind the cattle train. Raymond felt a wide smile appear on his face.

'A fort,' Ieuan said as he appeared at Raymond's back. He pointed back through the trees along the line of the river. Raymond nodded and picked up his sword. His armour, helmet, gambeson and shield were strapped to Fulk's packhorse as it had been far too warm to wear them as they travelled south. He missed their weight around his shoulders.

'Leave one man to tell Caradog where we've gone,' he told Ieuan, as usual underlining his French with hand signals, caricature and splashes of Welsh. He then waved to Grím to follow. The Ostman shook his head and pointed to the south towards a slight rise in the landscape. He said something in his own language which Raymond didn't understand.

Exasperated, Grím picked up a stick and drew a great triangle in the mud. At the top where the line ran parallel with the river he drew waves and said, 'Siúire.' Raymond nodded to let him know he understood. He poked a point on the top line and then pointed to himself and Raymond.

'That's where we are now, I get you.'

Grím smiled and pointed off into the trees in the same directions as had Ieuan. 'Dun,' he said.

'A fort,' Raymond replied. 'Dun Raymond,' he added with a smile.

The Ostman laughed and nodded. He then stabbed his stick into the far end of his drawing just above where the two arms of the triangle came together. 'Dun Blácaire,' he said and pointed directly south. He then mimed rowing with his hands, indicating that was where Gufraid's son had landed the ship.

Raymond smiled. He then pointed to the upper half of Grím's drawing and then to his own eyes. The Ostman seemed to understand for he copied Raymond's gesture before indicating towards the lower part of the map.

'I'll watch the north and you watch the south,' Raymond muttered. 'I don't suppose you will want to help with the cattle, will you?' Grím laughed and leaned forward, slapping him on the shoulder before disappearing into the trees. 'I'll take that as a no,' he said and turned towards the river. The cattle were almost halfway across. He spotted Caradog at the front of the train and decided that he was not needed by the drovers. He nodded to Ieuan. 'Lead the way. Let's check out this fort.'

They emerged from the trees after just a few minutes walking. Fields stretched away in every direction and Raymond was able to see the sense in Gufraid's selection of the island as their crossing point. Cattle would grow fat on the pasture available there. The fort was actually one building surrounded by a timber wall. It would suffice as a rallying point for the Welsh, should the need arise, but little more. There were a few cooking implements left scattered around and some straw bedding, but otherwise the fort had been emptied. Even the firewood had been taken away. He could see the places where Ieuan's men had dug out the soil, hunting for the buried hoard of silver that was always rumoured to be hidden in a Dane's fort.

'It will do,' he said, but received no response from Ieuan. 'Good,' he said instead, pointing at the ground inside the fort.

'Good,' his companion repeated before barking out orders to the bowmen in the Welsh tongue.

Raymond left them to their preparations and made his way back down towards the fording point. He heard the shouts of the Welsh cowhands before he spotted the first of the animals emerging into the open meadows. Caradog waved and crossed towards him. He was still dripping wet from the crossing but in cheerful mood. Flies buzzed all around him.

'I will sleep tonight,' the archer captain said with a smile. He took off his wide-brimmed hat and began fanning his face. 'I'd still prefer work that pays, but this will do for now.' Caradog turned to his men. 'Keep them coming up the hill. We'll get them settled and get a rest soon, boys.'

'You've done very well, Caradog,' Raymond replied. 'It has been a pleasure to watch you and your men work.' He felt a little rush of humour. 'At least we now know that there is a use for you Welshmen.'

Caradog laughed. 'And we still know that your folk are no use at all.'

'The only one I can think of is as a messenger. Would you like me to carry a note to Lord Strongbow on your behalf?'

'Yes. Tell him that Caradog ap Thomas thinks him a fool for treating Raymond de Carew as he has done. Tell him that I will forgive him if he sends us ale. A lot of it.'

'I will do. You deserve it.' Raymond nodded to the western side of the island. 'There is a small fort up there. I don't think there's enough space to house the cattle inside.'

The Welshman sniffed and looked around. 'There's plenty of grass and nowhere for the beasts to wander. I'll put a few men on guard at the ford and let the rest have the afternoon off.'

Raymond yawned. 'I'll take William and head west to find

Strongbow. I'll be back by sundown with our orders. We'll camp here tonight.'

'Take all the time you need. We'll make some cheese to keep us going during the siege.' Caradog replied before joining the train of men and animals that climbed up from the river.

As expected, Dreigiau had been difficult during the fording of the river. William de Vale was soaked to the skin and in a grumpy mood. He was leading both his own mare and Dreigiau. 'The little shit threw me and tried to bite me,' he complained. 'Halfway across and everything was fine and then suddenly, he just went crazy. I don't know how you handle him, Raymond.' At William's back were Alice and Fulk who both giggled at their companion's condition.

Raymond took hold of Dreigiau's bridle and gave him a pat on the neck. 'Are you all right, you big fool? Did William forget that you are a very special horse?'

'I could've been badly hurt, you know.'

Raymond smiled at William's comeback and hoisted himself onto Dreigiau's back. 'You seem fine to me. But you could always stay here with Caradog's boys while I go and find Lord Strongbow.'

His miles looked with concern at the cattle, perhaps tallying which option would lead to the greater workload. 'No, I'll come with you,' he finally said. 'I need to dry off anyway.'

'I'll come too,' Alice announced. 'We need to go over what you'll say to Strongbow. You need to convince him to allow you back into his inner circle. He must allow you to take part in the assault on the city. Only then will you have claim on the position of constable.'

Raymond's immediate impulse was to refuse her, but one look in her direction warned him to bite his tongue. 'It'll be a long ride. I don't know what dangers may find us.' He wondered if he wished her to stay because of her pregnancy or if he did not wish to be lectured.

'I'll be fine, I'm sure that we three will be able to outpace any potential assailants.'

He reluctantly nodded his head. 'Fulk, you'll stay here and get our things up to the fort. Make do with whatever space you can find. I hope we won't be here for very long.'

'Yes, Lord.'

Gufraid's men looked exhausted as they appeared in the fields above the ford. Each carried his own food, weapons and armour across his back and the extra weight of water tugging on their woollen clothes was not welcome.

Raymond broke the bad news to their jarl. 'It's a bit further, I'm afraid. Your son has taken over a fort at the south of the island.'

'Damn his eyes,' Gufraid panted. 'The boy has less brains than are in the keel of a knarr.' He looked over at his men and breathed deeply. 'Well, lead on then.'

What paths there were on the island were merely there to allow cattle to pass easily between the various fields, and Raymond followed one such route south. They didn't push the horses but strolled along the path behind the Ostmen. They soon heard voices in the trees and made their way down the slight slope to where Blácaire had tied the ship to a mooring on the southern course of the River Siúire. To Raymond's eye the river looked too dark to be fordable.

'You'll need ferrying across,' Jarl Gufraid said, confirming his impression.

Raymond frowned. 'If there were more of us to cross, yes. But we three? I think we can manage.'

'More swimming?' groaned William de Vale.

Alice laughed. 'The ship can ferry our saddles and your weapons across. No point in getting those wet.'

'Do you want me to go with you?' Gufraid asked Raymond. The jarl did not look overly excited about the idea of adding more miles to his legs that day.

Raymond assured him that it was not necessary. In truth he was glad that the Ostman didn't wish to travel any further, for he did not yet know what Strongbow would make of his alliance with Gufraid, or the promises that he had made in return for his warriors. He would keep that news to himself until he could find a way to restore himself to favour with his lord. He prayed that his delivery of the cattle train would prove his trustworthiness to Strongbow, but William's account of the earl's words to him at Dun Domhnall did not leave him in much hope of so rapid a return to his inner circle.

Gufraid wasted no time in ordering the few men lounging in the sunshine on the grassy shoreline to ready the boat for crossing the river. Raymond and his companions handed over their weapons and saddles to the Ostmen. They only kept their bridles on the horses. While Alice and William's horses went to eat grass, Dreigiau looked nervously at his master as if remembering a far-off time when Raymond had last got him to swim.

'It is years since I last rode bareback,' Raymond told Alice. 'This should be interesting,' he added as he gazed at the narrow waterway between the island and the mainland.

'I have never swum on the back of a horse,' she replied. 'Are you sure that Rufus will be able to carry me?'

'Very sure. It isn't that far,' he said as he dragged off his shirt and threw it into the ship. William copied him, revealing a pale body with lines of tan around his neck and forearms. Raymond assisted Alice onto Rufus's back before clambering on top of Dreigiau. 'Get going,' he told the eight Ostmen in the ship. 'We'll follow you across.'

Gufraid translated his words and then shook Raymond's hand. 'It's a stiff current. Watch yourselves.'

William and Alice joined him at the waterside. The Ostmen had untied the line holding them to the mooring. Immediately the ship was swept downriver by the weight of water and it wasn't until the men got the oars out that they righted their direction. Alice and William looked uncomfortable.

'You can see where the folk who live here usually land on the other side,' he told them. 'If they can make it so can we.' Neither responded but looked nervous at the prospect of the swim. 'We need to see how easy it will be for the cattle to cross.'

The ship was now twenty feet away with her bows pointed towards the far shore. Raymond clipped his heels to Dreigiau's flanks. The courser gingerly stepped forward and got his hooves wet. There was no great drop from the bank into the course of the river, but it still took several clicks of his tongue to encourage Dreigiau to go up to his middle in the water. His ears flicked madly and his head jerked up and down.

'It's all right,' Raymond soothed. 'It's just a nice dip on a

233

sunny day.' Behind him, he could hear similar words of reassurance from Alice towards Rufus. 'Come on,' Raymond repeated. 'Keep going forward.' Raymond's feet were already in the river and he could feel its weight against his calf. He gave Dreigiau a squeeze with his knees and felt him hop forward. He gasped as the cold water hit his middle, but the little courser did not seem to notice. Instead he powered his legs and they cruised forward at a mighty clip. He heard a splash and Alice squeak as Rufus followed him into the river. If his cursing was anything to go by, William was having trouble getting his mare to follow. Soon, however, he too was swimming and he whooped with excitement as they trailed in Alice's wake.

They emerged on the southern shore a few seconds later and Raymond dismounted to allow Dreigiau a few moments to recover. He pulled off his bridle and watched as the small courser shook wildly and then dashed up the shoreline, kicking his legs and shaking his mane. Alice was shivering when she and Rufus joined him at the river's edge, but refused Raymond's help. The black gelding did not wait for Alice to remove his bridle, he tucked his chin to his chest and trotted after Dreigiau. He quickly found an appropriate spot and dropped onto his back for a roll. William's mare did likewise. All three continue to roam and drip and eat grass as Raymond and William recovered all their belongings from the ship. They waited long enough for the Ostmen to return to the island before catching the horses and saddling them again.

The trio hugged the coastline as they started out for Veðrarfjord. The river curled in two wide sweeps, first north and then southwards, but the land was flat and they even got up to a canter for a few minutes. Mostly they were limited to walking and trotting. Where the river again turned north-west the landscape began to get boggy and Raymond led his companions upwards onto the shoulder of a long bluff. From there they could see for miles. Mountains rose way off to the west, but otherwise the landscape was lowland and forested for as far as he could see. Directly below them, Raymond beheld the unmistakable signs of a vast marshland stretching northwards to meet the Siúire.

It was where the marsh met the river that Raymond had his first view of the Ostman city. Veðrarfjord was still half a mile away, but he could see the east wall rise from the great swaying greenery of the marshland. He could see the two great towers on the northern wall which ran parallel with the river and the limit of the city in west above the thatched houses. A church was built near the north-eastern point of the triangular fortress-town and he fancied that he could hear its bells ringing.

'How is Lord Strongbow going to get in there?' William de Vale asked as he stared down at the city. 'It's huge.'

Even to Raymond, who had seen Westminster, London and the great Frankish cities of the Loire Valley, the Ostman city still seemed vast. It covered at least twenty acres and the three walls were over a thousand paces long.

'I don't know,' he told William with a shake of his head. He could feel Alice's eyes on him and cleared his throat. 'I don't know yet. Gufraid will help us find a way inside. There is always some weakness.' William looked doubtful and Raymond had no further answer to assuage his worries. 'Let's keep going,' he suggested. 'We need to find a way across the marsh first.'

It took Raymond as long to find a way through the bogland as it had to ride to the hillside from the island. They rode south for a mile, across several small streams, before picking up a long ridge of land which led back northwards. They kept climbing and emerged through the trees onto a little bluff with the city now downhill on their right.

Ahead, over several fields, Raymond could see a tented town. It was bigger than the little market that had grown up beside Striguil, larger than Monmouth or Caldicot. A small smile broke on his face, for it was obvious that Strongbow had brought a great army to Ireland. He clipped his heels to Dreigiau's flanks and the courser responded, breaking into a trot. He could see a group of scouts cantering on an intercept course a quarter-mile to the west and he raised a hand to let them know that he was a friend. Ahead, stone-walled fields had been used as a stable for the army's horses. There were hundreds of the animals in the temporary stalls and many looked up to watch as he and his companions rode towards him. The thump of hooves grew closer and Raymond slowed Dreigiau to a walk as the scouts reined in around him.

'Where the devil did you come from?' a haughty voice asked.

Raymond came to a halt and lifted his hands away from his reins. The leader of the scouts had settled the point of his lance a few inches from Raymond's his chest. Rather than react, Raymond swivelled in the saddle. William and Alice had also been threatened in a like manner. All the scouts were young, younger even than William. They had helmets and all had gambesons. Some even had mail. They were esquires, boys playing war.

'There is no need for weapons. I am Strongbow's man, Raymond de Carew, come to speak with the earl. And we came from the west through the marsh.' He looked at the boy. 'And if I were your master I would skin your back for not guarding that approach to the camp.'

The lance dipped away from his chest. 'Sir Walter said that the marsh was impassable and not to bother watching it.'

Raymond did not answer. Instead he clicked his tongue and squeezed Dreigiau's sides. The courser quickly went into a trot. He glanced over his shoulder to see Alice follow at the same pace.

'We'll make sure to watch the marsh from now on,' the boy called after him.

'Make sure you do,' William told them and puffed up his chest. 'Or you'll have me to deal with.'

They slowed to a walk for the last pull towards the brow, passing the horses as the land levelled out. There was a small fortified longhouse below, and it was surrounded by more tents. But it was not at them that Raymond stared. Down by the river an army was in full flight.

Strongbow had been defeated and was fleeing from Veðrarfjord.

They cheered him on the walls. They cheered him from the streets at his back. He was sure they cheered him in every household within his city. Sigtrygg lifted his weapons and accepted their salute, their admiration of his kingship. He had

236

sent the enemy running from Veðrarfjord's walls for the second time in two days. Sigtrygg had defeated the invader again. He tilted his head back and whooped like a cockerel welcoming the dawn. His warriors cheered even harder. He turned and spat a long twisting globule of spit over the wall at the backs of the retreating foreigners.

'Don't come back,' he bellowed and raised his axe and shield over his head, pumping them in the air. The fortifications on Veðrarfjord's western side rocked as the warriors took up his call, battering their shields and stamping their feet as they repeated his words. Even Máel Sechlainn's Gaels joined his chant. They watched the grey-clad foreigners as they galloped away through the burnt remnants of Irishtown.

Even after his men's shouting had subsided, Sigtrygg still watched the enemy. Smoke circled around him from the burning bales and pitch at the bottom of the wall, stinging his eyes, but he watched them go back up to their camp at Brickin's Place. Every part of his soul wished to pursue them, to take the fight to the enemy in the night with fire and axe. He wished to terrorise the foreigners as they had done his folk. With effort he dismissed the idea. Up and down the wall there were bodies, most with short, thick crossbow bolts standing in their chests or heads. Blood shone on the wooden allure, he could taste it on the air. He could smell the stink of human excrement. He wished to inflict the same destruction upon the Norman camp.

He had been asleep in Thorgest's Tower at the north-west point of the city when he heard Jarl Orm's warning that another attack was in motion. He had kept watch through most of the night, certain that the wily enemy would launch a night-time assault. The Normans had not so much as shot an arrow at their walls. In the hours before dawn Sigtrygg had awoken Máel Sechlainn as he had requested. The King of the Déisi had been so certain that the attack would come then when the warriors were at their least vigilant. But the foreigners had not stirred and Sigtrygg had gone to sleep. It was only at midday that he had stirred, and then only to perform Mass up on the hill beside the ranks of colourful banners. The second assault on Veðrarfjord had come soon after. As with their first attack, they

237

had come through Irishtown, this time with twice as many ladders. His and Máel Sechlainn's warriors had ducked behind the walls, expecting a shower of crossbow bolts to rain down upon them ahead of the escalade. The Earl Strongbow had adapted his attack, however, sending groups of crossbowmen alongside the infantrymen, and it had only been as the ladders had been pushed against the walls and the Ostmen had risen to meet them that the damage from their bolts had struck home. Sigtrygg had taken one on his shield. It had punched through the willow boards and gored his forearm.

'Those bastards could still return today,' Máel Sechlainn warned as he and his ever-present derb-fine walked down the palisade towards him. The Gael ignored the cries of the wounded, stepping over the bodies. There were Ostmen and Gaels and Normans, but he did not take his eyes off Sigtrygg. 'There is more than enough daylight left for them to come back. We need to be ready.'

Sigtrygg sniffed and grimaced. 'If they come back it will be the same as before.'

'My warriors are exhausted,' Máel Sechlainn said. 'I'm taking my men on the east wall and Toirdelbach's on the north and sending them here to replace those we have here. You should do the same.'

Máel Sechlainn's words appalled Sigtrygg. His blood was still on fire. How could any of his men feel any different? Who amongst them would not gladly take the fight to the enemy? How could any man claim tiredness when there was glory to be won? It was all that Sigtrygg could do to not command his men to follow him up to Brickin's Place right then.

'You don't order me around, Máel Sechlainn,' he warned the smaller man. 'I am konungr. In fact, take all your men to guard the other walls and send my warriors here. The west will be held by Veðrarfjord folk until the enemy are driven away.' Sigtrygg bared his teeth.

Máel Sechlainn blinked many times but didn't make any show that he had been in anyway intimidated by Sigtrygg's words. 'Very well,' he said simply. 'I will make the arrangements now.'

Sigtrygg was immediately suspicious but dared not

withdraw his demand. He watched as, with effort, Máel Sechlainn pulled a quarrel buried in the timber wall.

'The crossbows didn't help the Liathgall today,' the Gael said. 'They couldn't safely shoot with their men climbing to the top of the walls. If you stay behind the defences they will soon run out of bolts.' He threw the bolt over the edge and placed his hands on the fortifications. There was a patch of blood on the wall where he grasped. He stared at it briefly on his fingers. 'I burned three ladders and two others collapsed on my part of the wall. You?'

Sigtrygg looked over the palisade. 'I don't know. We destroyed a few.'

Máel Sechlainn nodded. 'I still haven't seen them send out any foraging parties. They must be starting to run out of food up there,' he said nodding in the direction of the hill to the west. 'Running out of food, running out of crossbow bolts, running out of ladders,' he mused. 'If we can hold out for another few days -'

'It will be the end of Strongbow,' Sigtrygg completed his sentence.

'You should get some sleep, Brother. They will be back.'

Sigtrygg watched as the derb-fine divided to allow their king to walk between them towards the southern end of the west wall. His eyes narrowed suspiciously at the back of his confident young brother-in-law. At the very back was Toirdelbach, the Uí Fhaolain Tánaiste. Sigtrygg noticed Toirdelbach's distaste as his cousin, Máel Sechlainn, passed by. There was rivalry between the two, Sigtrygg noted.

He watched the Uí Fhaolain go and then descended into the town by a walkway close to the main gates. At the foot of the wall the wailing of women and howls of the wounded was more intense. The townsfolk had come out of their homes and were trying to find news of their loved ones. He could see the priests from St Olav's had taken over three gardens. In one they had already begun piling the dead. In the others they worked on the wounded, binding cuts and offering prayers for those beyond their help. He looked down at his own bloody forearm, pulling his mail down over the injury as far as possible to cover it.

His bodyguard quickly circled around him as he came to the bottom of the steps. There were hundreds of townsfolk and warriors on the streets and they immediately closed on him, cheering his name and grasping for a touch of their victorious king. Sigtrygg remembered how, just a few short months before, these same people had been baying for his head and only Ragnall's intervention had stopped them from having it. Now they were lauding him as the saviour of their city!

'You've changed your tune,' he told one leading merchant who leaned forward to shake his hand. The man could not hear him over the cheers. Another barged him out of the way so that he could congratulate Sigtrygg. He disappeared after slapping him across the shoulders.

'Get moving,' Sigtrygg told his bodyguard.

More hands came over his bodyguard's shoulders, some between their bodies as they attempted to walk down the High Street. Eyes full of joy, others in tears, appeared from the crowd which gathered around Sigtrygg. There were smiles, women's smiles. They chanted his name and suddenly Sigtrygg began to grin and reach out to take hold of the hands which emerged from the throng, giving them a squeeze before the flow of people took him forward. To his left he saw two priests, men who, only a few days before, had been part of Bishop Tostig's uprising against him. They fell to their knees in the road as Sigtrygg's group passed and began beseeching the Heavens for Lord God to grant him His grace against the city's enemies. At the hall of the Meic Bjarne he could see the effects of Máel Sechlainn and Toirdelbach's purge of the leading families. The hall doors were still off their hinges and there was a black patch on the dusty path in front where Asgaill Mac Bjarne had been cut down by the Déisi. There was an old woman in the doorway. Perhaps it was Asgaill's widow? His bodyguard swept him past before he could get a good look at her.

Ahead was Ragnall's Hall with the great tower at its back. The hall was the biggest in the city, fit for a king and, when he had ended the foreigners' threat to Veðrarfjord, he would have Bishop Tostig crown him on the steps to the hall. His father would be there to see it. Ragnall's Hall had been built on a little knoll soon after the city had been founded, and like the tower at its back it was named for one of the ancient konungrs of Veðrarfjord. His father had been named in honour of that great man too. He would be there to see it become Sigtrygg's Hall and Sigtrygg's city. The guards at the fence stepped back to allow him and his men to enter the compound around the hall.

'Keep them out,' Sigtrygg ordered and pointed to the townsfolk who had followed him along the High Street. He had planned to get some sleep in the hall, but he found that he could not take his eyes off the great tower. 'I don't need you anymore,' he told his men. 'Get some kip. I'll want to go back to the wall in an hour or two.'

Sigtrygg walked around the shoulder of the knoll to pick up the little path which led to the tower entrance. Like the defences, the bottom was built of stone with the top finished in cut timber boards. Two men guarding the door climbed to their feet as Sigtrygg appeared. He heard them sigh in relief that he had not reprimanded them as he passed and entered the cool of the tower. The walls seemed to creak around him as he climbed the curling timber steps. The bottom floor held Bishop Tostig and his store of food and wine. The first floor contained his riches – his silver, skins and furs – and in the doorway was another sentry. Amlaith had sailed with him for eight years and had been his ship-master aboard *River-Wolf* for four. He was not there to watch over his hoard, however.

'All is well?' Amlaith asked.

Sigtrygg nodded and held out his large hand. 'Key,' he said simply.

He kept climbing. A door to his left led out on the northern wall and then he passed an exit onto the east fortifications. There were two windows on the stair, both facing into the city. He passed them both, pausing only to throw open the shutters to let the light into the stairway. At the top was a closed door, but the staircase continued on towards the roof. Sigtrygg raised his hand to knock before thinking better of it and slotting the great iron key in the lock. He turned it and then pushed open the door. Inside was quite dark and it stank. It was a large space with a cone-shaped roof. Sigtrygg could see the outline of the daylight around the window shutters and crossed to open them.

241

'Leave them,' his father's voice emerged from the bed on opposite side of the room.

Sigtrygg ignored the order and threw open the shutters. There was another set on the western side and he opened those too. 'It stinks in here.'

'It stinks everywhere.'

Ragnall's wife was over in the corner. She had been mending a shirt as Sigtrygg had entered, but he could see that she had stopped working. Her head was down and she was trying to remain as inconspicuous as she could. She did not move.

His father could see Sigtrygg's gaze was on her. 'It isn't right to have my wife cooped up in here with me,' said Ragnall. 'She should be with her sons.'

'Your sons are fine without her.'

'I don't believe you. I haven't seen or heard a word of them in weeks.'

Sigtrygg sniffed. 'I haven't come here to talk about your whelps.'

'I know why you are here,' Ragnall stated and climbed to his feet from the bed. His father had never been a large man, but even to Sigtrygg's eye he had diminished since his incarceration. 'You are here to kill us.'

'Kill you?' Even as he replied he realised that his fingers were white on his sword pommel. He released his grip.

'That's what usurpers do, boy. They keep their prisoners alive only as long as they serve a use.'

'I never had a use for you.' Sigtrygg drew himself up to his full height, flexing his muscles and his jaw. 'So have a care with your tone.'

Ragnall simply cackled and walked over to the west window so that he could stare out down the length of the wall over the Merchant's Quay. It was empty of people. 'A boy needs a mother. My boys need theirs.'

Sigtrygg did not turn to face him. 'They have everything they need from Jarl Orm.'

'A boy needs a woman's care or they grow up to be peculiar,' his father insisted. 'Orm is a good man though. He will treat them right, his mother too. Ragnall Óg and Óttar are

242

down at Áth Skipir, then?'

'Did I say that?' Sigtrygg could feel his ire rising with every word that came out of his father's mouth. 'I told you, I am not here to talk about those two little shits.'

'They are your brothers. Family is important, boy. Your brothers need their mother.'

'If you stop talking about it, I might consider it.'

Ragnall sniffed. 'So? Strongbow, you drove him off?'

Sigtrygg felt a smile spread across his face and he half turned to face his father. 'He has attacked twice and I have driven him off both times.'

'He was merely testing your defences, boy. He wants to see what you are about. Now he knows what these Déisi of yours can do he will come again.'

'The foreigners attacked with their full might,' Sigtrygg said and turned on his heels. 'And I defeated them. Did you not hear the townsfolk call out my name?'

'It sounded like the Déisi from up here. The good Veðrarfjord folk wouldn't have the man who betrayed their city and opened the gates to the Gael. Not for their hero.'

Sigtrygg growled and stepped towards his father. 'They will have me for their konungr.'

Ragnall said nothing for several moments, instead staring out the window. 'You should send your Déisi into the hills to attack the foreigners.'

'Ha!' Sigtrygg laughed. 'Now who is being peculiar? The foreigners would be upon them in minutes with horses and crossbowmen.'

'Not if they are led by someone who knows the country.'

'Like who?' Sigtrygg asked.

'Well, you would know better than me,' his father replied and relaxed with his shoulder against the wall.

Sigtrygg could feel his eyes narrow in suspicion. He looked at Ragnall's wife over on the other side of the room. As soon as he turned his eyes on her she dropped her gaze, acting as if she hadn't been looking in his direction. 'Next you'll be telling me that I should release Bishop Tostig, maybe that I should give him a dagger and then bare my back to make it easier for him to kill me?'

Ragnall coughed and spat out the window. A dribble caught on his wispy beard. 'You have him caged in here too, then? That's an interesting thing to do, boy.'

Sigtrygg snarled. 'He was working against me.'

'It sounds like you have everything in order,' his father said.

'I do,' Sigtrygg asserted. Ragnall didn't speak for several seconds but stared at him, black eyes searching his face.

'What?' Sigtrygg demanded. 'What do you want from me?'

Ragnall merely sniffed and turned back to looking out the window. 'I don't want anything from you, boy. I wonder if you want something from me.'

Sigtrygg couldn't believe his ears. He had been away from the city and his father's care for most of his adult life. Had he needed his father to rise from a mere boy at the oar to captain a ship of warriors? Had he needed his father to storm the walls of Dun Domhnall? He certainly had not needed Ragnall to inflict the defeats upon the invading Liathgall. No, he had done it all himself. He always had. Sigtrygg chewed on his bearded lip as his fury threatened to explode. 'I am the Konungr of Veðrarfjord. I don't want anything from you, Ragnall.'

'And yet here you stand, boy, come before me like a poet in need of work. Showing off your great works to prove to me that you are worth a position and some pay.' Ragnall's eyes bored into him and he chortled at Sigtrygg's stuttering attempt to respond to his insult.

'I don't need anything from anyone,' he finally managed, 'especially not from you. I have already taken everything of yours that's of value.'

Ragnall turned back to looking out of the window.

Sigtrygg could take no more. He bellowed incoherently and dragged his axe from his belt. Ragnall's wife screamed as Sigtrygg stalked over to her husband and grabbed him by his thin shoulder, thumping him up against the wall of the tower and holding him in place with a large hand pressed on his chest. He could feel Ragnall's heart beating hard beneath his shirt. His father's expression didn't change even as he raised the axe. It remained locked in the same toad-like, stretched, hostile look that it always did.

'Stay,' his father hissed.

For a moment Sigtrygg thought Ragnall was addressing him. However, his black eyes were looking across the room at his woman. They soon returned to meet Sigtrygg's. Several seconds passed with the axe still poised above them, ready to strike. It was only when the sound of feet stomping on the stairs came through the door that Sigtrygg released his grip on Ragnall's chest and stepped back.

'Stay here and rot then, you old horror,' he told his father as Amlaith came through the door with a long dagger ready in his hand.

'Is everything all right, Sigtrygg?'

'Yes,' he replied through his teeth. 'Get my bodyguard ready to go back to the west wall.' He hadn't taken his eyes off Ragnall. 'I have a war to win.' He turned on his heel and pushed past Amlaith, throwing the key to his father's jail to his ship-master. 'Make sure he keeps the windows open.'

'Wait,' Sigtrygg heard Ragnall call as his feet alighted upon the top step. He did not turn but paused on the stairs. He could smell the old rotting timber somewhere below. He could hear seagulls walking around on the roof of the tower.

'What is it?' he demanded. Sigtrygg could hear Ragnall's light footsteps as he crossed the room to the doorway.

'Don't forget,' his father said. 'My boys need their mother.'

Sigtrygg could feel his fury return. His knuckles turned to white as he clenched his fingers around the smooth ash haft of his axe. With effort he kept his anger from surfacing and pushed the weapon into his belt. He continued down the stairs without turning. His father's cackle followed him all the way to the bottom.

Disorder reigned. Despairing cries echoed around the Norman camp. The noise came from the dying and the wounded, and combined with the frightened and angry voices of those who had survived the escalade unscathed. They bellowed for help. They called for order. The smell of blood and vomit hung like a cloud around the hillside.

From Dreigiau's back Raymond could see some Cistercian brothers from Tyndyrn Abbey amongst the crowd. Their white robes were already covered in pink and red as they attended to the injured. Many led their patients in prayer as they worked, grunting with effort, their heads down rather than facing up towards the heavens. Armed with linen strips and wine skins, Raymond could see that the churchmen would soon be overcome as more injured men struggled back into camp. He could already smell cauterised flesh.

Raymond could feel Dreigiau's uneasiness at the sights and odours that surrounded him. He dismounted and soothed his courser with a pat on his sweaty neck. Raymond turned towards William de Vale.

'The horses are terrified. Take them up to the hilltop. Find them some shade and some water.'

Raymond could see the billowing dust cloud thrown up from the remains of Irishtown. He could see the dry soil flung into the air as hundreds of men fled back through the fields in his direction. He could hear the Ostmen's victory songs.

'William?' he asked when he received no answer to his orders. He looked towards his pale-faced miles.

'I can't believe that the Ostmen defeated our attack,' William replied. 'How could they win? Lord Strongbow has a thousand men!'

'Did you hear what I said?'

The young man nodded his head and got down from the saddle, taking Raymond's reins and adding Alice's to his grip. For once he had no argument to Raymond's commands and clicked his tongue to get the three horses moving in the direction of the hillock to the west.

'What now?' Alice asked as she joined Raymond.

Raymond's brow furrowed. 'We find the earl.'

'Where?'

The tented camp was already full of armed men and Raymond spun around to see if he could catch any sign. Wild eyes shone above dull grey armour as Raymond and Alice walked through the crowd searching for news of the earl. One man said that Strongbow had been killed, another that he had seen him fighting with the Ostman king. A Fleming was certain that the earl had helped him with a ladder, but could not rightly say what had become of him after they had made it back to camp. Hundreds of men had retreated from the walls of

Veðrarfjord and were gathering up on the hillside. A war of words had broken out near to Raymond and Alice. Punches and accusations were thrown before more men waded in, whether to intervene or to add their fists to the fight Raymond could not tell. The shouting raged just the same and his view was blocked by a bolting horse.

'Get him out of here,' Raymond called to the rider.

'This is chaos,' Alice appealed as they were brought to a halt by the press of men.

Raymond had never been around so many people. He had been to the city of Gloucester on several occasions for Strongbow and once it had been market day. He and Borard had been late getting down to the corn market and the streets had already been packed with people. They had been young men, warriors no less, with a decade of instruction and training in hand-to-hand combat, but it was all for naught in the crush in the marketplace. They had been jostled and separated and Borard had been pickpocketed. Raymond was reminded of that day, of the squeeze of the enemy warriors between the double fortifications of Dun Domhnall, the thunderous noise as the cattle had stampeded over the packed ranks of Gaels. He reached out and grabbed Alice's arm, hauling her out of the press and between two tents.

'Sir?' an esquire asked. He and two other boys were already snuggled in the gap out of the press of warriors. The boy was pale and Alice knelt down at his side.

'Let me see,' she demanded. The esquire shook his head and turned his shoulder, but Alice insisted and he grudgingly produced his left hand. Alice delicately unwound the strip of cloth around the esquire's fingers. The boy gasped in pain and looked to Raymond for help.

'Alice?'

She pulled the bandage away to reveal that the esquire was missing two digits. Blood poured from the stumps and the esquire grasped at the tent at his back to stop him from collapsing.

'Go on without me,' Alice shouted to Raymond. 'Find Strongbow.' She helped the esquire to his feet and scolded his companions for not insisting that he seek medical help from the

Cistercians.

Raymond nodded. 'Be careful and find William after you get the boy some help.' He waited for the trio of esquires to follow Alice into the traffic and took stock. The Norman camp had been built on a little plateau. To the east, less than half a mile away was the walls of the city. He spied the roof of the little fortified longhouse amongst the tents and decided to make his way there. The flow of men was coming in the opposite direction and so Raymond vaulted the guy ropes holding up the tents and joined another snaking column of warriors as they passed through the camp. Edging through the people, he finally was able to make a break for open countryside. He could see the river and the ridge of land running parallel with it on the far bank. He was so fixated on getting his bearings that he caught his foot on the last guy rope and fell flat on his face on the ground.

'Damn it all,' he grumbled. Despite the punishing sun which had made all the other ground hard, his hand had disappeared into loose soil. He could feel something soft and cold under his fingers and, as he lifted his body weight above the long grass, he suddenly caught glimpse of what was beneath his hand. He jerked his body away and wiped his hand on his shirt. Grimacing, he climbed to his feet and looked down to confirm that he had inadvertently stuck his hand into a grave. The body was barely a few inches below the surface and his impact had uncovered the man's face. He quickly scooped up a scattering of earth to conceal the grave again. Standing straight, Raymond realised that it was not an isolated burial. He quickly counted eighteen mounds on the hillside. The realisation that what he had seen had not been Strongbow's opening attack on the city, but his second, hit home. If Strongbow had suffered the same number of casualties as were in the graves during second reversal it was a high toll. He cleaned the loose dirt from his shirt and trousers and continued on his way past the line of tents and a mound of horse muck towards the longhouse.

As with the camp, the area around the thatched building was packed with people. Three milites were guarding the opening in the twisted wattle fence, denying the angry soldiers entry. The barrier was effective in keeping out men still exhausted from battle and encumbered with mail, but Raymond was neither armoured nor weary. He quickly hauled himself over and into the longhouse compound. The building was little more than a barn and was made of twisted branches and daub. He could see where a store of farming implements had once hung and a little pen for pigs stood empty. A small covered area had a sprinkling of grain and a place for a millstone. The base was still in place but the runner stone had been removed by the former occupants of the homestead.

Despite the din from the army circling the longhouse, Raymond could hear raised voices inside and he moved around the side to the door at the rear of the building. He quietly pulled it open and glanced into the darkness beyond. He stepped inside to find that he was in the head of the house's sleeping quarters. There was a large chest at the foot of the sleeping bench and on the wall was a mail hauberk. His head bumped into two rabbits hanging from the rafters. A wattle screen divided the little bedroom from the living quarters beyond and he carefully plotted a course between the wine skins and other foodstuffs that had been stored there. Raymond could see light coming through the little gaps in the screen from the main south-facing doorway. Closing the door at his back, he moved closer. He could see that a figure was seated in a high-backed chair placed against the other side of the screen. There were many voices all speaking at the same time beyond and without being able to see the speakers Raymond found it difficult to ascertain what was being said. Using his fingers he pulled one strand of willow down and then the one above upwards so that he could see out. The light coming through the far doorway made it difficult, but he could see ten men on the benches around the edge of the room. More were perched on the cold hearth in the middle. As his eyes adjusted he could see that those in the middle were pages, there only to serve the adults.

'Good people,' Raymond heard Strongbow appeal from his left. It was his lord who was seated in the chair. 'Good people, please!'

No one in the room was listening to the earl. They were arguing amongst themselves. One threw an accusation of cowardice across the room, something Raymond thought utterly scurrilous until he heard Sir Hervey de Montmorency attempt a rasped answer to the indictment.

'Good people, please!'

Raymond turned back into the room and picked up a skin of wine and several carved wooden cups. Taking a deep breath he pushed through the screen door and into the longhouse living quarters. Out of the corner of his eye he saw Strongbow jump at his sudden appearance and the others in the room quietened down too. Several reached for their swords, Sir Hervey de Montmorency among them.

Raymond offered the cups to the pages seated on the hearth. 'Give one to your masters please, lads,' he told them and plonked the skin in the arms of the oldest boy. 'I am sure you are all parched from your brave endeavours today,' he said loudly to the warriors. 'Lord Strongbow? I expect that you would like to get this conference started while your men are served?'

'Good God, Raymond, I thought you were a damned Dane,' Strongbow exclaimed into the brief silence that followed as his barons accepted and drank the wine that was offered around.

Raymond looked down. With his cache of weapons about his belt and lacking armour, he fancied he did look little different to the enemy. He was also unshaven from his many days raiding. 'I apologise for startling you all.' He bowed and backed away towards the wall. 'Please continue, my Lord.'

Strongbow sent an annoyed look in Raymond's direction before turning to the gathered warriors in the room. 'Good people, we must discuss what our next step -'

'The enemy are ready to break,' Sir Hervey interceded. 'My plan is working. We need only attack again as we have done and we shall roll over their defences. We must send another wave against their walls as soon as possible.'

'You said the same thing this morning,' another man announced. He was wearing a blue and yellow surcoat, but Raymond did not recognise him. 'You said the same thing before our first attack on the city.' A number of voices declared their support for the man.

Sir Hervey snarled back at the man. 'If your men had just

250

done their jobs, Sir Robert, then -'

'Uncle!' Strongbow barked. He waited for the undercurrent of disaffection to quiet before speaking again. 'I know that every man who scaled the ladders did his part to the very best of his ability. The question is how do we make the next attempt a success?'

Raymond opened his mouth to speak, but his voice was lost amongst the four other opinions that were offered at the same time. When they could not get their view across to the earl the barons turned on each other again, shouting for their comrades to be quiet. Their competing voices quickly descended into argument. Raymond crossed to the page with the wineskin and sent him around a second time to fill the barons' cups. As the noise in the room quelled, Strongbow was able to make his voice heard.

'Jean, how many men do you think we lost today?'

'Using all our ladders was a sensible change, since it meant that more of our men could get within range of the enemy,' Jean de Clahull replied, sending a malicious look in Sir Hervey's direction. 'But of course that also meant that more men were within range of their weapons too.'

Raymond was pleased to see Sir Jean and Richard de Maroine amongst the barons for he knew them to be clear-thinking and steady men. He could also see Sir Ralph de Bloet. He wondered if Ralph would remember him. They had not spoken since the day three years before when Dreigiau had headbutted the Lord of Raglan and run off.

Jean de Clahull continued with his assessment. 'We lost nearly twenty milites in yesterday's attack and maybe the same to injury. I think that we will have lost the same, if not more, upon their walls today.' Jean paused and Raymond could hear the disconcerting intake of air from the other warlords. 'If you want my opinion, the crossbowmen were deployed too close to the wall -'

'You agreed to that, the same as everyone else did,' Sir Hervey responded. A very large, bald old man shouted his support of Strongbow's uncle.

'I'm afraid that whatever tactics Sir Hervey comes up with for the next attack, my bowmen will only be able to play a small part.' The speaker was a thin man and he stepped into the middle of the room. He was wearing a short gambeson and chape, and had an empty bag for crossbow bolts at his hip. His French was accented like a Fleming. 'We are down to our last ten quarrels.'

The man's statement proved enough to bring the room to silence.

'It's time to try our luck attacking the main gates,' a voice rang out. 'We'll break it down with a battering ram.'

Another scoffed at that plan. 'No! We'll set fire to the buildings outside the north wall. They'll not be able to defend them if they are burning.'

Raymond could see Strongbow appealing for quiet again as the room was again overcome with arguments and opposing strategies. Just as Raymond drew breath to shout for quiet, a loud whistle sounded from the doorway. All eyes turned to see Milo de Cogan step inside. Raymond's cousin looked disdainfully at each man and jumped up onto the hearth at the far end of the room to Strongbow.

'Whatever you decide can keep for a few moments, my Lord. *King* Sigtrygg of Veðrarfjord has sent an emissary to treat with you.' A hush descended upon the gathered barons.

'An emissary?' Strongbow looked at his hands. 'What could he possibly have to say?'

'I don't know, Lord. But I had to stop Adam de la Roche's men from killing him as he came up the hill.' Milo sniffed. 'I could always let them finish the job?'

'No, no. Bring him in,' Strongbow stated before turning to the barons. 'Not a word about our plans to resume the attack.'

Raymond watched Sir Hervey cross the room to stand by his nephew's arm. Sir Hervey's bony fingers rested on Strongbow's shoulder as the barons took their seats on the sleeping benches. There was little enough space and so Raymond lounged by the wall. He could hear warriors' booing and jeers outside the longhouse, presumably caused by the approach of Sigtrygg's emissary. The man appeared as a dark shadow in the doorway, with Milo and an interpreter by his side. The sun was behind them and it wasn't until they entered the shade of the longhouse that Raymond realised that he knew the emissary. It was Jarl Háimar.

A murmur of discontent began amongst the barons as Milo unceremoniously directed the two men towards Strongbow. Háimar led the way, glancing nervously at the rows of fighting men to either side. Raymond could see his earrings and distinctive tattooed arms.

'Welcome, sir,' Strongbow stated as he climbed to his feet to greet his visitor.

As the two men exchanged pleasantries, Milo came across to stand beside Raymond. 'When the hell did you get here?' he asked, giving his cousin a comforting grip to the upper arm.

'A few minutes ago,' Raymond whispered. 'How are you?'

'Bloody starving – I hope you brought some grub?'

Raymond nodded.

'St Peter's beard, but that is good news. The Ostmen refuse to budge from atop the wall and let me in to find their stores. Several have tried to hit me with their axes! Not the sort of welcome I was expecting.'

'How rude of them,' Raymond joked. 'It's almost like they don't want you inside their city.'

A cough and annoyed look from Strongbow brought their short reunion to a close. The interpreter was delivering Jarl Háimar's opening salvo and all in the longhouse listened intently to his heavily accented translation. The man started by demanding that Strongbow retreat from Ostman territory to await a conference of bishops and brehons which would oversee the disagreement between the two peoples.

'Not bloody likely,' Milo scoffed before another stern expression from Strongbow got him to be quiet.

'Veðrarfjord has been sovereign territory since the days of St Anselm of Aosta when, as Archbishop of Canterbury, he consecrated this ground and rewarded the good people of the city with a bishop to oversee their spiritual needs,' the interpreter said. 'An assault on her walls is an assault on Holy Mother Church herself.'

Strongbow held up a hand to interrupt the man. 'I have heard that, in the days of Pope Adrian, King Henry was commanded to bring the Irish church back into the loving arms of Rome. They had, according to him, fallen from the path and required help to return to the true course. I would imagine that your people recognise the pre-eminence of the papal throne over that of Canterbury?'

Raymond watched Jarl Háimar as he listened to his interpreter's words. His face screwed up as he attempted to untangle Strongbow's response and formulate his own.

'In any event, you should withdraw to Wales and then send your own bishops back to begin negotiations.'

'They are just trying to stall for time,' one man called. His view was supported by a number of shouts from the barons.

Sir Hervey added his backing. 'Get him out of here. He's talking nothing but -'

'Uncle, please!' Strongbow stood and called for calm. 'We will not retreat and we shall not relent in our campaign,' he told Jarl Háimar. 'If your king is ready to capitulate I will give him until sundown to present his terms for the surrender of the city.' He turned to Sir Hervey who scowled before reluctantly nodding his head.

Jarl Háimar waited for the translation before giving Strongbow a surprised look and then bursting into a short, sarcastic laugh. Raymond could see that the earl was upset by the response.

'The walls of Veðrarfjord have proven a climb too high for you. Have you not lost enough men to our blades?' the translator asked. 'Have Ostmen axes not made enough widows? I will bring your offer to King Sigtrygg and will return with his answer before darkness falls, but I have already been told to advise you to go home with your lives, if not your honour, intact. King Sigtrygg promises that he will not attack you as you go back to your ships. And as a token of good faith he will even send you ten fat pigs from his vast stores to feed your starving warriors.' Somehow the monotone delivery by the translator made Jarl Háimar's words all the more difficult to hear. Raymond could see several of the barons dip their heads and adjust in their seats.

He turned towards Strongbow. The earl looked old and worry-worn. It had only been a few months since Raymond had seen him last but to his eye Strongbow's hair looked greyer, his face more lined, and his long body thinner.

Although he had been told by Alice and William that the army required his cattle, he had not truly understood the depth of that need. Strongbow's army was starving? Raymond could not believe it, but as he looked around the room he saw telltale signs of hunger. Robert FitzBernard was holding his arms across his chest as if it was a winter's day rather than the middle of summer. He stole a glance at Milo's face. He was pale and his eyes were sunken in his head. He imagined that if the barons were suffering, it would only be worse for the milites, archers, and esquires. Raymond cursed his vanity for he had never really considered that Strongbow would need his cattle so desperately. Alice had warned him, but he had dismissed it, concerning himself only with the perceived insult to his dignity. Truly, he had acted no better than a cowhand.

Strongbow was still being assailed by Jarl Háimar's mockery. His polite attempts to intercede were ignored by the Ostman and his translator.

'Fiodh-Ard Liag,' Raymond said suddenly. He hoped that he had said the name of Háimar's manor house correctly but it seemed to garner no response. 'Fiodh-Ard Liag,' he said again, much more loudly. The translator had stopped speaking and every eye in the longhouse had turned in Raymond's direction. 'It's your home, yes?'

There was a brief exchange between Háimar and his companion before the translator spoke again.

'Yes, it is Háimar's home. How do you know it?'

'Because I'm the man who burned it down.' Raymond could see the anger on Háimar's face as the man made the translation. Raymond didn't wait for a response but stepped towards the jarl, causing both men to make an involuntary step backwards. 'You won't remember since you spent the whole encounter flat on your back, but I was the man who smashed down your gates and burned your hall to the ground. Raymond de Carew is my name. I wanted to tell you that I have only just arrived in camp, but just as I did at Fiodh-Ard Liag, I will find a way into Veðrarfjord.' The translator began to reply but Raymond raised his voice so that only his could be heard. 'You should tell your King Sigtrygg that too. I hear that he has been telling all your folk that he killed me during the fight for Dun

255

Domhnall.' Raymond raised his hands. 'Well here I am, alive and ready to meet him again. Tell him that, Háimar. Tell him Raymond le Gros is coming for him.'

Jarl Háimar looked to Strongbow and then to Sir Hervey. The interpreter still babbled in his ear until the Ostman told him to be quiet. Raymond wondered what was going on in Háimar's mind. Did he recognise Raymond's name? He was the victor of Dun Domhnall after all and had beaten back the might of Veðrarfjord. The jarl might even have been part of that army. Perhaps Háimar even had the intelligence to realise that if Raymond had burned down his home then he had done it in union with Jarl Gufraid. Sigtrygg would certainly fear Gufraid's knowledge of the city. He would fear his desire for retribution.

'My Lord,' Raymond announced, glancing at the translator. 'I must ask for your permission to depart the camp. I promised that I would deliver a hundred and thirty head of the finest cattle in Ireland and it is past overdue that I lived up to that pledge.' He could see the hungry glances of the barons as he paused, waiting for Háimar's interpreter to catch up. 'There will be enough beef to feed your army for a few weeks and to give strength back into our warriors' sword arms.'

'You have my permission,' Strongbow muttered. 'Of course, you have my permission to go,' he said more forcefully.

Raymond bowed and turned to look at Jarl Háimar. Raymond smiled at him. 'Remember: tell Sigtrygg that I am coming for him,' he said and made for the door. Raymond smiled for an enemy unbalanced was an enemy ready to fall.

Alice of Abergavenny accepted the skin of water from Brother Charles. The cool liquid sloshed down her dry throat. She spluttered and handed the skin to the esquire. Without thinking he reached out with his injured left hand and howled in pain as he knocked the bandaged stumps of his fingers against the skin.

'You will be fine,' the Hospitaller Chaplain said and smiled. 'There are far worse off than you, my boy. Perhaps holding a shield might be a little more difficult from now on, but with a little bit of practice you will get it.'

The esquire winced and nodded his head. 'Yes, Brother Charles. Thank you for helping me.'

The old Hospitaller took the water from the boy and splashed it over his bare and bloody forearms. 'Off with you, then,' he told the esquire. 'And tell your lord that you will not be able to use that hand for at least two weeks. Keep it clean!' he added as the boy walked off.

'Yes, Brother Charles.' He nodded once at Alice before disappearing into the crowd.

'He should never have been anywhere near the top of the ladder. It's a hard lesson to learn for a boy as young as he is,' she said. The Hospitaller Chaplain was one of three from his order who had agreed to cross to Ireland with Strongbow. They, alongside the Cistercians, had made an infirmary of sorts on the southern slope on the outskirts of the camp. He wiped his hands on his brown robes, close to the cross above his heart. 'Hard lessons are lasting lessons,' he told Alice. 'If Our Lord made one mistake in His creation of mankind it was giving boys too thick a skull. I am certain he meant it to be difficult for the Devil to get through and manipulate a young man's soul,' he frowned, 'but it also makes it nigh impossible for good sense from mortal man to penetrate to their brains too.'

Alice smiled. 'It should not stop you from trying.'

'The only reason that I know the lessons is because I was exactly the same and had to learn them for myself.' He wore a heavy white cloth turban around his head and, looking over both shoulders, he lifted the corner. He was missing an ear and a large scar followed the line of his chin to the crown of his head. 'A bloody great Saracen did that to me at Damascus. I should've died. I didn't, thank all the saints, but my desire to wield a sword did.' He took a deep breath and closed his eyes. A cry from the far end of the tented infirmary pulled him out of his moment of rest.

'I must go,' he told Alice. 'You did the right thing in bringing the boy to me. If you should come across any more like him please do the same. Some are so knuckle-headed that they will wait until rot has set in before coming to receive care. You seem to have a knack for getting through to them. Use it!' he shouted over his shoulder as he walked away.

Alice nodded her head, but did not reply. More people were being helped into the infirmary, coming between the tents from all directions. She could see blood on the white canvas and, as she looked down, she could see blood on the grass beneath her feet. Men called for help. Men screeched for their mothers. Men simply moaned in delirium. People surrounded her. The smell was unbelievable. A set of legs thumped painfully across her back and Alice turned to complain. She managed to stop herself for, as she looked up, she saw that it was Asclettin FitzEustace. As he turned she saw that he cradled Dafydd FitzHywell in his arms.

'I need someone,' Asclettin bellowed.

At his back was Denis d'Auton. 'We have an injured man here.' Even as Alice turned away she knew that Denis had seen her. 'Alice?' he called. There was nowhere for her to go and Denis grabbed her by the wrist. 'You must help! It is Dafydd.'

Alice had no chance to protest and no choice but to follow as Denis dragged her towards Asclettin, who still carried Dafydd in his arms. Dafydd was the youngest of the milites, only a year older than William de Vale, only a little bit older than Alice, but he was already a large man, and heavily muscled from years of training with the conrois. She could see that his face and lips were blue and that he was struggling to breathe. His fingers clawed at Asclettin's collar.

'Find me a place to set him down,' Asclettin demanded. He was covered in sweat and blood and his whole body was shaking.

'Have you carried him the whole way from Veðrarfjord?' she asked. One angry and desperate look from Asclettin shut her up. 'Just set him down there.'

Asclettin all but collapsed under Dafydd's weight.

'We need to get his armour off,' Alice told Denis as Asclettin crawled from underneath their friend. 'And keep these people back. We don't want him trampled.'

The improvised infirmary was becoming overwhelmed with wounded men who milled around between the Cistercians' tents. While Asclettin kept the crowd away, Alice and Denis removed Dafydd's helmet and coif. His eyes were rolling in his head as he fought for a breath and he reached out with his hands, gesturing that he couldn't breathe. Alice could already see blood on the links in the middle of his chest.

'God damn it all,' Denis shouted as he failed to tug the mail hauberk from Dafydd's back in one go. 'Hold on!' he shouted and pulled the young miles into a sitting position. 'Grab his arms,' he ordered. Alice grabbed and lifted but it was only when Asclettin came to help that they manoeuvred the mail from his back. By the time they had him on his back again, Dafydd was unconscious. Pink froth was bubbling at his mouth.

'I don't know what more I can do,' she told Denis. 'There is a Brother-Chaplain of the Order of St John, Brother Charles. I must find him.' She climbed to her feet. 'Get his gambeson undone. I will return with help.'

Alice skipped nimbly between the people waiting for medical help. She passed more men in as poor condition as Dafydd. Others she passed had wounds that she imagined, if treated soon, would heal up quickly. She felt frustration arise that no one was organising the entry to the infirmary, sending those with minor injuries away so that those like Dafydd could be treated first.

'Brother Charles?' she cried as she reached the area where she had last seen the monk. Everywhere were people. She saw a flash of Cistercian white robe and considered abandoning her search for the Hospitaller and dragging the monk to look after Dafydd. As she turned, she caught sight of his distinctive turban and jinked between two milites to stand at his side. 'Brother Charles?'

The monk was part of a team working on another man. Three warriors held their friend still as Brother Charles extracted an arrow from the man's shoulder. He smiled at Alice and then grimaced as he dragged the barbed end of the projectile out of the wound. In his hand was a bloody knife used for opening the wound to extract the arrow.

'Do you have wine?' he asked one of the men who were assisting him.

The miles looked confused but called to an esquire standing nearby. The boy produced a small flask from his belt. Brother Charles took a swig and then poured some the remaining

259

contents onto his patient's shoulder. The man screamed in agony but the Hospitaller took no notice, splashing more of the wine onto the wound.

'Do you have thread, a needle?' Brother Charles asked of the esquire. The boy looked to the older men for support. Receiving none he nodded his head. 'Then you can close the wound. Keep it clean and dry,' he added, hoisting himself on his knee and patting the terrified boy on the shoulder. 'You wanted me?' he said, turning towards Alice.

She indicated back into the crowd of men. 'There is a friend, a miles. He is badly injured. He needs your help.'

Brother Charles glanced in both directions where wounded men were lying awaiting his assistance. He sighed and nodded. 'Lead on.'

Together, they pushed through the crowd in the direction of Denis and Asclettin, Alice out in front and Brother Charles just behind. Hands clasped at Alice, appealing for help. Angry voices demanded attention. Everyone fought for space. She spotted Asclettin first and could immediately tell that they were too late. The proud warrior was slumped at Dafydd's side with his head down. Denis stood over them both, haranguing a Fleming who seemed to have no idea what transgression had offended the miles so.

Alice pointed and Brother Charles knelt at the miles's side, delicately taking Asclettin's hands away from Dafydd. Denis had opened his gambeson and Alice caught sight of the inch-long stab wound in Dafydd's chest. The Hospitaller placed his face near Dafydd's and then put a hand above his heart.

'I'm sorry,' he told Asclettin. 'It is too late.' Brother Charles lifted his chin towards the sky and placed a hand on the cross upon his chest. He said a short prayer over the miles. 'He is with God now and his worries are over,' he said in Alice's direction. 'I must go. There are more wounded.' He climbed to his feet and took a pace away before stopping. 'I could use some assistance,' he said as he turned.

Alice looked at Asclettin and Denis, expecting them to answer Brother Charles' request. Both men kept their heads down and Alice turned to find that the Hospitaller was addressing her. 'What can I do?' she asked.

'One of a hundred tasks, I would wager. And I can imagine you might think of a hundred more which I have not considered.'

Alice opened her mouth. Her first impulse was to refuse. No voice emerged. She did not have time to perform menial tasks for the Hospitaller, cleaning wounds and mopping up excrement and blood. She had to be on hand to advise Raymond. He would certainly fail to regain Strongbow's favour if she was not there to give him counsel. And, she thought, what did she know about working in such a place as the infirmary? It was dirty and there seemed to be no order at all. In her opinion Raymond's Welsh archers' governed their cattle train better than Brother Charles did his hospital! No, Alice thought, it wouldn't suit her at all. And yet she couldn't bring herself to decline his offer outright.

'Would I have to take Holy Orders?'

Brother Charles snorted a laugh. 'We are not like the Cistercians. We have seen the good works of lay sisters,' he told her. 'We understand the contribution that you could make.'

Alice suddenly felt her breath leave her chest and she turned away from the Hospitaller to stop him seeing tears appear at the corners of her eyes. 'I'm sorry,' she said. She blinked her eyes and forced air down into her lungs to compose herself. She had no idea what had caused the overwhelming reaction.

'If you change your mind, you know where to find us,' Brother Charles said, misreading her words. 'I am so sorry about your friend. Go with God,' he added and stepped back into the press of men which milled around them.

Alice opened her mouth to speak but paused long enough for his white turban disappear. She turned back to Asclettin and Denis. They had already lifted Dafydd's body and were carrying it away through the crowd. Dafydd's head hung limply to the side as Denis hoisted him under the armpits. They hadn't even thought to say goodbye to her. At her feet she discovered Dafydd's armour and weapons, left behind by the milites.

'Denis,' she called but the noise of the army drowned out her shout. Despairing of all men and their carelessness, she knelt and hefted all of the items into her arms. They were so heavy that she almost fell on her face amongst the legs of the warriors in the infirmary. Alice managed to right herself and stumbled towards a gap between two tents. She gasped in relief as she allowed the mail armour to drop to the ground. Dafydd's gambeson was still covered in blood but she imagined that a soak would soon remove most of the discolouration. The damage to the linen would require a seamstress's skill, but Alice knew that such women would've accompanied the army from Wales and wouldn't cost that much to employ. Turning over the hauberk, she found the tiny corresponding hole in the mail rings. It seemed absurd to her that the tiny damage caused to the rings of steel could have led to the wound that Dafydd had sustained. She was able to poke a single digit through and wondered if it would even be necessary to mend the damage. A smith would be costly and she imagined that the chance of another weapon strike hitting the same point would be very small.

'It's not my decision, of course,' she muttered.

Alice waited for a few minutes for either Denis or Asclettin to return to retrieve their fallen comrade's armour, but neither they nor anyone else from the conrois appeared. She didn't think leaving the expensive armour unattended was a clever idea, however, she was beginning to worry that Raymond and William might be awaiting her return, or could be searching the camp for her. She did not want to leave the infirmary without making sure that Dafydd's possessions were in the right hands. She tarried a few minutes longer before making her decision. She put Dafydd's weapons belt over her shoulder and then hung the bloody gambeson around her neck. That load was heavy enough, but she could barely straighten up after picking up his hauberk. Alice had only moved a few steps when the coif spilled out of her arms and onto the ground. Having rescued the headgear and got moving again, she found her path blocked by guy ropes and in trying to traverse them, she dropped Dafydd's helmet.

'For goodness' sake,' she exclaimed and dumped the lot on the ground. A page was staring at her from the entrance to a tent opposite and she scolded the boy, telling him that he should get back to work before she tanned his hide. Having divested some of her frustrations in the page's direction, she stared down at the bundle of steel and linen. Alice again considered abandoning the armour between the tents. It was Denis and Asclettin's fault for leaving it behind after all. It wasn't her responsibility.

Sighing, Alice lifted the heavy gambeson and pushed her arms into the sleeves. It was a warm afternoon, but she could immediately feel the extra warmth. The garment stank of Dafydd's sweat. Blood crusted and flaked on the chest, but Alice ignored it and fixed the weapons belt over her shoulder so that it would not disrupt her stride. The spangenhelm went on her head and then, bracing herself, she heaved the hauberk and coif around her neck.

The walk to the meeting place up on the hill to the west was excruciating. The plateau on which the camp had been built fell away into a little glen with a river at the bottom. She crawled up the far bank and then began the long walk up the grassy hillside to where she could see the three horses eating grass. There was no sign of William or Raymond until her progress was noticed by the horses. Then their heads appeared at the treeline where they had been sitting in the shade. Thankfully, despite her load, they recognised that it was her and came downhill with the three coursers to meet her. Alice was breathing hard and threw Dafydd's armour from her shoulders. The spangenhelm followed.

'Are you all right?' Raymond asked as he reined in. 'We were getting worried that something might have happened.'

'I'm fine,' Alice replied, swiping the sweat from her brow.

'What are you wearing?' William asked. 'Have you decided to become a soldier?'

Alice did not answer William's joke and instead gave Raymond a look that he understood.

'William, be quiet. Alice?'

She quickly told them what she had seen at the infirmary and why she was wearing the blood-covered armour. 'I'm so sorry,' she told both men when she finished her tale. William had walked a little way off while Raymond stared at the ground where Alice had dropped Dafydd's gear. For many minutes neither spoke.

'That bloody fool,' Raymond said suddenly. His outburst

startled both Dreigiau and Alice.

'Who?'

'Sir Hervey. A lady's maid would have a better idea about how to conduct a siege than him. I lay Dafydd's death completely at his feet. William!' he snapped. 'Pick up his armour and we shall see it goes to a good man who can avenge poor Dafydd.' With that Raymond climbed back into the saddle.

'What are you going to do?' she asked with trepidation obvious in her voice. Raymond's bearing was angry, understandably so, but Alice was worried that he might be considering doing something in response to Dafydd's death.

Raymond turned his irate eyes on her. 'What I want to do is to find Sir Hervey de Montmorency and beat his head into a pulp. But that won't do any good, will it? So we are going back to the island. We will get the cattle and we shall get Caradog and Gufraid and we shall return here.' With that he clipped his heels to Dreigiau's side and began walking his horse southwards.

William crossed to Alice and handed her Rufus's reins. He knelt and picked up the mail armour and spangenhelm, quickly strapping them to his saddle. He paused as he lifted the gambeson, gaping at the extent of the blood on its front.

'He didn't suffer,' Alice lied. 'He was already unconscious by the time Asclettin and Denis got him to the infirmary.' William scowled and crammed the garment into one of his saddlebags. 'I'll carry his weapons,' Alice continued, looping Dafydd's swordbelt over her shoulder again.

'Thanks,' William muttered before clambering up onto his mare's back. He looked downhill to see how far away Raymond was and, adjudging him to be beyond earshot, William turned back towards Alice. There were tears in his eyes. 'He may not say it, but I will. Dafydd's death is your fault. If it weren't for you we would've been fighting alongside the conrois, not off leading a cattle train like bloody serfs. If it weren't for you, Raymond would've been part of the war council and able to tell Strongbow how to mount a proper escalade rather than have him listen to Sir Hervey.' He breathed deeply. 'And if Strongbow hadn't listened to Sir

264

Hervey then Dafydd would still be alive.' William did not wait for Alice to defend herself, but kicked his mare into a canter.

Alice could not believe William's words and it took her a few moments to collect her thoughts and climb onto Rufus's back. She thought that she would want to chase him down and force him to apologise to her, but there was a distinct absence of righteous anger. The gelding seemed to sense her distress and stamped his hooves on the dry earth. 'It's all right,' she whispered in his ear, squeezing her knees to prompt him to follow the other horses. 'We all say these things when we're sad.'

Raymond led them south without going near the camp. As they passed the stone-walled fields several of the horses stabled within whinnied and spluttered a welcome, but Raymond did not stop. Nor did Alice close the gap on William. She could see that he also stayed behind Raymond though the ridge of land that they followed was easily wide enough for them to ride side-by-side. They crossed the little river and then the marsh without incident. The only time that they spoke was when Raymond greeted the scouts who had taken his advice and posted sentries at the crossing.

'We'll be back before dark,' he told them. 'We'll have cattle. Keep your eyes open for us.'

Raymond steered them north and east again, always uphill, towards the little hill which hid the Siúire and the island from view. Rather than descend down to the river and follow its meandering course back to the island, he led them in a more direct route, around the shoulder of the hill. Alice could've done with a rest after an hour's riding but she held her tongue and steeled her body to continue. It was only late afternoon and she knew that they would have enough evening sunshine to get the cattle across the small straits and then back to Veðrarfjord. The thought of more riding did not appeal to her but she forced the impending exertions from her mind. They had entered some woods as they descended towards the island. It was a pleasant little grove of low-hanging oak and beech and Alice was lulled by the buzzing bugs and satisfying smells from wildflowers. The trees caused Raymond to slow down and Alice to close on her companions. None of the trio exchanged words. The only sound came from the tinkle of tack and the thud of hooves on dry ground. Rufus' nose almost touched the swishing tail of William's mare.

'Stop!'

Raymond's sudden whispered warning dragged Alice from her daydream just in time to stop her crashing into William de Vale's horse. Both men climbed down from their saddles. Alice looked in the direction of Raymond's intent gaze, but could see nothing through the heavy foliage. She copied her companions and dismounted.

'Where?' William hissed.

Raymond raised his left hand and gestured through the trees. 'Quarter of a mile.'

'What is it?' Alice asked.

Raymond did not answer but beckoned for Alice and William to join him. 'Alice, keep the horses quiet. William, you'll come with me,' he told the miles. 'Quick and quiet.' Raymond did not wait for agreement but dropped his reins and ran forward at a crouch, disappearing into the trees. William followed and Alice listened as the sound of their movement intermingled and then were lost to those of the woods.

'Easy,' she told William's mare as she took a few steps to follow her rider. Dreigiau stamped his feet in impatience. Alice trained her ears but could hear nothing that would've caused Raymond to stop. Wait! She had heard something. They were voices; many hundreds of voices, and the clip of hooves. Alice licked her lips. She pictured an Ostman army just like the one which had attacked Dun Domhnall for the sound was far greater than that which Caradog and Gufraid's men could make. She imagined the cruel axes of the men of Veðrarfjord and the savage cry of the Gaels. A cow cried out somewhere ahead. It was a long moan of distress. The enemy had discovered the cattle train, she thought, and had attacked the island. She pictured Dafydd bleeding on the grass. She saw her brother's murder again.

Alice rolled the leather reins around in her sweaty hand. She was not tired any longer. Fear coursed through her stomach like a cold drink on a warm day. She could hear the sound of feet running towards her, the scattering of leaves as a person

266

smashed through the woods at high pace. Alice backed between Rufus and Dreigiau, stifling a squeal. She wanted to call Raymond's name but she held her tongue. Instead she pulled a long dagger from Dafydd's swordbelt. Alice took a deep breath and waited as the footfalls came closer.

She gasped in relief as William de Vale emerged from the trees. 'Come quick,' he said, grabbing the reins attached to his mare and Dreigiau, hauling them back in the direction from where he had appeared. 'You've got to see. You are not going to believe it!' William was smiling, his angry words at the camp seemingly forgotten.

'What is it?' Alice demanded as she fumbled with the dagger, trying to return it to the small scabbard at her spine.

'Come on,' William replied unhelpfully as he again vanished into the trees.

Alice called for him to wait, but he did not reply. She took up Rufus's reins and led him through the trees. The black gelding followed happily, trotting alongside her with his ears twitching like little owls on his head. Through the gaps in the trees Alice kept catching and losing sight of William. The uneven terrain meant that she continually had to look down to stop her from falling over and Rufus wasn't helping her to stay upright. He was excited and kept bumping into her as they ran downhill.

'Careful!' she told her horse and eased him to a walk.

Ahead she could see the brown flow of the river and, without the noise from the rushing wind, she could hear more voices; happy voices. More, she could hear the jangle of armour and the sound of horses and cattle. She emerged from the trees close to where they had swum across the straits earlier that day. William de Vale and Raymond were part of a large group of men standing on the shore. Other than William and Raymond each man was covered from head to toe in armour. Nearby a large group of esquires saw to their coursers and weapons. Alice didn't recognise any of the men.

As she walked closer she saw one man, the only one other than Raymond and William to be not clothed in steel, detach and walk towards her. Alice's hand went to her mouth in shock.

'How are you here?' she mumbled. 'How are you here?'

'It is a very long story,' Father Nicholas said with a smile, 'but one which I can tell you on the way.'

'On the way?'

Nicholas looked confused and pointed his arm westwards. 'With them.'

Alice turned in the direction he indicated where, over the trampled marsh and muddy beach, she saw an army on the move. 'Who are they?' she asked. 'Where are we going?'

'Back to Veðrarfjord of course,' Father Nicholas replied. 'As to who they are,' he smiled and placed his hands on his hips, 'why, they are my army.'

Chapter Seven

The archers cheered as the last calf attempted to haul itself out of the stream. He was only a few months old and he clung to the bank, his legs quivering and grinding at the loose soil and weeds for purchase. He brayed once, but the rest of the herd was making such a racket that it drowned out his plea for his mother's help. Finally his kicking feet propelled him upwards away from the marsh and onto the firm ground above. He galloped uphill to join the rest of the herd. Raymond felt a slap across his shoulders and turned to see that Caradog had caught up.

'Thank God the job is done. I think my boys deserve a right good rest after it,' the archer captain said.

'You deserve more than that, but at the moment I have very little to offer,' Raymond replied. 'Not even the promise of rest. Be patient and I will get them their reward, however.'

Caradog laughed and stepped into the stream which reached to his waist. 'The boys are well fed. So it's already better here than back home.' He looked past Raymond into the depth of the marshland. His whistle was sharp and sudden. 'Get them moving, Bryn,' he shouted. 'We're almost there.'

A shout in the Cymric language came in return and Raymond moved aside as the band of a hundred and fifty archers marched past him on the sloppy, hoof-marked path left by the cattle. The men laughed and chatted, all their possessions slung at their sides next to their arrow bags. One or two nodded their heads towards Raymond. How Father Nicholas had accomplished the feat, Raymond still could not comprehend, but together with Caradog's man, Bryn, the good-mannered priest had managed to persuade some of the Welsh March's finest killers to band together and cross the sea to Ireland. They came from Gwent and Brycheiniog. They came from Ystrad Tywi and from Powys Wenwynwyn. They came

269

from far and wide with little else other than their bows. They were outlaws and murderers, sheep-rustlers and mercenaries. Most were fleeing Norman justice or Cymric clan law. And now they were part of Father Nicholas's warband.

Raymond could see the priest riding at the back of the column. At his side were Alice of Abergavenny and Philip, who the Welshmen had appointed as leader of their motley band. If that wasn't impressive enough for a man of his age, Caradog had even accepted Philip's seniority over him and his company of archers.

'You hear tales about Philip. Bad tales,' Caradog had described. 'He made mayhem in Powys, Cheshire and Shropshire. Best let him lead your archers for I don't want any of his sort of trouble. He seems happy for you to be their captain and they are saying that Father Nicholas is the only man who can control Philip the Welshman.'

Despite the failing evening light, Raymond spotted Philip's vast bulk in the midst of the archers. He was dark of hair and dark of nature. His eyes were close together and there seemed to be little to no gap between the fringe of his cropped hair and his beard which grew high up on his cheekbones. Raymond nodded his head in Philip's direction and the Welshman returned the gesture as he marched past. He could already hear the sound of men wading into the little stream.

Behind the archers came Jarl Gufraid and his forty Ostmen. They were quieter than the Welsh bowmen, their shoulders more slumped. They were not marching to war with the same hopes as their allies. They had no wish for plunder or conquest. For them Veðrarfjord was home, or at least a refuge when one was required. It was a place they had only ever thought to protect and none had ever considered that they would be attacking her walls. Raymond could imagine the battle taking place in their hearts since they had spotted the city over the marsh. Gufraid and his son Blácaire were at the front of their unit. Both had a stern look on their faces. A crop of spears hung above their men who were also cloaked in steel, wool and leather. The warrior Grím stood out because of his purple shirt and grey beard. He wore a white chape over his shoulders and long leather greaves on his forearms and grimaced as he passed by. Raymond didn't react but internally he prayed that the Ostmen would do their part as Gufraid had promised.

The sight of the last contingent made the smile return to Raymond's face. They were the smallest in number, not even thirty strong, but each was on horseback. At their head was his brother, Griffin de Carew. He was only twenty-two years old but was still the eldest of all the horsemen who had come to Ireland at Father Nicholas's bidding. Griffin took after their father's side of the family and could easily have been mistaken for the twin of the rider alongside him. William FitzMaurice was Raymond and Griffin's first cousin and like his famous father, Maurice FitzGerald, Constable of Pembroke, he was slender and dark-haired, with the sleepy-looking eyes and aloof brow. William's younger brother, Gerald FitzMaurice, was a full head shorter than Raymond, who wondered how it was possible that someone so small was able to carry the weight of his weaponry and armour and still fight effectively. Griffin had soothed Raymond's doubts by telling him that there was no warrior in Wales more valiant than Gerald *Bach* and that he was not to worry.

'But for God's sake do not let him hear you call him by that nickname,' Griffin had warned.

Behind 'Little Gerald' came William de Vale and Robert de Barri, another of Raymond's kinsmen. Robert had twice been told to go home to his father at Manorbier because he was too young to take ship to Ireland with the men who had conquered Waesfjord. Raymond did not share his uncles' opinion of young Robert's capabilities and had welcomed him with open arms as they marched on Veðrarfjord. The last two milites were Gervais d'Alton and Hostilo d'Angle. Both were steady lances with a number of older brothers and few prospects back in the March of Wales. Raymond knew that they would do well. Right at the back was a large group of esquires, twenty in number, their ponies laden with food and weaponry. Most were fast approaching the end of their apprenticeship and, having secured no offers of employment as milites from amongst the noble houses of Wales, had opted to join the campaign in Ireland rather than beg their families for the funds to travel with all the other landless men to Outremer. Two of William de

271

Vale's younger brothers were amongst the esquires and another two sons of Maurice FitzGerald. They were a young conrois, but they were hungry for glory and if deployed shrewdly, Raymond knew they would be just as effective as the experienced company he had lost to Sir Hervey de Montmorency.

'Griffin,' Raymond called, signalling for his brother to join him. It was still rather awkward between the two of them for though they were brothers and only two years apart in age, they hardly knew each other. Raymond had left Carew when he was seven to become a page at Striguil and had only been back to their family home on a handful of occasions over the ensuing decade and a half. Griffin had remained at Carew and had learned his arms from their father and manners from their mother. While Raymond had toiled away in Strongbow's household Griffin had grown up with the knowledge that he was destined to serve their elder brother, Odo, against the Welsh of Deheubarth. It was a fate that would've made Griffin comfortable, if not rich, for the remainder of his days. And yet he had abandoned Carew to join Raymond in Ireland.

'Brother?' Griffin asked as he pulled his horse alongside Raymond. 'Is everything all right?'

'It is. But we're almost at the camp and I just wanted to, well, we haven't exactly,' Raymond flapped his hands around. 'But I want to make you understand -'

Griffin smiled at Raymond's discomfort. 'Is that what you are doing?'

'What I mean to say is that I'm glad you are here.'

His brother swatted away his admission. 'Don't be silly. I couldn't wait to get away. When Father Nicholas came to Carew I was almost out the door before he had finished speaking.'

'Was there trouble from Father?'

'God, no! It was Odo the *Odious* who was the problem,' Griffin disclosed. 'He tried to stop me taking my horse and arms. Father had to get involved. Then he tried to prevent Alexander and Thomas coming with me,' he added, pointing at two of the esquires as they passed by in the direction of the stream. Raymond and Griffin were quiet as their warband trooped past. 'I hope you are not going to tell me I have annoyed Odo just to come here to herd cattle?'

Raymond felt his back prickle.

'I mean obviously you have duties and you can't just, well, you know,' Griffin attempted after recognising Raymond's discomfort. 'The boys just want to know that we will get to fight, that's all.'

'We'll get to fight,' Raymond said. *I hope we get to fight.* 'We'll let the Welshmen make camp in the meadow. You and I will organise the milites to drive the cattle up to the camp. It's less than a mile along the ridge,' he said pointing over the marsh and trees.

'The enemy will see us,' Griffin commented as he shifted in the saddle to look northwards.

'They will, but only briefly,' Raymond confirmed.

'They won't like that we have delivered more food to sustain the siege.'

'No. I should think not.'

Griffin looked at his brother. 'You are happy to let them know we have all these cattle?'

Raymond nodded. 'Do you remember the stories that Father used to tell us? There was one I always liked about Grandfather when he was Constable of Pembroke -'

'Holy Ghost, but he used to bore me with his long-winded tales. I hardly listened to any of them.'

'You didn't listen to them?' Raymond asked. 'Well I loved them. There was one when half Grandfather's warriors deserted him during the night. Pembroke was under siege by the Welsh and he tricked them into believing that they were well-fed when actually they were starving.'

'I remember that one. He cooked his last few pigs and then threw most of the unfinished carcasses over the wall, licking his fingers and patting his belly.' Griffin barked a laugh.

'The Welsh ran off during the night when they decided that only a garrison with many months of food left would do such a thing.'

'They had no idea that Grandfather was a cunning old bugger. So you'd like to do the same to the Ostmen of Veðrarfjord?'

Raymond nodded. 'In a way. I'm not sure it will cause them to surrender, but you never know.'

Griffin considered the information. 'They could sally out to attack us.'

'I'd be delighted if they came out from behind their walls to have a go. The marshland means the only way they could get to us is to go through Strongbow's camp. Uphill and over open ground? His milites would tear them apart.' Raymond tapped his heels to his courser's sides and pointed him in the direction of the stream. The reeds of the marsh rubbed along Dreigiau's chest as he waded into the water. The little courser hardly paused as he leapt up the opposite bank in one muscular movement and Raymond heard Griffin urge his mare up the bank with a click of his tongue. The trees by the river were mostly alder, but soon they were passing under birches with large chunks of bark missing and coppiced willow trees as the hill climb became steeper. The meadow beyond had, at some point, been cut for hay, but the cattle happily milled around. Both the archers and Ostmen had selected parts of the hillside for their camp and had dropped their equipment in order to claim the best spots.

'Get the milites moving the cattle up onto the ridge,' Raymond told Griffin and kicked Dreigiau into a trot. The Welshmen had taken up the area furthest west and he first called there to tell Philip, Caradog and Bryn of his plans.

'What will we eat?' Philip demanded.

'Send men to select six cows. Make sure to make the meat last,' he warned. 'It's all that you will get until we break into the city.' Raymond left smaller numbers of cattle with Jarl Gufraid's Ostmen and the younger esquires before joining the cattle train for the final part of the journey to Strongbow's camp. He passed the place where Alice and Father Nicholas had unsaddled their horses.

'I won't be sad to see the back of these great lumbering beasts,' he told William de Vale as they cajoled the animals northwards along the ridge. William looked bone-weary and merely nodded his head. Milites and esquires yipped and yelled to keep the cattle moving forward. Below them, the little stream ran parallel to their course, feeding the vast marshland that defended Veðrarfjord's eastern flank. It was still light enough for Raymond to see the mighty River Siúire, but there were already torches burning on the walls of the city and the sight of the enemy fortress quieted his conrois. Some even brought their horses to a halt to stare at the triangular fortifications, imagining, perhaps, how they would fare if ordered to attack them.

'Go on there!' Raymond shouted at the rear of the cattle train. 'Keep them going,' he ordered and whooped again. His cry was not required to keep the cattle train moving but it proved enough to arrest the quiet that had come over the conrois. Most had abandoned their watch and had instead stopped to stare at the vast city in the distance. Raymond's shout had reminded them of their duties and they again clipped their heels to their coursers' sides, trotting up and down the length of the train.

Raymond looked at his long shadow which was cast eastwards down in the direction of the marsh. There was no way that the Ostmen on the wall of Veðrarfjord would not be able to see his men and the long cattle train, although from the perspective of the enemy they would be little more than large shadows. Raymond hoped that each man would see them and understand what it meant: that the Normans would not retreat, that they would soon attack again; and, next time, they would be stronger. A heavy thump of hooves caused him to turn.

'I rode ahead,' Griffin told him. 'If we want to take the most direct route to the camp, we should turn north now.' He dropped his reins to indicate uphill. Raymond lifted his eyes in that direction and could see several strips of smoke indicating the site of Strongbow's base.

'You're right,' Raymond told his brother. 'We've given the Ostmen a good show already. Get up to the front and lead them towards camp,' he ordered. It took a few minutes' more before the cattle train began their ascent towards the plateau and in that time the sun dipped behind the hills to the west.

Raymond could hear the cheering of the warriors in the camp before he saw the first fires and he kicked Dreigiau into a canter. Ahead in the twilight he could see many moving figures. Shadows danced on the sides of linen tents and their celebratory shouting caused the cattle to call in fear and bunch up. Even at a distance, Raymond could see hungry warriors circling in on the herd. More were emerging from tents and walking towards them. For the moment the temperature in the growing crowd was one of relief.

'Raymond, Raymond!' one voice shouted. Several took up his call and more whistled and clapped their hands in support of the captain who had brought the much-needed supplies to their camp.

He ignored the applause and slowed to a trot. 'Keep the cattle moving,' he shouted at his young conrois. Ahead he could see one man already had hold on a calf and was attempting to haul it out of the herd. Raymond tapped his heels to Dreigiau's sides and directed the courser in the direction of the mewing calf. The warrior turned to face Raymond, who slowed to a walk then used his courser's bulk to force the man to let go. The calf immediately ran off to rejoin the cattle train, kicking its back legs.

'What are you doing?' the man demanded. 'I'm only trying to feed my warriors.'

Raymond ignored him and got Dreigiau into a gallop up the line of cattle. 'Keep back,' he called as he drove his courser between them and the animals. As quick as the praise had started, it had descended into jeering and anger. He could see several places where the young milites in his conrois were caught in arguments with Strongbow's soldiers. Resentment flared in both directions.

'Keep them back,' he yelled again. 'Don't stop to discuss if they are hungry. Just keep moving.'

He could already imagine the sort of chaos that could overcome the ravenous army if one man was able to get a cow away. Each would presume his right to the cattle and might fight Raymond's conrois for their cut. They might fight each other to stave off their hunger. More and more men had been drawn out of the tented area to see what the commotion was about. Many were coming down the hillside, afraid that they would miss their chance for beef. His seven milites were too few to keep back the growing crowd. Raymond could see Gerald FitzMaurice already had his sword out and was threatening a group of Flemings. Another had hold of William de Vale's reins, but his miles put the man on his back with a punch to the side of the head. The cattle train had slowed to a walk and it would not be long before it would come to a complete stop.

'Back, you bastards!' he had a familiar voice cry above the dry thump of hooves and suddenly there were horsemen at his side. He turned to see thirty milites with torches in their hands coming downhill. They were led by Milo de Cogan. He sent his fully armoured men to each side of the cattle train, immediately forcing the warriors to back away.

Milo had slowed his courser to a walk. 'I see you there, Gilbert le Breton,' he said as he trotted through the growing crowd his torch high in the air to cast its light as far as possible. 'Don't think I won't remember your face. And Simon de Boode, do you think Sir Richard de Maroine will be happy to hear of your antics this night?' Even in the growing gloom of the evening, Raymond saw Milo's cheerful wink. 'By God, Hugh de Hockley, how did you manage to get down the hillside? I hear you couldn't even get up the ladder yesterday! Yet here you are – the first to react when there is the chance of some grub. I will inform Sir Robert de Bermingham that all he needs do during the next attack is to lob a leg of lamb over the wall and you will be the first man into the city!'

Raymond could've laughed out loud in relief at Milo's intervention. His kinsman continued to prowl around the crowd, announcing the names of those around him and claiming that they were would-be looters and cattle thieves. Under his scrutiny, the crowd began to dissipate and soon the cattle began moving again with the added security of Milo's men alongside his own.

'That almost got out of hand,' Milo stated as he reined in alongside Raymond.

'It did. Thank you, Cousin.'

'No need for that. I'm taking the biggest, fattest cow that you have and eating the whole damn thing by myself. That is my reward.' Milo snarled suddenly and kicked his courser into life. 'Hey! Get away from there,' he roared as he moved on one crossbowman who persisted in trying to make off with a cow.

Raymond could already see the little longhouse where Strongbow was residing and that Milo's men were leading the cattle train in that direction. He urged Dreigiau into a canter and caught up with Milo.

'Can you take command of this lot?'

'Have I not already done that?' Milo flashed a smile and then inclined his head in the direction of the longhouse. 'Get going. Let the earl know that you have done well.'

Raymond nodded and called out for his milites to stay with his cousin. He then asked Dreigiau for one more effort which saw him quickly outstrip the cattle train. One of Strongbow's pages was loafing around outside the longhouse fence and Raymond left his courser with him and pushed past the two sentinels on the gate. Despite the lingering heat of the day, there was a fire in the hearth and as soon as he pushed through the wattle door Raymond could see that he had disturbed another conference of Strongbow's barons. At least twelve men were inside and all eyes turned towards him. He could see Sir Hervey de Montmorency and the earl at the far end of the little longhouse. There were flies buzzing around in the firelight.

'My apologies for the interruption,' he said as the noise in the longhouse subsided. 'I have just returned to camp with the cattle, Lord,' he glanced at Sir Hervey, 'as I promised I would.'

Strongbow looked extremely put out by Raymond's disruptive entrance, but it was his uncle who answered.

'We have more important things to discuss than beasts of the field. We have a siege to conduct,' Sir Hervey said.

Raymond ignored the snort of laughter that came from several men in the room. 'I would normally agree, Lord, but from what I have seen just now, unless you get the cattle out to the men you could have a full-blown rebellion on your hands.'

Sir Hervey guffawed loudly, but one baron nervously climbed to his feet. 'My men have been complaining of hunger for more than a day. I must see to their needs first,' he said in the unmistakable clipped accent of the Flemings of Dyfed. The man bowed and then pushed past Raymond in the direction of the door.

'Well, if Prendergast is not going to be here, then what is the point in anyone staying?' asked Jean de Clahull. Both he and Richard de Maroine got up and made for the exit. Soon all the barons had turned their backs on Strongbow and were withdrawing from the longhouse. They left only Sir Hervey, Raymond and Strongbow beside the hearth on the floor.

'Are your milites not hungry, Sir Hervey?' Raymond asked. 'If they are, I would suggest following the other barons before Milo gives away all the cattle.'

Sir Hervey tarried for a moment. His eyes narrowed to slits as he considered Raymond's words for deceit.

'Go, Uncle,' Strongbow finally said. 'There is little need for you to be here without the other barons.'

'I will be back soon,' he replied and with a final murderous look, Sir Hervey scuttled past Raymond and into the darkness of the night, leaving the door wide open. For several moments neither Strongbow nor Raymond said anything.

'Would you mind?' the earl asked.

Raymond's eyes had drifted to the rafters of the longhouse where two stretched skins had been stored by the former occupants. 'Pardon me, Lord?'

Strongbow gestured over Raymond's shoulder. 'The door. The insects are attracted to the fire.'

'Oh, I see.'

'It is quite difficult enough to sleep in such circumstances without them buzzing around my face all night. Not that it makes much difference since there are so many places for them to get in.' Raymond dragged the doors closed. It was only after he had done it that he realised that the earl meant for him to remain on the far side.

'I suppose our proximity to the marsh doesn't help with the flies.' *Or that shit Sir Hervey*, he thought. 'Or the river,' he said instead. There was another period of quiet between the two men. 'Or because of all the animals,' Raymond suggested.

'What's that?'

'The insects – they would be attracted to the horses.'

Strongbow nodded his head and stared into the hearth.

The silence stretched until Raymond could take it no more. 'How many men have you been able to assemble for your army, Lord?'

The earl's gaze flicked up to meet Raymond's. 'A

279

thousand.'

'That is most impressive. How many are cavalry?'

'Close to two hundred, with almost six hundred esquires and other ranks.' Strongbow returned his eyes to the hearth and shifted uneasily in his chair. 'Maurice de Prendergast has two hundred crossbowmen in his retinue.'

'His is the biggest division?'

As Strongbow mumbled an answer in the affirmative the sound of cattle calls could be heard from outside. 'Shouldn't you be helping Milo?'

'He said that he could handle it.' Raymond ignored the earl's frustrated sigh. 'I wasn't absent from my duty, Lord. When you arrived at Dun Domhnall – I hadn't abandoned my duties. It was quite the opposite in fact.'

'I hear one story from you and another from Sir Hervey. And I have made Sir Hervey commander of this army.' Strongbow raised a hand to stop Raymond's complaint before it began. 'No! He has the most experience of war and battles and sieges. He is my uncle. Sir Hervey is the obvious choice. And when he takes the city I will name him constable.'

Raymond gritted his teeth. 'And if Sir Hervey falls?'

The earl's eyes shot up from the fire again. They were filled with alarm rather than anger. 'You should not think such horrid things about my uncle.' Raymond did not retract his statement but waited for Strongbow to answer. 'In the unhappy event that Sir Hervey is injured command would fall to Milo de Cogan or perhaps Maurice de Prendergast since he has brought the next largest following.' The earl sighed and waved a hand towards the door. 'You really should be out there assisting Milo. You have no reason to be here. The barons will soon return to discuss our tactics for the attack tomorrow. If you are needed, I am sure that Sir Hervey will send his orders to you and your,' his wrist wafted around as he searched for the correct term, 'troop.'

The fireplace crackled and popped between them and Raymond could feel his own temperature rising. He could not believe the change in the earl since they had parted ways in Striguil almost three months before. Back in Wales, Strongbow had relied on Raymond. He had trusted him even when he knew there were risks in following his advice. Having crossed the sea with a handful of men, having defeated his enemies, and delivered his provisions, Raymond had imagined that he would be lauded by the earl, offered positions of power. But instead he found himself sidelined and denigrated. He could not allow the insult to stand! He inhaled and braced himself to deliver a counter to Strongbow's dismissal, but before he could unleash the door opened and two of the barons walked in.

'We shall eat well tonight,' Sir Walter de Ridlesford joked as he slapped Raymond across the shoulders.

'Very well done, young man,' Sir Ralph de Bloet said. 'It's Reynaud, isn't it? I think I remember you from my younger days at Striguil. We used to call you something back then, what was it now?'

'Raymond le Gros.'

'Yes, of course!' Ralph laughed. 'But then you were a very stout young man. And it was all in good fun, was it not, Reynaud? It's not as if you are so stout these days.'

Before Raymond could answer more barons came in having secured their portion of the herd of cattle from Milo for their men. Sir Hervey was right at the back. He called for quiet and Raymond, unnoticed for the moment, sat down amongst them to listen to the attack plan for the next day.

'Before we were so rudely interrupted I was telling you of my plans for the attack tomorrow,' Sir Hervey began. 'The earl agrees with me that we must keep attacking their western defences. The city is ready to fall,' he insisted. There were many groans and derisive replies from amongst the barons. To Raymond's right, Jean de Clahull stood up and indicated for those gathered to listen.

'If you are so certain that the enemy is ready to surrender, perhaps you should lead the attack, Sir Hervey, from the front rank.' Raymond noticed that most in the room laughed sardonically at the suggestion and he found himself chuckling along with them. The longhouse hushed as Strongbow got to his feet.

'That will not be necessary. I will lead the attack again,' he said quietly. He looked like he might say more, but he suddenly sat down again.

'My Lord, our concern is not really who leads but what follows,' Jean replied. 'What reason does Sir Hervey have that his plan will not fail again? What new tactic has he come up with that will let us defeat their advantage of numbers and position?'

All the eyes in the room turned towards Strongbow's uncle. Sir Hervey spluttered as if he thought Jean's question impertinent. 'That buffoon Robert FitzStephen took Waesfjord with half the men we have to deploy. If you want someone to blame for the lack of success I suggest you should look closer to home rather than at my attack plan.'

That caused uproar within the room and it took several minutes for the barons to stop fighting amongst themselves. Raymond stared at Sir Hervey during the argument. He had a look of contentment on his face, for he had deflected the question for which he had no answer and had hidden it beneath the consequent squabble. Every now and again, Sir Hervey would send another gibe into the war of words, causing another front to open up. On his chair Strongbow had his head down, his thumb and forefinger massaged the bridge of his nose.

'We need a diversionary attack,' Raymond stated loudly just as the barons' grumbles abated.

'Who said that?' Sir Hervey demanded. 'Who said it?'

'I did.'

Sir Hervey looked affronted by Raymond's presence. 'Why are you here? Shouldn't you be out mucking out the cows?'

Raymond waited for the few laughs from the barons to die down. 'A diversionary attack,' he stated again. 'Sir Jean asked for a new tactic. Would you agree to a simple diversionary attack?'

Sir Hervey coughed a laugh. 'You proved yourself a dullard at Dun Domhnall and you seem determined to prove that you are one here. Even Sir Jean realises that we cannot afford to have any men missing from the attack on the west wall. The enemy already outnumber us by three to one and you want us to send men off on a hopeless attack? Where would you have them target?' Sir Hervey guffawed. 'One of the great keep towers?'

'If you want the enemy drawn away, then yes, that would

282

work best,' Raymond said before turning his eyes towards Strongbow. 'But of course I am not suggesting that you lose any men from your attack on the west wall, Lord. I will volunteer to lead the diversion and I will only use my men.'

'Your men?' asked Strongbow.

'Yes, Lord.'

'Fifty Welsh bandits,' Sir Hervey interjected, 'led by a man who should never have been permitted to take charge of anything more complicated than digging a privy.'

Raymond did not rise to Sir Hervey's insults but kept looking at Strongbow. 'I actually have two hundred Welsh bandits, Lord, each armed with longbows.' He could feel all the barons' eyes turn towards him, for it was an intimidating number of archers. Most were Marcher lords and had felt the force of the favoured Welsh weapon. Most had learned to fear it. Not even Prendergast's crossbowmen could match the range, speed and accuracy of the bowmen. 'I also have forty Ostmen who know this city better than any man here. They are ready to fight for me, Lord, as long as it means killing Sigtrygg Mac Giolla Mhuire and being permitted to remain in the city under your lordship when the city is won.' He turned to the barons. 'And to lead the diversion, I have eight milites and twenty esquires from amongst my own kin, newly arrived from Wales.' Raymond waited for their rumble of support to build before turning back to face Sir Hervey. 'They will be commanded by me, a man who has actually done his fair share of digging privies. I have never heard one complaint about their quality.' Raymond inclined his head towards Strongbow and then sat down.

Whatever Sir Hervey tried to say in response to Raymond was drowned out by the howl of laughter from the assembled barons. It was only when Strongbow took to his feet and raised his hands that the noise died down.

'Uncle?'

Sir Hervey spun to stare at Strongbow. He was panting and his long, lank hair swung wildly at the nape of his neck. The earl raised his eyebrows inquisitively and sat back down.

'He almost got us killed,' he stammered and raised a finger in Raymond's direction. 'If not for a stroke of luck -'

'We could use a stroke of luck right now,' Sir Richard de Maroine growled, and he got support from Sir Ralph de Bloet.

'Perhaps Sir Hervey is suggesting that we allow Raymond's men to sit out the fight?' Sir Jean added. 'That would be utter folly. For God's sake! He has more men to bring to the fight than I do, more than any of the barons assembled here. We need some new ideas, and if Sir Hervey can't come up with them then I say let Raymond lead this little diversion. It might be the break we need.'

'And it loses us nothing,' Strongbow added. Even the earl seemed surprised by his words. All eyes turned towards him. 'I do not claim to be a great tactician or commander like Sir Hervey. I can climb a ladder and I can swing a sword, but I must leave the tactical decisions to my uncle whose experience of battle dwarfs even that of some of our most proven veterans.' Strongbow raised a hand towards Sir Jean and Sir Richard. 'Yet they think this is a good strategy. Therefore, unless Sir Hervey can suggest some good reason for not trying it, then I will support Raymond.' Strongbow turned his eyes on his uncle and raised his hands expectantly.

'Well, Sir Hervey?' he asked. 'Is there any reason?'

The water came up to his chest and it was bitterly cold. Not as bad as it had been before the sun had risen, but ice still crept to the centre of Raymond's bones. His shirt was sodden and his breath caught in his chest. Rushes and tall wide-leafed plants swayed around him in the dawn light.

Gufraid and Philip the Welshman were just a few paces ahead, but he kept losing sight of them as the thick marsh plants closed behind them like curtains. It was only when he pushed aside the reeds that he again caught a glimpse of his companions. Both men moved slowly, carefully. Both made far less noise than he. Water dripped from Raymond's sodden shirt and his every step seemed to come with a splash. Despite the noise, he did not think the enemy would hear their progress through the marsh. Life teemed amongst the rushes. Lizards and newts and frogs croaked on either side, birds cawed and circled above. All manner of mammals scurried and swam below unseen. Raymond did not like to think of what might swim around in the stale brown water beneath him. Around his face buzzed insects but he had long since grown used to their annoyance. Gufraid had a sword across his shoulders while Philip had brought his bow. Raymond had decided upon a spear and he was glad for it since it doubled as a crutch on the unsure footing.

Raymond supposed that the Ostmen could've drained the vast marshland if they had wished. It certainly did not take any great mind to dig out ditches or build dykes, but it seemed that the people of Veðrarfjord had encouraged the marsh to grow wild and wide. Fed by the little tributary which ran north towards the Siúire, the marshland covered a vast area to the east of the city, an almost insurmountable obstacle for any army trying to storm the walls of Veðrarfjord from that direction. Or so they believed.

Ahead of Raymond, Philip suddenly clicked his tongue and held up his hand, bringing their party to a halt. He was half-hidden by rushes but he indicated that Gufraid and Raymond should crouch lower in the water and come forward. It was only when he reached Philip that Raymond saw just how close to the walls of Veðrarfjord they had come. The fortifications soared skyward, at least three times as tall as a man, just a hundred paces from where they were hidden. There were only a handful of figures – Gaels, judging by their dress and strange haircuts – patrolling the walls. Raymond suspected that two directly opposite were dozing against their spears, but there would be more warriors close by, ready to race to defend the walls in the event of an attack coming from the east.

He reached forward and moved some of the rushes aside so that he could get a better look at the defences. Philip had brought them to a point almost exactly halfway along the wall. Without taking the difficulties in getting his men across the marsh into consideration, on first inspection the city looked unassailable from their position. As with the west, a stone glacis, taller than a man, held up a huge wooden timber rampart. However, the east had the extra protection of a brattice, a covered walkway, hanging from the top of the wall. At the northern point was a vast wooden keep, while directly across from him was a gate with two intimidating guard towers.

285

He could see a muddy stretch of beach running along the bottom of the wall. It would at least give his warriors somewhere almost solid to plant their ladders. Unfortunately it seemed like it would be an almost impossible task to get his ladders through the difficult terrain in the marsh and on to the beach to attempt an escalade. To make matters worse, the Ostmen had opened up the waterway directly underneath the keep to create a large pool where their ships could dock. The pool stretched over half the extent of the wall and if it was deep enough for shipping, he knew it would be too deep for his men to cross. Raymond could see three jetties jutting out into the dark water under the keep.

Gufraid leaned in close to Raymond's ear and pointed over the wide expanse of water in the general direction of the great keep. 'The sally ports are behind those boats.'

Raymond concentrated his eyes on that point. There were three hulking hulls dragged up onto the beach and overturned alongside the keep. Gufraid was convinced that the best course of action was for their little force to traverse the marsh and fight their way onto the beach. Then he suggested that they should run along the length of the wall to attack the sally ports, breaking down the wooden doors with axes and so break into the city. That done, Gufraid's plan was for their little band to fight their way through the streets and storm the keep, Rögnvald's Tower as he called it. Raymond could only just identify two gaps built into the stone glacis, but he could imagine the thick timber and tiny doors that would be built into the stone.

'He who holds Rögnvald's Tower holds Veðrarfjord,' the jarl said for the thirtieth time that morning. 'And we can claim it by getting through those sally ports.'

Raymond did not answer and instead cast his eyes southward, past the eastern gates, along the lower half of the wall. The brattice made it look even more intimidating than the western wall where Strongbow had made his two unsuccessful attempts to storm the city.

'I don't like it,' he mumbled.

If they were to follow Gufraid's plan his men would have to run along the beach for three hundred yards in full armour while the enemy rained down on them with all manner of missiles from the brattice. Then they would have to wait while two axemen smashed their way through the sally ports. He imagined that it would take many minutes for them to break through and it would take even longer for his men to push through the small doors once the axemen had completed their work. Raymond eyed Rögnvald's Tower. It loomed above the sally ports. With no cover and with next to no room to move on the small beach, his men would be easy prey for darts, arrows, spears, and slingers stationed on the brattice or on the tower. Gufraid's plan had seemed an ambitious strategy when he had told him of it in the Norman camp. Now, looking across at the defences, Raymond knew that to attack the sally ports would cost half his men their lives. And after facing that onslaught, they would still have to make their assault on the far greater defences at Rögnvald's Tower through the tight streets of the city.

A long thumb of dry land looped from the southern point of the city out into the marsh. Raymond could see the stumps of many trees which had been hewn down. In their place the Ostmen had pushed sharpened stakes into the ground to slow the progress of anyone hoping to use it to their advantage. He had little doubt that they would've also dug trenches and pits to further hinder any attacker.

'There's a wooden causeway from the gates out to the point on that spur of dry land,' Gufraid whispered when he saw where Raymond was looking. 'We could use it to get close. Then we make a break for the sally ports.'

'It would be a good place for the archers,' Philip confirmed.

Raymond nodded his head, but his gaze had drifted to a large structure built up against the walls on the beach close to the jetties. The city was still shaded by the shadow cast by the rising sun and he had missed it during his first examination of the defences. 'Is that a church?'

Gufraid followed his view. 'It's a warehouse. Visiting merchants lease it from Konungr Ragnall to store their merchandise through the night. Every city has thieves,' he shrugged.

On closer inspection, Raymond could see that Gufraid was

right. Propped up against the side of the warehouse were a number of handcarts. Horses were too heavy to walk on the three jetties and so every bit of cargo had to be moved from sea to land by hand. Raymond spotted a little enclosure built alongside the warehouse. He had imagined that it was for animals, but now he realised that it was most likely designed to house slaves. The thought sickened Raymond and he turned away from the warehouse to stare at the guard towers. However, something nagged at his brain and he quickly glanced back at the building by the waterside. The warehouse was certainly big enough to be a church, or an inn.

'It'll be empty,' Gufraid added as he watched Raymond stare at the warehouse. 'There'll be nothing inside to steal. We can use it as cover while we hack our way through.'

'I thought we were only supposed to be a distraction?' Philip asked. 'Why do we need to attack the sally ports at all?'

Raymond said nothing. He kept his eyes fixed on the warehouse built against the wall. He knew that the taciturn Welshman was right. But he could not drop the idea that he was meant to accomplish more than leading a mere diversion. Success was impossible, he reminded himself. The walls were too high, his men too few, the enemy too many. The marshland and the towers were impediments too great to overcome. Yet still the desire to storm the city remained. Strongbow had basically said that he would award the role of constable to the man who took the city. He had meant his uncle, of course, and Raymond imagined taking that honour away from Sir Hervey. That small revenge would be reward enough, but then there were all the other benefits of controlling the city: tariffs and trading opportunities, a fleet and warriors ready to do his bidding. Holding Veðrarfjord would make him a powerful warlord. Storming her walls would make him famous.

Glory was currency in Raymond's world, and the capture of a city would make the successful captain as wealthy as any great magnate at King Henry's court. Knights and lords around Christendom trained every day for war yet they could go their whole lives without the chance of fighting a battle. Most never did. Yet those who took the chance, fought the war, and emerged victorious were lauded throughout the royal courts of

Europe. Stories would flow down rivers and across seas, over mountains to the furthest reaches of the Christian world. Triumph in battle could give a man position, it could give him power. It would certainly give him prestige in his lifetime and could make him immortal in the eyes of those who heard the tales of his prowess. Victory could turn a younger son of a defeated knight from the Welsh Marches into a great baron and warlord. It might even allow him to change the fate of a disgraced earl. It could allow him to claim a kingdom.

Raymond pictured what it would be like to cut his way over the defences, enemy warriors tumbling away from his sword. He imagined what it would be like to defeat Sigtrygg in single combat; he visualised raising Strongbow's standard over Rögnvald's Tower. Why could he not dismiss the notion for the damn fool idea it was?

'Yes,' he told Philip with a disappointed sigh. 'We're only a diversion.'

'Then all we need do is get my archers out onto that spur,' the Welshman said. 'We can spray arrows on the defences and your lads can pretend to attack the gates. That'll draw the enemy to us. Then, when Strongbow breaks in through the west, we can withdraw and follow him over the walls. There will be plenty of plunder to go around.'

'No!' Gufraid replied so loudly that both Raymond and Philip hissed at him to lower his voice lest he be heard be the sentries on the wall. 'We can get to the sally ports and smash our way through,' he insisted. 'It is the only way.'

Since Raymond had helped him rescue his three sons, Gufraid had been a totally different character to the indecisive man he had discovered with his people in the Black Mountains. He had taken control of the cattle train, overseen their camp on the island, and now he wished to lead the attack on Veðrarfjord. Raymond could feel his determination to do it his way. He could understand that desire. To most of his people he would be seen as a traitor, but Gufraid wanted to be seen as their saviour, the man who killed the usurper Sigtrygg and ejected the trespassing Déisi. He wanted to be the man who put Ragnall back on the throne. He wanted it so badly that he had dismissed all the dangers that his plan would entail.

'We are attacking the sally ports,' Gufraid said.

Raymond could hear in his voice that there would be no changing the jarl's mind. Instead he gazed at the defences, urging his mind to find the part of the wall that had some weakness that he could exploit, some weakness that would help sway his ally from a forlorn attack. Raymond could not stop his eyes from being drawn back towards the warehouse on the muddy beach beside the jetties. It wasn't exactly a crowning achievement of building, but Raymond's eyes refused to be diverted away from the structure. It was big, two floors high with the first made from stone. He could imagine that the wattle and daub walls above the stone would be as thick as those of a castle, for no visiting merchant would place his goods inside a building where a man armed with a sharp axe might cut his way in during the night. Raymond could see that the King of Veðrarfjord had been stopped from making the ground floor bigger by the lack of space for people to pass by on the beach. Instead he had extended the first floor of the warehouse outwards, balancing the parts that projected out upon massive timber posts sunk deep into the unstable ground. But Ragnall had not stopped there. He had even utilised the place between the two sloping sides of the tiled roof. A doorway had been cut through the gable end to allow extra storage space there. Above the door there protruded a large beam, wrapped in ropes and with a large pulley at the end, to assist the slaves to winch bundles of merchandise to the upper floors.

'All right, we will make for the sally ports,' he told the two men. 'Philip's archers will cover us from the spur. Agreed?'

The Welshman nodded. 'I think you are mad to try it, but we shall do our part.'

'We shall not fail,' Gufraid said as he locked his eyes on Raymond. 'By nightfall we shall hold the city. And I will have killed my enemy.'

The Norman captain made no response. He merely nodded his head. 'Let's get back to camp. We have many arrangements to make before the attack begins.' Gufraid nodded and plunged back into the reeds with Philip on his heels.

Raymond waited for them to disappear before allowing a

sigh to escape. He looked back at the defences and knew that there would be no hope of his men breaking through. No matter what he had told Gufraid, theirs would merely be a diversionary attack. Whatever glory there was to be won would be on the west wall with Strongbow. With one final stare, he waded back through the marshland.

'Holy Lord, help us today as we enter into enemy territory,' the priest extolled. 'We face a wicked army led by a prince of darkness. We seek only to enter his realm armed with the gospel of the lost, forearmed with the sword of righteousness. Rise up, Almighty God! We are but lambs amongst the wolves …'

Strongbow opened his eyes and glanced at the men standing either side of him. They didn't seem to him to be mere sheep. In fact their grey armour seemed much more akin to the pelt of wolves than it did sheep's wool. Above the men, the banners of the barons and knights lolled and flipped like ravenous dogs' tongues. Their spear tips shone like fangs in the early afternoon sunshine.

'We are assured in our belief that even the demons of this barbaric people are subject to you, Lord Jesus,' the priest continued to howl towards the sky from his position on the cart, 'and that no army can prevail without your divine authority. Sanction us, Lord of Heaven, to take the Holy Gospel into this kingdom of darkness. You defeated the enemy on the cross – grant us now that same strength and protect us from the sway of Satan as we go about your good acts! In the name of the Sovereign King of Kings and the Lord of Lords' name, Jesus Christ, we pray.'

Some of the lesser men, towards the bottom of the hillside, had yet to receive the Blessed Sacraments from the priests and canons who passed among the army. The priest waited expectantly until the last of them had been treated to the blessing of God and he received a signal that he could finish the rites.

'Amen,' the priest called.

Most men in the army had only a few words of Latin, but each repeated the last word and then climbed from their knees to their feet. They were absolved of their sins. Should they now fall in battle, their souls would be safe. Many had tears in their eyes as their captains and barons called for them to make ready for the escalade.

The priest had climbed down from the cart and was walking away towards the tents that Strongbow had given over to his use. His deacons and canons followed, singing a sad lament which the earl recognised as one of King David's psalms: '*Lord, tear open the sky and come down,*' they sang. '*Touch the mountains so they will smoke. Send the lightning and scatter my enemies. Shoot your arrows and force them away.*'

Strongbow listened to their words and found that his legs refused to allow him to stand. They were quaking beneath him. All around him men were readying for battle, and he could not get up for fear of crumpling to the ground.

'*He protects me like a strong, walled city, and he loves me.*' The song drifted over Strongbow and he clutched his hands together so tightly that they turned bone-white. '*He is my defender and my Saviour, my shield and my protection.*'

'He is my defender and my Saviour, my shield and my protection,' Strongbow repeated again and again. 'St Peter, hear my words. Guard me today and I will build a great church, just as you have done, to the glory of God. And if you cannot shelter me, grant me passage into God's grace this day.' Strongbow pictured his mother and could feel tears at the sides of his eyes. He cuffed them away. All around him he could hear the sounds of men readying for battle. He could hear mail shimmering as milites slipped their hauberks over their heads, the rasp of whetstone upon blade. Strongbow kept his eyes firmly shut, his head bowed. An image of his father, angry and large, loomed across his mind in gold and red. The earl squeezed his eyelids tighter, urging the vision of Gilbert de Clare, his father, the first bearer of the name Strongbow, to fade.

'St Michael, tip your scales in my favour,' he whimpered. 'Grant me victory and I will bestow your church with great riches. I will pay the brothers to sing for the souls of the fallen for all time in your name. Help me overcome the battle that rages within, Holy Archangel, for I carry both the sin of pride and the sin of fear. Help me to use my desires for good, for God's glory, and to find my faith in the protection of your angelic wings.' Strongbow paused as his stomach rumbled in hunger. He had fasted through the night and the morning and he prayed that the soldier-saint would see his suffering a grant him a steady hand as he went into battle against the Ostmen. Around him horns began to blare and the sergeants and captains began to shout. Strongbow could hear the stomp of hundreds of feet, the rattle of weaponry. 'Grant me the skill to earn his praise,' he appealed. 'Make me worthy of the name of Strongbow.'

The earl turned his eyes heavenwards. His view of the sky was concealed by a banner bearing his family arms. It whipped about in the small wind like an excited dog's tail.

'Amen,' Strongbow whispered.

Taking a deep breath, the earl climbed to his feet. He was wobbly at first, but a hand on the thick pole which held the banner allowed him to steady his feet. He closed his eyes and dragged another lungful of air down into his body. He felt strength flow to his arms and legs again.

'I must do my part,' he whispered and turned to look downhill towards the walls of Veðrarfjord. The army was already moving in the direction of the walls under the orders of his barons. He could see the lines of milites, esquires, crossbowmen and infantry as they juddered forward. Despite the awkwardness of the ladders, they were already within three hundred paces of the wall. Even up on the hillside Strongbow could hear the enemy's chants of defiance, their songs of war. The breath caught in the earl's chest as he watched them plough forward into the burnt-out town outside the walls.

'Lord, should we move out? Sir Hervey has given the signal.'

Strongbow waved a hand at Gilbert Borard. He and the rest of Sir Hervey's conrois were waiting for the earl as they had been commanded. The milites and thirty esquires would be his bodyguard as he once again took to the ladders. He could see Christian de Moleyns, Amaury de Lyvet, and Hugh Cantwell, who had joined with their party again. The conrois were eager to join the attack, of that Strongbow was sure, for Asclettin

FitzEustace and Denis d'Auton already had the ladder spanned between their shoulders. Both men stared expectantly at him.

'A moment, if you please,' the earl called across to Borard, signalling for his esquire to bring his last few pieces of armour forward. The boy helped him with the padded cap and then to put on his mail coif. His hands shook slightly as he slotted the mail mittens on, but his esquire was sensible enough to make no mention of it. As Michael disappeared to get more of his equipment, Strongbow heard one of the conrois sigh in frustration and complain to Borard about the delay. The earl said nothing, for he could understand the milites' desire to get to the wall. Raymond de Carew had mentioned that they had lost a man during the second assault. Strongbow searched his mind for the warrior's name, but it was lost amongst the mountain that had stacked before his eyes over the last weeks.

'Michael, hurry up!' Strongbow shouted towards the tents, sending an apologetic smile towards the milites that still waited for him to prepare. If all had gone well, Raymond would soon been launching his diversionary attack. Strongbow concentrated his eyes on the far wall of the city, but he could see no sign of any trouble over the thatched roofs of Veðrarfjord. He could hear bells ringing to warn of the impending attack.

His esquire soon came running, his arms laden with shield and weapons. The boy dropped all of the implements on the ground beside Strongbow before rummaging amongst them and pulling his surcoat from the pile. Michael gave it a shake to remove the bits of grass and dust. As it billowed briefly in the air the golden field shone like the sun, its three crimson chevrons pointing directly towards the city of Veðrarfjord. The deep blue band at the top lined up perfectly with the Ostman fortifications and for a moment Strongbow was transported back to his youth, to the last time he had seen his father wearing those same colours. He had been eleven or thereabouts, and had been told to hold his father's helm while his mother had made her tearful farewell. His father had been bound for the north to fight the rebels with King Stephen, he recalled, and had attempted to ease his mother's worries by telling her that he was one of the few veterans of an actual battle in the army.

'It'll be a siege in any event,' his father had told Lady Pembroke. 'They'll make terms and we'll come home. The last thing anyone wants is for actual fighting to happen.'

He had then turned towards his son and had snatched the spangenhelm from his arms. Strongbow remembered quaking in his boots as his father had turned his face on him.

'No snivelling,' he had said, putting a finger underneath his chin. 'You are the lord and master now, Richard.' And then he was gone, leaving Strongbow standing with his weeping mother and sisters.

'Lord?'

Strongbow smiled and dipped his head as if in deference to his family's arms and allowed Michael to place the surcoat over his head. It felt heavy on his shoulders, far weightier than the mail. The esquire secured it to his middle with his swordbelt.

'Three bloody days of fighting and he still hasn't figured out how long it takes to dress,' he heard Asclettin moan. Several of the milites croaked their agreement until Borard snarled for them to save their energy.

Strongbow might have said something, but he marvelled at the bravery of the milites and wished he possessed half their nerve. He had always been in awe of fighting men like his father and remembered every story of their courageous actions. He recalled the tale of the action at Exmes, and of the defeat at Lincoln, and of, of …

He paused. Strongbow suddenly realised that his father had only really fought two battles in his entire life. Two! He had been mauled at Exmes and he had run away from Lincoln. The man that he had so feared had only ever fought two engagements? Could that be correct?

Strongbow recalled his father's words: 'The last thing anyone wants is for fighting to happen.'

The earl raised his hand and could feel that the shake had stopped. He placed it on the pommel of his sword. He thought back to those first days after his father had died, when he had succeeded as earl. He had been so intimidated by his father's milites and knights, of their great deeds, and for years had deferred to their experience over his own judgment. For decades those warriors had dined out on their battle stories. He had never comprehended that they had been just that: battle stories – one battle and many, many stories. They had raided churches and they had ransacked the homes of serfs, yes, but not one of them had braved the dangers that he and his army had, Strongbow realised. His army was about to make their third attempt on the walls in as many days. His father and his famed warriors hadn't fought as many battles in their entire lives! He doubted that any man in Henry's kingdom had. Strongbow squared his shoulders and raised his chin.

'Michael? My helm, if you please.'

His esquire handed Strongbow the spangenhelm and he slotted it onto his head. He was ready for battle. Strongbow stared at the walls of Veðrarfjord. The first line of attackers was less than fifty paces from the walls, passing through the burnt Irishtown. The dust cloud began rising again as their feet marched across the fire-scorched earth. He could see that the defenders' barrage of missiles had begun. So had the screaming.

'Touch the mountains so they will smoke. Send the lightning and scatter my enemies. Shoot your arrows and force them away,' Strongbow murmured. In seconds the ladders would be against the walls, his warriors would be climbing, the Ostmen fighting back. Strongbow knew that he had to be among them. His army had to see that he was fighting. He turned towards the conrois and drew breath to order them forward. However, as he did so, he heard a warning shout from his side.

'Master!'

It was his esquire, Michael de Barnewell, who had cried out with such terror in his voice that Strongbow turned in his direction.

'Michael?'

The boy had his finger pointed northwards to the great tower by the riverside. Strongbow stared in the direction Michael gestured and for several moments he could not breathe. All his hopes, all his dreams, would soon be in tatters, he perceived. For Sigtrygg of Veðrarfjord had sprung a trap. It would soon close around Strongbow's army.

Sigtrygg watched the Normans come forward. He wanted them to come. Twice the enemy had attacked the west wall and twice they had been repulsed. This would be their last attempt on his city. His Ostmen would hold them, just as they had done so for two days, and this time there would be no retreat back to their camp. This time there would be death. There would not be a fourth assault on Veðrarfjord, Sigtrygg promised.

He gripped the straps on the inside of his circular shield, his axe haft, as the lines of armoured men stomped towards him down the hill. White dust rose around the grey clothed men as they passed over the burned fields and Sigtrygg could feel his heart thud in his chest. At his back he could feel the light breeze coming up the Siúire Valley, could hear the sag and sway of the charging boar-banner at his back as it rolled around on the cross-pole. He could feel vibrations on the timbers of the barbican as men moved about on the west wall. It was hot. He knew the day would get hotter still.

Sigtrygg looked to his right. Jarl Háimar had command of Thorgest's Tower and the most northern part of the wall. Sigtrygg could see his flags with his crossed swords. The jarl was up on the tower, staring out at the approaching army and Sigtrygg raised his axe, waiting until Háimar returned the gesture. He then turned his eyes southwards to the part of the wall which Máel Sechlainn Ua Fhaolain's Déisi had held for the previous two days. Jarl Orm's blue longship banners now festooned the wall, dangling over the side near the lower gates. He was too distant to see the man from Áth Skipir, but he knew that the young jarl would do his part.

Five hundred sons of Veðrarfjord would face down the might of the invading Liathgall. But it would be Konungr Sigtrygg who would have the glory. It would be his name that would ring out in the songs of the people of the city. Nothing that Ragnall had accomplished in his long life had come close to this triumph, Sigtrygg knew. His reign as king would begin with victory. Glory would last his whole life.

'Victory!' he bellowed and raised his arms in the air. It was his crewmen from *River-Wolf* who first took up his cry, but soon every Ostman warrior was screaming. Some shouted blasphemy, some for the help of Holy Saint Olav. He could hear the name of Veðrarfjord being roared at the Normans. He could feel the stomp of feet on timber palisade. He could hear the crash of spear shafts on the back of shields. Hands drummed on the outside of the defences, pipes whined madly and horns blared flatly. Most of the warriors shouted profanities or simply issued blood-curdling incomprehensible screeches in the direction of the invaders.

'Victory!' Sigtrygg shouted as he left his place on the wall and began stomping up and down the wall, urging his warriors to battle frenzy. He pumped his axe in the air. 'Victory!' he thundered.

The enemy had entered the remains of Irishtown. They were close enough for Sigtrygg to see the ladders and crossbows in their hands. The roar of defiance from his people ached in his ears. He could see the few archers in his army had begun their bombardment of the Normans, shooting at the slow moving lines from wherever they could find a gap. Sigtrygg licked his lips and held his breath in expectancy. During the first attack, this was when the storm of quarrels had fallen on his men, killing at least a hundred before his folk could even respond. The second attack had been different. The crossbowmen had closed to within fifty paces of the wall and had shot over the heads of the warriors on the ladders as they had climbed, taking out anyone who stood to meet the enemy. But no arrow storm came and even those who had anticipated a spray of bolts were back on their feet, their songs reaching a crescendo as the enemy came within thirty paces of the walls. Then the few arrows coming from the defences were joined by a cloud of spears and darts hurled at the advancing Normans. The barrage was completed by bricks and stones and pieces of wood and sharpened bones taken from dead cattle. Sigtrygg was sure that he saw a stool fly through the air towards the enemy.

It did not stop their advance. The second line of Normans merged with the first and together they pushed forward, their leaf-shaped shields high in the air to defend them from the falling debris. They were soon within twenty feet and Sigtrygg took a deep breath. He grabbed his banner from where it was fixed to the walkway and began waving it in the air. Up on Thorgest's Tower he saw Jarl Háimar's hand rise into the air in answer to his signal. Seconds later his banners began waving and Sigtrygg spotted a Gael emerge from the base of the tower. He began running along the northern wall towards the east to deliver Sigtrygg's message.

Sigtrygg smiled and handed his banner to a nearby warrior. 'That stays in the air. It must be seen. Is that understood?' The man nodded and Sigtrygg returned to his spot on the wall to meet the attack. As he arrived the top of a ladder swung upwards to land just to his left. Sigtrygg felt its impact with the outside of the rampart and glanced over to see a Norman climbing towards him.

'Stone!' he called and held out his hands for a block which his men had collected just for this moment.

A young man hefted the large stone, as big as a head, and tried to carry it to his king. The weight of the block was such that the man struggled to cross to where Sigtrygg stood.

'Stone!' Sigtrygg demanded again as he set down his shield. He stole another glance. The Norman was halfway up the ladder.

'Stone,' he cried as the young man finally offloaded the rock into his arms.

Sigtrygg inhaled as he hoisted the block above his head and crossed to the defences. He had only just cleared the top of the wall when a crossbow bolt glanced off the rock and high into the air. Its force was so great that it put Sigtrygg off balance and he dropped the stone over his back. It smashed through the timbers of the walkway before disappearing through the thatch of a house built beneath the wall. 'They have crossbowmen on the ladders,' he bellowed as he peeked over the rampart. The first man on the wall was calmly reloading a crossbow as he hung just a matter of a few arm-lengths away.

'Beware arrows,' he called in warning.

Sigtrygg cursed and crossed to the pile of rocks. Selecting the biggest, he heaved it onto his shoulder and went back to the point above the crossbowman. Despite the awkwardness of his position, Sigtrygg could see that he had spanned the weapon and had a quarrel in his hand. He knew that the lightly armed man would soon be able to shoot again. He sniffed down a breath and raised the rock upwards. His arms shook with the effort and Sigtrygg roared as he rolled his shoulders forward, releasing the block so that it dropped directly downwards. His momentum made him stumble and he clung onto the spiked timbers, staring over the wall as the stone fell towards the crossbowman. The block did not strike the man, but it had the same effect as if it had. The weight of the stone was such that it crashed through one of the rails of the ladder, splintering it and making the crossbowman tumble fully twenty feet onto the ground below. Two men behind him disappeared as the remaining rail spun and then collapsed under their joint weight.

'It rains hard in Ireland!' Sigtrygg cried to the crowd gathering at the foot of the wall. He snorted a laugh as he watched the fallen crossbowman writhe about in pain. However, a glance to his left and right told him that he alone seemed to have dealt with the crossbowmen on the ladders. Everywhere else there were Normans already at the top, stabbing at his men with spears, swinging with swords or shooting their crossbows. Sigtrygg stepped back as another ladder slammed into the rampart in place of the fallen one. This time a fully armoured warrior came first with a crossbowman just behind, his weapon ready to shoot. 'Keep fighting,' he shouted as another took his place. 'Victory is near!'

Sigtrygg picked up his shield and began marching up the length of the palisade, bellowing encouragement to his folk as he walked towards Thorgest's Tower. 'Keep fighting them.'

The door to the tower was open and Sigtrygg made it up the winding stair in several large bounds. He emerged onto the flat roof of the tower and spotted Jarl Háimar above the west wall, casting rocks and wooden beams down into the Normans below. Sigtrygg ignored him and moved across to the part of the tower which overlooked the River Siúire. The northern defences seemed empty of warriors, but Sigtrygg didn't flinch at the sight. Instead he leaned over the rampart and stared down at the Merchant's Quay. With the sun in the south, the quayside was cloaked in shadow and in that darkness there lurked an army. Sigtrygg smiled. There were at least two hundred hidden on the Merchant's Quay and he could see more running along the length of the wall to gather for the attack.

Searching amongst the front line, Sigtrygg finally spotted Toirdelbach Ua Fhaolain's distinctive long hair with its shaved sides. He waved to the Déisi chieftain and indicated that he was to wait for his signal to charge. Sigtrygg crossed back to Jarl Háimar and his small party on the far side.

'Get your men to stop throwing,' he ordered.

Háimar turned with a confused look on his face. 'Stop throwing? It is the only thing keeping the foreign bastards from getting over the wall!' The jarl's face was coated in sweat from his efforts.

'Get your men down on to the wall if you want to fight,' Sigtrygg told him. He didn't wait for an answer but went back to the north side and found Toirdelbach again. The Uí Fhaolain Tánaiste was surrounded by his saffron-clothed derb-fine, his brothers and near kinsmen. Toirdelbach was a cousin of Máel Sechlainn Ua Fhaolain's and his elected successor, but he was no longer satisfied with waiting for his rival to vacate his position as King of the Déisi. He wanted that role for his own. He wanted the security and power of kingship. And he had made a pact with Sigtrygg in order to obtain it. They would defy Máel Sechlainn and bring the fight to the Liathgall outside the walls, and then, once the siege was lifted, Sigtrygg would use the power of Veðrarfjord to depose the King of the Déisi and put Toirdelbach in his place. The price of Sigtrygg's help in that cause would be Toirdelbach's everlasting obedience.

Sigtrygg had watched the Normans during their second attack on the walls. He had seen them throw their entire army at the west wall, almost a thousand men, without thought of defence or retreat. Sigtrygg had seen how, for almost an hour, the vast majority of the enemy had been standing stationary staring upwards as those on the ladders had engaged his Ostmen. Those left on the ground could do little to help other than huddle under cover and await the opportunity to get onto a ladder. None were prepared for attack from any direction other than from above. But Máel Sechlainn was not daring enough to see the opportunity. He wished only to hide behind the walls – Sigtrygg's walls – and wait for the enemy to grind themselves into submission. Where was the glory in that? Worse, Sigtrygg saw treachery in Máel Sechlainn's tactics. Each attack had killed Veðrarfjord folk – almost a hundred on the first day, and more on the second. Yes, there were as many dead amongst the Déisi, but Sigtrygg knew that the Gael could replace their warriors far more quickly than could Veðrarfjord. The city may be able to defeat the Norman threat, but at what cost? Might Máel Sechlainn be purposefully weakening the Ostmen in order to take the city for his own? Toirdelbach had all but confirmed his suspicions during their short conference during the night. There was no one he could trust. He had enemies everywhere. Sigtrygg promised that he would root them out, one by one. Only then could he secure Veðrarfjord and make her great again.

First he had to defeat the Normans and he had to do it quickly. To that end he had told Toirdelbach to take his four hundred warriors from their guard on the north and to use the sally ports below Rögnvald's Tower to leave the fortress. He knew that they could approach the undefended left flank of the Norman army out of sight along the Merchants' Quay. Sigtrygg's Ostmen on the wall would be the block, he had told Toirdelbach, and the Déisi would be the axe. And the time had come for the executioner to swing.

Sigtrygg put both arms in the air and signalled to Toirdelbach. The Gael turned and squawked his orders, raising a spear and a fistful of darts in the air. He did not wait for a response but began running towards Thorgest's Tower, his hair and saffron cloak billowing out as he went. And behind him flocked his people, hundreds of them, following their chieftain into battle. Sigtrygg followed them as they flowed around the base of the circular tower like a great torrent ready to smash into the Norman flank. He urged them on, his hands passing between the timbers as he orbited the top of the tower. They sprang over the flooded ditch which was fed by the river and onto the grass beyond.

'Go, go,' Sigtrygg urged. He was already looking down the length of the west wall, his teeth bared in anticipation of the carnage that the Déisi would wrought. He stared down at the enemy. He could see where they huddled in the fosse and under the wall, in the ash-clothed remains of Irishtown. He could see the flashes of steel where the Normans' bravest warriors battled for command of the wall. Sigtrygg could see an exposed flank of an army. He held his breath as Toirdelbach charged.

The noise from the fight on the wall was lost beneath the screaming attack of the Déisi. They were truly terrifying, even to Sigtrygg up on Thorgest's Tower, as they charged headlong into the packed ranks of the enemy. It was as devastating as the cattle stampede had been during the fight for Dun Domhnall. Toirdelbach was out in front, running down the length of the flooded fosse with the nimble footwork of a dancer. Such was the surprise that no Norman lifted a sword against him. He did not pause but launched his darts at the crowd of men standing around the ladders. His followers copied him and soon there were men toppling onto the ground, men falling from the top of the ladders, and men rolling downhill towards the fosse. But Toirdelbach did not allow the enemy to recover and pointed his spear towards Irishtown. There were hundreds committed to the attack on the defences and hundreds more in the remnants of the settlement outside the walls. Sigtrygg watched on for a few minutes as the Déisi strafed through the buildings, their spears and axes flashing left and right as they ran, their howls echoing dully on the burnt timbers and tumbledown wattle walls. Soon, the cloud of ash kicked up by their feet was too thick for Sigtrygg to see. It banked high in the sky, obscuring his view of everything below him.

But Sigtrygg knew that his enemy would soon break. He would have his victory.

'Victory,' he bellowed.

Raymond de Carew kept his eyes closed. All he could hear was the rustle of rushes as they swayed in the wind above him, the trickle of dirty marsh water as it dripped from his milites' armour. He listened to the sloshing movement of water as nervous archers adjusted their stance to try and get some feeling back into their legs. He tried to ignore the noises. He sought the sounds of battle.

'Quiet,' he heard Philip rumble at two men who whispered to each other. 'The bugs won't kill you. And it won't be long now.'

The Welshman had been addressing his bowmen, but the words had been equally for Raymond's benefit. *Hurry up*, they urged. *Give the order*. But Raymond did not move. He concentrated his ears on the east wall of the fortress, now only two arrow shots away.

His new surcoat, the one which Alice had spent so much time working on, was sodden and it was splattered all over with mud. She had met him with the surcoat as Gufraid, Philip and he had ridden back into their camp. Raymond had too many arrangements to make and initially he had ignored her as Alice had shouted his name. But her insistence eventually got his attention and while Fulk had helped him don his armour she had appeared, the surcoat in her hands.

'Win, Raymond,' she had told him as she had allowed the garment to unfurl before him. Even in the shadow of a large birch the golden surcoat was resplendent, making the three black lions stand out even more than they otherwise might have. As Raymond reached out to take the surcoat, muttering his thanks, Alice had grabbed hold of his hand.

'Be seen to win,' she had told him.

Alice had held his gaze for a few moments and then headed in the direction of Strongbow's camp. Raymond had watched her go. He had wanted to say more, but before he could Father Nicholas had launched into a blessing to his men and Raymond had to take his place on his knees with them. He had barely heard a word. Instead he had stared at the lion surcoat. His arms.

He half expected the colour to have completely drained from the tails of the new garment by the time he got out of the marshland. But there was no avoiding the stagnant water. Raymond hated putting his mail through such foul conditions even more. It would quickly cause rust to take hold, but he knew it would be utter folly to attempt the route that faced him without the protection of the armour. He opened his eyes and stared through the rushes. He could see the dark outline of the fortifications which stretched northwards for over three hundred yards to meet the wide River Siúire. Dead ahead was the spur of dry land covered in spiked stakes and beyond it was the eastern gate to the city. Raymond could not see the great keep, Rögnvald's Tower, nor the sally ports that it defended, or the jetties which jutted out into the deepwater pool from the muddy beach.

Their route through the marsh had been lengthy and tortuous. Raymond had soon become lost in the tight, sapping confines of the swamp where heavy, hanging trees hid the sky and rushes grew thick and reached well over even the tallest archer's head. Thankfully, Philip the Welshman had taken the lead, his instinctive sense of direction allowing the three hundred men to arrive as close to the eastern wall as possible. To have gone any nearer was to alert the enemy to their approach and if his plan was to succeed Raymond knew that even a few seconds extra without discovery could make all the difference. He concentrated his gaze at the top of the wall. If the enemy knew that an attack would fall in the east, they were not giving it away. The Gaels up on the wall patrolled its length just as they had been doing hours earlier when Raymond had scouted the position.

He closed his eyes again and listened. He could smell watermint growing close by. He could hear the trickle of water in the little stream which fed the marshland. He could hear animal life all around him and swatted at a large dragonfly buzzing around his face. He could hear the small noise of the archers, Ostmen, milites and esquires at his back and prayed that the defenders could not. What he really wanted was to hear the telltale signs that battle had commenced in the west. Shifting water lapped against Raymond's rear and he opened his eyes to see Jarl Gufraid wading towards him through a field of pennywort, between the tall reeds and bulrushes. The Ostman took his time, charting a course between the archers, but despite his efforts he made a great deal of noise, educing hisses from the Welshmen for him to be quiet. Raymond held his breath, for he knew that the ground underfoot was treacherous and should Gufraid fall the sound of a splash or his cry would carry to the distant defences. He prayed that the spreading waves caused by Gufraid's passage would not reach to the open water some fifty paces ahead of them.

'It is slippery,' Gufraid confirmed as he came to a halt beside Raymond. He looked through the heavy foliage towards

305

Veðrarfjord. 'I can't see much from here,' he muttered. 'Is it time?'

Raymond put a finger to his lips and shook his head. 'Not long now,' he whispered. *I hope.* He turned back towards the city. *It must be midday by now.* He strained his ears, certain that he must have missed something. Suddenly his ears pricked. Yes! There was a shout from within the town and moments later a riotous sound erupted from within the walls. It could only have been caused by the impending attack.

'Now?' asked Gufraid.

Raymond held up a hand and looked north and west. It was only a few minutes later that he saw the faint haze of dust and ash rising over the fortifications. It could only have been thrown into the air by Strongbow's army. There was an upsurge in the bellows, war cries and songs coming from the Ostmen. Raymond glanced as Gufraid. His eyes were bulging, his teeth bared and chattering together. There was a look of utter fury on his face. Raymond waited until he could hear the first high-pitched clash of steel on steel.

'Philip, lead them on,' he whispered. 'The archers go first, fast and quiet.'

The dark-haired archer captain grinned and turned towards his men, whispering in Welsh and pointing towards the walls. Twenty men waded past Raymond and Gufraid with barely a glance in their direction.

'See you on dry land,' Philip growled as he went by Raymond and disappeared into the reeds and waist-high water. Another hundred and eighty men of every shape and height followed him, but only few made a sound as they plunged into the depth of the marshland. All their bows were unstrung to save the bowstrings but it made no difference, for even the long bowstaves could not reach above the bulrushes to be seen by the Ostmen of Veðrarfjord. Only Caradog and Ieuan made any gesture of recognition towards Raymond as they passed.

'My men will go next,' Gufraid stated as the last bowman disappeared.

'Quickly,' Raymond insisted. 'Don't stop for anything.'

Gufraid called into the foliage and soon the reeds and rushes were knocked aside by axe haft and shield to allow Blácaire to appear. Beyond him, Raymond could hear his forty Ostman hacking marsh vegetation aside to allow them through. Blácaire had a short garbled conversation with his father before he followed the Welsh archers into the tangle of water and plants. Gufraid waited for his men to pass before grabbing Raymond by the forearm.

'You promise that my folk will be permitted to remain in the city?' His eyes searched Raymond's face. 'Do you swear it?'

Raymond nodded his head. 'I do.'

Jarl Gufraid licked his lips and shoved his helmet onto his bald head. 'Then let's get it done.'

As his ally vanished, Raymond could already hear warning cries coming from the eastern defences. Raymond whistled back into the depths of the marsh. He only had to wait a matter of moments before Griffin and Gerald Bach emerged and ploughed through the water towards him.

'Ready?' he asked his brother. He received a curt nod in reply. 'We go quickly and quietly. As soon as you hit dry land, make for the sally ports. Do not stop.' Raymond waited for both men to respond. 'Then let's go.'

His shield was across his back and weight of the water against it made it challenging to wade forward. Thankfully, the passage of the archers and the Ostmen had trampled a path through the tangle of reeds and rushes and, using his arms, Raymond was able to force his way through. The plantlife clung to his ankles, his heavy, soaking gambeson to his knees. Ahead, down the alley carved in the marsh by his men, he could see the Ostmen. It was hard to discern where the marshland ended and the little stream began, but they seemed to be in relatively open water. The bottom of the marshland suddenly slid away, plunging Raymond up to his chest in water. The tug on his shield doubled and Raymond half-turned to give a warning to Gerald Bach. He was too late, and his little cousin only managed to keep his feet thanks to Griffin's help. If not for the gravity of the situation and the danger that would soon be upon them, he would have laughed out loud at Gerald's attempt to keep his head above water.

Soon he was climbing again, through reeds and towards a

307

half-flattened wattle fence. The Ostmen and the archers were already on the spur of dry land which ballooned out towards the deepwater pool. Marshwater ran freely from the bottom of his clothes as he pushed through the last few feet of marshland to the fence. He panted hard and attempted to swipe the sweat from his brow.

'Gerald, Griffin,' he called loudly and waved for them to hurry. The defenders up on the wall knew that they were facing an attack. Raymond could hear their shouts and warnings. They intermingled with the Welsh commands coming from Philip, Caradog and Ieuan. Glancing over the fence, Raymond could see that the archers had spread out across the dry land, finding whatever cover they could to allow them to string their bows. And up ahead, leading his men through the field of sharpened stakes, was Jarl Gufraid and his band of Ostmen. They were headed towards the top end of the spur where he had said there was a causeway.

Water poured from his cousins' clothes as they arrived beside him and Raymond could see that more of the milites and esquires were close behind.

'Get to the causeway,' he ordered, indicating at the backs of Gufraid's Ostmen. 'Be careful. The enemy have cut trenches and pits. Fall in one and you will break your leg.'

Gerald Bach and Griffin were followed by Hostilo d'Angle, Robert de Barri and William FitzMaurice before the esquires came tumbling past. At the back were William de Vale and Gervais d'Alton, just as Raymond had commanded.

'Stay with them,' Raymond called to William pre-empting his complaints about being put in charge of the twenty younger men rather than at the front of their attack. He didn't want the esquires caught in the thick of the fighting unless it was in the unlikely event that Gufraid succeeded in breaking through the sally ports. 'Remember: stay on this side of the causeway.'

Raymond had looked up just in time to catch the flicker of movement in his peripheral vision and ducked as the dart thrown from the wall slashed through the space where his head had been moments before. He gingerly rose again. It was fully a hundred paces to the wall, well beyond what he thought possible for a hand-thrown projectile. He could hear more thudding into the dry ground of the spur and he scanned the wall where he could see the jig of slingers as they unleashed their bombardment. Griffin's group were crouching behind their shields, the large rocks cracking like hail on the wooden boards as the milites still tried to go forward. He had lost sight of Gufraid's Ostmen but he had little doubt they too were beset from above.

'Philip?' Raymond shouted across to the archer captain. 'Are you ready?'

The Welshman did not respond with words but rose from his knees with an arrow nocked on his bow. Raymond could see the muscles on his back ripple as he drew the weapon, raising his left arm in the air and pointing the sparkling arrow tip at the wall. His arm quivered for an instant before he released. It was a short distance for the Welshman to shoot and Raymond had no doubt that Philip's shot had struck home.

'Let's go,' he called to William de Vale and the esquires as he vaulted over the wattle fence. Ahead was a blur of deadly stakes and Welsh archers who rose to shoot before ducking back into whatever cover they could find. The noise from the attack on the west wall was loud and Raymond could hear very little as he glanced at the wall and the men ahead of him as well as keeping lookout for the menace of covered pits and trenches. He sprang over another twisted fence and fell down into a ditch half-flooded with water from the river. It was up to his knees. He grimaced as he forced his legs clear of the squelching morass and was already scrambling up the other side when the esquires tumbled in behind him.

Raymond was on his hands and knees as he pulled himself out of the ditch. Sweat spat off the end of his nasal guard as he gulped down air. Arrows whistled overhead and cries issued from the wall. Ahead, on the causeway, he could see the Ostmen, already more than halfway across. They had their circular shields covering their faces as they advanced into the barrage thrown from the two towers guarding the eastern gates. The defenders had an archer of their own on the towers and he was causing damage. Raymond could already see men were down, lying in the shallow water, though whether dead or injured he could not tell. His milites, led by Gerald Bach, were not far behind the Ostmen, having just stepped onto the causeway that spanned the marshland between the spur and the beach. They too had their shields up and, being fewer in number, were quickly gaining on Gufraid's group as they advanced towards the beach.

Raymond turned and shouted back into the ditch at his heels. 'Gervais, keep the esquires in there. It's safer than out in the open. Send someone back to Philip and tell him we need more cover from his archers.' He glanced over his shoulder at the wall. Hundreds of men now crowned the rampart. More bowmen had appeared and were shooting at Gufraid's men and the milites. Darts and rocks were launched through the air, adding to the bombardment. Raymond could see the splashes of water and puffs of mucky sand as rocks landed around them. He could hear them drum upon his men's shields. Raymond could already see that Gufraid's warriors had almost come to a halt as they pushed into the storm.

'William, follow me.' Raymond did not wait for his miles to respond but climbed to his feet and dashed after his men. It was only a twenty paces to the causeway, but the land between was peppered with shallow pits that could turn an ankle or break a leg. Raymond danced over them.

Mud sloshed out from underneath the wooden planks of the causeway as he leapt down onto them. The boards were slick birchwood and Raymond skidded onto his hip as his feet went from beneath him. On both sides was more boggy marshland with thick bulrushes poking head-high like spear staves. Raymond's legs disappeared into their midst. But then William de Vale was at his shoulder and was hoisting him back to his feet. He shouted something but Raymond could not hear it over the din of shouting coming from above, the thud and clatter of missiles ahead.

'Shield up,' Raymond shouted back and pulled his own from his back into a defensive position on his left arm. Sunlight sparkled on the dirty motionless water in the marsh as he strode forward. It was fifty yards to the beach and the first rocks began impacting on his shield in less than half that distance. He grunted as each blow shunted him backwards and to the sides. At his back, William cried out in alarm at the frequency and power of the projectiles.

'Come on,' Raymond shouted, with no real hope that William could hear him.

He knew his people were ahead, but to steal a glance was to risk injury. Instead he simply put his head down and pushed forward. He could already feel a bruise forming on his left shoulder from the impacts which rattled his shield. Nestled behind the leaf-shaped defence, he knew he was covered from above his head to below his knee. His whole world narrowed to a few inches between the wooden boards and his own golden-clothed chest, his shuffling feet and the birch causeway which squelched and spat muck under his weight. Even with his head wrapped in a gambeson cap, coif and spangenhelm, Raymond was deafened by the noise coming from the Gaels above. They taunted and cursed, sang and shouted, and crashed their hands and weapons against the ramparts with such ferocity that Raymond felt like his eyes were shaking in his head.

Raymond paused long enough for William to come alongside him and then he locked the rim of his shield to William's and threw his right arm over his miles's shoulder, taking hold of a fistful of his mail shirt.

'Ready? Let's go,' Raymond shouted, gritting his teeth. He called out the pace so that they moved forward together. Suddenly the impacts lost some of their sting and Raymond was able to push his shield off his forehead. 'Right, left,' he bellowed.

They passed bodies, Ostmen all, but they did not stop to check if the men were living or merely dazed. Darts, spears and arrows stood proud in the boards of the causeway, in the marshland to either side. They were so abundant in fact that to Raymond's eye they looked like a new species of tough bulrush growing in the wetlands of Veðrarfjord. And then suddenly, rather than the next slippery birch board, his foot met with soft, sliding mud. Another step saw his foot meet sand. He was on the beach. Raymond glanced past William's shoulders and could see all fifty of Gufraid's Ostmen and the milites. They were just a few steps away, but had come to a halt, crouching together, seeking shelter behind their shields. Bodies already littered the beach beneath them and as he watched an Ostman tumbled backwards into the shallows.

'Move,' he shouted into William's ear. The volume of missiles hurled in their direction had increased threefold. Sand scattered wildly as they walked towards the huddled warriors. Raymond could feel William stumbling and it took all his effort to keep him upright and pushing forward. Pain seared up through his knee. A rock had ricocheted off his shield, striking Raymond on the calf, and for a second he teetered on one leg. William screeched incoherently as their shields came apart and Raymond groaned as he forced his whole weight onto his injured left.

'Keep going,' he growled. At the nearer end of the cluster of warriors, he could see Robert de Barri on his knees, hiding behind his shield. Raymond directed William towards his cousin. 'You must get up,' he called to the young miles as they came to a halt beside him. 'If we stay here they will kill us one by one.'

'I know!' Robert shouted over the tumult. 'But the Ostmen stopped and won't move on.'

Raymond grimaced as he glanced past Robert. 'Then we'll just have to do it ourselves. Lock your shield to mine. Get the other milites to follow.'

Robert nodded and shook the shoulder of the man next to him. Gritting his teeth, he emerged back into the hail of missiles and put the right edge of his shield on top of Raymond's.

'All set,' he shouted as Griffin, William FitzMaurice and Hostilo d'Angle appeared from the crowd and joined the tiny shieldwall.

'Where's Gerald Bach?' Raymond called as he and William de Vale started shuffling around the Ostmen at the pace of a hedgehog.

'Look! Up ahead,' Robert replied despite the thunderous assault on their shields.

As they rounded the bank of Ostmen, Raymond espied him. Gerald Bach was out on his own, his shield pierced by twenty arrows and darts. He was surrounded on all sides by spear shafts and rocks. There were even burning torches that had been thrown at him from the defences. The only reason Gerald

Bach still lived was because his shield was bigger than he was. He was on one knee, but still fought to move forward up the beach.

'That daft little fool - he's going to get himself killed.' Raymond couldn't hide his admiration for Gerald Bach's brave one-man advance. 'Come on!' He began calling out the step to keep the six men together. Robert took up the chant with him. They covered the ground to get to Gerald in a few seconds. Coming to a halt in front of him, they drove the points of their long shields into the sand, angling them so that they defended him from all sides.

'Gerald?' Raymond called over his shoulder. 'Are you all right? You need to get up. We can't break formation to help you.' There was no answer from the other side of the shield. 'Gerald?'

The volley of missiles had increased again and he could hear the anguish from William de Vale and Robert de Barri as they fought to keep their feet. 'Gerald, we must get going again. Can you walk?' he demanded.

'Raymond! We must move.' Griffin called from the other end of the shieldwall. His voice was close to panic. 'Hostilo has been hit.' He suddenly cried out in pain as if he too had been wounded.

William de Vale was in equally dire straits. A bowman further up the wall was shooting over the top of the warehouse and William's end was taking the lion's share of his attention. Every couple of seconds another arrow smashed into his shield, almost knocking William off his feet. To go to ground was death and every moment they stood immobile on the beach made it all the more likely.

'Gerald!' Raymond bellowed, not daring to turn and break his link with William's shield. 'Get up now!' But there was no response. William de Vale cried out as an arrow sliced across his shoulder. Another clanged off his helmet. Robert de Barri was cursing and William FitzMaurice was praying. Raymond could still hear Griffin moaning in agony.

'Gerald!' he cried.

The Gaels' howls reached all the way uphill to where

313

Strongbow and the conrois stood. One second it was the Norman army on the attack and then, before his very eyes, everything had changed. From where the enemy had come, Strongbow did not know, but they had suddenly fallen upon his army's left flank. He had barely time to register the meaning of the cries of alarm before the cloud of ash had risen in Irishtown to bury all from his view.

Strongbow was frozen. The last image of the sudden Gaels' assault, of Norman milites tumbling from ladders, of darts flying through the air, replayed again and again in his mind. He could still hear screams resonating off the city walls as he stood at the top of the hill looking down at the scene. He did not know if his army had broken or were fighting back. He did not know if the attack continued or if, caught between the defenders on the wall and the sortie, his army had been mauled to death.

'Can you see what's going on?' he called across to the milites.

'Nothing,' Asclettin FitzEustace shouted back. 'Where did those bastards come from?'

Strongbow had no answer for the miles. 'Do you see Sir Hervey?'

Again Asclettin answered in the negative. 'What are we going to do?' he added. The ladder that the conrois should've been using for the assault was still hanging between his and Denis d'Auton's shoulders.

The earl did not know what he should do. He searched the landscape below for any sign of his uncle. Sir Hervey was the captain, the most experienced military man in the army. He would know how to oppose the Gaelic flanking attack, how to order the troops, and how to regain the upper hand.

'Where is he?' Strongbow mumbled. The high midday sun was making it even harder to search the land near the walls. It shone brilliant white and forced Strongbow to cringe in pain as the light seared across his eyeballs. Here and there, the dust cloud gaped open and Strongbow could see fighting going on in Irishtown. Through the little windows he could see that his army was being taken apart. Here and there great bands of Gaels fought tiny groups of Normans in the crumbling remains of the settlement. Above them, the attack on the wall had stalled; ladders lay on the ground or were empty of warriors scaling the defences. Then, all too quickly, the breeze-borne dust closed again, blocking his view of the battle.

'We need to find Sir Hervey,' Strongbow called to the milites, but there was no answer. They were transfixed by the fight going on below them. He could feel his heart rate rising for his men did not seem to realise the danger that loomed over the army. 'Michael, get down there and find Sir Hervey. Make sure he knows what has happened. Go!' His esquire tarried for just a moment before taking off downhill towards the frontline.

'Should we follow down and attack the fortifications?' one miles asked.

'We should wait for orders,' Asclettin cut him off.

Orders, the earl thought and searched the landscape below for any sign of his esquire. Should he take command? He was no captain! It had been several minutes since Michael de Barnewell had run off. Perhaps the boy had already alerted Sir Hervey to the threat to the left flank? Perhaps unseen behind the dust cloud, his army was fighting back. With every minute that passed the clash of steel on steel became more intense.

'What are our orders, my Lord?' Borard shouted. 'We should go to their aid!'

Strongbow did not know. His head told him that he needed to act, to lead his little band of warriors down into the dust cloud and re-establish control. But he hesitated. *Wait for Sir Hervey*, he repeated as the urge to act came again. He will know what to do. Wait.

'Lord?' Asclettin interrupted. 'Shouldn't we stay put?'

No, attack them, a voice sounded in Strongbow's head. 'We will wait for Sir Hervey's orders.' Down below he could see the ungainly figure of Michael de Barnewell running back towards the camp and he felt his whole body relax, for the boy would surely have news from his uncle, news that would let him know that his fears were unfounded, that the army had seen off the threat of the Gael and that the attack on Veðrarfjord had recommenced. Michael was breathing hard by the time he reached Strongbow.

'Well?' the earl asked. 'What does Sir Hervey suggest we

do?'

'I couldn't get to Sir Hervey,' Michael spluttered. 'I saw him in a doorway, but he was surrounded, Lord, and his men were fighting.' The esquire paused to cough and Strongbow could see black mucus at the sides of his mouth. 'I tried to get close, but there were too many Gaels.'

'But they will soon defeat them?'

Michael glanced over at Asclettin FitzEustace and the milites. 'I don't know. There is fighting everywhere.'

Strongbow closed his eyes. He knew what was happening. His army was losing and his ambitions for conquest were disappearing with it. He stared down at the half-concealed city. Conquest of Veðrarfjord should have been his greatest triumph but it was fast turning into a disaster. The earl was no general but he knew that no army could stand for long if they were assailed from two sides. Sir Hervey should have foreseen the dangers posed a flanking attack! He should've guarded against it, Strongbow raged. Was it not the obvious response from the Ostmen? Strongbow's could feel the anger grow in his chest. He had given everything to bring an army to Ireland. Everything! And now, because of his captains' incompetence, he might lose the army he had given so much to raise. Strongbow felt tired.

In his mind's eye he could hear the chatter and laughter of the lords of King Henry's court. He could hear their jibes that he had failed again, that he had not the ability to capture a savage town in uncivilised Ireland. Their insults would tumble from each and every one of them. *How far the House of Pembroke has fallen*, they would mock. *The son was not the equal of the father*, they would roar with laughter. He pictured the wide, scornful face of Henry FitzEmpress. Surrounded by all those sycophantic courtiers and lesser men who he preferred to raise above men of good birth, he imagined how the king would react when he heard that the Earl Strongbow had failed to claim his Irish throne. He remembered the king's taunts when they had met in Westminster Hall after the coronation of the Young King Harry. Strongbow had merely been asking for permission to leave England, to search for his fortune on foreign soil. The sound of King Henry's acerbic laughter still echoed around his head.

Henry would sneer and chuckle when he heard the news of Strongbow's defeat. *His lineage far outweighed his ability,* the king would say. *Strongbow was never good enough to deserve his family name.*

The earl could feel his fury begin to overwhelm his reason. He might not be able to prove that he merited the name of Strongbow. He might never be able to say that he warranted a crown. But he could certainly show that he was a proper Norman. That was something the Angevin monarch would never be able to claim.

'Get to the horses,' Strongbow bellowed towards the conrois. 'Everyone, all the esquires, get back up to the camp. We are going to clear the Gaels from the town.'

No one moved save Asclettin FitzEustace. 'Shouldn't we wait for Sir Hervey, Lord?'

'By the time we wait for Sir Hervey the war may well be over.' He turned towards Borard and waved for him to follow as he began to climb. 'Quickly now! Get the horses ready. Ditch the ladder and get your lances in hand. We are going to charge them.'

Strongbow had only one thing left to give to the cause. He could give his life, on horseback charging into battle, like a proper Norman. And when he faced his father in the life hereafter, he would tell him of his three battles and how, for a few moments, he deserved to shoulder his noble name.

The earl's long stride had already taken him half the distance to the camp when he stole a glance over his shoulder. Led by Borard and Asclettin, the small conrois were jogging to catch up with him as he increased his effort to take them in the direction of the stables.

'Esquires, run ahead and have the coursers ready,' Strongbow commanded. The forty-strong pack of adolescents soon galloped past him. Despite knowing it was already too late to change his plans, as Strongbow climbed he constantly questioned whether leading a charge was the correct move. He was still trying to decide when he mounted his courser and took his lance from Michael de Barnewell.

'Ready,' Borard shouted to him.

Strongbow turned in his saddle. They were seven milites and thirty esquires, each armed with shield and lance. Many didn't even have mail armour. It was a small conrois, but they were the men who had fought beside Raymond and Sir Hervey before the walls of Dun Domhnall. He saw Gilbert Borard and Christian de Moleyns, Asclettin FitzEustace, Amaury de Lyvet and Hugh Cantwell, while at the very back was the tall figure of Denis d'Auton. Each miles had five determined-looking esquires circling around him. Even the boys seemed more experienced than he. As if sensing Strongbow's nervousness, his courser began dancing around in front of the conrois and rather than fight the horse, Strongbow kicked him into action, cantering up and down in front of this warriors.

He drew breath to give his orders, to say something that would inspire them, but the words failed to surface. 'Lead them out, Borard,' he mumbled in the direction of the senior miles.

'Let's go,' Borard called, tapping his heels to his courser's flanks and half-turning in his saddle. 'We'll do it just like we did at Dun Domhnall: five esquires to each miles. Rollo, Geoffrey, Gui, Elias, you are with Lord Strongbow and his boy. He'll lead so you must keep on his tail and don't stop moving. Do not give the enemy time to think. That's when they will be dangerous. Once you get them running, keep them running.'

Borard delivered his orders over each shoulder but even the five esquires who had formed around Strongbow had not been listening. The earl knew that Borard's advice had been for him alone. He could feel a surge of embarrassment in his face as Borard urged his horse into a canter, taking him further down the line. To either side of Raymond there were little groups of horsemen. Amaury de Lyvet was to his left with his esquires in a line behind him. Their tack jangled loudly as their hoof beat synchronised. To his right was Hugh Cantwell. His esquires were lined out alongside him and he chatted away to them as they came within fifty yards of Irishtown.

The dust cloud had drifted a little way northwards and Strongbow could see much of the southern half of the wall. There were still ladders against the wall, but none of his warriors were climbing. And among the burnt-out remnants of the town, he could see faces. The enemy knew that they were coming.

'Keep close to me,' Strongbow told the esquires. 'Who is oldest?'

'I am,' said a confident voice from his right. 'Elias de Blanchville, Master,' he introduced himself.

'Elias, good. You stay at the back and make sure that everyone else keeps together. You will watch our rearguard and make sure we don't make any mistakes. Understood?'

'It is, sir. Thank you, sir,' Elias replied and dropped back into position. Strongbow could hear him delivering orders to the other esquires like a veteran of twenty battles.

He was interrupted by Borard who was calling out his final orders as he circled back towards the earl. 'Cantwell? Take your group and Lord Strongbow's south and come back through the town. Do you understand? Keep pushing north. Once you get to the river you can turn back.'

Strongbow blanched at the thought of fighting his way through the whole of Irishtown, but thankfully both Cantwell and Borard laughed at the outlandish suggestion. Strongbow joined in, a little bit too late, with their joshing.

They were only twenty yards away from the town when Borard's call came to attack. 'Go!'

'Go!' Cantwell called, clipping his heels to his horse's side and directing his group southwards.

'Go, go,' Strongbow added, shifting his reins to follow. Behind him, Elias called the same orders and the earl could feel the presence of the esquires behind him. Wind whistled through his spangenhelm, through his coif, and for the first time in quite some time, Strongbow felt joy pump through his chest. This was war! Each impact of galloping hoof on the summer-cooked ground sent a shiver across his vision and he whooped with delight. Beneath him his courser snorted and followed Cantwell's group as they entered Irishtown, hollering and shouting like bandits as the ash puffed thickly into the air like hot breath on a cold winter's day. Cantwell led his cluster of esquires into a street to the left, leaving Strongbow the route in the other direction, in the shadow of the town walls.

'Come on,' he cried and vaulted a blackened rafter that had fallen from a collapsed roof. There was a flash of movement from his left and Strongbow raised his shield just quick enough to deflect a spear thrust over his head. The esquire behind him yelled out in triumph as he stabbed downwards at the man. Strongbow tugged his reins to the right and began circling in the tight little street. His esquires followed and as they completed their circuit they could watch as Elias skewered the Gael. There were more men hiding with him and they spilled out into the dusty roadway, running as fast as they could northwards.

'Let them go,' Strongbow shouted and led his little troop to the right, within a spear throw of the walls of Veðrarfjord. 'Don't stop moving,' he mumbled under his breath. 'Do not give the enemy time to think. Once you get them running, keep them running,' he repeated Borard's orders. 'There!' he shouted as he spotted more Gaels. They had their backs to the street and were hurling darts at the milites sheltering below the ladders. He dipped his lance and got his courser moving in their direction. The enemy heard him coming and leapt away like startled birds, making for a side street. Strongbow stood in his stirrups and stabbed forward at the last of them, catching the man in the elbow before his momentum took him past.

He urged his courser onto a parallel thoroughfare. He could see over the top of the burnt home as the Gaels emerged into the north-bound street beyond. At his back the esquires were screeching and shouting like dogs - even his own attendant, young Michael de Barnewell, was joining in, and Strongbow added his own call.

'Get away,' he shouted. 'Go on, get out!'

He appeared behind the second group of Gaels and trotted his horse after them. He kept close enough to frighten them, but not so close as to force them to turn and make a stand. Within seconds the closer group had caught up with the first and both were running northwards. A rumble of hooves and ash exploded from the Gaels' left and Denis d'Auton's horsemen crashed into the enemy's flank. Strongbow could see flashes of steel and splashes of blood. He grimaced and led his little conrois away from the main street, back towards the walls. A larger group was fleeing south from Christian de Moleyns and together they squeezed them away from the wall and back northwards. As they emerged back onto the main thoroughfare, Strongbow could see a whole army fleeing down the length of the wall towards the river. He could not believe how far he had come in just a few minutes. They had been like foxes in a chicken coop. Sweat poured down his back, but his mind was aflame! The earl could see Borard and Asclettin emerge from the buildings to the north and then Cantwell came from his left. Dust hung in the air. A wave from Borard got all the horsemen moving up the street.

'Denis, Christian,' Borard ordered. 'Take your groups and keep them running. I don't want them coming back.' A brief nod was the only response from both men as they jolted their horses into action and disappeared into the ash cloud with their esquires. Their hoots and roars continued to echo for many minutes after their parting.

Borard lifted his spangenhelm and wiped perspiration from his forehead. 'What do we do now, my Lord?'

Strongbow looked to his right at the walls of Veðrarfjord. His warriors were beginning to emerge from cover through the dust of Irishtown. Each looked for orders.

'We should -'

'Retreat!' the voice came clear and loud, drowning Strongbow's own orders. 'Full retreat!' it sang out again.

Every face in Strongbow's conrois turned towards the voice as Sir Hervey de Montmorency came staggering into view a little bit to the north. His sword was in his hand and he looked, if anything, even more bedraggled than was usual.

'Come on,' he called. His voice was clear and determined. 'We must regroup at the camp.'

Strongbow glanced at the walls and could see it was already having an effect. Men, already scared by the Gaels' attack, did not need a second invitation and were bounding over the small defensive ditch and into the town. They were abandoning ladders. They were abandoning their friends. They were abandoning the attack.

'No!' Strongbow bellowed, kicking his courser into action. 'No retreat!'

Up on the wall the Ostmen had begun to sing and shout abuse. They thought that they had repulsed a third attack on their defences. They hammered the rampart with their weapons, created a thunderous din that heralded their victory.

'No retreat,' Strongbow shouted again, increasing his pace to a gallop as he passed Sir Hervey's position. 'Back to the wall,' he cried. 'They are ready to break.' A large group emerged into the main street and Strongbow pulled his courser to a halt beside them and pointed his lance towards the city. 'That is our target.' He threw a leg over his saddle and dropped to the ground, lobbing his reins at Michael de Barnewell. 'Are you not here for riches and glory? I can promise you that there are none in our camp! The only riches on offer are inside Veðrarfjord. To get at them we need to cross that wall. That is all that's stopping us. Come on,' he called to the men, 'I will lead you. After me!'

Strongbow raised his lance and began running, and did not wait to see if anyone followed.

'Gerald!' Raymond roared again. The clatter of steel and wood and masonry on their tiny shieldwall was colossal, ringing the six milites' ears despite the layers of linen, wool and metal that encased their heads.

Raymond could already feel his shield arm sagging. He had no doubt that the younger men to either side of him were equally tired. Hostilo d'Angle and Griffin had already been wounded and it was miraculous that William de Vale had not been killed. He was on the extreme right of the little group, the most perilous position, and had been targeted by an archer up on the wall. Arrow after arrow smashed into his shield. The impacts were so great that each threatened to knock William from his feet and onto the sliding sand beneath them. If that happened, their little shieldwall would almost certainly collapse. Another of the bowmen's shots crashed into William's shield, sending judders up through Raymond's arm as he locked his rim to that of his fellow miles.

'We're going to have to leave him behind,' Robert de Barri shouted into Raymond's ear. The six milites had formed up around Gerald Bach FitzMaurice, Raymond's young cousin, after he had tried a solo-advance into the barrage of missiles thrown by the Gaels from the walls of the city. 'If we stand here any longer waiting for him we are all going to die,' Robert boomed.

'Get up,' William FitzMaurice, Gerald Bach's elder brother yelled urgently from Robert's other shoulder. 'Get up now!'

Still there was no answer from the young warrior. He was surrounded by stones and spears, and his long-teardrop shield was punctured by at least twenty darts and arrows. More lay scattered around and beyond him.

Raymond knew that Robert was right. They could not hope to survive much longer under the bombardment. To his side, William de Vale cried out in agony as an arrow sliced across his hip. Raymond threw an arm across his shoulders and hugged him to his own chest.

'Stay on your feet,' he moaned as he felt William's weight slump towards the ground. 'And keep your damn shield up.' He knew that they were at breaking point. He would give one last chance to get Gerald back on his feet and to join them.

'Gerald Bach, you little dullard,' he yelled over his shoulder. 'You will climb onto those two twigs you call legs and join this shieldwall right now. We are all tired of waiting for you. So if you can, pick up your shield and take two steps forward to join us.' Raymond held his breath, hoping that his words had done the trick.

A roar of anger came from Gerald as soon as Raymond had stopped talking. 'Do not call me that name! I'll kill you!'

Raymond craned his neck so that he could see. Gerald's shield gingerly rose from the mucky sand and pushed forward. Stones and arrows rebounded in all directions and he tottered towards the shieldwall. However, instead of joining Hostilo and Griffin at the safer end of their formation, Gerald pushed towards William de Vale and locked his shield to the rest.

'I promise that I'll fillet you if you ever call me that name again,' Gerald roared. His voice was hoarse but it echoed off the inside of the locked shields.

Raymond smiled. Griffin had warned him never to use the small man's nickname, for he hated it. But on this occasion it had helped to get his diminutive cousin to his feet and that was all that mattered.

'If you don't lead us into cover you will never get the

chance to fillet me,' Raymond replied and shouted for his men to get ready to move. He was just about to call out the rhythm for their march when the impacts on their shields suddenly stopped. In their place Raymond heard cries of pain up on the wall. A few moments later he heard loud cracks on the timber brattice above them. He dared not look but he knew that it could only mean one thing: Philip the Welshman finally had his archers shooting at the defences.

'Make for the warehouse!' Raymond ordered and pointed towards the building fifty paces away. A second flight of arrows whistled overhead. They whacked into the wooden defences. 'Gerald, go! Griffin, Robert, everyone, we are going to make a break for it.' He still had a grip on William de Vale's shoulders and he used their joint weight to force Gerald Bach to separate from the shieldwall and to move further up the beach.

'But the missiles!' Robert de Barri shouted as Raymond detached, leaving his right side more vulnerable. 'They'll pick us off.'

But Raymond was not listening. 'Just move!' he shouted. His right arm burned under the strain of William's weight. 'To the warehouse.' Gerald Bach was already out ahead, stumbling along the beach towards the only available cover on the outside of the eastern wall. The warehouse was close, but to the exhausted milites it seemed like an insurmountable distance. Raymond glanced over his shoulder and saw that William FitzMaurice was helping Hostilo while Griffin and Robert de Barri jogged ahead of them. Sand scattered as they dragged their tired legs into a run.

'Keep going,' Raymond shouted and grimaced. William de Vale shrieked in pain each time his weight went onto his injured right side. 'Keep your shields up,' Raymond warned as he caught an arrow on his own shield boss. 'Don't stop!'

Raymond glanced up at the eastern wall as two hundred arrows clattered down onto the covered wooden walkway. The Gael were well defended from the archers in the brattice and it was becoming harder and harder for the Welsh bowmen to get under the defences the further Raymond's milites got up the beach. Already he could see Gaels ignoring the danger of the arrows to fling darts and sling stones at his little group as they ran. Breath burned in his chest as he heaved William into the cover provided by the warehouse wall. Gerald Bach was already there with his hands on his knees.

'What now?' he demanded.

Raymond shook his head and breathed deeply. Sweat ran freely down his face as he turned to look back down the beach. Robert, Griffin, William and Hostilo were still running towards the warehouse and he could see from the bursts of sand around them that the barrage had begun again despite the best efforts of the archers.

'Come on,' he yelled. 'Not far now.' Stones clattered on their shields as they crossed the last few steps and collapsed under the shade of the warehouse. They were, for the moment, safe.

Raymond could see the archers out on the headland of the spur. They were only fifty yards away but could not cross the causeway to the beach lest they come in range of the Gaels on the wall. The bowmen did not wear mail around or carry shields and would have no chance of making it along the beach to the warehouse. Gufraid's men were also in a difficult position. They were still sheltering from the bombardment behind their shields out by the causeway. At least ten men were down and Raymond's allies seemed unable to move up the beach to join them in the cover.

'It looks like we are on our own,' Raymond told his five young milites. 'Gufraid's Ostmen are stuck on the beach.'

'Do you think we should retreat?' Griffin asked. He had a large gash along his right cheek and blood seeped through his fingers as he pressed his hand to the wound. Beside him, Hostilo's pale face looked up. He had a wound across his upper left arm and another to his side. He shook his head as if the thought of crossing the beach a second time was too much for him. William de Vale was seated and dazed. He merely stared out over the deepwater pool that lapped up against the beach at his feet. Gerald Bach, William FitzMaurice and Robert de Barri were all unhurt but had stripped off their helmets and coifs to allow the cold air around their sweat-plastered heads.

'We can't assault the sally ports with just the four of us,'

Raymond replied.

'Surely we have done enough to make them think that it is a real attack,' suggested William FitzMaurice.

'No! Onwards,' Gerald Bach urged and dragged his coif back onto his head. 'We can catch them unawares. They'll never expect so few men to attack.'

Raymond did not answer. Gerald's passion was infectious and he felt the excitement build in his chest. To retreat back along the beach was just as dangerous as going onwards. He licked his lips. 'Wait here,' he said and began running along the covered walkway. The wooden planks creaked under his weight.

The warehouse had been erected with its back up against the east wall of Veðrarfjord and stretched almost to the water's edge. To allow more room for the first floor, Konungr Ragnall had planted wooden columns in the sand to support the overhanging balcony and it had created a covered gantry much like the cloister of a monastery. Raymond could see that the corridor could be used as a wharf for smaller vessels. He slowed down as he came to the end. Three jetties hovered above the deepwater pool and beyond them he could see the stone base of Rögnvald's Tower, vast and intimidating, above the wide river. He took a breath and turned his head around the corner of the warehouse. Through the slave enclosure he followed the length of the wall to where he could see the sally ports. They were only forty paces away! Nestled in the midst of the slanting stone glacis, he could see the weather-blackened doors. It was tantalising to see them so close. Perhaps Gerald Bach was right?

The answer to his question came moments later. Darts slammed into the wattle and daub wall ten feet from his head and was soon followed by a drum of several large stones thrown from Rögnvald's Tower. The warehouse shook with each hit. Raymond ducked back into cover just as an arrow thumped into the wooden walkway where his feet had been seconds before. More rocks splashed into the pool and clattered around in the slave enclosure. Up on the wall he could hear shouting and insults in the Gaelic tongue.

Raymond retreated back down the corridor to where the

milites waited. 'There is no way through,' he told Gerald.

'Our archers -'

'Would be as likely to hit us as they would the men in the brattice or on the tower,' Raymond finished his sentence.

'We've done all we can,' William FitzMaurice said. 'The rest is up to Strongbow. We should just worry about getting back to camp alive.'

But Gerald would not relent: 'I didn't come all this way just to be the second man into Wetherforth,' he frowned. 'Waderfud?'

'Veðrarfjord,' William corrected him.

'Whatever it's called, I came to Ireland because Father Nicholas told me that there would be opportunity and battles and land for any man brave enough to win them. He said that Raymond le Gros was the man to lead us.' Gerald pointed at the warehouse wall. 'All I know is if we take this place we will have a base. We take this place and we have access to riches. We take this place and we will be rewarded.'

Raymond shook his head. 'And I am telling you that there is no way in. Not unless you have some way of bringing down that tower.' As he turned to stick a hand out in the direction of Rögnvald's great keep, the walkway beneath his feet creaked and groaned. Raymond could distantly hear Gerald continuing his argument, but he could barely hear it. His last words rebounded around his head: *bringing down that tower*. He gently bounced up and down on the platform. It felt like the whole warehouse wall moved as he shifted his weight. He reached out to touch the whitewashed wall and jumped up and down again. There was definitely movement, and dust tumbled onto his mail sleeve from above. Raymond looked up to where the beams that held up the first floor protruded. There were places where the plasterwork had crumbled away to leave great gaping holes.

'We need to get inside,' he yelled to Gerald Bach and Robert de Barri as they continued their argument. Both men paused and looked at him. 'Come on! Forget the sally ports. I have an idea. Help me break down this door.' He did not wait but worked his shield onto his back and then drove his shoulder into the heavy door at the front of the warehouse. The second time he drove his weight into the door was alongside William FitzMaurice and then Gerald and Robert added their bulk to the effort. It only took a few more attempts before a large crack sounded where the lock met the wall and the door swung open.

Raymond stepped inside. The warehouse was totally empty but for dust which floated around inside. He could see where merchandise had recently been piled in the far corner, right up against the stone glacis. It was exactly what Raymond had been hoping to see. The builders had used the rampart of the city as the back wall of the warehouse. The glacis reached almost to the ceiling while four great posts stood in the middle of the warehouse, reaching through to the floor above.

'How do we get up to the next storey,' he demanded of Gerald and William who had followed him inside.

'There are steps at the side of the building,' said William.

Raymond nodded and made for the door. 'Gerald, come with me.' He paused at the end furthest away from Rögnvald's Tower where the injured milites still gathered. 'There are steps, but we are going to have to be quick,' he told his cousin. 'Ready?'

'Always,' Gerald Bach replied with relish.

'Go!' Raymond turned to his right and caught hold of the pine banister as his foot hit the second step. He immediately felt the tug of his mail on his shoulders and waist as he climbed. He could hear shouting up on the wall above him and as he turned onto the second flight the first darts clattered against the wall of the warehouse.

'Faster,' Gerald Bach screeched behind him.

Raymond pumped his legs with all his might and did not pause as he rammed his shoulder into the door blocking his way into the first floor. The door quivered but did not open and Raymond took a step back. He snarled as he stamped his foot onto the wooden frame. Thankfully the door gave way under his weight and both he and Gerald Bach tumbled inside. All manner of missiles crashed into the side of the building as they got into cover. Both men panted and paused out of danger. The door swung open as it was struck by another sling shot. Through it Raymond could see down the beach. Gufraid's men had finally decided they could not move any further up the beach and were halfway across the causeway and the safety of the trenches on the spur. Raymond nodded his head to draw Gerald's attention to it. He flapped a hand in their direction dismissively.

'What now?' he asked as he turned and looked around another empty warehouse room.

Rather than answer he again bounced up and down on the thick wooden beams beneath his feet and then crossed to the first of the four posts that came up through the middle of the floor and into the ceiling. Raymond placed his hands against it and gave it a push. A trickle of dust came from above. At the back of the first floor he could see that the builder had rendered thick daub straight onto the palisade wall. He put his ear to it. He could hear muffled voices and footsteps of the Gaelic defenders.

Gerald watched him as he crossed back to the waterfront side of the room and swung open the two goods doors. 'What are you doing?' the miles asked as Raymond slid his shield off his shoulders and reached out to take hold of a rope that dangled by the door. A large iron hook was suspended from the end.

'Stay here,' he told Gerald Bach as he swung out and began climbing.

It was hard work and the added weight of his armour and weapons, and not a little daunting. But Raymond kept telling himself that the rope could definitely take his bulk. He looked up as he climbed. The line was part of a winch system that was suspended from the side of the building in order to help dealers lift their merchandise to the first and second floors of the warehouse. The whole mechanism was held by a thick beam that projected out several yards from the top of the shingle-tiled roof. Raymond could imagine the hauliers at the top, hoisting their barrels and baskets upwards, and wished that he could call on their services now. He had begun to spin and collided painfully with the gable end of the building as he neared the top.

'Are you all right?' Gerald called from below.

Raymond could see him peering up at him and he gritted his teeth and heaved himself up the last few inches. Taking a deep breath he reached out and grabbed hold of the second floor goods entrance. He did not need to force his way in, for the doors swung open towards him on their hinges. Raymond was pushed outwards before alighting on the second floor like a seabird upon a cliff face. It was obvious that the topmost room in the warehouse hadn't been used for many years. He could see rat and bird faeces on the ground to either side and there was a distinct smell of mould and damp. The roof was built just like a barn, with four vertical posts holding up the entire structure. At the end closest the rampart Raymond could see a sliver of light where the rafters should've met the daub wall.

'Built on a beach,' he murmured as he stared upwards. He reached up and gave the horizontal crossbeam a shake. That he could move it at all was odd in a building the size of the warehouse. The only place that he could not see daylight was where the great beam used to lift the goods on the winch system disappeared through to the other side of the rampart. An idea had begun to take shape in Raymond's mind on the waterfront. It was a plan as desperate as the one that had caused him to unleash a herd of cattle into the massed ranks of Ostmen and Gaels at Dun Domhnall, a plan that would be equally dangerous to his own men as it would be to the enemy.

'Climb,' he muttered and nodded his head. 'Climb.'

He crossed back to the waterfront and untied the rope so that the great iron hook descended into the shallow water below. Securing it again, he swung out and quickly dropped down, calling for Gerald Bach to follow as he past the first floor. His feet hit water and he ducked onto the corridor-wharf. He waited for Gerald to join him and then he called for his five milites to listen.

'I have an idea and I need all of you to help me.' Raymond told them. He was breathing deeply and paused to catch his breath. He looked at the injured men. Hostilo and Griffin swapped a look and heaved themselves onto their feet.

William de Vale's eyes swam in his head but he put a fist in the air. 'Count me in,' he slurred.

A smile was wide across Gerald's face as he guessed what Raymond was about to say: 'We are attacking the city after all, aren't we?'

'Look at it this way: we had better start thinking of Strongbow's escapade on the west wall as the diversion and ours as the main assault.' He looked at the warehouse roof above them. 'Whatever we call it, I am going to make such a racket that it is likely that half of the warriors in Veðrarfjord are going to descend upon us.'

The thrum of hooves was loud and interspersed with wild hoots and howling. Sigtrygg could not see anything through the dense ash cloud over Irishtown, but images of the Norman attack at Dun Domhnall resurfaced in his mind as he stood alone atop Thorgest's Tower. Just weeks before, the grey pack of horsemen had wrought catastrophe on his father's great army, appearing like wraiths and so turning the tide of battle with almost supernatural ease. He prayed that his flanking force of Gaels under Toirdelbach Ua Fhaolain had not suffered the same fate in the ruins of Irishtown. Where the horsemen had come from, he could not tell, for he knew the Normans had brought no cavalry with their assault force. But suddenly, they were there, bringing ruin to his counterattack as if some underworld chasm had opened up and the enemy had spilled forth to fall upon Toirdelbach's men, bringing death with devilish delight. The ash had only helped to clothe them with the appearance of something old, mystical and evil from the nightmares of children. The dust cloud swirled and pumped around the Gaels, hiding all. It could not conceal the cries of despair and appeals for help in the Irish tongue. It could not mask the clash of arms that went unseen beyond.

The sickening smell of burnt wood clogged his airway and Sigtrygg began coughing uncontrollably. He spat and wiped his large forearm across his mouth. Down on the west wall of Veðrarfjord, he could see warriors with their hands pressed to their brows as they searched the bank of ash for sign of what had happened. Only minutes before those men had been cheering Toirdelbach's attack, but now they were all but silent. In fact there was more shouting coming from the distant eastern walls than there was on the west. Sigtrygg had only just turned to investigate the cause when he saw movement in his peripheral vision. Gaels were surfacing from the inside of the dust cloud. Sigtrygg's attention quickly turned to anger as he watched them run away.

'Where are you going?' he roared at them, reaching out to take hold of the top of the rampart that ringed Thorgest's Tower. All thought of the eastern wall was forgotten for the Déisi were fleeing the battlefield. His fingers wrapped tighter around the timbers, turning bone white. A long line of his allies had emerged from the ash haze and were taking flight northwards along the banks of the Siúire.

'Cowards,' Sigtrygg bellowed. His allies were hundreds in number and behind them came little more than a handful of Liathgall horsemen. The foreigners held their lances over their heads as if in celebration. Sigtrygg glanced back at the west wall. His outburst had only served to draw attention to the flight of the Déisi from the fighting. He could hear an undercurrent of disaffection build amongst his warriors on the wall as they watched the tiny number of enemy cavalry humiliate an army of Gaels. But Sigtrygg ignored it. An eerie quiet had descended over Irishtown. Nothing could be seen or heard from beyond the curtain of ash, and what sounds had pierced that blanket had stopped; there were no hooves and no voices, no piercing cry of steel weapons coming together. Dust swirled and sank, but otherwise it was an unchanging white-grey picture beyond the west wall. Sigtrygg licked his lips and stared outwards. He was only distantly aware of the noise coming from the other side of the city as the unnerving atmosphere continued.

Then suddenly a lone figure appeared from the ash. It was a man on foot. He stood out against the colourless curtain of dust for he had a bright gold and crimson surcoat covering his armour. For a moment, Sigtrygg felt a breath freeze in his chest, for he bore the same colours that Raymond the Fat had been wearing during the battle for Dun Domhnall. But where Raymond was stout and short, this man was tall and gangly. He was also out of his mind, Sigtrygg decided, for it looked like he meant to attack the walls of Veðrarfjord on his own. However, it was not this, but something in his awkward gait, his thin arms, that made Sigtrygg chuckle as he watched him. The foreigner was obviously brave but he looked ridiculous. With his long limbs and thin body there was something distinctly aquatic about the man.

Sigtrygg turned to look down at his warriors. They too had spotted the solitary attacker and many had their arms pointed in his direction. Several were mocking his running style. Others the fact that he had forgotten to bring a shield! A great peel of amusement sprang from his warriors and Sigtrygg turned back to see that the man in the surcoat had fallen as he attempted to vault the flooded ditch. He lay sprawled on the ground, kicking his legs like a frog making his escape from a pike. Sigtrygg added his voice to the howls of laughter as the man clambered back to his feet, righted his helmet and jogged the last few paces to one of the ladders still leaning against the west wall. He tried to begin climbing but his leg went between the second and third rungs.

The Ostmen of Veðrarfjord were still taunting his clumsy efforts to climb as hundreds of Norman warriors emerged from Irishtown and charged the defences.

Unlike the other attacks which Sigtrygg's people had faced, this time they came as an unordered rabble, bellowing unintelligible war cries, screaming like demons. Gone were the long lines and steady pace. This time the Liathgall were all steel and iron and linen gambeson. Barely any piece of flesh could be seen. The only thing that Sigtrygg could see to identify the enemy as human in any sense was the snarling teeth beneath their spangenhelms. The Konungr of Veðrarfjord took an involuntary step back from the rampart.

Sigtrygg glanced down the length of the defences. He could see enemy warriors were still coming out of the ash as the first were leaping over the great flooded ditch near the base of the wall. More were emerging from the cover under the defences and were climbing to meet his men. And in their midst he could see the tall, clumsy-looking warrior who led them. He hung from the middle of one ladder by one hand, looking for all the world like he might be blown off by the smallest puff of wind. His surcoat was brilliant amongst the grey, he drew his sword and for a second its entire blade sparkled in the sunlight.

'Strongbow!' he heard the enemy chant. The man on the ladder fumbled his sword as he began climbing. His feet hoisted him upwards with every cry. 'Strongbow, Strongbow, Strongbow!'

The sound of fighting began with a single faint strike of steel on stone. Then there were more noises of war, no more than a jangle of weapons coming together, the thump of axe on willow shield, the smack of spear on thick flesh. But within moments battle was blazing and the tumult had swollen to a deafening din of vying voices and arms.

Sigtrygg could feel his anger rising and he hefted his battleaxe in both hands. He kept his eyes on the golden warrior and promised that he would not take Sigtrygg's city. He made his way across the roof towards the stairs, picking up a shield as he went. The buildings of the city stretched out before him, a patchwork of thatch and shadowed streets as he looked eastwards. Beyond the houses and churches, inns and workshops, was the great marsh, a swaying green sea running next to the river all the way the horizon of low, blurry hills. It was all his and no one else's.

'I am konungr,' he hissed. 'I am Veðrarfjord.'

His feet had only just alighted on the top step when he heard a monumental crash. He craned his neck to look at the western wall, but there was seemingly no source for the noise. The battle for the wall went on seemingly without notice of the sound. Confused, Sigtrygg stepped back up onto the flat roof of Thorgest's Tower and twisted around to look out at Irishtown. In the absence of the Liathgall and with the little breeze, the ash had begun to settle and there was no obvious cause there either. Sigtrygg was beginning to believe that he had imagined the sound when he turned back towards the stair.

It was then that he saw it: on the far side of the city a great plume of dust was rising from the eastern defences between Rögnvald's Tower and the gates above the marshland. And through that discharge of brown dust Sigtrygg could already see daylight where there should've been solid timber ramparts.

Sigtrygg was frozen to the spot, for the walls of sovereign Veðrarfjord had been breached. His ship was holed. She was listing and taking on water and unless he could right her all hands would be lost.

Sigtrygg began running.

334

'Would it not be better if I stayed behind?'

It was at least the fifth time that Gerald Bach had asked the question of Raymond in the few minutes since he had told the milites of his plans. He did not look up to answer but kept on hacking at the timber column with the axe. Gerald had already taken care of two of the others and now watched Raymond work.

'I'm a faster runner than you are,' Gerald continued, 'and, well, you are the captain. What if you can't get out quick enough? Or you get stuck? Where will we be then? I can get through places that you can't -'

'Oh, really? Why would that be?' Raymond asked gruffly as a great chip flew past his face from the wide cut in the wood. There was no way that the Gaels up on the wall had not heard the sound of the chopping, but so far they had made no move to find out the cause.

'Well, because I'm littler -' Gerald frowned, annoyed that he had used that word. 'I mean, you are more, you know ...' He puffed out his cheeks and rounded his shoulders and arms.

'Come off it!'

'Well I wouldn't say you were thin, Cousin. I just worry what will happen if you get caught and we are forced to do without our captain. Will I take command?' Gerald Bach did not look displeased at that possibility.

'If I don't get out, you will find Milo de Cogan. Do not wait for Sir Hervey to tell you where to go. Find Milo - he will keep you right.' Raymond turned towards Gerald, handing him his shield and weapons belt. 'And just so we are clear, you are not faster than me. You are certainly not the fastest. William is,' he said, nodding to Gerald's spearshaft-thin elder brother who stood at the end of the warehouse's gantry corridor.

'I will be happy with being fast enough,' William suggested as he stared down the beach towards the causeway. 'That is a long way to go with only a shield to cover me.'

'It is,' Raymond agreed. 'I wouldn't ask you to do it if I didn't think you capable of getting there. And as soon as Philip sees you coming he will get his archers shooting again. That should be all the cover you need.'

William nodded his head and began snorting down air through his nostrils. 'I'm ready.'

Raymond could feel his heart begin to thump in his chest. He looked down at the axe, rolling it around in his hands. He thanked whatever providence had led the Ostmen to leave an axe used for splitting wood in an anteroom in the warehouse. Hidden behind the door, it had been an easy mistake to make, but if the axe could help Raymond accomplish his task then it would prove a costly error for the people of Veðrarfjord. 'Gerald, join the others. We'll all go at the same time. Run fast, don't stop.'

Gerald Bach looked like he was about to complain again, to make one last appeal, but a stern stare from Raymond convinced him to abandon his protest and he crossed to the other side of the warehouse to where Robert de Barri, William de Vale, Griffin and Hostilo waited. Robert was pulling William up to his feet, taking hold of him under the armpit. Raymond saw his old esquire still looked dazed. Gerald slotted his head under Hostilo's right arm, taking a stern grip on his wrist as it dangled over his shoulder. Griffin was on the other side. He turned towards his brother.

'We're ready,' he confirmed. 'Good luck, everyone.'

Raymond turned his eyes heavenwards. 'Keep an eye on us, St Maurice,' he prayed. 'We really need you with us now.' He sucked in one last breath and nodded his head. 'Go!'

Men spewed from the warehouse corridor in two directions. William FitzMaurice had the most dangerous route. His role was to make a break for the causeway, running down the beach in full sight of the defenders up in the brattice. But he was tall and fast, if fully armoured with the encumbrance of a shield on his right arm. The soft sand underfoot slowed him down too. His job was to get to Philip the Welshman and Jarl Gufraid and to tell them of Raymond's plan, of their part in them.

Griffin's group had less distance to cover and in the opposite direction. They used the slave enclosure for what little protection it could provide from enemies up on Rögnvald's Tower before angling back towards the waterside. Raymond had a brief sight of the little group kicking muddy water into the air as they plunged into the deepwater pool. Their role was to find whatever shelter they could from the enemy by hiding under the timber jetty nearest the warehouse. It would be uncomfortable and it would be cold, but they would be safe. If Raymond did not succeed in his task, they would wait for nightfall and then swim to safety after ditching their armour and weapons.

Raymond waited until the first missiles began raining down around William FitzMaurice before following him out onto the beach. He did not track his cousin, but began climbing up the steps to the first floor. All eyes must have been drawn towards William, for not one dart or arrow crashed around him as he scrambled up and through to the next level. He breathed deeply and watched through the door as William leapt from the beach onto the causeway. His young cousin momentarily lost his footing on the slippery boards, crashing onto his left side but, as more stones and spears splashed into the marshland around him, he nimbly got back to his feet and hurried across to the spur of land, diving headlong into a trench on the far side. There were cries of abuse from the defenders above but it quickly died down. Raymond smiled at William's small victory.

Gingerly, Raymond walked to the front of the warehouse, where the overhang was now balanced precariously on one remaining timber column. The others had been cut through or damaged so fully that Raymond thought his weight might be too great for them. The balcony creaked and squeaked beneath him as he walked forward and he could feel the whole platform shift minutely to the right. Raymond quickly backtracked deeper into the open space, away from the waterfront. He licked his lips as he stared at the four great posts that disappeared through the dusty oak floor. Above, he could see the beams that held up the top storey of the building. At the very back of the warehouse he reached out to touch one of the posts. He could already feel welts forming on his palms from where he gripped the axe. He had a strange sensation in his sweaty hands, the same as he always had after weapons training. It was a prickly, ringing sensation. He lowered the axe head to the floor and held it between his feet as he wiped his hands on his golden surcoat.

'Here goes,' he said as he heaved the axe skyward, bringing it down at an angle. It bit into the wood of the post. He brought it down again and again, ignoring the cut splinters of wood that shot into the air close to his face. He paused only to change hands and direction, each swing of the axe chewing a wider cut into the wood.

'Easy does it,' he said, bringing his work to a halt. He could already feel sweat trickling down his back, but he had taken a large enough slice from the post. Raymond crossed to the second post and began work on it too, hacking halfway across the great post. By the time he had finished the fourth post, Raymond was spluttering with fatigue and perspiration was thick on his brow. The axe head rang like a bell as he dropped it to the floor and rolled his shoulders. He looked at his work and hoped he had judged it well: too little damage and the first floor might not collapse; too much and the floor above might collapse as soon as he set foot on it.

Raymond could see the points on his hands where blisters were forming and wished that he had something to wrap around them and protect his palms. The goods door to the first floor was still open and he eyed the rope before looking back at his hands.

'This is going to hurt,' he said as he lifted the axe and walked towards the open end of the warehouse. The balcony floor creaked and dipped as he soon as he put weight on it. Carefully, Raymond edged forward, leaning out as far as he could so that he could reach up and hook the axe blade to the floor of the top storey where the goods doors swung open. It took every inch of his height to make sure the axe was secure. He then took hold of the rope, looking up at the pulley and praying that he had tied a good knot to fasten it to the wall. With a deep breath he swung out, simultaneously wrapping his feet around the rope. Pain seared through his hands but he ignored it and began edging higher.

He had only been on the rope a few seconds when the first arrow fizzed past him. Initially Raymond thought he had imagined it, but the next one went so close to his head that he could not mistake it for anything else. The rope was swinging him around in a circle, like a spider on a single thread of web,

338

but up on Rögnvald's Tower he caught sight of an archer. The man was nocking a third arrow upon his bowstring. The angle was against the Gael, with most of Raymond covered by the corner of the warehouse. But he obviously thought he could get him.

'Climb,' Raymond shouted as he saw the man loose another arrow.

This one deflected off the corner of the warehouse and went well wide but Raymond was barely looking any more. He was spinning wildly and trying to climb. His biceps burned with the effort while the noseguard of his spangenhelm rubbed the rope with each upward movement. Sweat blinded him. Each heave became shorter than the last until he was barely getting one hand over the other. His hands were slick and Raymond could see pink patches left on the rope. Soon he had to come to a complete stop. He hung there.

'Keep going, Raymond,' he heard Robert de Barri call from beneath the jetty. 'You can do it.'

'Do you want me to help you?' Gerald Bach shouted.

'No! Stay where you are,' Raymond barked back. His forehead was pressed against his left hand, his right against his chin as he gripped onto the rope. 'Climb,' he commanded through clenched teeth. Raymond squeezed his feet and pushed upwards, hugging the rope as tightly as a lover, but to no avail. His strength was failing. He sucked down more air and stared at the top where the rope passed through the pulley. The rope was spinning as another arrow flew past his shoulder. He thanked his lucky stars that the man up on the tower was not a Welshman. If he had been, Raymond would already be dead. But he knew that he could not stay suspended above the beach for long. The archer would eventually find his range.

'Come on. It's only a bit further,' he groaned. 'You've already done it once. Come on, you wretch. Climb! It's not like you are climbing a mountain,' he joked sarcastically as he reached upwards with his right hand. '*With deadly travail, in stress and pain, Count Roland sounded the mighty strain*.' The words to the *Song of Roland* hissed tunelessly between his teeth as he hauled his body up another few inches. He could hear Robert and Griffin begin cheering him on from beneath the

339

jetty. He raised his voice: '*Forth from his mouth the bright blood sprang, and his temples burst for the very pang.*' His left arm quivered with the effort as he raised himself again. '*On and onward was borne the blast, till Charlemagne hath heard as the gorge he passed, and Naimon and all his men of war. "It is Roland's horn," said the emperor, "And, save in battle, he hath not blown."*'

Raymond gasped as he reached out to clutch the doorframe on the second floor. With one almighty effort he launched himself through the gable end doors. There was a loud cracking of wood, somewhere below, as he landed hard on the floor but he was too exhausted to do anything but lie there. Little white dots danced across his eye sockets and he felt sick to his stomach.

After a few seconds his vision righted itself and he rolled onto the front, crawling deeper into the top room of the warehouse. 'Next time, just let Gerald have his way. Let him do the climbing.' He groaned as he pushed up onto his feet. He flexed his stiff fingers and arms while he studied the roof. The two arms of the wood-shingle roof met directly above him but there were three places where the structure was braced by crossbeams. The horizontal spars also supported the arm for the winch which passed through the wall at the far end of the triangular room.

'All right, Roland, it is time to make sure Charlemagne knows you need his help.' Raymond knelt and retrieved the axe from the doorway. Looking up at the crossbeam in the middle of the room, he laughed. 'Time to blow your oliphant horn.'

He raised the axe and hacked down, keeping up a rhythm until it was nearly cut through. He then hewed a large rent in the side of the spar at the back of the room. He had raised the axe for another cut when an unhealthy crack sounded beneath him, sending a shiver through the floor. Raymond rolled onto his heels and grabbed hold of the wall for balance. He knew it was time for him to play the final note, to hope his fanfare had the desired effect.

He stood underneath the last undamaged crossbeam with his axe in hand. '*Then to his lips the horn he drew, and full and lustily he blew,*' he said as he brought down the tool. '*The mountain peaks soared high around; thirty leagues was borne the sound. Charlemagne hath heard it, and all his band. "Our men have battle on hand."'* He threw the axe forward, feeling it bite into the heavy oak. His arms cried out in pain, but Raymond ignored it and drew back the weapon again. With every blow the warehouse shook and Raymond knew that it would soon fall. For his plan to work, the top two storeys had to collapse. He cut down.

'Break,' he roared as he chopped at the crossbeam again. 'Break, damn you!'

The thud of the axe intermingled with creaks and groans of wood under strain. The timbers on the first floor were screeching as he hewed and tore at the crossbeam. 'Break,' Raymond yelled. And then suddenly the warehouse floor seemed to lift under his feet and he was flung forward. But for the axe being buried deep in the beam above, Raymond would've been thrown through the goods doors and onto the beach below. But he held onto the axe haft buried in the crossbeam above him like King Arthur's sword in its anvil sheath. Another judder passed through the building, another gust of ripping wood. He twisted around just in time to see daylight pour into the room from behind him. There was the sound of twisting and breaking, like the crack of a whip. The floorboards began to buckle. And then the back wall began to collapse away. Raymond could feel the whole building moving. It fought valiantly to keep together, but he had caused too much damage, and the unstable ground beneath the warehouse was not its ally. Daub began to crumble and smash onto the floor in large dusty blocks. He could see the struts hidden in the walls appear, the wattle frame.

'Run,' Raymond shouted as the roof began to come down. He bellowed incoherently as the walls gave way around him. Thrown from side to side, he caught a glimpse the winch rope bouncing and swaying out through the doors. He did not have time to think. Raymond jumped.

When he had first learnt to swim, Raymond could not rightly remember. He had been able to for as long as far back as his memory stretched. He recalled summer days swimming in the

341

streams on the plains below the motte of Raglan with the other esquires and later, having become a miles at Striguil, losing his trews in the River Wye during a dip and being forced to walk back through the bailey with only his shirt to cover his nakedness. He delved back into his memories. Raymond was certain that he had swum during his time as a page to Countess Isabel, but he couldn't think of any occasion. He had an image from his youth, perhaps at Carew or Cilgerran, of swimming. His father had been watching over them. Odo had been there too, but he couldn't remember Griffin being with them. Perhaps he had been too young to accompany his brothers on that occasion? The reminiscence was distant and he recalled little other than Odo's tears and his own joy at being allowed into the river.

The memory contorted in his mind and suddenly he was on Dreigiau's back, urging him across the straits between Gufraid's island and the shore of the Siúire near Veðrarfjord. The landscape was ill-defined but he could see Alice and William de Vale alongside him. Suddenly the weather closed in around him and it started to get dark. He felt pain in his hands as the water surged around him. He clung to Dreigiau's reins but the flow of the water was too great and he was being pulled under. It was raining too, a great downpour, and he could barely see. Alice was laughing in the rain. But before he could demand her to tell him why, he felt a great kick to his chest as though Dreigiau had lashed out at him with his backs legs. He tried to shout for his courser to calm down, but his mouth was full of water. Another jolt hit him in the side and Raymond felt his temples scream as badly as they had when he had been recovering from his head wound. He was being struck from all sides and he could not shout. It was dark and he was being dragged under. No matter how much he kicked his legs and pulled with his arms he seemed to get deeper.

Panic surged through Raymond and he opened his eyes. He was underwater. There was weed everywhere and the water was a murky brown. His hands disappeared into the gloom as he attempted to swim. At his back was something sharp and he tried to swim for where he thought the surface was, but he could not get there. Something was holding him back. He

342

yelled out and kicked but if anything the hold on his leg increased. He leaned down to try to free his foot only to find that he was looking at a wall of broken timber struts and shingle roof. Raymond lurched away from the splintered beams and large pieces of wattle frame. Bubbles flowed from his mouth and down his chest until something grasping at his collar choked even that from him. He was being dragged deeper! He fought the sensation, but the hold on his foot and collar were too great. Raymond swung around to lash out just as he breached the surface of the water like a great feeding whale. Instead of landing a punch, Raymond's fist missed Robert de Barri's face and went over his shoulder. The fist quickly released and he clawed at Robert's mail, holding onto his cousin as he coughed and slugged down air. His nostrils burned as water shot out. His ears were so clogged that he was only distantly aware of Gerald Bach's shouting. All that concerned Raymond was the air surging into his lungs in great heaves.

'Go,' Gerald screeched. 'The whole thing might slide further at any second.'

Water splashed onto Raymond's face, blinding him as Robert and Gerald half-carried, half-lugged him through the shallows by his feet and shoulders. His vision was distorted by hexagon droplets that cast coloured stripes across his eyes, but above he could perceive a great dark mound of timber and daub. Its broken limbs stuck this way and that like a great exposed ribcage. His left hand was drawn over wood just beneath the water. Then suddenly he was clear of the river and Gerald Bach had dropped his feet and grabbed him around the shoulders. Raymond's own feet were carrying him again. Ahead was the great Rögnvald's Tower and Raymond could not understand why they would be taking him in that direction. He shook his head and squeezed the remnants of water from his eyes. He tried to refocus and managed to spot the other milites just a few paces away. They were waving their hands, encouraging Robert and Gerald to hurry.

'Watch your head,' Robert warned as they all ducked under the jetty.

'What took you so long?' Griffin demanded. To Raymond all the voices seemed distant and dulled.

343

Gerald answered. 'Not content with almost killing himself with that acrobatic rope swing, the bloody fool was trying to swim deeper into the water,'

'Why would he do that?'

'Who knows? He's lucky he wasn't buried beneath the debris.'

'He must've been heavy with all that armour,' Hostilo mumbled.

Raymond spluttered and wiped water from his face. 'I'm fine,' he croaked as he rubbed a hand over his chest. He could feel a bruise forming. 'Did it work? Did the warehouse come down?'

'Go see for yourself,' Griffin said.

Still spluttering, Raymond waded over to the edge of the jetty. The sun was high in the sky and shining almost directly into his eyes. It would've been utterly blinding as it reflected onto the water, but the pool was buried beneath three storeys. The warehouse had collapsed into the shallows. Raymond looked up to his right and could see that a wide breach had been torn in the wall of Veðrarfjord. Surprised Gaels still stared down at the rent in the defences as though it might magically repair itself. Raymond could see the great spar that had protruded from the gable end for the winch. It sprouted from the wreckage like a giant's spear shaft buried in the ground. The shingle roof had stayed intact other than where it had been punctured by vertical posts, and it sloped upwards from the water to above the stone glacis. If Raymond had been asked to sketch the ideal breach through which his warriors could attack, he would've drawn that one. The slope of the wreckage that would get them there looked acute but scalable.

Raymond could hear shouting up on the wall. It was in the Irish tongue, but he didn't need a translator to tell him what was being communicated. The enemy knew what would happen next and they were trying to come up with a plan to prevent it.

'There's no time to waste,' Raymond told his milites. 'We need to get through before they have the chance to get ready. Where are my weapons?' he demanded. His brother handed over his shield and unlooped his belt from around his neck.

Raymond quickly buckled his weapons around his middle.

'What do you want us to do?' Griffin asked. His face wound was still seeping blood and he was pale.

'You stay here with William and Hostilo,' Raymond told him. 'Keep them safe. Robert, Gerald, we are going through the breach.'

Gerald Bach whooped and scooped up his shield, giving Robert de Barri a triumphant shake on his shoulders. 'We are going to be rich!'

'Wait,' Griffin said sternly as he grabbed his brother by the shoulder. 'You cannot attack the city with just three men!'

Raymond was soaking and he was bone-weary. He was bruised and blistered and he was half-deaf with water in his ears. But he wanted to prove himself to be fit for more than to lead a diversion, more than to be a commander of a cattle train. Raymond wanted to prove that he was a conqueror. All the insults, all the abandoned friendships, all the hardships, they would all be worth it if he was the man to bring defeat to Veðrarfjord. And then no one – not Strongbow, and not Sir Hervey de Montmorency – could deny him his reward.

'I'm going,' Raymond told Griffin, 'alone if needs be. But I will get into the city.'

'And we'll have the pick of the prizes,' Gerald Bach said as he waded across to stand at Raymond's side. Alone of the Normans under the jetty, Gerald could stand upright, but in that moment Raymond wished he had ten men the equal of his tiny cousin.

'If you live,' Griffin warned.

'They'll live,' William de Vale replied as he warily got to his feet. 'Because I'll be there with them.'

'Well, if Gerald is going, I suppose I'd better go too,' Robert de Barri stated.

'Damn it all,' Griffin added and withdrew his hand from his face. The bleeding was crusty and black on his face. 'I knew we should have left Gerald back in Pembroke. Hostilo?' He turned to his friend.

'I'll go with you.'

Raymond nodded his head in appreciation. 'Jarl Gufraid's men will be right behind us too. All we have to do is keep that breach open until they join us. Are you ready?' he asked as he looked around the men under the jetty. Each nodded their head. 'Then let's go.'

As Raymond's feet hit the beach, the first missiles began falling around him and he swung his shield onto his right side. It felt unfamiliar there on his sword arm but Raymond just kept running. He could hear the other milites' feet pad on the sand behind him.

'Won't they ever run out of things to throw at us?' Robert shouted as darts and stones rattled his shield.

'Maybe once we get up there we will find them all unarmed,' Raymond replied as a flight of arrows soared overhead from the spur. Philip had his archers about their work again, forcing the defenders to seek cover. Moments after the first wave had landed on the defences, a second crashed home and it was followed by a third. Philip had even men shooting over their heads at Rögnvald's Tower. The bowmen stationed there were no match for the Welshmen and they too ducked behind the wall or died with arrow shafts buried deep in their chests.

Raymond reached the collapsed warehouse and allowed his shield to swing back onto his back as he bounded upwards, grabbing on to whatever he could to help him climb. There was a piece of floorboard poking up through the shingle and he caught hold of it, using it as a swing to propel his feet up. His stomach muscles objected but he was able to manoeuvre his way onto the flat roof. Raymond reached down to offer Robert a hand while, at his back, Gerald's head popped up between two parts of the wall. He looked like a hare popping his head out of his burrow to check the air for predators. He nipped up onto the structure and deflected away a spear.

'Shieldwall,' Raymond commanded as he dragged Robert up beside him. There were missiles coming from left and right but Raymond gritted his teeth and swung his shield onto his left arm. Gerald and Robert did likewise. Moments later Hostilo joined them, and then William and Griffin.

'Forward,' Raymond called. 'Go quick.' Surprise was everything now. There was no time for order.

The bombardment wasn't as heavy as it had been when they

had been on the beach, but the climb was sapping and the terrain difficult; everywhere there were broken spars and unstable pieces of timber ready to trip or impede their progress.

'Keep going,' Raymond yelled as Robert went to his knees again. Even as he helped haul him upwards, Raymond lurched to his right as a panel of wattle gave way underneath his own foot. It was chaos. Gerald Bach was off running with Robert de Barri on his heels, calling for his cousin to slow down. Hostilo and Griffin went forward more carefully with Hostilo, as he had promised, watching Griffin's back.

'I'm with you,' William de Vale announced from Raymond's side. 'Come on. We can't let that short-arse get there first.'

Raymond leapt over a gap in the warehouse roof. A slinger – who had emerged from the brattice now that arrows had stopped falling – had identified him as his target and continually pelted him with stones. Raymond heard one rebound high in the air off the great spar as he ducked underneath. His thigh muscles were burning, his biceps straining, as he climbed. The first sign to tell him that there were defenders counterattacking was Gerald Bach's battle cry.

'St Maurice,' he shouted as his sword rang. Raymond deflected another stone over his head and glanced across at his cousins. Gerald and Robert were fighting four Gaels who hacked at them with axe and spear and sword. Ahead Raymond could see more warriors leaping down from the fortifications which had survived the collapse and onto the warehouse wreckage.

'William, front up,' he called and drew his sword. 'Enemies ahead.'

Raymond was in awe of the Gaels. They had no armour or shields and several weren't even wearing shirts on their backs. But they did not break stride as they came down to meet the advancing Normans. They howled and unloaded all their remaining darts before jamming their spears forward. Raymond's arm was already jarred from their initial attack but he took two massive spear blows on his shield before he could even get in range to fight back. When he did the two men opposing him danced away as he slashed wildly at them. One

347

was laughing at his pathetic attempts, keening in his strange tongue.

He gritted his teeth and waited his opportunity. It came moments later. One man went high and another low with their spears, hoping, Raymond supposed, that one could draw his shield into a defensive position so that the other could skewer him. But Raymond was ready. This time, just before they stabbed forward, he stepped backwards, far enough so that their spear tips did not reach him. One of the Gaels fell flat on his face while the other attempted to right himself by using his weapon like a crutch. Raymond swept his sword through the spear shaft and then cut down to finish the man. The other had rolled away towards William. A kick to the face dealt with his threat.

Breathing heavily, Raymond looked up. The way to the top was clear and he called for William to go to Gerald Bach and Robert's aid.

'Keep going,' William replied and veered off to the right.

He began climbing. More missiles flew through the air but Raymond swatted them aside derisively. He looped his elbow over one spar sprouting from the floor, hauling himself onwards. His shield and sword hindered him, caught in the debris, but he fought on, always climbing, always in the direction of the breach.

'Go, go, go,' he heard Griffin call from behind, urging him onwards.

Raymond used the great beam that had crowned the warehouse to cover his right as he climbed for the pinnacle, and hung from it when a panel gave way and almost sent him plummeting deep into the void beneath the wreckage. He gritted his teeth and launched himself forwards, over the yawning gap.

'No,' he heard Gerald Bach snarling for he wished to be the first man into Veðrarfjord.

'Climb,' Raymond bellowed. There were only a few paces to the top. He hauled himself over the ruin of the brattice. He could see the dead and the wounded Gaels inside the collapsed covered walkway, but he did not pause. He would be the first man into Veðrarfjord. He would succeed. He would be

348

remembered.

And then suddenly Raymond wasn't climbing any more. His feet were planted on top of the stone glacis. To either side were the broken timber posts of the wall, behind him the remnants of the warehouse.

'I did it,' Raymond mumbled as he stood there, sweat pouring from his temples, staring into Veðrarfjord.

A breeze grasped at his surcoat and shield as he stood on the precipice above the city. Ahead the thatched roofs of the city longhouses stretched out before him. There were gardens of herbs and animals in little wattle pens. There were granaries and coops and stables and workshops. A large church was surrounded by a head-high stone wall and he could see streets running in straight lines like veins in all directions. The walls of Veðrarfjord enclosed him on every side.

'We did it,' William de Vale whooped as he joined Raymond on the glacis. Behind him came Gerald Bach and Robert de Barri. Both had bloody swords in their hands and were panting from their exploits.

'Well, I can still be the first man in there,' Gerald stated and pointed north to where the walls intersected. Rögnvald's Tower was dark against the sky. Gerald didn't wait for Raymond's order but dropped onto his backside and used the slope of the glacis to slide down into the city. Robert de Barri skidded after him with Raymond and William just behind. Griffin and Hostilo were both breathing hard as they landed beside the rest of the milites.

Gerald Bach and Robert de Barri left dark trails of water on the dusty ground from their wet clothes as they skirted around the nearest house.

'Come on,' Raymond called and leapt over a fence and into a garden. He could see a face in a window of the attached longhouse, whether a woman or a child he could not tell before it disappeared from sight. His feet crushed turnips and kicked over Welsh arrows which had missed their target and had landed inside the city. He vaulted over the next wall and back into the street, already ahead of Gerald and Robert. The big hall was just ahead, Rögnvald's Tower looming behind it like a great sarsen stone.

He had just turned to shout orders to his milites to hurry when he saw them. The charging boar device appeared first, just visible over the rooftops atop the cross-pole standard. It was followed by a long length of pole and then, as the bearer rounded the corner into the street, a helmet. Below it he saw the face of his enemy, the red, knotted beard hanging like tusks, and the massive frame of Sigtrygg Mac Giolla Mhuire. He had brought fifty armoured Ostmen to plug the gap in the east wall of Veðrarfjord.

Both peoples were armoured, both equidistant from the breach in the fortifications. Both seemed surprised to see the other and for a moment everyone came to a halt, staring across the fifty yards of open roadway that divided them. Raymond's eyes flicked to the breach and then to Rögnvald's Tower before settling back on Sigtrygg and his large company of men.

'Where are you, Gufraid?' he whispered. He knew that if Sigtrygg's men made for the breach, the chances of his allies forcing their way through would be small. Yet he didn't have enough men to prevent it. Raymond knew he had to provoke Sigtrygg to leave it open, even for a few moments. He had to get him to do something stupid. He had only one idea.

'How's that nose of yours, Sigtrygg?' he called. Whether or not his enemy could hear his words, Raymond did not know but certainly he could see that Sigtrygg had spotted him. 'Do you remember me? I'm the one who gave you that snout of a nose. I'm the man you've been boasting about killing.' Raymond realised that no one would recognise him in his new surcoat and so he sheathed his sword in order to whip off his helmet and pull his coif away from his ears. Everyone could see his face and a hint of fair hair. Despite the distance he could see a flicker of recognition pass over Sigtrygg's large face. 'I told you I would be coming for you! I am Raymond de Carew, victor over Sigtrygg at Cluainmín, victor over Sigtrygg at Dun Domhnall. God be good, I will be victor over him today at Veðrarfjord too.'

He had been hoping for a reaction, but the swiftness and anger of the one that erupted from Sigtrygg and the Ostmen surprised even Raymond. Suddenly there were men running headlong towards him, fifty stampeding Ostmen. There was no order given, no command to follow. It was just a snarling pack seeking to defend their den.

Raymond's mail leapt and landed heavily with every running step that took him and the five milites towards Rögnvald's Tower. There was a wattle fence dividing the great hall from the rest of the town. If there had been a guard at the gate he was long gone and Raymond barrelled through unimpeded.

'Come on,' he called to his milites as he pushed one of the gates closed. Gerald and Robert were next and they turned on their heels to yell encouragement to their three kinsmen. Griffin, William and Hostilo were barely through before Raymond banged shut the second gate. Robert and Gerald had the locking bar in the air and slotted it down.

'We're in trouble here,' Griffin called. 'There's no way that will hold them.'

Raymond could see that his brother was correct. The wattle fence was high but the Ostmen were surging against the outside and already it was giving way, sagging and bulging like a mainsail in an erratic wind. He could hear the sound of axes cutting into the thin hazel and willow branches. There were hands on the top as men tried to climb over. He turned and looked behind him.

'Get to the tower,' Raymond called and began running.

Raymond led his five companions around the side of great south-facing longhouse. It was by far the biggest building in the city, but there was no way that they could defend it against attack by fifty men who each knew the place better than they. Their only hope was Rögnvald's Tower. If they could get inside Raymond knew that they would be able to barricade the doors and hold out.

He was dimly aware of fighting on the western wall but there was no chance that Raymond was going to pause to take a look. He and his milites were running for their lives.

'Look out!' a call came from his side. Some instinct told him to raise his shield and he was fortunate to have done so. A stone thrown from the battlements above the tower struck the boss of his shield and ricocheted away. The height from which it fell was so great that it almost forced Raymond to his knees. He knew he would've been killed or at least knocked out cold had it hit him, for he still had not had the chance to pull up his coif or return his spangenhelm to his head.

'Keep going,' he roared, fearing that his men would halt in the cover of the longhouse rather than face another barrage from above. Raymond knew that if they stopped that would be where they would make their last stand, surrounded on all sides by Sigtrygg's fifty warriors. No, their only hope was the tower.

'They're coming through,' he heard Griffin shout from behind. He knew what it meant and prayed that they would have enough time to get into the refuge before Sigtrygg's men were upon them.

He had a clear view of the stone foundations of the great wooden tower now. His shield blocked his view of the upper levels and the fortifications on top from where the enemy pelted them with all manner of missiles. The bottom floor was built much like the wall, with a sloped stone front. Into that impenetrable shell was built a doorway and thankfully the heavy oak entrance was still open.

Raymond thanked whatever saints were watching over him as he pumped his legs harder to cover the remaining twenty yards as they began climbing the small hill upon which Rögnvald's Tower was perched. It was obvious that the defenders on top of the tower knew of their mistake, for they were throwing everything they had at the milites. Arrows and two-handed battle axes crashed into the grass around them. Spears and darts and stones walloped into their shields. Raymond even saw a conical helmet bounce off Gerald Bach's shield. As he got closer a huge piece of tree trunk bounced just in front of him and went past his shoulder. It almost collided with William de Vale's legs as it landed but his former esquire was agile enough to leap over the missile.

Raymond was breathing heavily as he entered the little anteroom inside the tower. William and Gerald were just behind him and he imagined that Griffin, Robert and Hostilo would be on their heels.

'William, get the door closed as soon as they are through,' he ordered. There was a closed door to his right and a winding staircase leading upwards on his left. He told Gerald Bach to watch the stairs while he investigated any threats inside the room, but just as he turned towards it the door opened and a grey-bearded Ostman came out. He had a heavy set of keys in one hand and a wineskin in the other and he stopped dead in his tracks when he laid eyes on Raymond.

'They are coming down the stairs,' Gerald Bach called from his position on the far side of the room.

Raymond half-turned in Gerald's direction just as the Ostman threw himself across the small anteroom to tackle him to the ground. Raymond felt his back collide with William, dragging him down with his opponent in a great tangle of arms and shields. Keys rattled as they struck the wall and wine sloshed across Raymond's face, blinding him and stinging his eyes. A punch caught him in the cheek and then another in the stomach. The Ostman was screaming incoherently, lashing out at him wildly, and Raymond could hear Gerald Bach shout out a challenge to whoever was coming down the stairs from above to fight. Another punch caught Raymond on the end of his chin before there was a shuffling of feet near his head and a cry of pain. The pressure on his chest suddenly disappeared and Raymond was able to swipe the wine from his face. His brother, Griffin, stood above him, his sword red. To his side the man who had attacked him was holding the stump where his hand used to be. Blood poured from the wound and he began howling in pain. Griffin silenced him with a single stab downwards into his neck. Griffin didn't pause to see if Raymond was hurt, however. He bounded across the anteroom, shouting Gerald's name with his sword ready. Raymond could see that his diminutive cousin was valiantly trying to hold off at least four Ostmen who had come down from the fortifications at the top of the tower to attack. He tried to claw his way back to his feet to go to Gerald's aid when his hand found the set of keys resting in the puddle of wine. Raymond quickly stashed them on his belt before helping William to his feet.

'They are right on our backs,' Robert called as he backed through the tower entrance with Hostilo. Both had their shields raised.

Raymond had just time to turn when a spear came through

the doorway. He caught the end as it went past his midriff and pulled the bearer through the door, smashing his spangenhelm into his face as if it were a mace. The Ostman collapsed onto the floor as Raymond fixed his shield to his arm and made for the door. But he couldn't get close enough to swing it shut. Another Ostman was already through and he slammed his shield into Raymond's and for several seconds they powered against each other in the middle of the room. Raymond could feel his feet sliding backwards as a third man burst into the room, stabbing wildly at his legs and unprotected head with a spear. William de Vale brought his sword down on the man's arm and there was a cry as he tumbled away. But more of Sigtrygg's warriors were coming in and none of the milites could get to the door to get it closed over.

An axe flashed downwards and was buried in William's shield, forcing him backwards and allowing two further Ostmen to enter and suddenly Raymond was going in reverse too. He roared with the effort and Hostilo leapt to his side, cutting down with his sword onto a helmeted head. Robert planted his shield on Raymond's back, holding him in place and pushing with all his might to maintain their foothold inside Rögnvald's Tower. But no matter how hard the four men pushed, the weight of men outside was greater and, step by step, they were forced back from the door.

A spear sliced over a shoulder and went past Raymond's ear. As it was withdrawn, he could feel the long pine spearshaft rasp against his mail at his neck. He doubted the man who had launched it would miss a second time, but he had nowhere to hide and he could not move. He managed to raise his shield by half an inch and by some miracle that proved enough to bounce the second spearthrust away from his face.

Sweat mixed with the wine that had been spilled all over him and stung his eyes. Such were the close confines of the fight that no one spoke or shouted insults over their shield rims. Grunts and snorts of effort was all that could be heard. Soon an odour of perspiring bodies was rank in the air. For several seconds it seemed like no side had the upper hand but then there was a roar of vehemence from the doorway and the massive figure of Sigtrygg Mac Giolla Mhuire rose, a head

354

taller than everyone else in the anteroom.

Raymond felt himself take a step backwards. He could feel Robert de Barri's breath hot on his neck as he still fought to keep their position. He had long since lost his helmet and he could feel someone kicking at his legs. The man attempting to kill him was just a few inches away, the span of two shields pressed together. His opponent had a dagger in his hand but in the crush he could not bend his arm in the right way to stab at Raymond. Instead the long steel blade hung above them both, twisting in the air like a worm on a hook.

'This way!' Gerald Bach's call rang like a bell inside the small stone room. 'Come on, up the stairs,' he shouted.

Raymond shifted his eyes in that direction and could see that Griffin and Gerald had cleared the stairway and that his brother and William de Vale were already climbing up past Gerald with their swords outstretched to meet any new threats.

'Go,' he called to Robert and felt the pressure on his back relent. 'Back,' he snarled at Hostilo and together they retreated towards the small stair, step by step. 'You first,' Raymond gasped as the flat on an axe blade clubbed him lightly on top of his head. It did no damage, however. The man facing him had taken most of the impact from the wooden haft on his head and crumpled to the ground. It gave Hostilo and Raymond just the opening they needed to backtrack onto the stair. Even as he climbed, moving backwards and upwards, he could hear more fighting going on above them. Hostilo had a hold on his collar and half-directed, half-hauled him up the curling staircase. He was glad of the help, for twice he almost tripped over the bodies of men killed by Griffin and Gerald for control of the staircase.

Raymond's thighs and calves were burning with the effort and he had to crouch low to defend his ankles from the thrusts that came from below. A sword slashed around the corner and cut into the right side of his shield, carving out a large chunk of rim. Then there was a bearded Ostman in front of him, hacking and stabbing.

'Keep climbing,' he bellowed as he felt Hostilo come to a halt at his back.

The man facing him smiled as he prepared a two-handed

355

thrust upwards at Raymond. Just as he pulled back Raymond stepped forward and drove his shield into the Ostman's defenceless, front knocking him backwards. The man's hand grasped for purchase on the smooth wooden walls, his feet on the tiny steps, as he tipped over. He found no hold and went sprawling down the uneven stairs. Raymond could not see the damage the man's fall had caused for Hostilo was moving again.

'There's no way through,' a shout came from above.

'The door is locked,' another moaned.

'Heaven help us,' Hostilo screeched in Raymond's ear. 'Are we trapped?'

Raymond could hear the dull sound of a shoulder thumping into a heavy door somewhere just above him as another Ostman came around the corner and began stabbing at him with a spear.

'I'll try the next one,' Griffin's voice came, followed by the sound of running feet, and soon Raymond could feel the pull on his collar again. As they wound their way around tower and up the stairs, Raymond was aware of passing a closed door to the room on the first floor, as well as two small windows and doors that he presumed led out onto the north and east walls of the city.

'Hostilo,' he garbled as he was choked by the miles's hold on his hauberk collar. 'Hostilo, I have keys on my -'

The spearman returned and stabbed forward again. This time Raymond was ready, catching hold of the wooden shaft as it went past his right shoulder and holding it fast. He could feel the spearman trying to haul it out of his grasp but instead of letting go Raymond rammed his shield rim into the part below the steel tip and snapped the spear in two.

Left with just the pine handle, the Ostman came at him. Raymond raised his shield high and stabbed low with the Ostman's own spear tip, catching him under his armpit. His opponent cried out and fell back down the stairs with the shattered spear tip still in his side.

'What's going on?' Raymond yelled over his shoulder for Hostilo came to a halt. 'Can we get through?'

The sound of men hammering at thick wood with their

shoulders came echoing down the tight stairwell. It was answer enough.

At his left elbow was another doorway, leading into the second floor room, he supposed. Keeping his eyes on the passageway beneath him, he quickly unhooked the set of iron keys from his belt. There were seven on the ring that he had taken from the Ostman with the wineskin. He selected one key and slotted it into the lock. It would not turn but he thumped his shoulder against the door twice just to make sure. He was sure he heard a woman squeak on the other side as he did so. He quickly tried a second key and then a third which turned once in the lock. However, he had no time to investigate further for he could see a shadow creeping up the wall of the stair.

Even before he saw the charging boar device on the front of his circular shield, Raymond knew who was approaching. He could almost feel his menace, his vast frame, as his step caused the stairs to creak and strain beneath him. The bangs of shoulders striking the locked door above mirrored the tolling of Raymond's heart. As he turned the corner the blade of an axe came into view and then it was Sigtrygg's massive right arm, bulging with muscle. His helmeted head crept around the corner just a few paces beneath Raymond. The Norman captain caught sight of his little piggy eyes beneath his steel helmet before it disappeared back behind the curve of the stone staircase.

'Is that you, Raymond the Fat?'

Sigtrygg's voice boomed around the walls. It caused Hostilo and Raymond to take another step up the stair. Above them, the impacts on the door stopped in response to his words.

'It is you, isn't it?' Sigtrygg's laugh was scathing and loud. 'You should tell your men to stop trying to get through to the roof. There is no escape that way,' Sigtrygg laughed as the milites' attempts to break through the door began again, more frequent and with greater gusto than before.

'Ten minutes ago, there was no way to break through the city walls,' Raymond replied as he took another step away from the door and from Sigtrygg, 'but I found the means.' He glanced at the set of keys swinging in the lock just to his left and licked his lips as he quietly reached across and tried to

357

remove them from the lock. The key would not come out and he twisted it until it clicked. 'This is not the end,' he said.

Sigtrygg laughed again. 'The boy I killed at Dun Domhnall – the brave one – you probably told him the same thing. But it was his end, wasn't it, Raymond the Fat. He stood beside you and then you just left him to die by my hand.'

Raymond gripped the thick leather enarmes inside his shield as he remembered Alice's screams and the sight of her brother, Geoffrey, being murdered by Sigtrygg. He felt his teeth grind against each other, but he said nothing. Desperation pulsed around his chest as the key kept turning in the lock. *Come out*, he urged. He knew that soon Sigtrygg would identify the jangle of keys as they turned in the lock and what it meant.

'Blácaire,' he said loudly to cover the sound. 'Oistin and Bárid – do you recognise those names?'

Spittle hit the wall of the tower. 'Gufraid's whelps.'

'I take great comfort in knowing that I was able to save those boys from a similar fate to Geoffrey's. And I know that because of your treatment of those boys my new friend Jarl Gufraid will not stop fighting until he has -'

Raymond was suddenly interrupted by a roar of bellicose rage as the immense figure of Sigtrygg of Veðrarfjord exploded around the corner towards him. He barely had time to abandon his hold on the keys as his enemy came forward, slashing wildly with his axe. He was keening as he brought the axe down on the steps at Raymond's feet, and then rammed it back across the stairwell where it cut into the wall of the tower, shaking the whole structure and showering him in woodchips. Raymond could hear Hostilo and Robert screeching his name as Sigtrygg hauled the axe back across the face of his shield and then cut upwards towards his head, narrowly missing his chin. Sigtrygg's attack was all power and mad energy, but it drove Raymond onto his heels. Whether because of his efforts to break down the wall, or his injuries, or his tiredness after weeks in the wilderness, he simply had no response to Sigtrygg's brute strength. As the Ostman's next lunge crashed into the wall to Raymond's left, the Norman captain drew a dagger from his belt and dived forward desperately, but Sigtrygg was ready and he butted Raymond away with his

358

shield so that his thrust found the thick oak panels of wooden door rather than Sigtrygg's breast. The dagger was stuck fast and Sigtrygg brought up his shield rim, smashing it into Raymond's right elbow. The Norman captain's fingers immediately went numb and he abandoned his hold on the dagger which remained horizontal in the door as he tumbled backwards, burying Hostilo and Robert beneath him as he fell.

Sigtrygg pinned Raymond's shield and arms to his chest with his foot. 'I thought this would be more difficult,' the Ostman said as he bared his teeth and raised his axe.

Raymond saw death in Sigtrygg's little eyes as he fought to free himself. The weight of the Ostman was too great and no amount of squirming allowed him to escape Sigtrygg's hold. The axe blade hovered above him, poised to strike down on Raymond's defenceless head. There was nothing that he could do but stare up at the thin strip of steel which would claim his life.

His forlorn tussle continued but his thoughts were elsewhere. The image that was conjured in his mind's eye surprised him. It was not Alice or Basilia nor any other desire upon which his ambitions had so frequently rested. It wasn't of his friends, the Welshmen or those in his old conrois, or of his kin who stood beside him at the end in Rögnvald's Tower. It wasn't his late mother or father or even his siblings, and it certainly wasn't any fantasy of future riches and renown. Instead Raymond's mind presented him with a memory from many years before, of the solar at Striguil Castle and of the Dowager Countess and her children, enjoying an evening song by a Welsh bard. The Earl Strongbow, then a callow youth on the verge of manhood, was over by the hearth while his sister Isabel was curled up in their mother's embrace on a fur-backed chair. Raymond had been a boy, a page standing by and ready to serve wine to the family from a clay jug. In that instant he fancied that he could smell the contents as if he was actually in the room.

The flood of memories from the scene in the solar puzzled Raymond, and the look that crossed his face must've confused Sigtrygg too, for rather than chop down with his axe and finish his enemy, he paused.

'What?' the Ostman demanded angrily of his victim.

That moment of hesitation was all the time that Ragnall of Veðrarfjord needed to swing open the door at Raymond's left knee and stab his son in the throat with Raymond's dagger.

Several things happened at once. A woman was screaming and Sigtrygg was tumbling backwards down the steps of Rögnvald's Tower. An axe clattered across Raymond's front. There was blood on the walls and Robert de Barri was shouting. Ragnall was standing over him, raging in the tongue of the Ostmen. The noise echoed and amplified around the wooden walls.

It was all a blur to Raymond. His mind was caught between the image which he thought would be his last and the one that had actually happened above him: Ragnall throwing open the door and wrenching free the dagger to bury it in Sigtrygg's neck. It was as if time had slowed down for Raymond. And yet he struggled to comprehend what he had seen.

Ragnall, bald and bearded, did not allow him the chance to understand that he was going to live. He did not grant him time for relief. The deposed king stood over him, shouting directly at his face. Raymond had no idea what he was saying. His right arm hung limply at his side and he tried to roll back to his feet only to find that he was obstructed by his shield. Hostilo was moaning in pain at his back. Above them the thumping of mailed shoulder on wooden door still sounded.

'Wake up, you fool of a foreigner.' Ragnall's voice was distant but he followed it up with a slap across Raymond's jaw. 'Do you hear me? Wake up.'

'I hear you, I hear you!'

'Good,' Ragnall told him as his unpleasant features quickly looked up at Robert de Barri's outstretched sword and then down the steps where Sigtrygg had disappeared. He wiped his hand, still fresh with his son's blood, across his thin lips. 'I surrender to you. Do you hear me? I surrender.'

'You surrender?' Raymond garbled.

Ragnall looked to the roof. 'Holy St Ibar save me! Yes, I surrender to you, Raymond de Carew, but you should remember who saved you when you were looking death

360

straight in the eyes. Me. And God is always watching, boy, and he will know if you betray that good deed.'

'Meaning?'

'Meaning it's up to you to keep me alive.' Somehow Ragnall managed to turn that unfortunate circumstance into a gesture of defiance. His toady mouth stretched into a smile behind his wispy beard as he offered out his hand.

Raymond looked at the gnarled knuckles, the slick shine of crimson which covered them, and what it would mean. It was the hand of a king, a king who would be his prisoner. All the laws of Christendom and war said that by doing so Ragnall was, in effect, transferring his kingdom into Raymond's hands. He was offering power and wealth and fame, the chance to climb to the very top of society in one swift bound. Yet Raymond hesitated. The image of the solar of Striguil still lingered in his thoughts, of the family at ease and safe together.

'Perhaps you would prefer to remain as Strongbow's cowhand?' Ragnall accused.

Raymond lifted his gaze from Ragnall's hand to his face. His smile was disappearing into a grimace.

'I'm giving you my surrender, boy. If you are clever you will take it before the offer is withdrawn.'

Something in Ragnall's manner reminded him of Alice's words, of her claim that she was smarter than him, of her challenge for him to win at all costs. He remembered their agreement and that she would soon give birth to their child. He had a responsibility to provide for the infant. It wasn't just about what Raymond wanted and he shook his head to clear the image of the solar from his mind. He withdrew his left arm from the straps of his shield and grabbed hold of Ragnall's hand.

'I accept your surrender, Lord King, and that of your city, and, by my honour, I swear that I will keep you safe.'

Ragnall cackled and hauled Raymond up to his feet. Blood surged back to his right arm, causing the captain to wince in pain as feeling returned to his fingers. Behind Ragnall, Raymond could see a woman, hiding in the shadows of the second floor room.

'Robert, help Hostilo. Make sure our prisoners are kept

safe.' He leant past Ragnall and extracted the key from the door.

His prisoner nodded his head and stepped back into the room. 'Is Gufraid really with you?' he asked as Raymond reached for the door handle. 'Did you really save his boys?'

'We did and yes, the jarl is with us now.'

Ragnall nodded his head. 'I have two sons out there somewhere too. I have lost one today. I need to know that my family is safe.'

He was an unpleasant-looking man, but at that moment Raymond felt deep sympathy for Ragnall Mac Giolla Mhuire. 'I'll search for your children and return them to you, if I can,' he said.

Ragnall's eyes narrowed suspiciously. 'I don't yet know if you are weak or strong, Raymond de Carew. Somehow I worry for you and am worried by you,' he said and leaned forward and closed the door. Raymond did not bother to lock the room. He could see Gerald Bach's face and he tossed the ring of keys up to him. 'Open the door to the roof, Gerald.. Then follow me down to the ground floor with William. We must secure the tower.'

Raymond knelt and picked up Sigtrygg's abandoned axe. His right arm was still buzzing as if tiny grains of sand were running down the veins from his shoulder to his fingers. He imagined that the Ostman weapon would be must more easily deployed in his left hand than his sword and gave two cursory sweeps to test the weight of the axe.

There was blood spatter on the walls and the steps as he descended through the building. He passed several bodies of men that had been killed as his conrois had retreated. The smell of iron and sweat was rich in the air and as he passed Raymond forced open the shutters on the windows to clear the stink. Otherwise he went quietly and slowly, certain that soon he would come across Sigtrygg's body or one of his Ostman warriors. He could hear shouting below, but the sound was dulled by the thickness of the stone walls on the first floor. Raymond put his back to the curling inside wall of the stair as he neared the ground, listening for sign of men below. With every step his apprehension grew. He edged downwards. It was only when Raymond caught sight of the small anteroom that he realised that Sigtrygg's men had fled the tower.

There were still bodies on the ground and discarded weapons and shields. One man was still alive, a broken shaft of spear buried in his side and pink bubbles at his lips. He stared blankly up at Raymond as he emerged from the stairs. The only sign that he was still alive was the movement in his tired eyelids.

There was still no sign of Sigtrygg and that made Raymond uneasy, but he pressed towards the door which still hung open. The sun had swung further to the west and he exited the shade of the slanted stone glacis into bright light. Past Ragnall's Hall and over its timber defences, Raymond could see the survivors of Sigtrygg's attack. They were on their knees in the streets, surrounded by more of their kin. For a moment Raymond was confused by what he saw, but then he saw Jarl Gufraid barking out orders with his son Blácaire and Grím by his side. His eyes crossed to the breach in the eastern defences. Esquires were still pouring through the gap and onto the streets of Veðrarfjord under the direction of Gervais d'Alton and below them he could see archers streaming through the streets and into homes, searching for plunder. He could see the giant figure of Philip the Welshman pointing out targets and Caradog ap Thomas as he tried to break down the gates into the church in the centre of the city. Beyond them he could see Gaels fleeing through the eastern gates and out onto the muddy waterfront. This was not their city and the Déisi could tell that the battle had been lost.

'Raymond,' he heard Gerald Bach call from his rear. His cousin was pressed up against the wall at the back of the anteroom with his sword in his hand. Gerald's eyes were locked on the door to the ground floor room. It hung ajar. Gerald lifted its chin in its direction and mouthed that he had heard movement inside. Raymond nodded that he understood and moved closer to investigate.

Gerald Bach led the way, pushing open the door and then darting inside with a loud challenge. Raymond followed him, his injured right arm now held across his front and the axe ready in his left. There were boxes and barrels of food inside the little room, a treasure trove of food, with wineskins and breads and sacks of grain. Smoked sides of beef and pork hung from the rafters above them. Gerald was over to Raymond's left threatening an old whimpering man with his sword. He was dressed richly in vaguely clerical apparel.

'Easy, Gerald,' he warned. 'He might be valuable.'

But Raymond's interest was in the other side of the room. There was a trail of blood leading between the vast racks of foodstuffs and he followed it, his axe out ahead of him. He passed the abandoned shield bearing the charging boar and then a spangenhelm spinning gently on the stone floor. Several packs of oats had fallen over, spilling their contents. Raymond stepped over and there, at the very back of the room, sat between a large box of onions and a container of apples, he found Sigtrygg.

His enemy was still alive, but he didn't have long. He was pale and blood ran freely from his neck wound. The dagger was still stuck in Sigtrygg's throat with the hilt pointing out towards Raymond. He was dying, but Sigtrygg's little eyes were alive with loathing. They stayed locked on the Norman captain as he came closer.

'The city is taken,' Raymond told him. 'Ragnall has surrendered and my men are through the breach. It is the end.'

Sigtrygg had his mouth clamped shut with one hand over the wound to his neck. He wanted to speak, Raymond knew, but he could not. His lips peeled open and blood began seeping between his teeth. His other hand gripped the basket of onions at his side.

'I cannot save you, Sigtrygg, but I can help you on your way faster.' He showed the axe to the dying man and stepped closer so that he was only a pace away. 'You do not need to suffer.'

The Ostman stared up at Raymond. His eyes were swollen and bloodshot. Sweat poured down his brow and Raymond could not tell if it was tears or perspiration that dripped from the end of his disfigured nose. Hatred and resentment were clear upon his face. Sigtrygg had twice bested Raymond in single combat yet he was the one dying on the floor surrounded by animal carcasses and vegetables.

'*Gamla vis Hruga uskit'r,*' Sigtrygg mumbled as he reached

up and drew the dagger from his own neck. Even as he leant forward to slash at Raymond he was choking, his eyes no longer filled with anger but with terror. Blood spilled from his mouth and from his neck as he collapsed at Raymond's feet, gurgling and spluttering as the life drained from him. With one final drawn out sigh and shuffle of his feet, Sigtrygg Mac Giolla Mhuire – the despot, the usurper, the would-be King of Veðrarfjord – died.

He had sworn revenge when Sigtrygg had killed Geoffrey, but Raymond could find no joy in his enemy's death. He rescued his dagger from Sigtrygg's hand, wrapping up the bloody weapon in a thick piece of cloth before stowing it in his belt.

'What now?' Gerald called from the other side of the room.

Raymond pushed his way back to the doorway and pointed at Gerald's prisoner. 'Bring him with us. We'll put him with Ragnall until we find out who he is and if we can use him.' He looked around the provisions in the room. 'Lock the door. No one gets in here unless he asks me first.'

Gerald obliged and Raymond left him to fulfil the rest of his orders while he left the tower and walked down the little hillock towards the city. He passed the longhouse and then went through the twisted limbs of the fence which divided the north-east point from the rest of the city. The strange feeling had left his right arm and although still painful it was masked by all the other aches that fought for his attention. Raymond raised that same arm in greeting to Jarl Gufraid.

'I've taken the tower and have secured Ragnall,' he called across to his ally. 'Get your men through into the hall compound,' he ordered poking a thumb over his shoulder. 'We must hold our position.'

Raymond didn't wait for Gufraid's response but made for the breach where he found the esquires with Gervais and William FitzMaurice. 'Run to the tower,' he ordered. His attention was taken by a growing din from the west wall. Since breaking into the city there had been the noise of distant battle from the west. But now a new sound had arisen – the sound of chanting. One of the big streets ran in more or less a straight line from the tower to the western gates and Raymond stood in the middle of thoroughfare, staring towards the afternoon sun. There was much activity on the west wall, flashes of light on steel and the movement of men. But above it all he heard one word being shouted over and over again: Strongbow.

Raymond smiled, for he knew what the chanting meant. The earl who had risked everything had won. Veðrarfjord had been conquered. The Earl Strongbow was lord.

The line of Ostman warriors and their families stretched for half a mile until it disappeared into the trees on the horizon. Alice watched them from the top of Thorgest's Tower. She wondered where they would wander now that their homes had been taken, their city conquered and the Ostmen expelled from Veðrarfjord.

'It is a sad sight,' the Hospitaller Chaplain, Brother Charles, said as he came across to join her.

Alice nodded her head. 'Where will they go?'

'There are many little villages and manors outside the walls. They will find somewhere to roost, I am sure.' He turned around to look back over the city. 'And they will be safer out there than here.'

Alice couldn't disagree. After the city's fall Strongbow's victorious warriors had gone berserk. She had not been present but had heard the screams echoing through the night as she had tried to sleep up in the Norman camp. Brother Charles had tried to comfort her, telling her that the sack of Veðrarfjord could not be stopped, but that soon the soldiers would drink themselves into a stupor and it would relent. Alice had imagined far worse crimes than drunkenness being inflicted on the people of the city and the high-pitched cries for help and mercy which emanated from the town seemed to confirm her worst fears. They were women's cries. They were children's.

It was only at first light that Raymond had sent word for those remaining on the hillside to break camp and make their way down. He had despatched his handsome cousin, William FitzMaurice, and a platoon of esquires to help Alice and the monks to move into the city. All along their path they had seen evidence of a great pillaging in Veðrarfjord. Everywhere Alice had looked there were bodies, men, women, children and animals alike. She had seen death on a mass scale at Dun Domhnall but this was worse again. She had seen the young wandering the streets screaming for parents who would never return. Many of the wounded had died unaided and alone during the night and more would be beyond their help. Yet still more wailed for help. Some of those Alice thought to have been dead were merely fall down drunk and as they had travelled through the city she had seen some of them seemingly rise from the dead and wobble down the street to rejoin their units. Not even St Olav's Church had been left untouched by the violence. The clerics who had hidden within had not escaped the vengeance of the men who had been forced to gamble with their lives to claim the city. They wanted compensation for their efforts. Reprisals were owed for the men who had fallen.

Thorgest's Tower had been partially burned during the night, but the damage had been primarily cosmetic and Brother Charles had gratefully accepted it as the base for his new infirmary. The sick would occupy the first two floors while the Cistercians and the Hospitallers would sleep in the top storey. Alice had set up a temporary shelter on the roof and Brother Charles had even given her the key so that she would not be disturbed by anyone unless she wished it.

'Have you had time to consider my request?' Brother Charles asked her.

Alice's mind was elsewhere and she had to ask the Hospitaller to repeat himself.

'That you stay with us here and help me with the infirmary,' he said. 'I have never been in any one place long enough to learn how to run a household, but if I'm going to oversee a preceptory here in Ireland as the earl requests I will need someone to help me.'

'Brother Charles,' Alice began. 'I don't wish to -'

'Before you give your answer I would repeat that there is no requirement for you to swear any vow. I know of many noble ladies like you who serve the Order as lay sisters and can leave at any time. Adelaide of Arles was one such woman. Like her you would not be beholden to stay with us any longer than you wish. But you would be given responsibility.' Brother Charles paused. 'You would be mistress of the house in all but name.'

Again Alice felt her stomach knot. 'Would I be paid?'

'A little. But you will not want for anything while you serve the Order.'

Alice could feel tears forming at the sides of her eyes and she turned away from Brother Charles so that she faced the river. 'Where would you build this preceptory?'

'I always pictured it by the seaside. Close enough to this city for its protection and far enough away to be outside its control.'

'And if I were to require more time,' she asked, putting a hand across her stomach. 'Perhaps as much as seven months?'

'I would make allowances for whatever you need,' Brother Charles told her. 'We are in a very strange land here and most of those with us are military men. They think conquest comes at the point of a sword but I have seen that it can come at the hands of kindness and care. You are one of the very few people here who I can enlist to help me. You are one of the very few I think that can help.' He crossed the rooftop to join her above the fast-flowing Siúire. 'And as long as I am prior, your secrets will be our secrets. And I will wait as long as I must for your answer.'

Alice thought of Raymond and her commitment to him, to their understanding. She did not yet know what Strongbow had in mind for him. If he handled himself correctly, Alice believed that Raymond could demand whatever he liked from the earl. Brother Charles had been down into the city and had returned to tell her that his name was on every man's lips. They were already recanting stories of his heroic deeds, saying that he had stormed through the breach on his own, that he had killed King Sigtrygg in single combat, and had claimed Rögnvald's Tower by scaling its outer walls. Many spoke of Strongbow's courage in the west, Brother Charles told her, but most were saying that the only reason that assault was successful was because Raymond's daring attack had drawn so many defenders to the east.

They had already talked of his appointment as Constable of Veðrarfjord, and Alice now prayed that Raymond had the self-assurance to demand that role of Strongbow. It would give him great wealth and influence, perhaps even a large estate of his own. Alice's hand still rested on her midriff. Raymond offered protection for Alice and her child, safety in a perilous world, and the chance of great wealth in the future. But the Hospitallers offered independence, not importance perhaps, but freedom and responsibility, her own money, her own household. Her own life.

Alice smiled at Brother Charles. 'Then, with my thanks, I will visit your new preceptory in the spring with my answer.'

The Hospitaller seemed content with that and nodded his turban-clad head. 'Look. It's beginning,' he said and lifted a finger to point down onto the wharf on the Merchant's Quay.

She followed his outstretched hand and saw a small group of men making their way towards the jetties which jutted out into the river. There was already a small fleet docked there, made up of the men in the merchant vessels which had transported Strongbow's army to Ireland. They barely took up a third of the space available. The crews of those vessels had come out to see what was going on and watched as the warriors selected one of the jetties close to Thorgest's Tower and began marching up it. Alice could hear the dull thump of their armoured feet on the wooden boards. She looked for Raymond but there was no sign of him. In their midst, however, she could see several long-haired men and one pushing a handcart with a person slumped inside.

'I don't think I want to watch this,' Alice said. She did not move away.

The Merchant's Quay was perfectly designed for cargo ships, with long jetties and deep water. Each berth also had access to small, rudimentary winches which could help the traders lift their wares from the innermost parts of their vessels and onto the jetty. They were slung from eight-foot high posts driven deep into the bottom of the river and secured to the great posts upon which each dock was moored.

It was the perfect place for Sir Hervey to conduct an execution.

'The men in the city are saying that Ragnall demanded it,' Brother Charles told Alice. 'But I was party to a conversation between Strongbow and Sir Hervey before the second attack.

They were planning to kill the Ostman leaders anyway. That's Jarl Háimar,' he added, pointing to a small brown-haired warrior with his hands in fetters. He was kicking and shouting as he was dragged forward by Sir Hervey's men, a knotted rope placed around his neck. The end was then looped over the hook and without any ceremony he was winched into the air.

Alice gasped as Háimar kicked wildly and circled in the air. The noise of the small group continuing to the next berth covered the sound of Háimar choking to death. She nonetheless looked away.

'Jarl Orm,' Brother Charles said, causing her to look back. 'Brave lad. Too brave for this bad business.'

She could see the young man of whom he spoke. Unlike Háimar, Orm stood by his executioners as if accepting of his fate. His chin was high and he looked to the walls of the city as they looped the rope over his neck. Two youngsters ran out of the little pack to grab hold of Orm's sides as if in an embrace before they were hauled away by an unpleasant-looking bald man. 'Are those his children?'

'No, they are Ragnall's sons. Orm was their keeper during the siege.'

As he spoke the Normans abruptly winched the young jarl into the air. Alice closed her eyes, but the wail of the two boys reached easily to her ears up on Thorgest's Tower. By the time she opened her eyes both Háimar and Orm were still and the group had moved to the last berth on the jetty. It took them more time to prepare the last hanging than it had done the first two. It required three men to lift the body from the handcart and get a rope around his neck. The last man to be hanged put up no fight at all.

'This is indecent,' Brother Charles said and walked away.

Alice did not join him. His was the execution that she had prepared herself to watch. The three warriors continued to hold the last man as two more began hauling at the ropes which looped through the pulley system. It required their joint effort to drag the huge frame of Sigtrygg Mac Giolla Mhuire into the air on the winch. He hung there, his feet dangling over the River Siúire, for all to see. He had died the day before, but Strongbow and Sir Hervey had hanged him anyway. Alice did not care to know of their reasons for hanging a dead man. Sigtrygg had killed her brother and it seemed like justice.

Long after the crew of the merchant vessels had returned to their work, after Brother Charles had left her side. Long after the party of executioners had returned to the city, Alice remained on the roof of Thorgest's Tower, staring down at Sigtrygg's lifeless body. She imagined what might've happened had Geoffrey survived, of how Raymond might've been able to use his new-found influence to help her brother win back Abergavenny from their usurper cousin. Where would she have been then? What would that have made her? Would her brother have valued *her*, or would he have merely valued the alliances she could bring to his house through marriage? Tears began to flow from her eyes

'No, you will keep going,' she scolded. 'You have a new dream.'

Alice was about to end her vigil over Sigtrygg's body when movement on the far bank caught her eye. At first she thought it was the effect of her crying and she had dabbed away her tears with her cuff. But no, on the far bank of the river she could see people amongst the trees. She glanced down to the wharf below. The men on the jetties had noticed too and were calling up to Norman lookouts on the north wall of the city. Alice could see esquires running down the length of the fortifications with the news. Strongbow had taken up residence in Ragnall's Hall and she could see one boy climbing down the steps in that direction. Another was running towards Raymond's lodgings in Rögnvald's Tower.

Orders were called and men were running. Strongbow had conquered Veðrarfjord. Now his army were preparing to defend it. Loud blasts of many horns sounded, drawing Alice's eyes back to the northern shore. At the edge of the long shoulder of high ground opposite her see could hear drums beating and the call of hundreds of cattle. From the woods Gaels were emerging, thousands of them. They made no effort to remain unseen, but sang and shouted, waving their arms and weapons in the air. The wail of a piper crossed the water. It was so piercing, it was if the man was standing by Alice's shoulder.

From her position up on Thorgest's Tower she had a better

view than most and Alice was aghast at the size of the army that faced Veðrarfjord across the wide stretch of river. It was a whole nation on the march.

She trained her eyes on a large group of horsemen coming through the throng. Most were wearing the saffron robes so prevalent amongst the Gaelic nobles, yet amongst them Alice could've sworn she saw something else. She swiped her eyes of any remaining tears and concentrated on the little group that plodded its way towards the riverbank. Yes! Her eyes did not deceive her. She had seen Norman surcoats amongst them.

Cheering sounded to Alice's right and she looked down the wall to see the Normans within Strongbow's army dancing and shouting joyfully as they too realised that the army were not enemies; they were allies. For the King of Laighin had come to Veðrarfjord. Diarmait Mac Murchada had come to secure his pact with Strongbow.

There were not many women that Raymond de Carew thought could outshine Alice of Abergavenny for beauty. There were none that he believed came close to the delicate loveliness and regal bearing of Strongbow's daughter, Basilia. But at that moment in the midst of Ragnall's Hall in Veðrarfjord, he truly believed that Princess Aoife of Laighin might be the most striking of them all.

King Diarmait's daughter was different to either of the women in Raymond's life. While Alice was fair and Basilia dark of hair, Aoife had long auburn curls that reached down her back. The princess also carried herself with more confidence than either Alice or Basilia and she was tall, as tall as Raymond's uncle, Robert FitzStephen. He could barely take his eyes off her. She was utterly captivating.

He watched her over the central hearth as she took Strongbow's hands to receive Father Nicholas's blessing. Most women of her age might have been embarrassed at being the centre of attention to so many warriors, but not Aoife. She was not so meek and met the earl's gaze unwaveringly.

'Then I beseech the Heavens, all the panoply of Holy Saints, and the Trinity – Father, Son and Holy Ghost – to protect and keep them in their loving care as they go forward as man and wife.' Father Nicholas paused for a moment. 'We ask it in His Holy Name. Amen.'

Strongbow beamed as King Diarmait and his kin whooped and hollered. The earl was older than his new bride by at least twenty years, but somehow he seemed younger than that as he stood beside Aoife. It had only been one year since Strongbow and Diarmait had made their promise in the great hall at Striguil. They had agreed that in return for an army to help put him back on the throne of Laighin, Diarmait would arrange this marriage and then name Strongbow as heir to his kingdom. And perhaps it was the completion of that pact in Veðrarfjord that had caused the change in the earl. It no doubt helped that he was smiling. All those cares and worries that he had carried for so long had been shed like a wet cloak allowing him to stand straight and tall on the dais, accepting the celebratory cheer of Diarmait's folk as well as the more solemn congratulations from his barons. It had been a long time since Raymond had seen his lord so happy and he was drawn back to the image of Strongbow and his mother and sister in the solar of Striguil years before.

'So you are alive then,' Fionntán Ua Donnchaidh said as he emerged from the crowd and slotted a mug of wine into Raymond's hands, interrupting his reminiscences.

Raymond smiled and crashed the goblet against Fionntán's ale cup, sinking a large slurp. 'I am!'

'But it was a close-run thing again, I hear.'

'Well, I had to think on my feet -'

'I wonder if sometime you might consider coming up with a plan in advance of putting it into action?' Fionntán said. 'You might live longer.'

'Or I could just keep you with me for advice?'

'That would do the trick, yes,' laughed Fionntán. 'It is good to see you have recovered your sense of humour. I was worried that it had gone for ever.' He dropped his voice so that only Raymond could hear. 'You might want to use it on your uncle.'

'Robert?' he asked. 'What is wrong with him?'

Fionntán looked over both shoulders to make sure no one was listening in. 'He crept out before Aoife came in. Diarmait wasn't pleased.' Raymond must've still looked confused and

Fionntán shook his head in exasperation. 'Robert's in love with the princess and now she's been married off to Strongbow…'

Raymond hardly knew Sir Robert FitzStephen. He and Raymond's father were half-brothers and many years apart in age. His uncle had been Constable of Aberteifi, a fortress in the extreme west of Wales, perhaps two days ride from Carew, and as a result the brothers were rarely in contact. Raymond, growing up in Striguil, was even further away again. Robert had not even thought to ask him to come to Ireland during his invasion of the summer before, when almost all of their kinsmen had accompanied him to defeat the Ostmen of Waesfjord.

'What can I do?'

Fionntán snorted. 'Maybe you could give him some tips to get over it. You are not going to tell me you aren't in love with Alice of Abergavenny, are you?' He nodded his head up towards the dais where Strongbow was introducing Raymond's former mistress to his new wife. At Alice's side was the Hospitaller, Brother Charles, with his great bulbous turban.

Raymond felt his cheeks blush and he took another long draught from his mug. 'It's not like that with us,' he mumbled.

His friend chuckled again. 'You can mark my words: Robert will only be at Diarmait's side as long as he has to be. As soon as he can he will run off to Waesfjord so he doesn't have to see Strongbow and Aoife together.'

One of Diarmait's retinue had picked up a harp and had started singing. The song started out quite slow but the bard was well practiced and he soon had changed up to a faster tune which matched the mood in Ragnall's Hall. Raymond had no idea what his words meant but the Gaels were singing along with him, bawling out words and laughing at the jokes contained in its story. Even Fionntán was mumbling along and tapping his foot in time with the piece.

Men from seven different nations talked and feasted and drank. Raymond could see Jarl Gufraid and his sons sitting quietly in one corner with Philip the Welshman and the Fleming commander, Maurice de Prendergast. Prendergast had picked the point furthest from the dais as he could find and still stole nervous glances up at Diarmait and his party. Gerald Bach and William de Vale were drunk and were dancing in the middle of the hall, calling out to Aoife of their love for her in the manner of the courtly troubadour. Raymond's brother Griffin and Milo de Cogan howled in laughter at their desperate attempts to get even the slightest rise out of the princess. Amongst their number were Asclettin and Denis d'Auton, the milites from his old conrois, now serving Sir Hervey.

'I'm going to get some air,' Raymond told his companion. The beds that had once crowded the walls of the longhouse had been removed and replaced by benches. Raymond picked his way through but did not get very far. Everybody wanted to speak to him, to shake his hand. He was the hero of the hour, they said, and each asked him to share a mug of wine with them before he could move on. By the time he reached the door, Raymond could feel the drink taking hold. He spied two mugs and a full skin of wine and snatched them up before exiting.

It was dark outside but he had only a little bother finding the steps that took him up past Rögnvald's Tower and onto the northern wall. The river sparkled silver in the mix of moonlight and firelight. Raymond returned the acknowledgement by the sentinels on the wall as he wandered along the palisade. He had no idea if he was on Robert's trail, but he hadn't gone very far before a hand fell upon his shoulder.

'I think you have had enough to drink, Nephew.'

Raymond turned and greeted Robert FitzStephen with a hug. Unfortunately, FitzStephen being much taller and Raymond being slightly drunk meant that rather than go over his shoulders Raymond's arms slipped around his chest, like a child cuddling its mother. FitzStephen laughed as Raymond withdrew from the clumsy embrace.

'I thought I'd bring you a drink,' Raymond said. Most of the wine from the skin went over his uncle's sleeve but enough found its mug for the knight to get at least a few mouthfuls.

'Were you not enjoying the feast?' FitzStephen asked. His surcoat was bright blue with a large silver star across the centre of his chest. It spun slightly as Raymond tried to focus on it.

'I prefer to limit the amount of time I spend in the same room as Sir Hervey de Montmorency.'

'We have that in common.'

'And more besides,' Raymond said, crashing his mug against FitzStephen's. 'We're both famous conquerors of cities.'

The knight chuckled and nodded. 'In my experience that is the easy part. Then you have to run the place. Lists and numbers and clerks,' he said as he stared down at the wharf on the Merchant's Quay. 'Make sure to get yourself a good clerk.'

Raymond nodded his head seriously. 'Of course, a good clerk. Got it.'

'Of course, if King Diarmait gets his way you won't be here for very long.' FitzStephen paused and shook his head. 'No, I've said too much.'

'No, please, go on.'

FitzStephen smiled. 'I'm sure you'll hear in good time. But tell me, does Strongbow treat you well? How has he rewarded his famous conqueror?'

Raymond frowned. 'He hasn't actually spoken to me since the city was taken.'

'Well, presumably there was a lot he had to do, particularly with Diarmait arriving,' FitzStephen said, flapping a hand in the direction of the hall. 'But if he forgets, or you don't feel valued here, don't forget that your uncle Maurice and I would have you and your men with us in Waesfjord.'

Raymond recalled Alice's assessment of that outcome when he had threatened to leave Strongbow's service. If she was correct, then there was little territory into which his uncles could expand. To the north was Diarmait's clan and to the west, Strongbow's newly won realm. He decided on a more diplomatic tack. 'You've plenty of people to look out for without worrying about me and my problems.'

FitzStephen did not press the matter. 'Think on it.'

'Fionntán would probably tell me that too.'

'Fionntán thinks too much and would tell you that those around him think too little.' FitzStephen put a hand on Raymond's shoulder. 'I came to Ireland because I had, truth be told, no other option. But here in Ireland, I don't have to ask King Henry's permission to do what I want. I don't have to ask for anyone's approval. Do you know what brought you here,

Raymond?'

An image of Basilia surged to the front of his mind, but it seemed distant, less defined than it once had. It was quickly replaced by Alice's face. Raymond licked his lips. 'Recognition,' he told FitzStephen.

His uncle nodded his head slowly as he stared down at him. 'What you need to do is figure out what you want, no, what you need, and then devote all your energy towards getting it.'

'Is that what you did?'

FitzStephen grimaced. 'I have found that there is a great deal of difference between what you want,' his eyes flicked back towards Ragnall's Hall, 'and what you need.' He cleared his throat and sank what remained of his wine. 'Two years ago I was a prisoner of the Welsh. Now I have a castle and an army and a king who needs me. For the first time I have land to leave to my sons and I even have some money in my purse.' FitzStephen held out his mug to Raymond. The nephew refilled his uncle's cup from the skin. 'That is what I need. You think on what you need and, if you are lucky, the Earl Strongbow will help you to win it.'

A quiet cough sounded from beyond FitzStephen. 'I very much hope that to be the case.'

Both Raymond and his uncle spun to look at Strongbow and his new wife, Aoife of Laighin. The earl had a cloak over his shoulders but Aoife had no wimple or mantle to guard against the cold. She was wearing a long green gown with a richly woven shirt over the top. Gold thread followed the line of her hips and ran down her thighs where it met a swirling pattern of beads. The design shone in the light of the moon above. Raymond ducked into a bow as FitzStephen stared at the princess and her new husband.

'My wife asked that I introduce her to the man who captured Veðrarfjord,' Strongbow stammered. 'I was unable to find you inside, Raymond, but Sir Hervey helpfully pointed me in this direction.' FitzStephen shifted uneasily at the mention of Strongbow's uncle. 'This is Raymond, my love, the man who brought down the walls of the city and stormed the tower.'

Aoife inclined her head towards Raymond, but he could see that her gaze flicked towards FitzStephen at his side. 'It is good to meet your acquaintance, sir, and congratulate you on your wondrous feat of -'

'It is I who should be congratulating you, my Lady,' Raymond interrupted. 'I wish you the greatest happiness and success in your marriage, and that you have many -'

'Yes, we shall be very happy together, no doubt, and successful and wealthy. And in time we shall be King and Queen of Laighin, perhaps even more than that.' At her side Strongbow beamed, holding her arm and staring at Aoife with great pride. 'Won't we, my love.'

'Oh yes,' Strongbow told her as he followed Aoife's gaze towards FitzStephen. 'I'm sorry, we haven't been introduced.'

'Sir Robert FitzStephen.'

'Ah yes, Diarmait's man.'

'And my uncle, my Lord,' Raymond added.

'It is good to have you here, Sir Robert,' Strongbow said seriously, 'and I hope that in the future we can help each other as you have helped King Diarmait.'

FitzStephen nodded his head slowly. 'I will do what I can to help you both.'

For several seconds no one spoke until Raymond could take it no longer and loudly clapped his hands together: 'Perhaps we should get back to the feast?'

Strongbow raised his hand. 'In a moment. As we sought you out Princess Aoife - my wife, Lady Pembroke - reminded me that I had not yet rewarded you for your efforts yesterday.' The earl turned to the young woman on his arm. She inclined her head. 'And so I am here to thank you and to ask what you would have of us?'

'Well, my Lord,' Raymond began. His eyes flicked towards FitzStephen. His uncle merely raised his eyebrows and stepped back from his nephew. 'I don't really -'

Strongbow cleared his throat. 'Perhaps I might ask Sir Robert to escort my wife back to the hall while we talk of such matters?' Both Aoife and FitzStephen bristled at that proposal, but there was little argument to be made as the earl left his wife's side and took Raymond by the arm, directing him further up the palisade of Veðrarfjord in the direction of Thorgest's Tower. 'I can't imagine the countess would have any interest in military appointments and what not.'

Raymond stole a glance of Aoife as he was turned and led away by her husband. He spotted a distinct look of fury on her face as she was left to FitzStephen's care. Strongbow's long gait quickly swept them out of earshot and the earl deliberately picked a spot halfway between two sentries on the north wall.

'Robert de Bermingham's men,' he told Raymond quietly as he nodded at the lookouts and put a single digit to his lips. 'I owe you an apology,' he began, raising a hand to stop Raymond's argument to the contrary. 'No, I did not treat you fairly. And to think that you repaid my scorn with -' Strongbow's voice drifted away as he raised both his palms, indicating towards the thatched roofs of the city. 'I will not forget it, Raymond, but before we discuss anything else I need your opinion on something.'

Raymond was surprised how the earl's short statement had affected him. His words caught in his throat and he had to repeat himself: 'Anything, my Lord.'

Strongbow's brow furrowed. 'Dubhlinn – you have heard of it?'

He had. The city was said to be Ireland's greatest, as large as London and home to the biggest market in Christendom. It lay somewhere to the north, Raymond did not know how far, on the coast facing England across the Irish Sea. Wealthy beyond even Veðrarfjord's reckoning, it was the home of pirates and smugglers, slave traders and warriors, of lordless men and rebel bandits.

'I know of it,' he replied.

'Diarmait demands that I take my army there,' the earl said. He glanced back down the length of the palisade as if checking to see if his new wife was listening in to their conversation.

Raymond's eyes narrowed. 'Are we to invest the city on King Diarmait's behalf? Or will he allow you to hold it once it is taken?'

Strongbow shrugged. 'I tried to press him on that exact point, but he is crafty and would not be pinned down.'

'We have dealt with craftier men than he,' Raymond smiled. 'Remember our audience with King Henry in Westminster?' The earl did not say anything but continued to stare at him. Raymond realised that the question was too serious for his joking. 'We know that Diarmait and Sir Robert's combined forces are not strong enough to storm the city. If they were they would already have done so -'

'So they need us,' Strongbow said wistfully as if he had never considered it.

'News of Veðrarfjord will travel fast, my Lord. And the more time we give them to prepare, the more difficult it will be to take the city. I say we go for it, use Diarmait's might, and FitzStephen's men, and then when all's said and done we will demand it for our own. For you own,' he corrected.

'If we do this I will need to leave a body of men here to make sure that the Ostmen do not recapture Veðrarfjord.'

Raymond nodded his head. 'He should be someone you trust, Lord.'

Strongbow placed the ends of fingers together and paused, thinking. 'Let us talk of your reward, Raymond,' he eventually suggested. 'What would you have of me? You would seem to be the sensible choice to leave as Constable of Veðrarfjord.' It was exactly what Alice had advocated that he demand but Raymond did not speak as Strongbow continued. 'You won the city and have some experience of the building work that will be required to fix the walls. You have a relationship with the Earl Gerald -'

'Jarl Gufraid, Lord.'

'Yes, Jarl Gufraid, and you have enough warriors to see that Veðrarfjord is kept safe while the rest of the army is in the north.' Strongbow placed his back against the rampart. 'As constable you would be a wealthy man, Raymond. You could even marry.'

Raymond turned his eyes on Strongbow for in that second he had thought that the earl was about to propose some future marriage to his daughter, Basilia. He would've blurted out his acceptance there and then had not Strongbow completely misread his expression and spoken first:

'Not that it's any of my business what you and Mistress Alice get up to,' Strongbow exclaimed and blushed. 'No, that's not what I mean either. I didn't mean to presume that you were,' he said and dropped his hands to his sides. 'Oh, dear, I fear I've offended you.'

'No, Lord, not at all,' Raymond said, smiling sadly. 'You merely reminded me of some advice Sir Robert just gave me.' He did not elaborate or even start thinking of the miles and impossibilities that separated him from Basilia. His mind then drifted to Alice, who had tried to convince him that this offer was everything for which he could hope. He thought of their unborn child whose future he could secure with a single word. He thought of his followers who he could reward for their efforts, of Caradog, Gufraid, and William de Vale. He wanted it all. But what he really needed remained outside his grasp.

'Lord, I cannot accept the position of constable.' The arrow was loosed, the bowstring quivering. So many factors might affect if it ever struck its intended target.

Strongbow sighed. 'I suppose Sir Hervey might be convinced to take it.'

'Sir Hervey commands the army, Lord. He must come with us.'

The earl's brow puckered in confusion. 'You wish him to continue as commander? I thought you of all people would wish him,' Strongbow paused and smirked, 'promoted to a higher role.'

'I will serve under him, Lord, but as my reward I would like to be appointed as his lieutenant along with Milo de Cogan. We will each have command over a battalion of six hundred men. The barons will listen to us as we besiege Dubhlinn, rather than we to them.'

Strongbow was perhaps thinking back to the many diverging views that had plagued his war councils since landing in Ireland for he did not take more than a few moments to agree. 'The barons will agree or they will be told to go back to Wales. That still leaves the question of who to leave in command of Veðrarfjord.'

Raymond paused, for he had not considered who would fill the role that he had rejected. He ran his mind over everything that had happened since he had first set foot in Ireland. It seemed like a decade had passed rather than a few months. He smiled as he thought back to the building of the fort at Dun Domhnall and the milites' support of his captaincy over Sir

Hervey's claims. Geoffrey of Abergavenny and Bertram d'Alton's faces came to him as he remembered those who had fallen in their great defence of the bridgehead. Raymond considered his actions when the Ostmen prisoners had been killed and the subsequent argument with the conrois, Alice's guidance and William de Vale's constancy. Caradog and Ieuan had become treasured friends during their time cattle-rustling in the north, and he would never forget the moment that he met Father Nicholas on the beach by the River Siúire with his newly recruited army.

He had never stopped to think just how lucky he was in his friends. He could never have accomplished anything without them, Raymond knew, and his greatest failure during his time in Ireland was that he had managed to forsake his oldest friends amongst his old conrois. Raymond smiled as he thought of a name to propose as constable came to him.

'Gilbert de Borard, Lord.'

Strongbow looked nonplussed. 'I don't follow you.'

'As Constable of Veðrarfjord, Lord,' Raymond said again, liking the idea the more he thought about it. 'Gilbert de Borard.'

'The man who serves in Sir Hervey's conrois?'

Raymond nodded his head. 'They are your most trusted men, Lord Strongbow, and Borard would need them all at his side to keep the city safe.'

It was the perfect reward, Raymond knew. The conrois had shared Raymond's every danger on Strongbow's business for years yet they had rarely had enough money to repair their armour or shoe their horses. Now, they could settle in the safety of the city they had helped conquer. They would be awarded lands nearby and could start families. Rather than the border raiders of ill-repute that they had been in Wales, they would be the first men of Veðrarfjord. They would be respected. Borard would make sure that each man would get their cut of the fortune generated by his rule. That the loss of the conrois would also weaken Sir Hervey did not escape Raymond either.

'If you think he is the man to do it, I will agree to Borard,' Strongbow said with a slight shake of his head. 'Would you

382

like to pass on the good news to him?'

'I think it would be best coming from you, Lord Strongbow.'

The earl nodded his head. 'If you are sure this is what you want.'

Raymond de Carew inhaled deeply. 'No, this is what I need,' he told Strongbow. For perhaps the first time he had seen clearly what he was meant to do with his life. It was not his fate to oversee building work or collect tariffs. It was not his aim to mediate between the subjugated Ostmen and the needs of the Bristol merchants. Raymond wanted more. Raymond wanted action and renown and the chance, just the chance, of making Basilia his. And he could not do that by remaining in conquered Veðrarfjord.

Ahead were battles and glory. He had picked out his target and his arrow was in the air, soaring against the clouds. He did not yet know if it would strike true, but at least he knew now where he was aiming. And he would prove his worth at Dubhlinn in the service of his lord, the Earl Strongbow.

Historical Note

For much of the summer of 1170 the real Raymond de Carew didn't do very much. Having landed in Ireland around the beginning of May, he built a headland fort at Dun Domhnall and then defended it from an attack by an army many times the size of his own (as depicted in *Lord of the Sea Castle*), presumably at some point in June. It wouldn't be until August 23rd that his master, Richard de Clare, would finally join him and their campaign to capture the city of Waterford could begin.

So what did he get up to during those quiet months? Only one event is relayed to us – the massacre of seventy Ostman prisoners. In Gerald of Wales's *Expugnatio Hibernica*, written less than twenty years after the event, the blame for the crime is placed firmly on Hervey de Montmorency's shoulders. In this account, Raymond de Carew tries in vain to force Hervey to do the honourable thing and have the prisoners ransomed back to their families. But his efforts were to no avail. Gerald even describes how Hervey has the Normans break the legs of their prisoners, casting their bodies over the edge of the cliff and into the sea below where they drown.

It is only in a later version that Alice of Abergavenny suddenly appears in the story. Writing in the first half of the thirteenth century, the unknown author of the *Song of Dermot and the Earl* records:

Of the Irish there were taken,
Quite as many as seventy,
But the noble knights,
Had them beheaded.
To a wench they gave
An axe of tempered steel,
And she beheaded them all,
Then threw their bodies over the cliff,
Because she had that day
Lost her lover in combat.
Alice of Abergavenny was her name
Who served the Irish thus.

Alice is a strange omission on Gerald's behalf, given his fondness for the melodramatic. Surely having a half-mad camp follower murder the men would be a better story than a brief conversation between Raymond and Hervey? Blaming Alice would certainly have exonerated Gerald's beloved cousin, Raymond, of any part in the crime. But no – Gerald blames Hervey de Montmorency rather than the 'wench' Alice. If not an omission by Gerald then Alice's inclusion in the second account is even more interesting. In my view it can only be because the author of *The Song* does not wish to blame either Raymond or Hervey for the hideous crime of murder, probably because of their familial link to the House of Strongbow which came about after Gerald's time. My own feeling is that Alice of Abergavenny never existed, certainly not in the role she is assigned in *The Song* and, while that is ultimately disappointing, I felt that I should try to right the wrong in this book and put the blame back on the shoulders of the person I think actually conducted the massacre: Raymond de Carew. Yet Alice is too good a character to abandon completely. Her elements within this novel are entirely fictitious.

Raymond probably didn't have any children although several families are still reported on genealogical sites as his descendants. For the record, I think it much more likely that the *Grace* surname is a variation on the Welsh 'ap Rhys' (much like the modern Welsh variation, Price), rather than it is taken from le Gros (or le Gras). While on the subject of names, Strongbow was never known by that moniker in his lifetime. In all likelihood it was a much later invention or perhaps a mistake by Camden or Geraghty based on the old name for Chepstow – Striguil. Nevertheless I have chosen to keep that name in this book as *Strongbow* is simply too evocative a name, and too closely linked to the story of the Norman invasion of Ireland to be left out.

We are not told if Raymond conducted a cattle raid into Carlow and Kilkenny as I have described. Rather, after the incident with the Waterford Vikings, he seems to have 'holed up' in his fort for almost three months awaiting Strongbow's arrival from Wales. Raymond's rescue of Jarl Gufraid's people is made up. However, there was a citizen of Waterford named Gerald MacGillamurray (more likely Gufraid Mac Giolla Mhuire) who was mentioned in a piece I read in the *Decies Journal* of the Old Waterford Society by Ciaran Parker. This Gerald was one of the few Ostmen who were not expelled from the city by Strongbow, presumably because he had assisted in the Norman takeover in some manner. In Dublin during this period the ruling Ostman elite were more than happy to make deals with more powerful Gaelic families and often invited them to become involved militarily in their internal disputes. I have no evidence to suggest that this could've happened in this case, other than the fact that Gerald/Gufraid remained a powerful man in the city at least until 1174.

Ragnall and Sihtric (Sigtrygg) were the rulers of Waterford at this time. Very little is known about them, or their relationship, but they are believed to have been from the same Mac Giolla Mhuire stock as Gerald/Gufraid. According to Gerald of Wales, Sihtric, and another earl of the same name, were executed by Strongbow's men after the Normans were forced into an assault on Rögnvald's Tower. Ragnall (who was never a prisoner of Sigtrygg's) and Máel Sechlainn Ua Fhaolain were only saved from a similar fate by the timely arrival of Dermot MacMurrough. Ragnall remained an influential character in the city for some time after the Norman conquest – but that's a story for another day.

MacMurrough, only recently reinstated as King of Leinster, did bring his daughter Aoife with him to Waterford in August 1170 and there, amongst the blood and gore of battle, we are told that she was married to Strongbow. She was an 'exceeding beauty' and probably younger than twenty when she married the forty-year-old Strongbow. What she thought of it all is difficult to know, and as much time has been spent discussing that particular subject elsewhere I won't do so here.

I couldn't find any reference to where Strongbow's camp was located so I decided to place it at Ballybrickin. This point would've overlooked the west wall of the city, which was really the only side that an army could attack Waterford from. Unlike how it played out in this book, Raymond was almost certainly present for – and may even have masterminded – all three attacks on Waterford. Gerald of Wales even has him arriving at the city before Strongbow! Unsurprisingly, Gerald gives the lion's share of the glory to Raymond. He tells us that Raymond caused a building (a dwelling rather than a warehouse) to fall, taking part of the defences with it, thus allowing his milites to force their way through the breach. *The Song of Dermot and the Earl* merely says that Strongbow took Waterford by assault. Neither account states where exactly Raymond broke through so I have placed it on the eastern side.

Rögnvald's Tower is now known as Reginald's Tower. The building in the Ostman town was probably constructed from a mix of stone and wood (much like the city walls of the period) and the Normans replaced it soon after their conquest with the stone tower which still stands on the same spot. Reginald's Tower is open to the public and, like Waterford, is a fantastic place to visit. Unfortunately Thorgest's Tower (latterly known as Turgesius's Tower) is gone. Here and there on the city streets you can still spot parts of the medieval stone walls and if you are really lucky when you visit Waterford you might even find one of the members of the Deise Medieval group prowling the streets their ancient ancestors founded. I'd like to thank them for all their help in bringing this book to life in a number of different ways. The marshland that would've defended Waterford's eastern wall was drained as the city expanded in the centuries following Strongbow, but it would've probably stretched from The Mall to where De La Salle College now stands.

It may have been that Strongbow's ships transported Raymond and his cattle from Dun Domhnall to Waterford. However, during this period Great Island in County Wexford was an actual island (it isn't any more) and the straits between Little Island (where Waterford Castle now stands) and the northern bank in County Kilkenny were fordable. I couldn't resist having a little wander through south Kilkenny and I suspect it would be relatively easy to drive the animals by this path to Waterford's walls. I'm indebted to Andrew Doherty from Waterford Tides n Tales for his help with all things to do with the Three Sisters river system. Any mistake in this regard is entirely my own. Thanks also to my fellow classmates in the

Creative Writing MA class at Queen's University Belfast, who were the first to give their opinions on *The Earl Strongbow* during our prose classes. Chapter One would've been very different if not for their brilliant suggestions!

The end of this novel has the main players in the Norman invasion of Ireland finally in one place, but their adventurous spirit will take them further again. Diarmait and Strongbow, Raymond and Robert FitzStephen, Aoife and Alice, especially Gerald Bach – they will not be happy with just one kingdom or one city. And with the fires still burning around conquered Waterford, they have already set their sights on the next target, Ireland's greatest city, Dublin.

Ruadh Butler, September 2018

Proudly published by Accent Press

www.accentpress.co.uk